Praise for Emma Miller and her novels

"This is truly an enjoyable tale overall."

—*RT Book Reviews* on *A Love for Leah*

"The concept of having two suitors…provides a fresh twist. It is fun trying to figure out who [the heroine] will choose."

—*RT Book Reviews* on *The Amish Bride*

"A captivating story."

—*RT Book Reviews* on *Miriam's Heart*

Praise for Alison Stone and her novels

"Stone's latest is so fast-paced and action-packed that it is hard to put down. Numerous red herrings and palpable suspense combine in this thoroughly engaging nail-biter."

—*RT Book Reviews* on *Plain Sanctuary*

"This tale quickly engages the reader with its attention-grabbing details and original twists."

—*RT Book Reviews* on *Plain Cover-Up*

"[A] well-researched tale with an engaging pace…. It contains sweet romance, palpable suspense."

—*RT Book Reviews* on *Plain Peril*

Emma Miller lives quietly in her old farmhouse in rural Delaware. Fortunate enough to be born into a family of strong faith, she grew up on a dairy farm, surrounded by loving parents, siblings, grandparents, aunts, uncles and cousins. Emma was educated in local schools and once taught in an Amish schoolhouse. When she's not caring for her large family, reading and writing are her favorite pastimes.

Alison Stone lives with her husband of more than twenty years and their four children in Western New York. Besides writing, Alison keeps busy volunteering at her children's schools, driving her girls to dance and watching her boys race motocross. Alison loves to hear from her readers at Alison@AlisonStone.com. For more information, please visit her website, alisonstone.com. She's also chatty on Twitter, @alison_stone. Find her on Facebook at Facebook.com/alisonstoneauthor.

EMMA MILLER

A Man for Honor

&

ALISON STONE

Plain Jeopardy

HARLEQUIN® LOVE INSPIRED®

Recycling programs for this product may not exist in your area.

ISBN-13: 978-1-335-47007-2

A Man for Honor and Plain Jeopardy

This edition published by arrangement with Love Inspired Books.

www.Harlequin.com

Printed in U.S.A.

CONTENTS

A MAN FOR HONOR

Emma Miller

Then came Peter to him, and said, Lord,
how oft shall my brother sin against me,
and I forgive him? till seven times? Jesus saith
unto him, I say not unto thee, Until seven times:
but, Until seventy times seven.

—*Matthew* 18:21–22

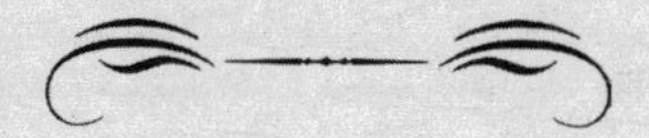

Chapter One

Luke Weaver lifted the collar of his lined jean jacket to his neck, pulled down his still-wet black hat and made his way toward the exit of the convenience store and the raw December morning.

"That *is* you, isn't it?" the college-aged boy behind the register called after Luke. He pointed to the TV screen mounted above the snacks section. "Look!" he proclaimed to several customers. "That guy's the mystery cowboy they're looking for! He's the hero that rescued those people from the bus wreck in Pennsylvania last night!"

Luke kept walking. The last thing he wanted was to be recognized in his hometown of Dover, Delaware. When a tractor trailer had skidded on an icy highway the previous night, causing a multivehicle collision, he'd been in the midst of it. The bus he'd been riding had flipped on its side and slid down an embankment into a deep drainage pond. With icy water fast pouring in and people panicking, he hadn't considered that his photo might end up being plastered all over the national news.

Luke had acted without thinking. He'd pulled the unconscious driver to safety and then broken a window to assist a mother and several small children out of the sinking bus. He'd gone back into the rapidly submerging vehicle twice to help other trapped passengers before state troopers and paramedics arrived. One of the officers had asked who he was, but not wanting to draw attention to himself, he'd refused to give his name. And that had only made things worse because the news media had made a big thing of it. Now everyone was hunting for the *mystery cowboy*, calling him a real-life superhero.

"Hey, mister! Are you the super cowboy?" a woman headed toward the doors to the convenience store asked as he stepped out. "You look just like him."

Luke strode down Lepore Street. He was supposed to meet someone from the Seven Poplars Amish community at the bus stop, but he wasn't hanging around. He'd find his own way to Sara Yoder's home.

Beads of freezing sleet stung his face and hands, but he kept walking. Winters in Delaware weren't as cold as those in Kansas, and he could dry off when he got to the matchmaker's. He hoped someone had some spare clothes he could change into, because the trousers he was wearing were ripped and stained, and his duffle bag with spare clothes was still in the bus's luggage compartment, probably resting at the bottom of that drainage pond.

Luke had just crossed the street and turned onto North State when he caught sight of a mule and buggy coming at a sharp pace. Guessing that that must be his ride, he waved the driver to a stop. To his surprise, the only occupant of the buggy was a plump, middle-aged

Amish woman with dark curly hair, a nutmeg-colored complexion, and eyes as dark and shiny as ripe blackberries. "Sara?"

She nodded. "You must be Luke," she said in *Deitsch* and then switched to English. "Jump in before we cause a traffic jam."

He glanced up and down the street. Not a single vehicle was coming in either direction. He looked back at Sara as he swung up onto the bench seat. The interior of the buggy was plain black, neat and well maintained, pretty much what he'd expected of the woman he only knew from correspondence. "Dover hasn't grown all that much in the time I've been gone," he said.

"*Atch.* According to my neighbors, it *has* grown. They say the traffic has increased," she replied. "I moved here from a rural area of Wisconsin a few years back, so Kent County still seems busy to me. You're certain you want to trade the wide-open spaces of the Midwest for our little state?"

He nodded. "*Ya*, I do."

"You said in your first letter that you grew up here."

"I did, and I've always thought of Kent County as home," he answered. "Kansas can be pretty dry. I miss the green and the rain."

A line of cars slowed behind them, but Sara didn't seem to notice. "Rain we have aplenty," she said after a bit.

"And a strong church community." He stretched out his long legs and rubbed absently at his aching shoulder. When the collision happened, he'd been thrown violently against the corner of the seat frame across the aisle. Nothing seemed broken, but he guessed he was going to have quite a bruise. "At least, that's the way I remember it," he finished.

"It is. And everyone will welcome you. We're always glad to add to our family. You say you're a master carpenter?"

"More of a cabinetmaker, but I can do any type of construction."

Sara looked at him with frank curiosity. "I'm curious as to why you'd need my services. A nice-looking man like you with a good trade? Back in Kansas, mothers must have been parading their daughters in front of you. Girls must have been lining up hoping you'd take them home from a singing."

But not the woman I want, he thought. To Sara, he said, "I'm ready to marry and start a family, but I thought the whole process would be easier if I used a matchmaker."

"Mmm." Sara's brow arched. "I've checked up on you. Wrote a couple of letters. Your bishop tells me that you're baptized and a solid member of your church." She pursed her lips. "A matchmaker can certainly make it easier finding the right wife, but why me? Why not someone in Kansas?"

"The nearest Amish matchmaker to where I lived just celebrated her eighty-second birthday, and she doesn't hear or see well. Besides, I want to move back to Delaware and marry a woman from here." He glanced at her. "You have a good reputation. People speak of you as one of the best, and you specialize in hard-to-place cases."

Her eyes narrowed. "Are you a difficult case, Luke Weaver?" She gave him an appraising look. "I'll admit you do look a little worse for wear."

"Ya." He ran a hand over the three-cornered tear in the knee of his go-to-church trousers. There was a stain on the other leg he suspected might be blood and his wide-brimmed black wool hat had taken a beating. The brim was sagging and it was shrinking as it dried; it wasn't meant to be submerged in water.

"I suppose I do," he admitted. He considered whether or not to explain his condition to Sara. His first impressions of her were good, but he didn't know that he was ready to tell anyone what had happened on the highway the previous night. The idea of talking about it made him uncomfortable; he'd done what any man would have done. End of story.

Sara turned off State Street onto Division. Traffic was still light for the center of town. A few pedestrians stopped and watched as the mule and buggy passed. A little boy in a fire-engine red rain slicker and yellow boots waved from the sidewalk, and Sara waved back.

"A lot of new construction in Dover," he commented as the grand Victorian houses gave way to commercial buildings and smaller frame homes. "I'm hoping I'll be able to find steady employment."

"There's always work for a carpenter," she replied. "A good friend of mine has a construction crew. You'll meet him at church tomorrow." Her shrewd gaze raked him again. "If you're planning on joining us for worship. It's being held at Samuel Mast's, not far from my place. You know Samuel?"

"I do. Good man. And *ya*, I do want to attend service. If you can find me something decent to wear. We, um…had some trouble… The bus." He cleared his throat. "I'm afraid my duffle bag with all my clothes is lost. I don't want to impose. I know I've picked an awkward time to arrive, two days after Christmas, but… it was time I came."

"Not a problem. I can find clothes, and I've got a warm bed for you. All my prospective brides have either married or gone back to their families for the holidays. It's much too quiet in my house. Even our little schoolteacher has gone visiting relatives. As I told you in my letter, I have a bunkhouse for my hired hand and male clients from out of state. Some stay for the weekend, others a few weeks or longer. It's far enough from the house for propriety, but close enough so that your meals won't be cold before you get to the table. Prospective brides stay in the house with me."

"The bunkhouse sounds great. I appreciate it," he said. "And I appreciate you coming to get me. It's a miserable day for you to be on the road."

Sara reined the mule to a stop as the light ahead turned from yellow to red. "I could have sent Hiram for you. He's my hired man. But his judgment's not the best. He might have decided to take the buggy down the DuPont Highway to stop at the mall. And the madhouse of a highway is no place for a mule, even a sensible one." She glanced at Luke. "And the truth is, I was looking for an excuse to get out of the house."

They rode in comfortable silence for a few minutes and then Luke spoke up again. He wasn't one to keep quiet on things. Sometimes he was criticized for speaking too easily from his heart, with his feelings. It wasn't something necessarily encouraged in Amish men, but he was who he was. "I hope you're going to be able to help me make a match," he said. If she couldn't, he didn't know what he'd do.

"No reason why I shouldn't, is there?" She glanced

at him again. "I'll admit, Luke, you are something of a mystery to me. You do make me curious."

He winced at the word *mystery* but said nothing.

"You know, young women seeking husbands are plentiful, but eligible bachelors with a solid trade seeking brides aren't as easy to find. From what I see with my eyes, and from what I've learned from your letters and my own inquiries, you're almost too good to be true."

"I don't know about that. I'm as flawed as any man. But I assure you, I've not told you any untruths."

"I didn't say you had," Sara said. "My first thought would be that I can think of a good dozen young women who would jump at the opportunity to meet you. But something tells me that there's more to you, that you've not told me everything I need to know if I'm going to make the right match for you."

He grimaced. "There is something I haven't said."

"And that is?"

"There's a particular someone I've set my mind on, someone special I used to know." He stopped and started again. "Someone I haven't been able to forget."

Sara reined the mule off the street and into a parking place in a car dealership lot. She looped the leathers over a hook on the dash, folded her arms and turned to face him. "I take it that this *someone* is of legal age, Amish and free to marry?"

"She is."

"But you didn't think that I should have that information before you arrived?"

He tugged on the sagging brim of his hat. It was a shame it was ruined because he'd bought it new before he left Kansas. "I thought it would be easier if I could explain in person." He looked away and then back at the matchmaker. "Her name is Honor. Honor King."

Sara didn't hide her surprise. "I know Honor. A widow. She doesn't belong to our church community, but I have introduced her to several prospects. Honor's husband passed a year and a half ago."

"Nineteen months."

Sara frowned. "And you know that Honor has children. Four of them."

"*Ya*, I do. That doesn't matter to me."

"Well, it should," she harrumphed. "It takes a special kind of a man to be a father to another man's children. Especially as they get up in age."

He felt himself flush. "I know that. What I said about the children, that didn't come out right. Her children are part of her. I want to be a good father to them. And a good husband to her."

Sara raised a dark eyebrow. "You're familiar with Honor's children? You've met them?"

There was something in her tone that made him hesitate. "*Ne*...but I hope to have many children."

She sniffed. "Easily said by a man who has none. As the preachers tell us, children are blessings from God. That said, they can be a handful. Some more than others." She pursed her lips. "Any other revelations you'd like to share with me?"

He hesitated. "Well..."

"Like this, perhaps?" She reached under the seat and came up with a copy of the *Delaware State News*. The photo snapped by one of the bus passengers stared back at him. It was clearly his face, with a fire truck and a Pennsylvania State Police car in the background. In his arms was a screaming child. Under the photo, a bold headline proclaimed Mystery Cowboy Rides to the Rescue!

"You saw it," he said.

"*Ya*, saw it and read it. What I didn't know was that I would be welcoming the mystery cowboy into my home. You know our community takes a dim view of photographs. They are forbidden."

"In my church, as well," he agreed. "But I didn't give anyone permission to take a picture. And I didn't ask for people to talk about what happened. There was an accident. I did what seemed right."

"But it will make talk." She allowed herself the hint of a smile. "A lot of talk."

"I was afraid of that."

"That the hat you were wearing?" She frowned, looking up at him. "Doesn't look much like a *gunslinger's* hat. Or a rodeo rider's."

"Ne."

She had a sense of humor, this perky little matchmaker. He liked her. Better yet, he had the strongest feeling that he could trust her in what might be the biggest step of his life.

Sara chuckled. "*Englishers*. Mistook your church hat for a cowboy hat, I suppose, and thought you were a cowboy."

"*Ya*. Someone who isn't familiar with our people."

She nodded. "I can see that. Better for you that it doesn't say *Amish*. Better for us."

"Maybe so," he said.

"I know so." Her eyes lit with mischief. "But good of you to save the *Englishers* from the accident. They are God's children, too."

"I didn't want the fuss. Anybody would have done what I did."

"But according to the newspaper, you're the one who took charge. Who kept his head, did what needed to be done and kept the unconscious bus driver from drowning. Not everyone would have the courage to do that." She paused and then went on. "There'll be questions we'll have to answer from our neighbors, but if you don't wear snakeskin boots, rope cows or sign autographs, the talk will pass and people will find something else to gossip about."

"I hope so."

She reached over and patted his arm reassuringly. "If you didn't want your photograph taken, there's no reason to feel guilty about it. Any of our people with sense will come to realize it." She gathered the reins again and clicked to the mule. And as they pulled out onto the street again, she said, "One question for you. The widow, Honor King, will she look favorably on your suit?"

"I doubt it," he admitted, gazing out at the road ahead. "She returns my letters unopened."

Two days later, Luke and Sara drove west from her house in Seven Poplars. Eventually, they passed a millpond and mill, and then went another two miles down a winding country road to a farm that sat far back off the blacktop.

"I don't know what her husband, Silas, was thinking to buy so far from other Amish families," Sara mused. "I haven't been here to Honor's home, because she lives out of our church district, but Freeman and Katie at the mill are her nearest Amish neighbors. It must be difficult for Honor since her husband passed away, being so isolated." She turned her mule into the driveway. *"Atch,"* she muttered. "Look at this mud. I hope we don't get stuck in the ruts." The lane, lined on either side by sagging fence rails and overgrown barbed wire, was filled with puddles.

"If we do, I'll dig us out," Luke promised, adjusting the shrunken hat that barely fitted on his head anymore. Now that they were almost to Honor's home, he was nervous. What if she refused to let him walk through her doorway? What if he'd sold everything he owned, turned his life upside down and moved to Delaware just to find that she'd have nothing to do with him?

Honor's farmhouse was a rambling, two-story frame structure with tall brick chimneys at either end. Behind and to the sides, loomed several barns, sheds and outbuildings. A derelict windmill, missing more than half its blades, leaned precariously over the narrow entrance to the farmyard.

"I'd have to agree with what you told me yesterday, Sara. She needs a handyman," Luke said, sliding his door open so he could get a better look. He'd heard that Honor's husband had purchased a big farm in western Kent County, near the Maryland state line. But no one had told him that the property was in such bad shape.

How could a woman alone with four children possibly manage such a farm? How could she care for her family? Why had Silas brought his young bride here? Fixing up this place would have been a huge undertaking for a healthy man, not to mention one who'd suffered from a chronic disease since he was born.

The wind shifted and the intermittent rain dampened Luke's trousers and wet his face. He pulled the brim of his hat low to shield his eyes as the mule plodded on up the drive, laying her ears back against the rain and splashing through the puddles. As the buggy neared the farmhouse, Luke noticed missing shingles on the roof and a broken window on the second floor. His chest tightened and he felt an overwhelming need to do whatever he could to help Honor, regardless of how she received him.

As they passed between the gateposts that marked the entrance to the farmyard, Luke could hear the rusty mechanism of the windmill creak and grind. The gate, or what remained of it, sagged, one end on the ground and overgrown with weeds and what looked like poison ivy.

"If I'd known things were this bad here, I would have asked Caleb to organize a work frolic to clean this place up," Sara observed. "Caleb's our young preacher, married one of the Yoder girls. You know Hannah Yoder? Her daughters are all married now, have families of their own."

"Knew Jonas Yoder well. He was good to me when I was growing up."

"Jonas was like that," Sara mused. "Hannah and I are cousins."

Luke continued to study the farm. "You've never been here before?"

"*Ne*, I haven't. She's been to my place, though. I'd heard Honor doesn't have church services here, but I always assumed it was due to Silas's illness and then her struggle to carry on without him."

Luke didn't know how long Honor's husband had been sick before he'd been carried off by a bout of pneumonia, but either he'd been sick a long time or he hadn't attended to his duties. The state of things on this farm was a disgrace.

A child's shriek caught his attention, and he glanced at the barn where a hayloft door hung open. Suddenly, a squirming bundle of energy cannonballed out of the loft, landed on a hay wagon heaped with wet straw and then vaulted off to land with a squeal of laughter in a mud puddle. Water splashed, ducks and chickens flew, squawking and quacking, in every direction, and a miniature donkey shied away from the building and added a shrill braying to the uproar.

The small figure climbed out of the puddle and shouted to someone in the loft. Luke thought the muddy creature must be a boy, because he was wearing trousers and a shirt, but couldn't make out his face or the color of his hair because it was covered in mud.

"What are you doing?" Sara called to the child. "Does your mother know—"

She didn't get to finish her sentence because a second squealing child leaped from the loft opening. He hit the heap of straw in the wagon and landed in the puddle with a satisfying splash and an even louder protest from the donkey. This child was shirtless and wearing only one shoe. When a third child appeared in the loft, this one the smallest of the three, Luke managed to leap out of the buggy and get to the wagon in time to catch him in midair.

This little one, in a baby's gown, was bareheaded, with clumps of bright red-orange hair standing up like the bristles on a horse's mane and oversize boots on the wrong feet. The rescued toddler began to wail. With a yell, the shirtless boy launched himself at Luke, fists and feet flying, and bit his knee.

"Let go of him!" the leader of the pack screamed in *Deitsch*. "*Mam!* A man is taking Elijah!"

Luke deposited Elijah safely on the ground. "Stop that!" he ordered in *Deitsch*, lifting his attacker into the air and tucking him under one arm.

"What do you think you're doing?"

Luke turned toward the back porch. A young woman appeared, a crying baby in her arms, wet hair hanging loose around her shoulders. "Let go of my son this minute!"

For a moment Luke stood there, stunned, the boy still flailing against his arm. Luke had been expecting to see a changed Honor, one weighed down by the grief of widowhood and aged by the birth of four children in six years, but he hadn't been prepared for this bold beauty. He opened his mouth to answer, but as he did, a handful of mud struck him in the cheek.

"Put Justice down!" the biggest boy shouted as he scooped up a handful of mud and threw it at Luke. "You let my brother go!"

The little one did the same.

Luke spit mud and tried to wipe the muck out of his eyes, only succeeding in making it worse.

Sara, now out of the buggy, clapped her hands. "*Kinner!* Stop this at once! Inside with you. You'll catch your deaths of ague." She reached out for Justice, and Luke gladly handed him, still kicking and screaming, over to her.

Honor came down the steps, carefully stepping over a hole where a board was missing. "Sara? I didn't realize—" She broke off. "You?" she said to Luke, raising her voice. "You dare to come here?"

He sucked in a deep breath. "*Goot mariye*, Honor. I know you weren't expecting me, but—"

"But nothing," Honor flung back. Red-haired Elijah's cry became a shriek, and a dog ran out of the house and began to bark. Honor raised her voice further to be heard over the noise. "What are doing here, Luke?"

"Calm down," he soothed, raising both hands, palms up, in an attempt to dampen the fire of her temper. "Hear me out, before—"

"There will be no *hearing you out*," she said, interrupting him again. "You're not welcome here, Luke Weaver."

"Now, Honor—"

"Why did you bring him here, Sara?" Honor demanded.

To add to the confusion, the rainfall suddenly became a downpour. Sara looked up at the dark sky and then at Honor. "If you've any charity, I think we'd best get under your roof before we all drown," she said.

Honor grimaced and reached out for the child struggling in Sara's arms. "Could you grab Elijah?" she asked the matchmaker. "Stop that, Justice," she said, balancing her middle child on one hip and the baby against her shoulder. "Why are you half-dressed? Where's Greta? And where's your coat?" She glanced up. "*Ya*, come in, all of you. Elijah! Tanner!" She rolled her eyes. "You, too, Luke. Although it would serve you right if I did leave you out here to drown."

Chapter Two

Honor set Justice down on the top step and herded him and the other two boys into the narrow passageway that served as a place to hang coats, wash clothing and store buckets, kindling and fifty other items she didn't want in her kitchen. "Watch your step," she warned Sara. "The cat had kittens, and they're constantly underfoot."

Her late husband had disliked cats in the house. The thought that this was her house and she could do as she pleased now, in spite of what he thought, gave her a small gratification in the midst of the constant turmoil. "Tanner? Where's Greta?" She glanced back at Sara who was setting Elijah on his feet. "Greta's Silas's niece. She helps me with the children and the housework." She raised her free hand in a hopeless gesture. "She was supposed to be checking on the sheep. She must have taken the little ones outside with her."

Kittens, sheep, Greta and the condition of her kitchen were easier for Honor to think about than Luke Weaver. She couldn't focus on him right now. Barely could imagine him back in Kent County, let alone in her house. What had possessed Sara to bring him here?

Queasiness coiled in the pit of Honor's stomach and made her throat tighten. It had taken her years to put Luke in her past…to try to forget him. And how many hours had she prayed to forgive him? That was still a work in progress. But she wouldn't let him upset her life. Not now. Not ever again. And yet, here he was in her home. *God, give me the strength*, she pleaded silently.

Confusion reigned in the damp laundry room where the ceiling sagged and the single window was cracked and leaked air around the rotting frame. Her baby daughter, Anke, began to wail again, and Justice was whining.

"Inside," Honor ordered, pointing. "You'll have to forgive the state of the house," she said over her shoulder to Sara. She chose to ignore Luke as she led the way into the kitchen. "The roof has a leak. Leaks." Her cheeks burned with embarrassment. Water dripped from the ceiling into an assortment of buckets and containers. Not that she had to tell Sara that the roof leaked. She could see it for herself. She could hear the cascade of falling drops.

Honor gazed around the kitchen, seeing it as her visitors must, a high-ceilinged room with exposed beams overhead, a bricked-up fireplace and cupboards with sagging doors. She'd painted the room a pale lemon yellow, polished the windowpanes until they shone and done her best with the patchy, cracked linoleum floor, but it was plain that soap and elbow grease did little against forty years of neglect. What must Sara think of her? As for Luke, she told herself that she didn't care what he thought.

But she did.

"Tanner," Honor said brusquely. "Take your brothers to the bathroom. Greta will give you all a bath and clean clothes. As soon as I find her," she added. "But you've not heard the end of this," she warned, shaking a finger. It was an empty threat. She knew it and the children did, too, but it seemed like something a mother should say. She put the baby into her play yard and looked around. Where was that girl? Greta, sixteen, was not nearly as much help as Honor had hoped she would be when she'd agreed to have the girl come live with her. Sometimes, Honor felt as if Greta was just another child to tend to. "Tanner, where is Greta?"

Tanner flushed and suddenly took a great interest in a tear in the linoleum between his feet.

Justice piped up. "Feed room."

Tanner lifted his head to glare at his brother.

"What did you say?" Honor asked.

"Feed room." Justice clapped his hands over his mouth and giggled.

"What's she doing in the feed room?" Honor frowned, fearing the answer as she spoke.

Justice shrugged. "Can't get out." He cast a knowing look at his older brother, Tanner, whose face was growing redder by the second.

Honor brought the heel of her hand to her forehead. "Did you lock her in again?"

Tanner's blue eyes widened as he pointed at Elijah. "Not me. He did it."

"And you let him? Shame on you. You're the big boy. You're supposed to—"

"Wait, someone's locked in the feed room?" Luke interrupted, using his handkerchief to wipe the splatters of mud off his face.

"Tanner, you go this minute and let Greta out," Honor ordered, still ignoring the fact that Luke, *her* Luke, was standing in her kitchen. "And the three of you are in big trouble. There will be no apple pie for any of you tonight."

"I'll go," Luke offered, shoving his handkerchief into the pants he'd borrowed from Sara's hired hand. "Where's the feed room?"

"Barn," Tanner supplied.

"The'th in the barn," Elijah lisped.

Luke turned back toward the outer door.

Honor watched him go. The way it was pouring rain, he'd get soaked. She didn't care. She turned back to her boys. "Upstairs!" she said. "Go find dry clothes. Now. I'll send Greta up to run your bath. And you haven't heard the last of this. I promise you that."

They ran.

Honor exhaled and glanced at Sara. "I'm not as terrible a mother as I must seem. I was changing Anke's diaper. I thought Elijah was in his bed napping and the other two playing upstairs. Fully dressed. They *were* dressed the last time I saw them." She pressed her hand to her forehead again. "Really, they were."

Sara looked around the kitchen. She didn't have to say anything. Honor wanted to sink through the floor. Not that her kitchen was dirty. It wasn't, except that she'd been making bread. Who wouldn't scatter a little flour on the counter or floor? There were no dirty dishes in the sink, no sour diaper smell, and if her boys looked like muddy scarecrows, at least the baby was clean and neat. But the buckets all over the room…

"I hired someone to fix the roof and make the repairs to the house," Honor explained. "But—" She gave a wave. "It's a long story, but basically, it won't be happening anytime soon."

"I know," Sara supplied. "I heard. Robert Swartzentruber fell off a ladder and broke his ankle. A pity."

"*Ya*, a pity. Poor man. I've been looking for a replacement, but—" she opened her arms "—I've been a little busy."

"Which is exactly why I brought Luke Weaver," Sara said smoothly.

Honor studied her. Did Sara know about her and Luke? She *must* know. But it had all happened before Sara came to Seven Poplars. Maybe she didn't know. "Why him?" she asked.

"He's a master carpenter. And he's new to town and looking for work."

"I'm sorry. No, that's not possible." Honor picked up a small tree branch, brought in by one of her boys, and tossed it in the trash can. She checked her tone before she spoke again, because she'd been accused more than once of speaking too sharply to people. Of having too strong an opinion. "Luke Weaver is not working on my house," she declared. "I don't want him here. He's the last carpenter I'd—"

"Honor." Sara cut her off. "Think of your children. If you have a leak in the kitchen, you must have them elsewhere in the house. And your back step is broken. And you've got a cracked windowpane in your laundry room and another on the second floor. And the bad winter weather hasn't even set in on us."

"Half the house is broken," Honor answered honestly. Her late husband had bought the farm without her ever seeing the place. He'd promised to fix it up, but he hadn't kept many promises. And now she was left to deal with it.

"Don't let pride or an old disagreement keep you from doing what's best for your children," Sara cautioned.

So she knew *something*. The question was, what had he told her? "Just not him," Honor repeated. "Anyone else. I can pay. I don't need…" It was difficult to keep from raising her voice. Sara didn't understand. Couldn't understand. Honor didn't need Luke. Couldn't have him here. Why would he ever believe she would let him walk in and then hire him?

"I'm not asking you to marry him," Sara said with an amused look. "I know you have a history—"

"A *history*?" Honor flared, feeling her cheeks grow warm. "Is *that* what he told you?"

"The details aren't my business." Sara's face softened. "Honor, I know how difficult it can be for a widow alone. I've been there. But you have to make choices that are in your best interest. And those of your children. If Luke's willing to make the repairs you need and you pay a fair wage, you're not obligated to him. He's an employee, nothing more. He could do the job and then move on. And you and your children would be much better off."

Honor shook her head. The insides of her eyelids stung and she could feel the emotions building up inside her, but she wouldn't cry. There was no way Luke would make her cry again. "He didn't tell you what he did to me, did he?"

"He wanted to, but I wouldn't hear of it," Sara said. "As I said, I don't need to know. What I do know is that he seems to be a good man."

"I believed that, too. Once, a long time ago." Honor gripped the back of a chair. "But then he walked out on me nine years ago." Against her will, tears filled her eyes. "The morning we were to be married."

As soon as Luke walked into the barn, he could tell where the feed room was by the muffled shouts and thuds. He found his way past a dappled gray horse, a placid Jersey cow, stray hens and a pen of sheep to a door with a wooden bar across it. He swung the bar up, and the door burst open. Out spilled a slight, sandy-haired, teenage girl with tear-streaked cheeks.

"They locked me in again!" she declared. She seemed about to elaborate on her plight when she suddenly saw him and stopped short in her tracks, eyes wide. *"Atch!"* she cried and clapped a hand over her mouth.

"I'm Luke," he said. "Honor sent me to let you out." That wasn't exactly true, but close enough without going into a detailed explanation. "Are you all right?"

"They are bad children! Bad!" she flung back without answering his question. "And that oldest is the worst. Every day, they lock me in the feed room." She thrust out her lower lip, sniffed and began to weep again. "I want to go home."

"Don't cry," Luke said. "You say they lock you in the feed room every day? So why…why did you give them the opportunity to lock you in? Again and again?"

"*Aagschmiert.* Tricked. I was tricked." She wiped

her nose with the back of the sleeve of her oversize barn coat. "And it's dark in there. I hate the dark."

"Ya." Luke nodded. "I'm not overly fond of it myself. At least I wouldn't be if someone locked me in." He reached out and removed a large spiderweb from the girl's headscarf.

She shuddered when she saw it. *"Wildheet,"* she insisted. "Wild, bad *kinner*." She pointed at a chicken. "See? They let the chickens out of their pen, too. And yesterday it was the cow. Everything, they let loose. Me, they lock in."

Luke pressed his lips tightly together and tried not to laugh. "As I said, I'm Luke. I came to make repairs to the house. And who are you?"

"Greta. Silas's niece. From Ohio." Another tear rolled down her cheek. "But going home, I think. Soon."

"Well, Greta from Ohio, best we get back in the house before they send someone else out in the rain to see if I'm locked up somewhere, too."

Still muttering under her breath about bad children, Greta led the way through the cluttered barn and, hunching her back against the downpour, made a dash for the house.

They went inside, leaving their wet coats and his hat hanging on hooks in the laundry room, and made a beeline for the woodstove in the kitchen. Greta's teeth were chattering. Luke had the shivers, but he clamped his teeth together and refused to give in to the chill. He put his hands out to the radiating heat, grateful for the semidry kitchen, and glanced sideways at Honor.

In the time since he'd gone to the barn and returned, she'd twisted up her hair and covered it with a woolen scarf. Her plain blue dress had seen better days and her apron was streaked with flour and mud. Her black wool stockings were faded; her slender feet were laced into high black leather shoes. Honor had always been a small woman, and now she was even more slender and more graceful. Life and motherhood had pared away the girlish roundness of her face, leaving her stunning to his eye, more beautiful than he'd dreamed.

"Again?" she said to the girl. "You let them lock you in *again*?"

Greta began to sniffle.

"None of that," Honor said, not unkindly. "Go change into dry things and then find the boys. They need a bath and clean clothes."

"The wash is still damp," Greta protested. "I hung it in the attic like you said, but it's still wet."

"Then bathe them and put them into their nightshirts. I won't have them running around the house in those muddy clothes."

"They won't listen to me," Greta muttered. "Justice won't get in the tub and the little one will run off as soon as I turn my back to him."

"Never you mind, child," Sara said. "I'll come along and lend a hand. I've bathed my share of unwilling *kinner*. And, I promise you, they won't get the best of me." She fixed Luke with a determined gaze. "Honor and Luke have some matters to discuss in private, anyway. Don't you?"

He nodded, feeling a little intimidated by Sara. She reminded him of his late mother.

"I wrote to you," he said when they were alone, as he held out his cold fingers to the warm woodstove. "I wrote every month since I heard that...that your husband passed. You refused my letters and they were returned." He searched her face, looking for some hint that she still cared for him…that she could forgive him. "I apologized for—"

"I didn't want to hear what you had to say then or now," she answered brusquely.

He exhaled. "Honor, I was wrong. I regret what I did, but I can't change the past." Only a few feet separated them. He wanted to go to her, to clasp her hands in his. But he didn't; he stood where he was. "I'm sorry, Honor. What more can I say?"

"That you'll go back to Kansas and leave me in peace."

"I can't do that." He gestured to the nearest leak in the ceiling. "You need help. And I'm here to do whatever you need. I'm a good carpenter. I can fix whatever's broken."

"Can you?" she asked softly.

And, for just a second, he saw moisture gleam in her large blue eyes. Emotion pricked the back of his throat. They weren't talking about the house anymore. They were talking about their hearts.

"I can try," he said softly.

She shook her head. "It's over, Luke. Whatever we had, whatever I felt for you, it's gone."

He stared at the floor. Despite her words, he still felt a connection to Honor. And he had a sense that what she was saying wasn't necessarily how she felt. So he took a leap of faith. He lifted his head to look into her eyes. "I'll be here first thing tomorrow morning with my tools. I know you hate me, but—"

"I don't hate you, Luke."

"Good, then we've a place to start. As I said, I'll be here early in the morning to start patching your roof."

"Patching won't do," she said, looking up and gesturing. "Look at this. The whole thing needs replacing."

"We'll see. If it can't be patched, I'll find a crew and we'll put on a new roof."

She faced him squarely, arms folded, chin up. "I want no favors from you."

"Then you'll have none. You can pay me whatever the going hourly wage is. I'll start in this kitchen and go from there. I'll mend whatever needs doing."

She pursed her lips, lips he'd once kissed and wanted desperately to kiss again. "You will, will you? And what if I lock the door on you?"

"You won't."

Darker blue clouds swirled in the depths of her beautiful eyes. "And what makes you so certain of that?"

"Because you'll think better of it. You didn't expect to see me here, and you're still angry. I get that. But you always had good sense, Honor. When you consider what's best for you and your children, you'll decide I'm the lesser of two evils."

"Which is?"

"Putting up with me doing your repairs is better than living with a leaky roof and a fallen windmill." He smiled at her. "And you will agree to let me do it. Because turning me away isn't smart, and you've always been the smartest woman I've ever known."

Chapter Three

Honor pulled back the curtain and peered out the kitchen window. *Maybe he won't come*, she told herself. *By this morning, he's realized he doesn't belong here. He'll give up and go back to Kansas. Go somewhere.* She certainly didn't want him here in Kent County. She didn't want to take the chance of running into him at Byler's Store or on the street in Dover. Luke Weaver was out of her life, and there was no way that she would ever let him back in again. She couldn't.

"Mam!" Elijah wailed. "My turn. My turn!"

"It's not!" Justice countered. "He went first. I want to feed the lamb. I want to feed—" with each word, her middle son's voice grew louder until he was shouting "—the lamb!"

"You already did. He did," Tanner said. "Besides, he's too little. They're both too little. It's my job to—"

"Please stop," Honor admonished as she turned away from the window, letting the curtain fall. It was foolish to keep looking for Luke. He wasn't coming. She didn't want him to come. She didn't know why was she looking for him. "I warned the three of you about fighting over the bottle." She crossed the kitchen and took the bottle out of Tanner's hands. "If you can't get along, none of you get to feed her. Go and wash your hands. *With soap.*"

The children scattered. The lamb bleated and wagged her stub of a tail. The old wooden playpen that had once confined her oldest son had been pressed into service as a temporary pen for the orphan lamb that had been silly enough to come into the world the previous night. It wasn't really an orphan, but the mother had refused to let it nurse, so it was either tend to it or see it die.

And the truth was that Honor had a soft spot for animals. She couldn't bear to see them in distress. She had to do whatever she could to save them. And the barn was too cold for a smaller-than-usual lamb with a careless mother. So it was added to the confusion that already reigned in her kitchen. It wasn't a good option, but she could think of no other.

Honor held the bottle at an angle, letting the lamb suck and wondering whether it would be possible to put a diaper on the fluffy animal. Probably not, she decided. She'd just have to change the straw bedding multiple times a day. At least here in her kitchen, near the woodstove, she wouldn't have to worry about keeping the little creature warm. And the rain had stopped, assuring that both animal and children wouldn't have to endure trickles of water dripping on their heads. "Thank You, God," she murmured.

There was a clatter of boots on the stairs and the three boys spilled into the kitchen again. "We're hungry," Tanner declared. He held up his damp hands to show that he'd washed.

Greta wandered into the room behind them, baby Anke in her arms. Anke giggled and threw up her hands for Honor to take her.

"Just a minute, *kuche*," Honor said. "I have to finish giving the lamb her breakfast."

"I want breakfatht," Elijah reminded her.

Greta had made a huge batch of oatmeal earlier, but she'd burned it. It wasn't ruined, simply not pleasant. *Raisins and cinnamon could make it edible*, Honor supposed. But then she weakened. "I'll make you egg and biscuit," she offered.

"With scrapple," Justice urged. "Scrapple."

Justice liked to say the word. He didn't like scrapple, wouldn't eat meat of any kind, but the other boys did.

The other two took up the chant. "Scrapple, scrapple!"

Justice grinned. Sometimes, looking at him, Honor wondered just what would become of him when he was grown. He was a born mischief maker and unlikely to become a bishop. That was for certain.

The lamb drained the last of the formula from the bottle, butted her small head against the back of Honor's hand and kicked up her heels.

"She wants more," Tanner proclaimed, but Honor shook her head. Lambs, like children, often wanted to eat more than was good for them. She went to the sink and washed her hands, then looked around for a clean hand towel.

"All in the attic drying," Greta supplied. "Still wet."

Honor prayed for patience, dried her hands on her apron and turned on the flame under the cast-iron frying pan. "Get the eggs for me, will you, Greta?" she asked. That was a request she regretted a moment later when the girl stumbled, sending the egg carton flying out of her hand and bouncing off the back of a chair. Eggs splattered everywhere and the boys shrieked with excitement. Anke wailed.

Greta stood there and stared at the mess, looking as if she was about to burst into tears. "It was the cat's fault," she insisted. "Or maybe I slipped on a wet spot on the floor."

One remaining egg teetered on the edge of the table. Justice made a dive for it and missed. The egg rolled off. Tanner grabbed it in midair and the egg cracked between his fingers. The cat darted toward one of the broken eggs, only to be confronted by the dog. The cat hissed, and the dog began to bark, barely drowning out the shouts of the children.

"Clean it up, please," Honor told Greta. "And stop crying. It's only eggs." She scooped her daughter out of Greta's arms as a loud knock came at the back door. *"Ne,"* she muttered, closing her eyes for a moment. "It can't be." *Maybe it's someone from Sara's, come to tell me that Luke changed his mind*, she thought as she pushed open the back door.

But there he was, taller and handsomer than he'd seemed last night. He had just shaved; an Amish man didn't grow a beard until he married. She could smell the scent of his shaving cream. His blond hair, showing from beneath the too-small hat, was as yellow as June butter. She drew in a deep breath.

"Are you going to let me in?" he asked. And then that familiar grin started at the left corner of his mouth and spread, as sweet and slow as warm honey, across his face. "You look surprised to see me, Honor. I told you I'd be here."

Behind her, the kitchen chaos continued: Greta whining, the boys quarreling, the cat hissing at the dog and the lamb bleating. For a few seconds, she felt as if she were trapped in a block of ice. She couldn't let him in. There was no way she could invite him into her house…into her life. She'd lived through Luke Weaver once. She could never do it again. She'd crack and break like those eggs on the floor if she tried.

"Honor?" His green eyes seemed to dare her to turn him away. Or were they daring her to let him in?

She turned and walked slowly back to the kitchen, where the frying pan was smoking. Justice had pulled off his shoes and was dancing barefoot in a mess of egg yolk and crushed shell, and Elijah was trying to climb into the lamb's playpen.

"Turn off the burner!" Honor called to Greta. "The pan's too hot. There's smoke…" She trailed off and did it herself.

Patience, she cautioned herself. If she wasn't gentle with Greta, the girl would run weeping to her bed and she'd be no help all the rest of the day. Not that she was much help, but at least she was another pair of hands. And there were never enough hands to do all that was needed in the house or outside on the farm.

She thrust the baby into Greta's arms. "Put her in her high chair and give her a biscuit. Break it up, or she'll try to get it all in her mouth at once."

She realized that Justice and Tanner were staring at something behind her. She glanced back and saw that Luke had followed her into the kitchen. A leather tool belt—weighed down with a carpenter's hammer, screwdriver and pliers—was slung over one shoulder. In his other hand he carried a metal toolbox. What was he doing in here? She'd closed the door on him, hadn't she? She opened her mouth to ask him what he thought he was doing, but clamped it shut just as quickly. She'd left the door open behind her...an invitation.

"Is that coffee I smell?" he asked.

"If you want some, pour it yourself. Cups are up there." She pointed to a line of mugs hanging on hooks.

"You remember that I like mine sweet." His tone was teasing.

"Cream is in the refrigerator. Sugar on the table." She turned her back on him, refusing to acknowledge his charm. She waved the smoke away from the stove.

"Honey?"

She snapped around, a hot retort ready to spring from her throat. But then she realized he was grinning at her and pointing to the plastic bee bottle on top of the refrigerator. Honey. Luke had always preferred honey in his coffee. She retrieved Elijah from the playpen, saving the lamb from certain destruction. *"Ne,"* she admonished. "You cannot ride her. She's not a pony."

"What if she was a pig?" Justice asked, leaning on the playpen. "You can ride a pig."

"You can't ride pigs!" Tanner corrected.

"Hungry," Elijah reminded her.

"Justice, put your boots on. The floor's cold."

"Once I fix those holes, it will be a lot warmer." Luke squirted honey into his coffee. "I need to get up on the roof now that the rain has passed. If it can't be patched, I'll have to look into getting a roofing crew together."

"Ask Freeman at the mill." Honor turned the flame on under the frying pan again and went to the refrigerator for scrapple. "Tanner, run out to the barn and see if you can find more eggs. Greta, go with him. You carry the eggs, and don't let him lock you in anywhere." She turned her gaze back to Luke. "James Hostetler has the best contracting bunch, but he's busy for months. I already tried him. If anyone is available and has the skill to hold a hammer, Freeman will know it."

"Freeman Kemp? I know him," he said, taking a seat at the table. "Did know him."

She turned her back on Luke again. She felt almost breathless with anger or something else, something she didn't want to confront. "*Ya*, Freeman owns the mill, so he's usually there."

"That's right. I forgot his family has the mill. I'll stop and talk with him on the way back to Sara's."

"If you're stopping there, you might as well pick up some chicken feed and save me the trip. I'll give you the money. That one can't drive a horse and wagon." She nodded in Greta's direction. "She's afraid of horses," she said, managing to keep any disapproval from her tone. She needed to work on judging people. But who ever heard of an Amish girl who was afraid of horses?

With the pan the right temperature, Honor added thick slices of scrapple. She tried to concentrate on what she was doing, because what sense would it make to burn herself making breakfast through foolishness over a man she'd put aside long ago? Rather, one who had put *her* aside. She winced inwardly. The hurt was still there, mended over with strong thread, almost forgotten, but still having the power to cause her pain if she dwelled on it.

"Good coffee," he remarked. "And that scrapple smells good, too. You always did have a steady hand at the stove."

She glanced over her shoulder and glared at him. "No doubt Sara already fed you a substantial breakfast. She's known for her bountiful table."

Luke shrugged and offered that lethal grin of his. "I could eat a little something, if you're offering. A man can't do better than to start the day with a scrapple-and-egg biscuit."

"With catsup," Justice added. He carried a large bottle to the table and plopped it down in front of Luke. "I like catsup on my biscuit."

"That sounds good." Luke smiled at her son.

"That bottle's almost empty," Honor said. She was feeling a little steadier now. Children grounded a person. "Get *Mommi* another bottle from the pantry."

Justice darted off to get the catsup. Elijah climbed onto a chair and grabbed a biscuit from the plate on the table.

"Watch it doesn't burn." Luke pointed to Honor. "The scrapple."

She turned away from him and carefully turned the browning meat. "Your shoes are muddy," she said to Luke. "I'd appreciate it if you'd leave them in the laundry room. I scrubbed this floor once this morning."

Luke chuckled. "You've been busy. It's still early and you've made biscuits and mopped the floor and I don't know what else."

"Milked the cow and fed the livestock," Honor said, "and changed diapers and made beds. And if you don't take off those boots, I'll be scrubbing this floor again, too."

He got up from the table, went out of the room and removed his shoes. "Honor," he said as he returned in his stocking feet. His voice had lost the teasing note and become serious. "We need to talk. You know we need to talk about what happened, right?"

She shook her head. "*Ne*, I have nothing to say to you on that matter. It's long in the past. As for the present, do you want the job of fixing this house? If you do a decent job at a fair wage, I'll let you."

"You'll *let* me?"

She pressed her lips together. "I didn't ask you to come here."

"I couldn't stay away." He crossed the room to stand only an arm's length away from her. "You have to let me explain what happened. Why I did it."

She whirled around, hot spatula gripped in her hand, barely in control. *"Ne,"* she murmured. "I don't. I'll make use of your carpentry skills for the sake of my children. But there will be nothing more between us. Either you respect that, or you leave now."

His green eyes darkened with emotion.

Her breath caught in her throat.

"Honor," he said softly.

"*Ne*, Luke." She looked away. "You decide. Either we have a business arrangement or none at all."

"You know why I came back here."

His words gently nudged her, touching feelings she'd buried so long ago.

"Luke, I can't—"

The back door banged open and Tanner came flying in. "Eggs, *Mommi.* Lots of eggs. I found where the black hen had her nest."

"Good." Honor took a breath. "Wash your hands. Greta, put those eggs in the sink. Carefully." She laid the spatula on the table and clapped her hands. "Breakfast will be ready in two shakes of the lamb's tail, boys."

Luke was still standing there. Too close. "We *will* have that talk," he said so that only she heard him. "I promise you that."

A few minutes later, her children around her, eggs fried, breakfast to put on the table, Honor's foolishness receded and her confidence returned. "Luke, you're welcome to a breakfast sandwich, the same as the rest of us." She indicated the chair he had been sitting in before. "Greta, bring Anke's high chair here." She waved to the space beside her own seat, trusting her daughter's sloppy eating habits to keep Luke at a proper distance, letting him see the wall between them. She ushered her family to the table, shushing the children with a glance and bowing her head for silent grace.

Please God, she whispered inwardly. *Give me strength to deal with Luke, to move on with my life, to use him for what we need and then send him on his way, gracefully.* She opened her eyes to find Luke watching her, and she used the excuse of her children to look away. Her heart raced as her hands performed the familiar tasks of stacking eggs, scrapple and cheese on biscuits and pouring milk for her sons and daughter.

Luke went to the stove for another cup of coffee. "Some for you?" he asked.

She hated to ask any favors of him, but she did want the coffee. She needed more than one cup to get through the morning. Reluctantly, she nodded. *"Danke."*

He carried it to the table, added cream and placed the mug carefully in front of her plate. The children and Greta chattered. Anke giggled and cooed and tossed pieces of biscuit and egg onto the floor where the dog and cat vied for the best crumbs.

"I thought I'd start here in the kitchen, if that suits you," Luke said after finishing off his second egg-and-scrapple sandwich.

"It would suit me best if you weren't here at all," she reminded him and then realized how ungrateful she sounded. She needed the work done. The state of the kitchen was hardly fit for her children—for anyone to prepare food or eat in. "I'm sorry," she said. "That was unkind. *Ya*, it would be good if you started in here. It certainly needs it."

So much of what Silas had promised had been left undone. And not for lack of funds, a truth she hadn't realized until after he had passed and she had taken the family finances into her hands. They were by no means poor, as he'd always led her to believe. Whatever his reasons for making her think that, he'd taken them with him to Heaven. And it would do no good to think ill of him. "Excuse me, Anke needs tidying up. Greta, see to the children."

She lifted a squirming Anke out of her high chair and carried her out of the kitchen and upstairs to the bathroom. There, she placed the toddler on a clean towel and proceeded to wash her face and hands, and wipe most of the egg and biscuit from her infant's gown. "It's going to be a new start for us, isn't it, baby?" she said to the child. "We'll make our house all sound and tidy and the matchmaker will find you a new *daddi*. Won't you like that?"

Anke needed a father, and the boys certainly needed one. That was what she had told Sara when she'd sat down in her office over a month ago to discuss an appropriate match. They needed a father with a steady but kind hand. Honor spoiled her children. Everyone said so. And she knew she did, but that was because Silas hadn't…

She bit off that line of thought. She wouldn't allow herself to wallow in self-pity. She had her faith, her children and her future to think of. She summoned a smile for Anke, tickled her soft belly and thrilled to the sound of baby laughter. She'd dealt with problems before, surely some greater than having Luke Weaver in her house. She'd find a way to manage him.

"After all," she said to her daughter, "how long can he be here? A few days? A few weeks? And then…" She lifted Anke in the air and nuzzled her midsection so that the baby giggled again. "And then we're done with him."

Freeman Kemp swung the bag of chicken feed into the back of Sara's wagon. "It's good of you to take this to Honor. Saves her a trip. And I'm glad you're going to do repairs on the house. That farm was in bad shape when Silas bought it, and I don't think he made many improvements before he took sick."

"It has to be difficult for a young widow with the children, just trying to get to the daily chores," Luke replied. "I can't imagine trying to get to bigger projects." He'd liked Freeman the moment he met him. Met him again. They had known each other as teenagers. Not well, but they'd once played on the same softball team.

"Our church community is getting so big that it's time we split off," Freeman said. "And it's natural that those of us farther out should form the new church. We're all hoping Honor will find a husband willing to settle here. You know how it goes. One young Amish family settles in an area and others usually follow."

Freeman tugged the brim of his hat down to shade his eyes from the glare of the setting sun. "You know," he said slowly. "Honor's mourning time is over. And you're a single man. Maybe you ought to think about courting her. 'Course you'd need a new hat." He offered a half smile. "She'd make someone a good wife. Honor's a sensible woman. Smart. Capable. And she speaks her mind."

"That she does." Luke grinned. Some men didn't like a woman who didn't hold back with their opinions, but he didn't have a problem with it. In fact, he wanted a wife who could be his partner. And it was a partner's duty sometimes to present the opposite side of an argument. "Honor and I knew each other from childhood."

Freeman shrugged. "Sometimes that's best. No secrets between you, then." He hesitated, as if sizing Luke up. Then he went on. "I'll be honest with you. I didn't care all that much for Silas. He was moody. Always seemed an odd match to me, him being older and on the serious side. But who am I to say? My family had given me up for a lifelong bachelor until my wife, Katie, came along and set me straight. Why don't you join us for church next month when we have service here at our place? We always appreciate a new face."

"I'd like that," Luke said. "I've promised Sara I'll attend Seven Poplars so long as I'm staying with her, though."

"That's no problem, then," Freeman answered. "We hold ours on a different schedule." He thought for a moment. "Long trip every day. And I see you have Sara's rig." He pointed to the wagon. "If you think you'd like to be closer, we've got a spare room you're welcome to. I'd have to check with my wife, but I'm sure it would be okay with her."

Luke met Freeman's gaze. "I might just take you up on that. Once… I get an idea of how long I'm going to be working for Honor." *Once I get an idea if she's going to kick me off her property*, he thought.

"Well, we can talk about it. I'm sure I'll see you at Sara's Epiphany party Saturday. Nobody wants to miss that." He offered Luke his hand. "Glad you're back. It's good to meet you again."

"And you," Luke said.

"Just a word to the wise," Freeman said as he opened the gate that led onto the hardtop road.

"Ya?"

"Honor's children can be a handful." He pointed at him. "Don't turn your back on them."

"Oh, I've already seen evidence of it. But boys can be mischievous. And those three are still little."

Freeman laughed. "Don't say I didn't warn you."

Chapter Four

Honor glanced out the window to where her three red-cheeked boys were playing in the snow. Justice had climbed up on the gate, and Tanner was pushing it open and shut while Elijah threw snowballs at them both.

At least, she guessed he was attempting to throw snowballs. His aim was good, but he hadn't quite mastered the art of forming fresh snow into a ball. It was probably for the best, she thought, because no one was crying yet. Even Greta, who was in the barnyard, tossing shelled corn to the chickens and ducks, seemed to be having a good time.

Honor was glad. It wasn't often that she saw Greta enjoying herself. The girl had been so homesick when she first arrived that Honor had seriously considered sending her home. However, Silas's sister had made it clear that she had a lot of mouths to feed and the wages Honor paid Greta were a blessing to the family. There were nine children still at home, and the father was disabled, his only income coming from what he earned fixing clocks. And as inexperienced as Greta seemed to be with most chores, she was better than no help at all for Honor.

"Have you got time to help me for a couple of minutes?" Luke asked, interrupting Honor's thoughts. "This would go faster if you could hold that end of the board."

She glanced at him standing at a window, a freshly cut board in his hand. She tried not to smile. She still didn't want him here, but she was astonished at the amount of work he'd gotten done in only three days. And it was amazing how easily he seemed to be easing into the household. The children were already trailing after him as if they had known him their whole lives. That rankled most of all. "Of course," she said as she put Anke in her play yard.

Honor wondered why she hadn't found someone to do this carpentry work sooner. But she knew why. It was her own fear of spending all her savings, leaving nothing to live on, as Silas had warned she would. Silas had made all the financial decisions in their marriage. He'd even given her an allowance for groceries and household items. And now that she was free to make her own decisions, it had taken some time begin to trust her own judgment.

"Just hold this end," Luke instructed, indicating a length of wood. "The kitchen will feel a lot snugger once these leaks around the window are patched. Just some decent framing and some caulk is all you needed here."

It already felt a lot warmer. The first thing that Luke did every morning when he arrived was to chop wood and fill the wood box. She could cut wood, and she was capable of carrying it. But it was hard work. Luke made it seem easy. Of course, she had propane heat to fall back on, but firewood from her own property was free.

Honor grabbed her end of the board and held it in place.

"Something smells wonderful," he said between the strikes of his hammer. The nails went in true and straight. "Downright delicious," he persisted.

She sighed. "I'm making a rice pudding. I put it in the oven while you were rehanging the gate."

He glanced out the window to where all three of the children were now swinging on the gate. "It looks like those hinges are getting a thorough quality-control inspection."

Honor laughed. "That's a nice way of putting it. Most people aren't quite so charitable."

"They ought to be. They're fine youngsters."

"Danke." She thought so, even if they were full of mischief. But that was natural, wasn't it? Boys were mischief makers. It was their nature.

Luke pushed another piece of trim into her hands. "Line the bottom of that up with the horizontal board."

"Like this?"

"Just a little higher. There. That's perfect." He quickly drove several finishing nails into place. "A little paint and this window will give you another ten years of service."

"I can do the painting," she offered. "At least in here." She wanted the trim and ceiling white. The walls were a pale green, lighter than celery. She liked green, and the white trim would set it off and make the room look fresh.

"You're welcome to it, if you can find the time. Painting isn't one of my favorite tasks. I can do it if I have to, but I'm happier with the woodworking." He motioned to the corner of the room where he'd pulled up a section of cracked and worn linoleum. "The original floor is under here. White pine, I think. Wide boards. If we took up all the linoleum and refinished the floor, it would be a lot cheaper than putting down another floor covering." He met her gaze. "What do you think?"

She considered. "A saving when there was so much money to go out would be a blessing, but..." She frowned, trying to think how to word her thought delicately, then just said what was on her mind. "You think the children will ruin it?"

"I suppose it's possible," he said with a twinkle in his eyes. "But more than one family of children has lived in this kitchen over the last two hundred years, so I doubt it. The hardwood would come up beautiful."

"And plain?"

"As plain as pine." He chuckled and she found herself smiling with him. "Plain enough to suit a bishop."

"And we want to do that, don't we?" she replied.

Staying within the community rules was a necessary part of Amish life, one that she'd never felt restricted her. Rather, it made her feel safe. The elders of the church, the preachers and the bishop, told the congregation what God expected of them. All she had to do was follow their teaching, and someday, when she passed out of this earthly existence, she would be welcomed into Heaven. It was a comforting certainty, one that she had dedicated her life to living.

Anke pulled herself to her feet and tossed a rag doll out of her play yard onto the floor. Luke scooped it up and handed it back to her. She promptly threw it a second time, giggling when he retrieved it yet again.

"It's a game," Honor said. "She'd keep it up all day if you'd let her." She wiped her hands on her apron. "Look at the time. I'd best get the dumplings rolled for dinner."

Luke handed the doll to Anke again, then tickled her belly through the mesh side of the play yard. The baby giggled. "She was born after her father passed, wasn't she?" he mused.

Honor nodded. "She was."

"It must have been terribly difficult for you, not having him with you. And after, when Anke was an infant."

Honor thought carefully before she responded. She wasn't going to lie to make her late husband out to be someone he wasn't, but she wouldn't disrespect him, either. "Silas was a good man, but he believed that small children were the responsibility of the mother. He said he would take them in hand when they were older."

How old, she wasn't certain. Tanner hadn't been old enough to command his father's attention beyond Silas's insistence that their little boy hold his tongue at the table, in church and whenever adults were present. As for Justice and Elijah, she couldn't recall Silas ever holding one of them in his arms or taking them on his lap. Not to read to them. Certainly not to snuggle with them. Looking back, she could see that her decision to marry Silas had been impulsive, she'd agreed without really thinking through her options. If she was honest with herself, the truth was, she married Silas because he was the first man to ask. After Luke.

"I'm so sorry that you had to—"

"Don't be sorry for me, Luke," she interrupted, shaking her head. "We all have trials to live through. They say that God never gives anyone more than they can bear."

His green eyes filled with compassion. "I'm still sorry."

"Silas left me a home and four healthy children. Riches beyond counting," she murmured, turning away from him to take a dish towel from the back of one of the kitchen chairs. "I'm truly blessed."

Luke was quiet for a moment and then said, "So what do you think?"

"About what?" She turned back to him.

"The floor? Will you be satisfied with the old wood planks?"

"How will you finish them?"

"A high-grade poly. But it still won't cost much."

She held up her hand. "Say no more. We can try it. If I don't like it, I can always cover the floor again." She lifted a heavy cast-iron kettle from the countertop.

"Let me get that." Luke took it from her and carried it to the stove. "What's going with those slippery dumplings?"

"Fried chicken, peas, mashed potatoes and biscuits," she said, fighting a smile as she washed her hands at the sink. The man did like to eat.

"Mmm, sounds good. You don't suppose you could spare a bowl of dumplings."

"Didn't Sara pack you a lunch?"

He grinned. "She did. But it's a ham sandwich and an apple. Cold. Hot chicken and slippery dumplings sounds much tastier. Especially on a chilly day like this."

He was right. It did. Her stomach rumbled at the thought of hot biscuits dripping with butter and chicken fried crispy brown. She loved to eat, too, and she had no doubt that by the time she reached middle age, she'd have lost her girlish figure. Not that she looked much like the slim, wide-eyed girl who'd married Silas King. Four children coming so quickly had added inches to her waist and hips. It was only long hours and hard work that kept her from becoming round.

"So, am I to fast on Sara's charity, or are you willing to give me just the tiniest cup of dumplings?" Luke began plaintively.

He sounded so much like a little boy that Honor had to chuckle. "All right, all right, you can have dinner with us. But you'd best not waste Sara's ham sandwich." Honor began to remove flour and salt from the Hoosier cabinet she'd brought with her to the marriage. The piece had been her great-grandmother's, and it had been carefully cared for over four generations. The paint was a little faded, but she loved it just the way it was.

"I'll eat it on the way back to her house," Luke promised. He tucked several nails into his mouth and finished up the last piece of trim work on the window frame. "I replaced the sash cord so the window will go up and down easier," he said. "And you won't have to prop it open with a stick anymore."

"Danke," she said. Now, if he could just do something with the ceiling. It was low, which made the room darker than she liked. And crumbles of plaster sometimes fell on them. Once, she'd had to throw away a whole pot of chicken soup when a big chunk dropped into their supper.

The kitchen was one of the worst rooms in the house. Silas had promised that he'd get to it, but he never had. The parlor, he'd remodeled. Partially. Silas had said that he was making it a proper place for the bishop to preach, but he'd never asked the bishop to come. Instead, the room had become Silas's retreat from the children and from her. He would close the door and huddle in there with a blanket around his shoulders against the chill while he went over his financial records.

"What do you think?" Luke asked her.

Honor blinked. She wasn't sure what he'd asked her but didn't want to admit that she'd been woolgathering. "I'm not sure," she ventured as she measured out three level cups of flour.

"It would save time. And I'd get more work done here because I could work until dark."

She turned to him, realizing she had no idea what he was talking about. "I'm sorry?"

"If I stayed at the mill instead of driving back and forth to Sara Yoder's every day. Freeman invited me. He said I was welcome to stay in the farmhouse, but I didn't want to be a burden on Katie. And they're not married that long, so I think they should have their privacy. But…there's a little house for a hired man. Just a single room. The boy who works for him still lives with his parents a mile away, so the place is empty. I offered to rent it from them, but Freeman wouldn't have it. He says if I help them out a few hours on Saturday morning, when they have the most customers, I can live there for free."

"It sounds a sensible arrangement, but you won't

be working on my house for long. What would you do then? Wouldn't you be better situated closer to Dover?"

"The mill will be fine. I don't know how long it will take to finish your house, but honestly…" He scratched his head. "There's a lot that needs fixing around here, Honor. Some things, like that windmill, have to be rebuilt. I can't go on using Sara's mule. It's not fair to her."

"What were you doing for transportation in Kansas?"

"I have horses. A neighbor is keeping them for me until I can find someone reliable to transport them to Delaware. Freeman says I can keep them at his place once they arrive." He shrugged. "Meanwhile, I can easily walk from the mill to your place."

"In bad weather?"

"Rain and snow don't bother me. After Kansas, Delaware weather will be mild."

"I'll remind you of that when you're soaking to the skin and wading through mud puddles." She shrugged. "Do as you please," she said, but secretly she thought it was a splendid idea. Who could complain about getting more work out of a hired man? And that's all Luke was, she told herself firmly. All he could ever be to her.

"You're certain you don't want to ride with us?" Freeman asked. "Plenty of room." He stood just inside the door of the little house he'd helped Luke to move into the night before.

The small log structure stood in the shadow of the mill within the sound of the millrace and shaded by willows in summer and spring. Wood-floored and low-ceilinged, the single room contained a bed, a braided rug on the floor, a table and two chairs, a propane stove and a built-in cupboard. It was sparse but spotless with a cheery red-and-white quilt and plain white curtains at the two narrow windows. Hand-carved pegs held his coat, water-damaged hat and spare shirt. It was a solid place for a man who needed a roof over his head close to a certain woman's house and one that Luke hoped he wouldn't have need of for long.

Luke shook his head. "*Ne*, you and your family go on. I'll be fine. I want to shine my boots and shave. I'll catch a ride with Honor and the children."

Freeman nodded. "I can understand how you'd rather go with them." He grinned and glanced around the cabin. "I hope you'll be comfortable here. Anything you want, you know you're welcome to come up to the house. And we expect you to eat with us whenever the widow doesn't feed you."

He chuckled. "Sara Yoder thinks highly of you. And it's not always easy to make an impression on our matchmaker. Well—" he slapped the doorjamb "—see you there. Sara's Epiphany suppers are talked about all year. Every woman that comes brings her special dish, and we make up for the morning's fasting by stuffing ourselves like Thanksgiving turkeys."

"I can't wait." Luke remembered Honor saying something about the sweet potato pies she was planning on making the previous night, after he left and the children went to bed. "And thanks again for your hospitality," he said to Freeman.

The miller tugged on his hat and went out, and Luke hunted up the shoe polish and cleaning cloth he'd seen on the shelf in the miniscule bathroom. He'd lost all his good clothes in the bus accident and hadn't had the time to replace them. Until he bought a new wardrobe, he'd have to make do with the borrowed shirts and trousers that didn't quite fit. Not that he wasn't grateful to Sara and Hiram and Freeman for their kindness, but it was hard for him to be on the receiving end of charity when he'd been accustomed to being the one giving a helping hand to those who needed it.

Luke waited until he heard Freeman's buggy roll out of the mill yard before donning his coat and hat. He hoped he hadn't waited too long and missed Honor. But he was counting on the children to keep her from leaving early. He hadn't exactly made arrangements to ride with her, and it would be a long walk to Sara's if things didn't work out. Or if Honor said no. Which he wasn't even going to consider.

The wind was rising as he strode away from the cabin and past the mill. There would be no customers today. The "closed, come again" sign hung at the entrance to the drive. Across the way and down, at the dirt pull off, he saw a blue pickup parked, and beyond it, at the pond's edge, a man and a small boy. It was too cold for fishing but they stood close together, tossing pebbles into the water and laughing about something.

A father and his son, Luke thought. A pang of regret knifed through him. If he'd not made the decision he had, Honor's children might have been his own. He could have been the man standing with his son beside the millpond, laughing with him, lifting him high in the air. So many years lost…so many possibilities that could never be. He swallowed hard as a lump formed in his throat.

For an instant, he could picture Honor's beautiful face the day before he'd ruined everything. She'd been radiant, joy in her movement, her features. And he'd crushed her happiness, turning her shining day to one of tearful sorrow. God forgive him, the fault was his. But…

He sighed deeply. If he were given the chance to relive that day, would he do any different? He'd never know, because that wasn't a possibility. All he had was hope that he could make a new beginning here and now.

Luke walked out onto the main road and headed toward Seven Poplars, hoping to he hadn't missed her buggy. As he walked, he wondered why Silas King had ever picked a farm this far away from Dover.

The nearest Amish school was a distance away. Tanner hadn't started school yet, although he was old enough, but when he did, it would be quite the walk for a first grader. Unless Honor planned on driving him at least part of the way, though that would mean leaving the other children in Greta's care or hauling them all back and forth every day.

It didn't make a lot of sense, but the boy had to attend school eventually. The Amish here had won the right to keep their children in their own schools from kindergarten through the eighth grade. And every child had to attend, so Tanner would have to start soon or someone from the state would be paying a call on Honor.

He'd ask her what she planned to do. But he'd have to do so in a way that didn't seem to be critical of her parenting. Honor was touchy over her children. Not that she wasn't a good mother. It was clear to him that her world revolved around them. But he had to agree with the warnings he'd gotten about them so far—the children *were* a little wild. And he couldn't help noticing that the consequences she promised for bad behavior never seemed to materialize.

Luke stopped and looked behind him. Still no sign of Honor. The fear that she had already passed this spot nagged at him. Wouldn't he look foolish, turning down Freeman's offer of a ride and then having to walk all those miles?

He was truly starving. He'd had no breakfast today. Not even coffee. Nothing more than a pint of cold water from a Mason jar. Freeman was probably halfway to Sara's by now. Maybe even pulling into the yard. Luke could imagine filling his plate with ham, turkey, roast beef and all the sides. He'd save room for a slice or two of Honor's sweet potato pie.

The sound of something coming behind him made him stop his daydreaming and look over his shoulder. But it wasn't a horse and buggy, just a car. The driver waved and drove on past. Luke glanced at the sky. What time was it? Well past noon. Why hadn't he left Freeman's place sooner? All he could think about was spending the day with Honor, and now it seemed he'd—

His heart leaped at another sound. There was a buggy coming. Grinning, he turned back toward Sara's house and started walking, taking long strides. He hadn't missed her. Things were working out exactly as he planned. There was no way she could pass him by without stopping to give him a ride. Not on Epiphany.

He started whistling a tune. He could hear the sound of horse's hooves on the blacktop. He didn't look back, just kept walking until the horse pulled alongside him. Then he turned, feigned surprise and waved at Honor and the children.

The children shouted, “Luke! Luke! Happy Epiphany!”

He grinned. “Happy Epiphany!” And then his smile faded as Honor smiled and waved and kept driving. The buggy rolled past him and on, down the road with the laughing children peering out the back and waving, leaving him behind.

Chapter Five

Honor waved at Luke and smiled back. Then she drove right by him without reining in the horse one bit. The nerve of the man. He'd wheedled his way into her house, forced her to hire him to make the repairs and now was manipulating her, so that she'd have to bring him to Sara's Epiphany supper.

He'd probably planned this whole thing; he'd probably been waiting there on the road for her since dawn. But she wasn't going to give him a ride. Why should she? Arriving together would give everyone in the community the idea that they were seeing each other. And that was definitely, positively, absolutely not happening.

"Mommi!" Tanner yelled. "That was Luke. You have to stop for him."

"Luke! Luke!" Justice had the back window partially open and was waving frantically.

Anke began to fuss. And she'd almost been asleep in Greta's arms before the boys had started such a racket.

"You should stop for him," Greta said.

Honor turned to look at Greta and guilt settled over

her shoulders. What was wrong with her? She wouldn't leave any Amish person walking when she could offer a ride, especially when she knew Luke was going to the same destination she was.

Before she realized what she was doing, she pulled back on the leathers. "Whoa, whoa."

The children in the back of the buggy cheered and Greta uttered a small sound that might have been astonishment. Honor leaned out. "Well, what are you waiting for?" she called. "Hurry up. Get in. We're late as it is."

"What shall I do?" Greta whispered to Honor. "Should I get in the back?" The cheering behind them had become a chant of Luke's name. All three boys were bouncing up and down and waving their arms.

"Quiet, all of you," Honor warned. "*Ne*, you will not get in the back, Greta. Just slide over toward me. There's plenty of room for him. You don't take up as much room as a small rabbit." Honor made her face stern and stared straight ahead at the horse.

Luke got up into the buggy, taking the place beside Greta on the bench seat. *"Danke,"* he said with a grin. "I thought you were going to leave me to walk to Sara's."

"I considered it," Honor admitted, not looking at him. She clicked to the horse. "Walk on," she commanded. She was gripping the reins tighter than she needed to. Her palms were damp where the leathers lay against them.

"I can drive, if you like," Luke said.

"And why would I let you do that?" she asked. Then she felt a little silly. She had no proof that he'd deliberately trapped her into driving him. Maybe he'd missed Freeman. Or maybe the miller's plans had changed.

Anke was still fussing, and now she was trying to climb out of Greta's arms into Honor's.

"Suit yourself," Luke said, still maintaining that good-natured air that made her wish she belonged to a less peaceful people, because a tiny, unpleasant part of her wanted to give him a sharp kick in the shins.

Anke's griping became a wail. Greta struggled to hold on to the baby.

"You're right," Honor said, giving up and passing Luke the reins. "You should be driving." She held out her arms for her daughter and Greta gratefully passed her over. Honor reached into her coat pocket and found a pacifier. She popped it into the baby's mouth, and soon the tempest passed.

Greta shrank down so that she left a space between herself and Luke. She sniffed and wiped at her nose. Honor found a handkerchief in her other coat pocket and passed it to the girl. Luke drove in silence, his hands gentle on the reins. In the back, the boys grew silent.

Honor wondered at her own show of bad temper. How could she have done such a spiteful thing? What kind of example was that for a mother? "I'm sorry," she said softly to Luke. "I thought you'd deliberately waited for me on the road and..."

"You always did jump to conclusions," Luke said. "You should wait and find out, before you fly off the handle. Simon Beechy lives a ways down on this road. I met Simon at the mill the other day and he told me I was welcome to ride with him to Sara's." Luke looked at her with an amused expression. "Maybe I was taking him up on that offer."

She hesitated, looking him in the eyes. "And were

you?" she asked. "Because it will be no trouble to let you out at Simon's."

"Ne, danke," he answered solemnly, looking straight ahead again. "I think I'd rather ride with you and the children."

Anke gurgled and began to clap her hands together. Greta didn't make a sound. Honor glanced at her to make sure she was still breathing. The girl was very pale, but her round eyes were large in her face. She seemed scared to death to be sitting so close to Luke. Honor felt sorry for her. Greta really would need to toughen up.

Everyone was quiet again. The sound of the buggy wheels and the rapid clip-clop of the horse's hooves against the hardtop were all Honor could hear. She waited for Luke to say something. If this was a game of wits, she wanted to win. But he shouldn't give up so easily.

"So, which was it?" Honor pressed when she could hold her tongue no longer. "You wanted to get to Simon's, or it was a trick to get me to feel sorry for you?" This time she didn't look at Luke, but kept her gaze on Anke.

Tanner giggled, and Justice and Elijah took up the laughter.

"Hush, boys," Luke admonished softly.

To Honor's astonishment, they obeyed.

"I guess we'll never know the answer to that," Luke said, looking her way.

And, in spite of herself, Honor chuckled. One thing you could say for Luke. He might be infuriating, but he was never dull.

When they arrived at Sara's, her hired man, Hiram,

and another man were taking charge of the guests' horses. Luke helped Greta out of the buggy and then came around to assist Honor. The boys scrambled out of the back, and Luke insisted on carrying the baskets with the sweet potato pies inside.

Sara's house was crowded with people, all talking at once in a mixture of *Deitsch* and English. Children, hers and others', crawled under the tables and hid behind the couch and easy chairs, peeked shyly at each other and then slipped away to play. Seniors sat or stood in clusters and younger women hugged and called out to friends.

The rooms smelled deliciously of gingerbread, pumpkin pie and baking ham, and everyone was relaxed and eager to share the day with each other. Although Seven Poplars wasn't the community that Honor had been raised in, she knew many of Sara's friends and immediately felt at home.

Hannah, Sara's cousin, who lived nearby, asked to take the baby, and Anke seemed delighted to be snatched away and displayed for everyone to admire. The schoolteacher, Ellie, who was a little person, showed Honor where to put her coat and introduced her to several young women Honor hadn't yet met. Luke deposited the pies on a counter on the porch with other desserts and vanished, presumably to find other men. In social occasions, Amish men and women were free to circulate as they pleased, but usually they ended up talking with those of their own gender. For Honor, having other women to talk to was wonderful, given her isolation on the farm.

Sara greeted her with a kiss on the cheek and a request for help with biscuit dough that was almost ready to go into the oven. Honor readily accepted the task, found an apron to cover her good clothes and joined Ellie in hand rolling baking powder biscuits and putting them on trays to go into the oven. Rebecca, one of the Yoder sisters, joined them in the kitchen.

Rebecca was wife to a Seven Poplars preacher and they had three children. Honor had met her before, but they'd never really had a chance to talk. With her in the kitchen now, Honor soon learned that Rebecca had a delightful sense of humor.

It was such a treat to be there, enjoying Sara's hospitality. Before her marriage to Silas, Honor had always enjoyed visiting friends and relatives and sharing the joy of holidays such as Little Christmas. Silas hadn't. He preferred to remain at home, and he preferred her in the house with her duties and her children. Church and the occasional grocery-shopping trip had been the rare times when she'd gotten out. Why she'd waited so long after his passing to return to the community, she wasn't sure. But she was here, and she was determined to make the most of every moment.

Men were setting up extra tables in the living room and the sitting room at the bottom of the stairs. Honor noticed a woman in a black elder's *kapp* and knit shawl sitting in the midst of several young mothers. The old woman, who was in a wheelchair, fussed loudly as one of them arranged a blanket over her knees and passed a baby into her arms.

"That's Anna Mast's grandmother Lovina Yoder," Ellie explained. "She lives with Anna and her Samuel."

"I remember her. She's Martha Coblenz's mother, isn't she?" Honor asked.

"Ya," Ellie agreed. "And Hannah's mother-in-law. Not Albert's mother, but her first husband's."

Honor lowered her voice. "Lovina's always terrified me."

Ellie chuckled. "*Ya*, she can be that way. But Hannah says Anna gets along *goot* with her."

Sara took Lovina a cup of hot mulled cider and retrieved the baby. Lovina complained that the cider wasn't hot enough and demanded to know when supper was to be served.

"Soon, soon," Sara soothed, patting the elderly woman's hand. "We're just waiting on the biscuits and a few more families."

"I should hope so," Lovina declared. "I didn't come out on such a cold day to go home with an empty stomach. My Jonas is hungry, too. He told me so. He's out in the barn. Milking the cows. But he will be in soon, and he wants his supper."

Honor looked at Ellie and whispered, "I thought Jonas passed away long ago."

"He did," Ellie said. "But Lovina likes to think he's still with us. Her memory isn't what it used to be, so Anna thinks it's kinder if we all just go along with it."

A woman brought a new, partially knit baby cap for Lovina to admire, and the elderly woman stopped grumbling and turned all her attention to the pattern.

Another couple came in out of the cold, bringing plates of German sausages, a tub of sauerkraut and a huge platter of *fastnacht kucha.* Since honey doughnuts were Honor's weakness, she couldn't wait for dessert.

Honor wasn't certain how any more guests would fit into Sara's house, but no one seemed to mind that the rooms were quickly filling up or that yet another table had to be squeezed in.

Between the exchange of recipes and neighborhood news, Honor couldn't help hearing snatches of Luke's voice or catching glimpses of him. To her own astonishment, she found herself following him with her gaze. Was it possible that she still cared for him after what had happened between them? She knew the answer to that question, but it had nothing to do with her resolve that he could have no part in her future other than to mend a few broken fences or patch a hole in a wall.

"I see you came with Luke Weaver," Rebecca teased as they completed the final tray of biscuits and slid it into the hot oven.

"What?" Honor felt herself flush. Had it been so obvious that she was watching him? "Um, we came upon him walking. On the road."

Ellie chuckled. "And, naturally, you gave him a ride."

Honor offered a quick smile. "Naturally." She spotted Anke in Martha Coblenz's arms and took the opportunity to escape the conversation by swooping to reclaim her daughter. "*Aenti* Martha. It's good to see you." Honor raised on tiptoe to kissed the older woman's cheek. "How is *Onkel* Reuben?" Martha wasn't really a relative, but she'd been a good friend of Honor's late mother, and Honor had always addressed them as Aunt and Uncle.

"Not well," Martha replied. "Not well, at all. His back and his knees. He suffers in cold weather."

Honor smiled and nodded as though she hadn't seen *Onkel* Reuben carrying one end of a heavy table just a few minutes before. Like his wife, Reuben was full of complaints. As Honor's mother had always said, Reuben had never been one for work, but he'd always eaten for two men and seemed to do whatever he wanted. But despite their dour outlooks on life, Honor had always believed the couple had good hearts.

"Sara's hunting you a husband, is she?" Martha asked. "About time." She was a tall, spare woman with an ample chin and a nose like a hawk's, who never missed an item of interest that went on in the county.

Honor nodded. "I've asked Sara to find me a settled, older man, possibly a widower with children. I need someone with experience to be a father to my children."

Martha harrumphed, "That you do, because they are sore in need of a man's hand, I can tell you that. Remember what the Good Book says—spare the rod and spoil the child."

"Martha!" Hannah Yoder Hartman entered the kitchen, bundled in cape and bonnet, her nose and cheeks red from the cold winter air. She was carrying a cast-aluminum turkey roaster. "Could you get this lid? I think it's slipping."

Martha grabbed a hot mitt off the counter and successfully caught the sliding cover. Hannah deposited the turkey onto Sara's second stove.

"Come with me," Martha urged her sister-in-law. "It's warm in here, and I have something to tell you. You'll never guess…"

Hannah followed Martha out of the kitchen, and Honor gave a sigh of relief. She feared that bringing Luke in her buggy might start gossip, but she hoped that she'd stopped that rumor before it got started.

Greta appeared at Honor's side. "Can I take Anke?"

she asked. "I was telling some girls my age about her, and they wanted to see her."

Surprised that Greta would ask for her daughter, Honor happily handed her over as she made the introductions to the others in the kitchen. "Greta is Silas's niece, come to help me with the children," she explained. "She doesn't know many people here in Seven Poplars yet."

"But I met Jane now," Greta said. "And her sister May. They have a little sister the same age as Anke. And there's a girl, Zipporah, who lives near us, I think. They asked if I could bring her." She pointed to the front room. "There are blocks. For Anke to play with."

"Of course," Honor agreed. "I'm glad you're making new friends." She watched until Greta was safely out of earshot and then smiled at Rebecca. "That's a blessing. The girl's been so homesick that I was afraid I'd have to send her back to her mother. She didn't want to come today. I do hope she has a good time."

"She will," Rebecca said.

"Ya," Ellie chimed in. "Jane and May are my students. They're nice girls. And they are experienced with babies, so your Anke's in safe hands."

Rebecca turned to the sink and began to wash the large stainless steel bowl that had held the biscuit dough. "I was surprised to hear that Luke Weaver's come back from Kansas. Is he planning on staying in Delaware?"

Honor shrugged. "I wouldn't know. He's doing some carpentry work for me."

"Mmm-hmm," Rebecca answered. She and Ellie exchanged glances and both women chuckled.

"*Ne*, really," Honor protested. She suddenly felt her

throat and cheeks growing warm again and told herself that it was the heat of the oven. "It's just a business arrangement."

Ellie's voice dropped to a whisper. "But you have to admit, he *is* cute."

Honor shrugged. "I suppose, in a boyish sort of way."

Ellie giggled. "Not boyish by the width of those shoulders."

Sara walked back into the kitchen with a pitcher in her hands. "Honor, would you go down to the cellar for more apple cider? That door over there. Watch the steps. There isn't much light from the basement window today."

Ellie looked up from unwrapping squares of homemade butter pressed with a leaf print. "I can go, if you like."

"*Ne*, I don't mind." Honor took the green pitcher and slid the latch on the cellar door. She waited a few seconds at the top of the steps while her eyes adjusted to the dim lighting. When they'd arrived at Sara's, the sun had been shining, but now the afternoon was growing cloudy and there wasn't much light coming in through the windows.

Honor descended the stairs and quickly found the keg of cider. She filled the pitcher and started for the steps, but, as she put her hand on the banister, someone opened the door. She stepped back and saw that it was Luke. He was carrying a green pitcher.

"I didn't know you were down here," he said.

"I was just bringing up this pitcher of apple cider. For Sara."

For an instant, a puzzled expression crossed his face,

but then he smiled. “Funny,” he said. “Sara must have forgotten.” He tilted his pitcher so that she could see that it was empty. “Because she just sent *me* for cider.”

He chuckled, and then, against her will, she began to laugh with him. “If I didn’t know better,” she said, “I’d think Sara is trying to set us up.”

Chapter Six

Leaving the door open, Luke came down the stairs and settled on one of the lower steps. He cradled the empty pitcher between his hands. "I suppose it's *possible* that Sara is trying to match us up. It is what she does for a living. And, from what I hear..." He met Honor's suspicious gaze full on. "She knows what she's doing. She has a reputation for seeing solid matches where others don't."

Honor pursed her lips, but her eyes were open wide, not narrowed, and she didn't appear to be disapproving.

Luke took it as a positive sign and forged ahead. "I already know we'd be a good fit. Perfect, in fact, if it wasn't for what happened last time you agreed to marry me. Which you have every reason to be angry about."

"I'm not angry. At least not anymore," she corrected, standing in front of him, holding a pitcher identical to the one Sara had given him. "That was a long time ago, and I've moved on with my life."

"I still feel like we need to talk about what happened," he urged, coming to his feet. "If you'd let me apologize for—"

"Ne," she interrupted firmly. "I'm afraid I'm not *that* far past it. Not today, at least." She sighed. "I don't want to feel those emotions again, Luke. Anger. Bitterness. That's not helpful for either of us. I'm simply not in the mood to drag all that up. This is too special of a day to ruin it with an old disagreement."

"We have to talk about it someday," he insisted.

"Maybe, maybe not." She shrugged. "But definitely not today. I'm having a wonderful time, and I don't want anything to ruin it."

He crossed the cellar to the barrel and filled his pitcher with cider. "This is delicious, you know," he said. "I had a glass upstairs. Some of the best I've had in years. Sara said she liked to blend different kinds of apples to get just the right flavor."

"Ya." Some of the tension eased from Honor's posture. She gave him a shy smile. "I had some, too, and it was good."

"Tanner definitely likes it. I think I saw him drink three cups." Luke grimaced. "I hope that won't cause trouble later."

"I don't think so," Honor replied, setting her pitcher on a stool. "He has a stomach like his father. Silas could eat anything and it never bothered him. Once, at his brother-in-law's house, the two of them were eating scrapple sandwiches and they hadn't bothered to cook the scrapple." She shook her head. "I like scrapple, but I want mine crispy and cooked all the way through. I was certain Silas would be sick, but it never even gave him indigestion. He said I was too finicky. That I'd make our boys weak."

"They hardly look weak to me." Luke tightened the shutoff on the cider barrel. "Justice can already lift

Tanner, and in another year, Tanner won't be able to hold his own when they wrestle. And that little one, Elijah, he's amazing for his age. Anything the older two do, he's right there, trying to imitate them." He carried the pitcher back to the bottom of the steps and placed it carefully on the floor before sitting down again. He patted the step beside him. "Sit with me? I won't bite. Unless you think you'd better go up and check on the children."

Honor folded her arms and regarded him for a long moment. Then she lowered herself on the step beside him. "*Ne*, I don't want to check on the children. I don't hear any screams, and I don't hear anything breaking. There are enough pairs of eyes to watch them, and truthfully, I'm enjoying having someone else do it." She glanced away and he noticed a slight rosy tint on her cheeks. "Now I've said it," she murmured. "You'll think me a terrible mother."

"I don't. I think you're a wonderful mother…if a little—" He bit off what he was going to say, knowing that he was wading into uncertain depths.

"You think I spoil them?"

"Not spoil, exactly. But they are…" He let his last thought go unspoken.

"Bad? Wild? Unruly?" She laughed. "Go ahead, say it. You won't hurt my feelings. And you won't be the first to say it. I know that I sometimes let them go too far, but I don't believe a parent should always be telling a child not to do something. Don't you think it's better to be an example of how they should live than to be constantly dictating to them?"

"You're right, of course," he said. "And I don't think they're bad children. Wild, certainly. But not bad and not mean. They have your good nature. And they don't whine. I hardly ever hear them cry, not even the baby."

She arched a brow. "And you've had a lot of experience parenting small children?"

"*Ne*, of course not." It was his turn to shrug. "But I had a lot of cousins out in Kansas, and most of them are older than me. We had our fair share of children in our church community. Our preacher gave a lot of sermons on the responsibilities of being a mother or father and on the importance of bringing up children who would honor their parents and our traditions."

"Honoring your parents and doing what you're told was always important to Silas," Honor said. "But my mother and father always put love first. It's what I've tried to do with my little ones. It's not always easy, especially now, being both father and mother." She steepled her hands. "You'd be surprised at how much advice I get, especially from those who have no children of their own."

"Ouch," he said, grimacing. "Point taken." He chuckled and she laughed with him. "But I do think you're a wonderful mother," he said. "An amazing person who never deserved what I did to you."

Her eyes narrowed. "Didn't we agree we weren't going to discuss this?"

"Not really. You said we weren't. I never agreed." Half-surprised she didn't just stand and go upstairs, he pushed on. "I don't want to put a damper on your holiday, Honor. I'll make this quick, I promise, but I need to say it to you. Face-to-face." He took a breath and turned to her. "I made a terrible mistake the day we were supposed to marry, and it's troubled me all these years. I owe you an apology. I hurt you, and I'm sorry. I know it doesn't make up for what I did, but I hope you can find it in your heart to forgive me. If not now, someday."

She looked away.

"I also need to try to explain how it was. I'm not trying to make excuses for myself, but looking back, I think I was too young to get married. *We* were too young. I thought I was ready, but as the day of our marriage got closer, I began to have doubts."

"About me," she said quietly. "Whether I was the right one."

"*Ne.* Never." He took her hand. "It was always about me. At the time, I wasn't positive I could live the Amish life. If I had the faith. Honor, I didn't know if I had the strength to be the kind of husband you deserved." He squeezed her hand. "I never doubted my faith in God, but I wondered if we were clinging to old ways too long when the rest of the world had moved on. And when it came time to go to the wedding that morning, I just couldn't…" His voice cracked and his eyes teared up. "I couldn't do it."

She raised her head and looked at him. He was afraid of what he would see in her eyes; he hadn't dared to hope for the sympathy, the compassion he found there.

"We *were* young," she said. "Me, especially. I had no idea what being a wife really meant. Not until I married Silas and found out." She gave him her other hand, and they sat there for a few seconds, not speaking, just feeling the warmth and security of each others' hands. "Thinking, back, I wonder if we'd just—"

The door at the top of the cellar steps abruptly slammed shut, interrupting her. Then they heard the latch slide into place and the sound of a child's laughter.

Luke got to his feet. "What's going on?"

"Justice would be my guess," Honor said, sounding amused.

Luke reached the top of the steps and tried the door. "Locked." He banged on the door. "Hey!" he called. "Let us… Let me out!" He glanced down at Honor. "Sorry."

"Not your fault." She pressed her lips together. "Unless I miss my guess, my little troublemaker is at it again."

He chuckled. "When you think about it, it is pretty funny."

She flashed him a smile so full of life and hope that it nearly brought tears to his eyes, a smile he'd been praying for all these years.

"I suppose it is," she agreed. "At least, it will be if someone lets us out before we become the scandal of the county."

"Right." He turned back to the door and rapped sharply. Seconds later, he was rewarded by the click of the latch and Sara's face in the doorway.

"I asked you to bring up cider," Sara said smoothly. "Not to lock yourselves in." She peered down to see Honor picking up the pitchers of cider and bringing them up the stairs. "Hurry along. We're just sitting down to the tables, and you don't want to miss silent prayer."

Luke met Honor halfway and took both pitchers from her. As they passed from hand to hand, he met her gaze. There was a twinkling in her eyes that made him think he might have accomplished what he hoped to today. Now that she was ready to forgive him, he was ready to bring up the possibility of courting. But not today. Today, he'd have to be content with the memory of the feel of her hand in his and her beautiful smile.

There was a last-minute flurry of activity before the sit-down meal: babies reunited with their mothers, preschool children seated at small tables with teenage girls to assist them, older boys separated from their sisters and cousins, and the best seats found for the elders. Satisfied that her little ones were all cared for and didn't need her, Honor allowed Rebecca to usher her to a table of young women near the kitchen. Honor had offered to help with serving, but Sara refused her.

"All the food is on the tables," Sara had answered. "Plates have been fixed for the toddlers and *Grossmama* Yoder. The rest can help themselves. Now, you just sit, eat and enjoy."

Rebecca's husband, Caleb, called for grace, and everyone hushed their chattering and lowered their heads. He didn't deliver a prayer, but he said a few words of welcome on Sara's behalf, reminding the guests of the significance of Epiphany after everyone had kept the traditional moments of silence. "Sara is so pleased that you could all be here to share Old Christmas with her," the young preacher concluded. "Now, let's give credit to the cooks and this good food, and eat."

As plates of turkey, roast pork, beef, bread and vegetables were passed around, Honor couldn't help but notice that Luke was seated on the end of the younger men's table, facing her. Rebecca, seated beside her, kept up a lively discourse with her half sister, Grace, another sister Leah, and their cousin Addy. Honor knew Addy because she was Aunt Martha's daughter, and Addy and her husband owned a butcher shop in Dover.

Addy was expecting another baby sometime soon, and Honor had seen Aunt Martha fussing over her.

"It's not like this is your first," Rebecca said to Addy. "You had no problems giving birth once before, and look at Honor here. She's had four and is none the worse for wear."

"*Ya*, I know, I know. It's not me who's worried," Addy replied. "It's my mother. I'm sure it's because I'm her only daughter. But then, Gideon is nearly as bad. The other day, he was fussing because I carried in a tray of scrapple. Honestly, I feel fine, and my midwife says everything looks perfectly normal."

Honor took a forkful of mashed potatoes, glanced up and met Luke's gaze. He smiled at her, and she averted her eyes, but not before she smiled back at him. Talking to him in the cellar had been nice. As much as she'd told him that she didn't want to discuss their breakup, it had made her feel better to hear him admit that it had been his fault.

She took a sip of cider and toyed with her coleslaw, turning her fork around and around and staring at her plate. In all fairness, she had been the one who pressed him for the wedding. She should have known that he wasn't as enthusiastic as she was about marrying, even after he'd agreed. He'd even suggested they wait another year while he worked and saved more money. But she had been young and immature and had insisted, because she'd been infatuated by the idea of being a wife. She'd wanted to be able to call herself Luke's wife, but looking back, she realized that she'd had no idea what the role really meant. She'd wanted to marry him, and she'd wanted to do it that fall, not the next. So she had to accept some of the fault.

"Honor?" Grace held a saltshaker in her hand. "Could you pass this to Violet, please?"

"*Atch*, of course." Honor realized that she'd been lost in her own thoughts. She made an effort to pay closer attention to her tablemates and resolved not to keep stealing peeks at Luke. What if someone noticed? They might get the wrong idea. Making her peace with what had happened between her and Luke was one thing. It certainly didn't mean that she was interested in him. She didn't want to invite curiosity. Bad enough that Sara might have some notion of matching the two of them. Sara, she could deal with. But she didn't want to encourage Luke to think that he had a chance with her, because he didn't. Absolutely not. It was impossible. End of subject.

But not the end of the repercussions of her time alone with him in the cellar.

When the meal was finished and being cleared away, Aunt Martha cornered Honor and insisted she step into Sara's office so that they could talk without being overheard.

"I really need to pack up the children," Honor protested. "Baby Anke—"

Martha cut her off. "Your Anke is fine. Greta has her. What's the girl for if not to take some of the load off you? I've told my son-in-law—my Dorcas needs a girl to help her."

Honor nodded. When Aunt Martha said Dorcas, she meant Addy. Apparently, when Addy had met her husband-to-be, he preferred her middle name, so she'd asked everyone to call her Addy instead of Dorcas. Most people had, other than her mother. But then, Aunt Martha rarely did what people asked her. She had her own mind that was pretty much set in concrete on how things should be done.

Aunt Martha latched onto Honor's arm and clung to her elbow with a death grip. For a woman in her sixties, she was surprisingly strong. Tall and gaunt, with a sharp nose, recessed eyes and bony chin, Martha may have looked frail, but she was far from it. "You just come in here," she insisted. "Sara won't mind. You need to hear this. It's my duty as your mother's friend to tell you what people are saying."

Honor glanced around the room, caught sight of Sara and grimaced in a silent plea for help. Sara chuckled and threw up her hands as if to say, "You're on your own." Seeing her last hope of escape fading, and not wanting to attract any more attention than necessary Honor allowed the older woman to tug her into the office.

Once inside, Martha twisted around and used one hip to shut the door before planting herself solidly in front of it. From inside her voluminous skirt pocket she produced a much-folded and wrinkled sheet of newspaper and waved it in the air. "You haven't seen this, have you? I know you haven't. You're much too smart to ignore something like this."

Honor reached for the paper, but Aunt Martha pulled it back. "Shocking, really," she pronounced. "Although, considering the source, I don't suppose any of us should be surprised. What Sara can be thinking of, I'm sure I don't know. I thought she had more sense of decorum. Of course, she's not really a Yoder, you know. Just a Yoder by marriage. Her family doesn't have a lot of *goot* German stock, not like the Yoders."

Honor thought she recognized the paper in Honor's hand as being part of the *Delaware State News*. "There's an article about Sara?" she asked.

Martha's mouth drew into a small pucker before she launched into another harangue. "Sara? Why ever would you think it was Sara? I've no bone to pick with Sara—other than her dubious choices in young men to marry off to our girls." She huffed. "*Ne*, not Sara. Luke. Luke Weaver."

Honor's brows knit. "The article is about Luke?"

Martha rested a hand on her hip as one shoe tapped the hardwood floor impatiently. "Honestly, Honor. Are you paying attention at all? Naturally, he wanted to keep it a secret. We take the paper. My Reuben always reads the paper after breakfast. And I'd used it to line the bottom of my egg basket, just as I always do. But then my Dorcas came by to get some extra eggs. She wanted to make a pound cake for Gideon. Dorcas makes the loveliest cakes. Anyway, she used up the last of the eggs, and then she saw it." Triumphantly, Martha held out the page. "There he is. Mystery cowboy, my eye. That's Luke Weaver. Dorcas recognized him right off. See for yourself." She pushed the news sheet at Honor.

Honor took it, went to Sara's desk and spread the page out, taking care to smooth the wrinkles. "It says this man saved the other passengers and the driver when the bus went into the water. The paper calls him a hero."

"The photograph. That's the real sin. And him probably bragging about his deeds and trying to take credit." Martha scoffed. "Probably exaggerated. That's what the *Englisher* do in their news. Everything is made to be bigger and worse than it is. Don't you remember when those two ducks got run over on Route One? The paper that day read Doomsday for Local Wildlife!"

Honor reread the news story and then scrutinized the photo. There was no doubt in her mind. The picture was of Luke, but where the *Englishers* had gotten the idea that he was a cowboy, she had no clue. "Surely, saving all those people is a good thing," she ventured.

Martha looked unconvinced. "You should never have let him do that work on your house. Not after what he did. Not him being what he is."

"And what is he?" Honor asked. Everyone in Seven Poplars knew that Martha often had her own interpretation of events and sometimes facts. One was wise to take what she said with a grain of salt. Still, that *was* Luke's photo, so there was some truth to the event.

"A deceiver." Aunt Martha waggled her finger. "A man whose word can't be trusted. And a man who enjoys being made a fuss over."

"That doesn't sound like the Luke I know," Honor said.

"Make no graven image. That's what the Bible tells us," Martha continued, ignoring Honor's comment. "And that." She pointed at the news page. "*That* is a graven image."

Honor considered the photo. Luke looked wet; the brim of his hat was drooping. But even as bedraggled as he was, he still looked pretty fine. "Maybe he couldn't help it. Maybe the English just took his picture without asking. It happens. Remember the Beachy twins at Spence's Auction last summer?"

Aunt Martha's eyes when round. "You aren't considering courting one of the Beachy twins!"

Honor was suddenly at a loss for words. "I'm not courting… Luke and I aren't…" she began, and then added, "Luke's just doing carpentry work for me."

"I wouldn't let him set one foot on my farm, if I were you," Martha warned. "After he shamed you by leaving you on the day of your wedding. Shamed your family. All that creamed celery that we spent days preparing. I can tell you, it was a long time before your mother could hold up her head at quilting bees."

"I didn't know about this," Honor said as she glanced down at the news story. "He didn't say anything."

"And would he? He's sneaky, that's what he is. Luke Weaver is a sneak. No proper match for you. Your mother would turn over in her grave, you courting him again."

"But I'm not courting Luke."

Martha folded her arms. "Thank Providence for that. No telling what further trouble and shame I've saved you."

Honor folded the paper and handed it back to Martha, but the older woman shook her head.

"*Ne*, best you keep it. Show it to him. See what he has to say for himself." She reached for the door handle. "And while you're at it, ask him about his brother."

"What about his brother?" She knew that Luke had at least one older half brother, but she'd never met him.

"A lot he keeps hidden, I'd say. And everyone knows about that brother. He left the Amish to go to Nashville. A singer." She nodded to emphasize her words. "With one of those country-and-western bands. Maybe he's the one who lured Luke into pretending to be a cowboy."

"That doesn't sound right," Honor protested weakly. "I'm sure there's some mix-up…a mistake."

"Oh, there's a mistake, all right," Martha said. "It was when Sara Yoder brought Luke Weaver to your house." She yanked open the door. "And now it's up to you to send him packing."

Chapter Seven

It was late when families finally set aside their game boards and loaded sleepy children and the elderly into buggies. Greta had found a new friend, Zipporah King, a cousin to Susanna Yoder's husband, who had recently moved to the area. Zipporah and Greta were the same age and shared many of the same interests. When Greta had begged to have Zipporah come home to spend the night, Honor was pleased. Freckle-faced and giggly, Zipporah seemed just the remedy for Greta's homesickness.

"I'm seeing you all safely home," Luke had said firmly. "This is no hour for women and children to be on the road and going into an empty house alone."

With so many chaperones, Honor felt it was only sensible to accept his offer. Despite her concern over the newspaper article and Aunt Martha's warnings against Luke, Honor hadn't been looking forward to entering the dark farmhouse. For safety's sake, she'd left a battery-powered lamp on, but there would be the gloomy barn to face when she put away the horse.

As often as Silas had made her grit her teeth and

pray for patience, she missed his solid presence and his protection. It might be a foolish fear for a woman grown with a flock of children, but she'd always been a little afraid of the dark.

As they turned out of Sara's long driveway and onto the road, it began to snow again. A thin, pale covering of snowflakes frosted the road and the dried grass on either side.

"This is nasty weather," Honor said. "I hate to think of you walking back to the mill in this. Maybe we should drop you off and then go the rest of the way on our own."

"Ne." Luke shook his head, closing his gloved hands more tightly on the reins. "I'll see you inside with heat and light before I leave."

Honor felt a small twinge of relief. She'd tried. If he had to walk two miles home, it was on him. "You could take the horse," she suggested. "And the buggy."

"I could," Luke agreed with a slight nod. "We'll see what it's like after we get you and the children settled. We had a lot of snow in Kansas. Far more than this. And tonight is hardly a blizzard. It's barely freezing."

It felt colder to Honor. It was good to snuggle down under the blanket and let Luke drive the horse. Anke was already fast asleep, and Honor could feel her daughter's warm breath on her cheek. For once she felt calm and all seemed right in the world. Honor rocked her baby and uttered a silent prayer for this precious child and the others murmuring in the back of the buggy. How she loved her children. Until she became a mother, she'd not really known what love was. She would do anything to protect them, make any sacrifice.

Ahead of them was Samuel Mast's buggy, and behind them were some of the large Beachy family. More than a dozen buggies rolled and bumped down Sara's driveway and then separated to continue on home. There were no cars in sight. It was close to midnight, far too late for the children to be awake, but everyone had been having such a wonderful time at Sara's party that no one had wanted to be the first to leave. Tomorrow, for those who had church services in their districts, there would be yawns and sleepy eyes, but good memories. After all, Epiphany came but once a year.

"Let's sing, shall we?" Luke said. And then to her, quietly, he said, "If we can keep the children awake until we get them home, they should be easier for you to get into bed."

Again, she wondered at Luke's ease with her children. He always seemed to know what was best to do or say to them to gain cooperation or turn disruptive behavior to good. Anke was still shy with him, but Elijah, Tanner and Justice seemed to have accepted him as part of the family. She knew that might cause some difficulty when he finished the work on the house and barns and had to leave, but she had decided to be grateful for it while she had it.

Their own father had never had much patience with them or with childish games, and he certainly had not encouraged them to sing with him. Had Silas *ever* raised his voice in song? In service, certainly, as was expected of a church member. But had he ever sung for the fun of it or to soothe tired children? She didn't think so.

"Oh, Susanna," Luke sang loudly in English, "Don't you cry for me. I come from Alabama, with a banjo on my knee..."

"What's a banjo?" Justice demanded.

"I think it's an English chicken," Tanner supplied in *Deitsch.*

Honor chuckled. "A banjo isn't a chicken. It's an *Englisher* thing that makes sound…music."

Luke picked up the word and supplied *chicken* for *banjo* through the remaining verses, much to the delight of Zipporah and Greta, who sang backup.

One by one, the other buggies turned off the road and their blue and red flashing lights grew dim in the falling snow. Then Honor and Luke and the children were alone in the night, the horse moving gaily along, everyone inside the buggy warm and happy, singing together. "Oh, Susanna" was followed by "She'll Be Coming Around the Mountain" and then "Silent Night" in *Deitsch.* As the miles passed, the singers in the back grew fewer, and finally, it was just her and Luke to finish off the last chorus of "Jesus Loves Me" to the sound of Greta's snoring.

For a few moments there was only the swish of the battery-operated wipers and the muffled clicking of the horse's hooves, and then Luke said, "I guess my plan didn't work."

"I guess not," Honor replied and then chuckled. "But it *was* fun." So much fun, in fact, she admitted, that she was sorry when Luke reined in the horse to turn into her lane.

"It was," he murmured.

The snow was a little deeper in the driveway, but the fence posts on either side made it easy for the horse to see where it was going. The animal, sensing the warm barn and perhaps a scoop of grain, picked up the pace.

Go slower, Honor thought to herself. *Don't be in such a hurry, Luke.*

She didn't want the evening to end, and she didn't want to deal with more serious subjects like the length of Luke's employment and the newspaper article that she needed to talk to him about. Better to just enjoy the moment than to consider the consequences of what she might be encouraging. She was tired of making decisions all the time, of being responsible, of being in charge.

Anke stirred and sighed in Honor's arms, bringing back her sense of duty. She couldn't allow herself to be swayed by foolish thoughts or emotions that swirled like the snowflakes on the night air. Instead, she turned her mind to what Aunt Martha had told her. And of the photograph in the newspaper. "Luke, is it true?" she asked, her voice a little harsher than she'd intended.

"Is what true?"

Honor forced her voice to a whisper. "Martha showed me a photograph. In the newspaper. It looked like you. They said that there was an accident. With a bus."

He reined in the horse and they came to halt on the far side of the gate. *"Ya,"* he answered, turning to her on the bench seat. "It's true."

"You did those things? You saved those people from the water?"

"I could hardly climb out myself and leave them. There was a woman with a baby. And others. The driver was unconscious. He could have drowned. I had to do what I had to do." Luke sighed. "But I didn't ask to have my picture taken. You know how they are with their cell phones. The English. They take pictures of everything."

"You didn't give them your name," she observed. "If you had wanted to show off, I would think you would have told the newspaper people who you were."

"And I wouldn't have said I was a cowboy." She could feel him looking at her, even though she couldn't really see his eyes. "Believe me, Honor. All it did was make me feel foolish."

She narrowed her gaze. "So why did they call you a cowboy?"

He shrugged. "My church hat, I suppose. Someone not used to Amish clothing?"

She smiled in the darkness. The English could sometimes have some pretty funny ideas about the Amish. "Why didn't you say anything to me about saving those people?"

"How would I have brought up the subject? You would have thought I was bragging."

She thought about that for a moment. Maybe that first day she would have thought so. But not now. Now she knew him again. Better. "I think it was brave of you to help those people," she said softly. "You could have gotten out of that bus and left the *Englishers* to save themselves."

"Ne," he said simply. "I couldn't."

"Now I feel ashamed." She rested her chin on Anke's little head. "To question you. I should have known you would never do anything to draw attention to yourself."

"I'm glad you asked. Better to ask than to wonder what the truth is," he said as he took the leathers between his hands again. "It's what I've always admired about you, that you speak your mind."

She sat up a little straighter on the buggy seat and shifted Anke's weight to her other shoulder. The baby whimpered in her sleep and Honor patted her back to soothe her. "Silas always said that I was too forward for a woman. That I should think and talk less."

"I don't believe Silas and I would have had much in common."

"He was a good man, a faithful member of the church. And he was always first to lend a hand to anyone in need," she defended her husband. "He took his role as a man of our faith seriously. Isn't that what the preachers tell us a man should do?"

"Ya," Luke agreed. "But there's no harm in taking joy in it. Having a wife and young children is a great responsibility, but they can also give great joy if you let them."

"You might think differently if you had children of your own."

"I don't believe so. Think about your own father, for example. He was one to enjoy life," Luke reminded her. "I'll never forget the time he organized a trip to Delaware Bay for our school. He had us all rescuing horseshoe crabs by turning them over and letting them go back to the water. Remember how he took off his shoes, rolled up his pant legs and waded in the water with a crab net? He scooped up all those small creatures and let us see them before he put them back."

"I do," she said, smiling at the memory. "*Dat* always found a way to make whatever he did fun. Once, we had a tomato-throwing contest with rotten ones we found in the field. And he made a tire swing for me when I was really too old to be playing children's games."

"I was so sorry to hear that he passed away." Luke's voice grew husky with emotion. "Such a small thing to take his life."

Honor nodded. Sometime after Luke had moved away, her father had been helping a neighbor pull old wire from a fence around a cow pasture. Her *dat* had sliced his thumb on a nail, a puncture wound that had been slow to heal. And then, suddenly, a midnight trip to the emergency room had turned into days in the hospital and then he was dead of tetanus. Her mother had never recovered from the shock. And years later, when the doctors said she suffered a heart attack, Honor wondered if it was the loss of her mother's beloved husband that had killed her.

"It *was* a small thing to take the life of such a healthy man," she said. "And you're right. *Dat* did find pleasure in the smallest things. And he loved children, not just me, but all children."

"But you were privileged to have him as long as you did," Luke said. "I always admired your father. His only failing was his bad eye for horseflesh." He chuckled. "Remember when he bought that blind horse from Reuben Coblenz?"

She joined in his amusement. "You still remember that?"

Luke grinned. "It was only blind in one eye. But he bought the horse for a ten-year-old, and the beast had seen three times those years and had bad knees, to boot." He pulled the buggy up close to the back door. "You stay here while I go in and turn on more lights and stoke the fire. Then I'll help you get the children up to bed."

"I appreciate it," she said. "Then you should take the horse and buggy back to the mill. You can bring them home tomorrow morning." She twisted around. "Wake up, girls," she called to Zipporah and Greta. "We're here."

A short time later, Luke carried a sleeping Elijah and Justice, with a drowsy Tanner tagging close behind. He removed their coats, hats, mittens and boots, and tucked them in while Honor did the same for Anke. Ordinarily, all the children would have changed into sleeping gowns, but not tonight. They were tired, and it wouldn't hurt them to sleep in their clothes, for once.

"I feel bad sending you out into the snow," Honor said, when the teenage girls and children were all tended to and abed. She and Luke stood in the kitchen, warming themselves in front of the woodstove. "I'm serious about you taking the horse and buggy."

"Nah." Luke held his hands out to the stove and rubbed them together. "It's not that cold, and a little snow never hurt anyone. I'll put the horse up, rub him down and give him a good measure of oats. He served us well tonight, and I'll not ask more of him. Besides, I'm wide-awake, and after so much good food, the walk will do me good."

"You're certain?" She was oddly reluctant to have him leave. She should have been exhausted, but she, too, was far from sleepy. "How about a cup of herbal tea before you leave, then? It will warm you inside and..." She trailed off and picked up the kettle.

He turned to her, his face gentle. "I'd like that, Honor."

"I've apple pie, if you're interested."

"Not another bite," he protested, holding up both hands. "I'll burst. Just let me run out and put the horse up."

He was back in ten minutes, which was perfect timing because the teakettle was just whistling. He took two mugs and a bottle of honey from the shelf. "Milk?"

She shook her head.

"No, not with herbal tea, I suppose. Me, either." He took the tea bags from a tin container labeled *Tee* and decorated with red and yellow painted tulips. "Sit," he said. "I can pour."

She did as he bade her, feeling light and a little giddy. She couldn't recall once in her marriage when Silas had poured her a cup of tea.

"I had a good time tonight," Luke said as he brought the mugs to the table. "And I think you did, too."

"Ya." She nodded. "I did." He handed her the small plastic container of honey and she squeezed some into her tea and stirred it with the spoon he'd brought for them to share. "And I'm glad you saved those people."

He took the spoon she offered and didn't answer.

She couldn't resist the barest smile. "Aunt Martha told me something else when she showed me your picture. She said that your brother ran away from the Amish to sing in a country-and-western band in Nashville."

Luke had just taken a sip of tea, and he was so surprised that he nearly choked on it. "My brother did *what*?"

She giggled. Saying it out loud made it seem all the more ridiculous. "That's what she said. I'm sure it's wrong, but… I guess I thought I should ask you for myself."

"Wait, wait." He wiped the drops of tea off his chin. "Was she talking about my cousin Harvey?"

"She said your brother."

"My brother can't carry a tune." Luke was laughing now, laughing so hard that he could hardly speak. "My *cousin* joined a Mennonite choir, when he was still *rumspringa*. Years ago."

"So, he isn't in Nashville?"

"He is not. Nor is my brother," Luke said. "Harvey, who *can* sing, is still Old Order, has a wife and five children and serves as deacon in his church."

Honor leaned forward and covered her face with her hands, suppressing another giggle. "I should have known. Aunt Martha is usually wrong with her stories, but she had the newspaper article and I thought—"

"Shhh." Luke reached his hand across the table and took hers. "It's not your fault. I should have told you about the bus accident. But I knew you were already so angry with me, I didn't… I guess I didn't want to… complicate things."

His hands were warm on hers and tendrils of excitement trickled down her spine and made her knees weak. "I'm sorry I've been so angry with you for so many years. You were wrong," she murmured. "But so was I." Her throat constricted. Long ago, when they were hardly out of their teens, she had realized she loved him. She could still remember their first kiss. "I think… I think you'd better go," she managed.

He sighed, released her hand and stood. "I should. But I'll be back tomorrow to work on the house."

"Great!" she exclaimed, looking at him over her shoulder.

"And to court you."

His words settled over her like warm rain on a summer afternoon. She turned back to him. "That's why Sara brought you here, isn't it? That was your plan from the beginning."

"*Ya.* I hoped Sara could help me get my foot in the door," he admitted. "But now this is about you and me." He exhaled. "Honor, I want to court you. It's why I came back. And you know that." He went on faster. "Let me make what I did up to you, and give me the chance to show you that I've changed. I'm not the boy I was nine years ago."

She drew in a ragged breath, wondering if he could hear the pounding of her heart. "And I'm not that girl," she said softly.

He snatched up his coat and hat, holding them against his chest. "I love you, Honor. I always have. I always will and I think we would make a good couple. Husband and wife."

She gripped the edge of the table and rose slowly. Her legs seemed too wobbly to stand. "I can't promise anything, Luke."

He was silent for a moment. "But you'll think about it?"

Moisture clouded her eyes. "I'll think about it, but… you'll have to give me time." Then she smiled. "Go with God, Luke. Take care."

"And I'll see you tomorrow?" he asked, putting on his hat.

"Until tomorrow," she answered. There was a gust

of wind as the door closed behind him and she was left alone with her doubts and fears and hopes. “Tomorrow,” she whispered into the gas-lit room.

Chapter Eight

"Boys. Look at those hands!" Honor placed the sauerbraten, a time-consuming roast beef dish, on the table. She pointed with the hot mitt on her hand. "Bathroom. Wash. Now."

Luke, who was standing in the kitchen doorway, opened his hands, palms up. "I washed. Soap and everything."

Greta giggled and Honor rolled her eyes. "You know who I was talking to." She turned her attention back to her two eldest. "Justice, Tanner, move along."

Slowly the boys climbed down from the bench and made their way out of the kitchen. Honor headed for the stove to pull scalloped potatoes baked in a cast-iron frying pan out of the oven. Usually, she liked to serve the main meal of the day just after noon. But the roast had taken longer to cook than she'd expected, so they'd made do with soup and corn bread. The roast beef she'd started marinating three days ago was finally done, though supper was a full hour later than usual. Why on earth she'd decided to make sauerbraten midweek, she didn't know.

Actually, she did. She'd made it to please Luke and possibly even to show off her cooking skills. What was it that her mother used to say about *hochmut*? With pride there's always a fall? How impressed would Luke be that she couldn't plan meals or get them on the table on time? Why was she trying to impress him, anyway?

"Can I help you with anything?" Luke asked.

"Ne." She blushed, embarrassed to have been caught woolgathering. "I didn't hire you to serve meals. I hired you to fix up my house," she said, her tone a little short.

Now that Luke had moved to the mill and was working even longer hours than before, it had seemed natural to invite him to eat dinner with the family. Sometimes he even stayed for supper before starting back to the mill. She was already making a big meal, why wouldn't she share it with him?

She carried the potatoes to the table, checking to see if she'd forgotten anything. Along with the roast beef and scalloped potatoes, there were green beans, a loaf of raisin bread and stewed squash. Leftover corn bread would round out the hearty meal. She'd wanted to make a cherry pie for dessert, but there hadn't been time.

Tanner and Justice's angry voices came from the bathroom down the hall. "Boys!" Honor called. "Behave yourselves. Stop that bickering."

Justice began to wail and Honor let her hands drop to her sides in exasperation. With four children, it seemed as if *someone* was always crying.

"I'll go." Luke volunteered. And before she could say she would handle it, he was out of the kitchen and heading in the direction of the disturbance.

Honor carried the corn bread to the table, pausing to nudge a wooden giraffe out of the way with her foot. The animal went with the toy Noah's ark Elijah had gotten for Christmas. The boys had been playing with the ark earlier, and she'd asked them to put all the pieces away. As usual, they hadn't gotten thoroughly picked up. "Elijah, put your giraffe away," she told him.

Elijah stared at the toy from his place on the bench.

Greta, already in her seat, was eyeing the corn bread.

"No eating until after grace," Honor reminded the girl.

When Greta had first arrived, she could hardly get the girl to eat enough to keep a sparrow alive, but now she ate like a blacksmith. It was a healthy thing to have a *goot* appetite. Maybe now Greta would put some meat on her bones. She suspected that meals were scanty at Greta's parents because there were so many children to feed. Thank the Lord that had never been a problem under Honor's roof.

Luke's voice rumbled over those of Justice and Tanner, but Honor couldn't make out the words. Whatever he was saying to them, it must have been the right thing because the fussing stopped. She sighed as she went to the refrigerator. She hated to admit it, but having Luke around *did* make her life easier. It was such a blessing to have another adult to lend a hand, and her boys trailed him around and pestered him instead of her. Plus, Luke had taken over milking and feeding the animals morning and night, leaving her free to do what needed doing in the house. Having an extra set of strong hands really helped on a farm.

Luke returned to the table with the two troublemakers. Both boys had apparently gotten over their disagreement because they were smiling as they climbed onto the bench and held up damp hands for inspection. Tanner's were not as clean as Honor would have liked, but she wasn't prepared to stall her meal any longer. She'd worked too hard to put it on the table.

Luke had also worked hard for the meal and he had to be starving. Since breakfast, he'd cleaned the horse and cow stalls, replaced a rotting windowsill in the front parlor, put weather stripping around the door so that wind and snow no longer blew into the hall and applied another coat of white paint in the bathroom.

"You know the old chicken house isn't in such bad shape," Luke said once Honor had taken her place at the table and grace was over. "The boys and I could clean it, make a few repairs and move the chickens out of the barn. All you'd need is wire and staples, and I saw two rolls of stock fence in the loft. It wouldn't cost much, and the cow and horse would be a lot happier without the chickens dirtying their stalls."

"That sounds like a good idea," Honor agreed. How many times had she had to wash down the buggy before she could be seen in public? Chickens were necessary, but they could make a mess. *Like children*, she thought and then smiled as she looked around the table at her little ones.

"I can definitely get a crew together to put a new roof on, but with the weather being unpredictable, it may have to wait until April or even May. I've got supplies being delivered to do a good patch job for the meantime."

Honor noted that Luke's mention of doing the roof in May indicated he thought he'd still be around in the spring. She decided not to make a comment on that.

"Whatever you think is best to keep the buckets out of my kitchen," she said.

"Honor... I was wondering," Greta said.

"Yes?" Honor secured Anke's plate to the table. The dish had a suction cup on the bottom, a useful device for keeping a toddler from throwing her entire dinner onto the floor. She handed her daughter a baby spoon. Cheerfully, Anke dropped the spoon, scooped up a handful of potatoes and stuffed them into her mouth.

"Spoon," Honor said as she put it back into the little girl's hand. "I'm sorry, Greta. What were you—" From the corner of her eye, she saw Justice slip a slice of sauerbraten off the platter and drop it on the floor. "Justice, stop feeding the dog from the table," she admonished gently.

Justice stiffened and looked straight ahead. "I'm not."

"Ith too." Elijah pointed an accusing finger at his brother. "I thaw him."

"Did not!" Justice shouted.

Honor put a finger to her lips. "Enough."

Tanner elbowed Justice, who howled in outrage.

"Boys, please," Honor said.

Baby Anke threw her spoon again. Luke's hand shot out and he caught it in midair. He handed the spoon to Honor.

"Use your spoon like a big girl," Honor said patiently as she gave it back to her daughter.

Just as Honor scooped some potatoes onto her own plate, Elijah turned over his glass of buttermilk. She jumped out of her chair to get a clean towel to clean it up, and Elijah started to cry. Justice took another piece of meat off the platter and dropped it under the table as Tanner neatly grabbed the slice of raisin bread that Greta had just finished buttering.

"Give that back," Luke instructed, pointing at Tanner with his fork.

Tanner took a big bite and Greta tried to take the bread back. In an effort to play a game of keep-away, Tanner dropped the disputed raisin bread. Before anyone could retrieve it, the dog snatched the bread off the bench and ran to the far corner of the kitchen to eat it.

"Enough!" Honor threw up her hands in exasperation. So much for a peaceful, pleasant supper. "Any more nonsense, and you can leave the table. All of you." She mopped up the spilled milk and refilled Elijah's glass. He was still crying. "You're fine," she told him, softening her tone. "Accidents happen. Eat your supper."

As Honor slipped back into her chair, Justice pushed Tanner and Tanner pushed him back. Justice reached across to take something off his brother's plate and spilled his milk into his plate. The baby began dropping pieces of sweet potato onto the floor, and while Honor was trying to pick them up, Elijah dumped half the sugar bowl onto the table.

"I'm going for my wooden spoon!" Honor went to the cabinet drawer and came back with a big spoon. She rapped it on the table. Elijah giggled.

"*Mam's* got the spoon," Justice warned, looking down at his plate.

Tanner grinned.

"What does this mean?" Honor demanded as she tapped the spoon on the table. "It means be *goot* or else," she threatened. "I *will* send you boys from this table without dessert."

She hated to have to get the spoon. She'd never threatened her children with paddling or even a tap on the knuckles. Using physical force against a helpless child was just wrong. But the sight of the wooden spoon made them consider the possibility that they just might get a spanking one of these days.

"Boys, you should all be—" Luke bit off his words, put his head down and went back to his meal.

Honor removed Justice's plate and got him another from the cabinet. "What were you going to say, Luke?"

"I'm not hungry," Tanner said. "Can I have pudding?"

"Eat," Honor told Tanner. "Otherwise, you'll be hungry when you go to bed."

"But I want rice pudding," he whined. "With raisins."

Honor grimaced. "I'm going to count to five and—"

"Flies!" Justice made a face. "You put flies in our pudding."

"I don't like flieth," Elijah wailed.

Anke shrieked with laughter and threw her spoon to the floor.

"Visiting Sunday," Greta announced. "On Sunday. Can I go?"

Flustered, Honor turned her attention to the girl. "I'm sorry. Can you what?"

"Go see Zipporah," Greta answered. "On Sunday. That's what I wanted to ask you. I could walk. You wouldn't have to take me."

"I don't know." Honor sat down yet again. She hadn't yet taken more than a single bite and she was starving. She looked down at her plate. Some of the sugar Elijah had dumped had made it to her potatoes.

She'd have to eat them that way. She couldn't show the children that it was right to waste good food. "It's too far to walk in this weather," she told Greta.

"I think it would be nice if she went." Luke helped himself to more green beans.

Tanner nudged Justice with his elbow again, and Justice punched him.

"Stop that!" Honor set her fork down sharply on the table. "Hitting is wrong. You shouldn't hit your brother. Tanner, stop teasing him." She glanced back at Greta.

"I promised Zipporah I'd come see her," Greta said, staring at her plate.

"Surely you can spare her on Sunday," Luke suggested. "Greta deserves some fun."

"Let me think about it." Honor shook her head. "Three miles is a long way for a girl to walk alone." As she pushed a forkful of potatoes into her mouth, she saw Justice slide under the table and out of sight. "Justice, back on the bench. You weren't excused yet."

"If I could borrow your buggy, I could drive her," Luke offered.

"I don't eat flies in pudding," came a small, muffled voice. "Yuck."

Luke glanced under the table. "Justice, did you hear your mother?"

There was a note of irritation in Luke's voice, and Honor didn't care for it one bit. "Not appropriate. Greta isn't a child any longer," she said. The baby was starting to fuss, so she got up and took her out of the high chair. She used the clean end of the towel to wipe off Anke's face and hands and deposited her in the play yard.

"Maybe...maybe you could drive me, then," Greta

suggested, meeting Honor's gaze. "Or I could take the buggy?"

"You told me you didn't know how to drive a buggy." Honor said. She shook her head when the girl's face crumpled with disappointment. "I didn't say you couldn't go. But loading all of us up and driving you to the Kings', it's a lot for me to do, Greta."

"How about this?" Luke offered, buttering a second piece of corn bread. "I'll come on Sunday and watch the boys. You take the baby and drive Greta to her friend's. You and Anke can visit with Katie at the mill or anywhere you want, and then stop for Greta when you're ready to come home."

Honor picked up her fork. "But it's a visiting Sunday. You work here all week. On Sunday, you should be visiting someone."

"I will be," Luke answered with a wink at Tanner. "I'll be visiting my favorite boys."

Tanner threw his hands up and cheered. An echo came from under the table. Anke, imitating Tanner, clapped and shrieked with laughter.

Honor saw the joy on Greta's face and couldn't resist. "*Ya*, I suppose we could do that." Her gaze strayed to Luke and she saw that he was watching her.

He smiled and she smiled back, and then she settled in to get at least a few bites of supper. Somehow, they got through the rest of the meal and things quieted down as everyone enjoyed their rice pudding.

Afterward, Luke offered to help with the dishes, but Honor refused. "You work hard enough around here," she said. "You don't need to do my work, as well. I have Greta to help me."

"And Tanner," he suggested. "He's old enough to take some responsibility."

She frowned. "He'll be a man soon enough. I think a child should enjoy being a child as long as they can."

Luke didn't look convinced. She was sure he had something to add, but when she waited for him to argue with her, he simply shrugged and reached for his hat and coat. "I'll be going," he said. "Thank you for the meal. It was the best I've had since I can't remember when. Best sauerbraten I've eaten, for certain."

"Tomorrow I'll make pies," she promised, feeling her cheeks grow warm from his compliment. Suddenly all the planning to make the roast beef dish seemed worth it. "Sweet potato, I think. We've got a few baskets left in the root cellar, and they always turn out *goot* for me. You do like sweet potato pie, don't you?"

"Love it," Luke answered. "But then, there are few pies I don't like."

Tanner had come to stand beside her, leaning against her affectionately. "What kind don't you like, Luke?" she asked.

Luke pulled on his hat and pulled a face. "Shoofly pie. Too sweet. And too many flies."

Tanner giggled. "There's no flies in shoofly pie."

Luke glanced at the door, then at Honor. "Well, I guess I'll be going. See you in the morning. Bright and early?"

"Bright and early? What's bright and early to you?" she teased. "Justice is usually up by five."

Luke grinned. "That's a little early for me. At least, if I'm walking. It won't be a problem soon, though."

"You've found someone to transport your driving horses?"

"*Ne*, I decided to sell them. My cousin already arranged for a buyer. Charley Byler deals in horses here. He says he has a half Morgan, half standardbred mare that's good for riding or driving. And she's trained to a plow. I'm going to take a look at her on Saturday." He opened the back door. "G'night, and thanks again for that wonderful supper."

"'Night," she called. When the back door closed, everyone scooted off, and Honor cleaned away the remainder of the supper, wiped down the table, and set it with clean dishes and silverware for breakfast. She'd wanted a few moments of peace and quiet, but her thoughts weren't quiet. She kept thinking about Luke and how, even with the children's mischief at supper, she had enjoyed the day. Usually, when it was time to put the kids to bed, she was exhausted, but not tonight. Tonight she felt restless, almost wishing she'd asked Luke to stay for a game of checkers and some popcorn.

She was just sweeping the last bit of dust into the dustpan when there was a quick rap at the back door and Luke stepped into the laundry room. "Honor?"

She paused, broom in hand. "Everything okay?"

"Fine," he said. "Quick. Put on your coat and come with me. There's something I want you to see."

"Outside? In the dark?" She looked around to see if any of the children were in sight. For once, the household was quiet. She could hear Greta upstairs, singing softly to the little one and her boys were playing a game in the front room.

"Trust me. Come on." He flashed a smile that was infectious. "You'll be glad you did."

"All right," she agreed, surprised by her own impulsiveness. She set the broom aside, shrugged into her coat, wrapped a scarf around her neck and followed him out into the night. The air was cold, but the moon was out, nearly full, illuminating the frosty landscape and making the icicles that draped from the trees and the eaves of the barn and house sparkle like the dust from angels' wings.

"Watch your step," he cautioned as she hurried down the porch steps. "Everything's slippery."

"I'm fine," she answered. Her cheeks stung from the brisk air, but curiosity and excitement made her eager to see what all the fuss was about.

Together they crossed the icy yard, cut between the barn and windmill, and passed the two old apple trees, bare now of every leaf, limbs gnarled and twisted against the winter sky.

"Where are we going?" she asked.

"Shh." He caught her hand as they moved over a low spot in the meadow just beyond the old chicken coop.

Surges of warmth shot up Honor's wrist and arm as Luke's fingers tightened around her hand. She would have protested his familiarity, but her right foot hit a patch of ice and she did almost lose her footing. Luke pulled her against him and then gently put a hand on her shoulder and pushed her to a crouching position. Before she could pull free, he released her and pointed to a rise in the field.

"Ahh," she gasped. A cloud of condensation issued from her lips. Clearly visible above the winter grass, a fox—no, two of them—raced and leaped in the moonlight.

Luke smiled and put a finger to his lips.

Her eyes widened as she watched the foxes playfully chase each other back and forth over the crest of a small hill. In the moonlight, the beautiful and graceful animals were dark shadows against a silvery background. She couldn't tell whether they were the native gray foxes or the smaller English reds, but it didn't matter.

She and Luke remained there for long moments; how many, she couldn't say. Her knees cramped and her fingers grew numb from the cold, but it didn't matter. She'd been born and raised in the country, but she'd never seen such a sight. She might have remained until she suffered from frostbite if Luke hadn't caught her elbow and raised her to her feet.

"They may be at this all night," he said softly. "You should probably get inside. It's cold out."

"I'm not cold," she whispered.

The foxes must have heard their voices. One gave a sharp yip, and they halted, almost in midair, whirled and dashed away into the darkness. In an instant, the meadow was silent and as still as a painting on a January calendar page.

"Thank you," she murmured, stamping her feet to bring back the feeling. "That was...magnificent."

He chuckled. "Too good to watch alone. I thought you might enjoy it."

"I did." She glanced back in the direction of the house. "I guess I'd better get back."

"Ya," he agreed. "You should. And I should move along. I'll see you safely to the door."

She made a sound of impatience. "You think I can't walk a few hundred yards to my own back door?"

"I'm sure you can," he answered. "But just the same, I'll walk you there. I'd not have you come to harm, Honor, not for all the wheat in Kansas."

She laughed. "That's a lot of wheat. You're certain you wouldn't consider it?"

He held her arm as they trekked back, following their own footprints in the light snow. "Woman, you would argue with a bishop, wouldn't you?"

"Maybe I would and maybe I wouldn't," she teased, refusing to look up at him, even though she wanted to. "But fortunately for me, you, Luke Weaver, are no bishop."

Luke ended up getting his way about visiting Sunday. Honor left him with the three boys and drove Greta to her friend's house. Zipporah was thrilled to see her, and Zipporah's mother, Wilma, a jolly, round woman in a dark purple dress and apron, invited Honor and baby Anke to join them for the noonday meal. Honor refused, explaining that she'd be back around two for Greta. She was just turning to go when Freeman's wife, Katie, appeared in the doorway behind Wilma.

"Honor! How nice to see you." Katie stepped around Wilma and gave Honor a hug. "The girls seem to have hit it off. I'm so glad. Teenagers need friends their own age."

"Oh, just come sit for a moment, Honor," Wilma insisted, adjusting her round wire-frame glasses. "You're already here. Just long enough for coffee. We're still only half-unpacked from the move, but I know you won't judge me a poor housekeeper." She led the way into a sunny kitchen. "My Zipporah, she's so happy to make a new friend. And Katie tells me we will be worshipping together in the same church family."

"Ya," Honor agreed. "We will be so glad to have you." Anke squirmed in her arms.

"Take off that baby's coat," Wilma urged. "A few minutes won't hurt. Such a sweet little girl." She smiled at Anke and then chattered on. "My husband was glad to find this farm, such good soil with no flooding. We were near a river before, and every spring, terrible floods." She ushered them into a tidy parlor with upholstered furniture. A cheerful fire blazed on a brick hearth, thanks to a propane fireplace insert. "Now, you just sit yourself down and make yourself at home while I fetch that coffee."

"She seems nice," Honor said when Wilma left the room.

"She is," Katie agreed, reaching to take Anke from her. "And she says her husband's brother is anxious to move here. They were in Canada before, but Wilma has relatives in Apple Grove." She took a seat on a worn green chair. "Sara's Epiphany party was fun, wasn't it?"

"It was," Honor agreed.

"I noticed you and Luke seemed to be having a good time together." Katie smiled warmly and bounced Anke on her knee. "You make a nice couple. My Freeman says Luke is a good man. He likes him. Hardworking."

"We aren't a couple," Honor hastened to correct her. "He just works for me."

Katie grimaced. "*Atch.* I'm sorry. Martha said—Never mind. You don't want to know."

Honor's eyes widened. "Don't tell me that Aunt Martha said we were dating?"

Katie chuckled. "*Ne*, she didn't. Not exactly. But to me, it looked..." She shrugged. "Forgive me. Freeman says I am too careless of what I say." She hesitated. "But I know what I know, and the way you and Luke

Weaver were making eyes at each other…" She smiled. "I'm sure I'm not the only one who thought maybe where there was an understanding between you."

"But we don't," Honor protested. "I mean, there isn't. Luke and I… I knew him years ago, and…" She sighed. "It's complicated, but *ne*, there definitely is not an understanding between us."

Katie studied her, opened her mouth as if she was going to say something more, but then pressed her fingers to her lips and rolled her eyes. "There I go again, speaking without thinking. It's your business, of course, but…" Her eyes twinkled. "If I were you, and I had such a respectable young man driving me and my children around on visiting Sundays, a candidate that Sara Yoder highly recommends, I'd give him some serious consideration."

Chapter Nine

By the time Honor arrived back at the farm that afternoon, the light was already fading and the temperature was dropping. Both she and Greta had had a wonderful day with the Kings and had followed that visit with one to the Kemps.

Anke had been on her best behavior and had been bounced and fed and made much of at one house and then the other. Now Anke had given up and fallen asleep in Greta's arms. It was too late for the baby to be napping, but there was no help for that now. She'd just have to stay up later tonight.

This had turned out to be such a nice week for Honor; for the first time in longer than she could remember, she actually felt like herself. First, there had been the Epiphany party, then her pleasant trip to Byler's for groceries and now today's visiting. She and Katie had known each other as teenagers and discovered they had much to talk about. Although Katie had no children of her own yet, she had toys for Anke to play with and seemed tickled to have a little one in her house. Honor liked Katie's mother-in-law, Ivy, and

Freeman's uncle Jehu, who lived on the property. Since they all shared the same worship community, and services were to be at the mill the following week, Honor had even volunteered to come and help with food preparation the following Saturday. It had been too long since she'd done anything to contribute to lives outside her own family.

"You've been in mourning too long for one so young," Ivy had pronounced with an affectionate hug. "It's time you and your family took a more active role in the community."

Uncle Jehu had agreed. "We've got some bass in this mill pond that need catching. When spring comes, you bring those boys over. I'll teach them where the biggest fish hide. I've got a secret bait that never fails."

"My boys would love that," she'd agreed.

Her visits with Katie and with Zipporah's mother had given her a lot to think about, Honor decided as she reined the horse up near the barn. Luke had given her such a treat by watching her sons so that she could have a day for herself.

"I just hope Luke has survived the boys," Honor commented to Greta, who sat beside her in the buggy. "You know how they can be." She looked around the farmyard and was relieved not to see anything out of place. Thank God they hadn't burned the house down or dismantled the windmill while she was away. There were no chickens running loose in the yard, and for once, the donkey was quiet.

Greta nodded over the top of Anke's bonnet. "*Ya*, they can be."

Honor glanced at her. "*Can* be?"

The girl nibbled her bottom lip. "Trouble."

"Mmm," Honor agreed with a chuckle. "They are lively, that's for certain. And I know they've given you a hard time."

"But they aren't bad," Greta assured her. "Just…just full of themselves."

Honor took a moment to consider what effect Greta's coming so far from home and being thrown into an active household might mean to a girl who'd never been away from her family. "We've been so busy lately that I haven't had time to turn around twice. But I want you to know, Greta, that I appreciate the help you've given me since you arrived. And I ask you to be patient with me. Too often, I'm quick to criticize you, instead of taking the time to show you what I want you to do."

A faint smile played over the girl's lips. "I'm glad I came," she answered hesitantly. "I know I'm not a fast learner, and…sometimes I'm clumsy, but…"

Honor shook her head. "You aren't clumsy. You're still growing. It's the way with all teenagers. And it's better to be slow than to rush into things like I usually do. You don't make nearly as many mistakes by taking things slowly."

Greta blushed with pleasure at the compliment. "I thought you weren't happy with me. That maybe you'd send me back."

Honor gently tightened the reins, slowing the horse as they came up the driveway. "Do you want to go back home?"

Greta shook her head. "*Ne*. I like you and the baby. And now I have a new friend. Zipporah."

"*Ya*, she seems like a nice girl. And in our church group. The two of you will be together often." Honor smiled at Greta. "You know, I have a nice length of lavender cloth. I'm sure we can find time to cut and pin it tomorrow afternoon, and then I can get it sewed in time for next Sunday. You're getting taller. It's time you had a new dress and apron for church. And we'll have to see about getting you some new shoes, as well." Honor glanced down. "The toes of those are about worn out."

"New? For me?" Greta beamed. "I never had a dress made new just for me before. Or new shoes. These are my sister Mary's shoes, ones she outgrew. But they were Joan's before that, so we got *goot* use out of them."

Honor was struck with a pang of guilt. *Lord, forgive me for not taking better care of this child who is in my keeping,* she thought. Why hadn't she noticed how shabby Greta's best dress was before this? Had she been so wrapped up in her own struggles that she hadn't thought about this girl's needs? Greta's parents might be hard put to keep all their growing girls in decent clothing, but she wasn't. "You'll have the dress this week, if I have anything to say about it," she promised. "The lavender will be so pretty with your fair coloring. And we'll look for some new shoes the next time we get in to Dover."

"Thank you," Greta murmured. The sparkle in her pale eyes and the red of her cheeks made her almost pretty, and Honor resolved to do more for her. The difference in their ages wasn't all that great; she might be able to think of Greta as a younger sister, the sister she'd never had and always wanted.

Arriving in the barnyard, Honor climbed down from the buggy and walked around to take Anke from Greta. Anke sighed and made small smacking noises with her lips, but didn't wake as Honor settled her against one shoulder. She was getting so heavy, growing every day. Soon, Honor thought, Anke wouldn't be a baby any longer; she'd be a little girl.

Honor's throat tightened. She'd loved all of her babies, but this one was especially dear to her because Anke was born after Silas had passed. All children were a gift from God, but her little girl had been a special blessing. She wondered if Anke would be her last and hoped not. There was something so precious about a baby. People thought it was difficult taking care of them, but compared to mischievous boys, babies were easy.

Greta slid down from the buggy seat. "Do you want me to unharness the horse?"

"Ne," Honor replied. "It's getting cold out. Best you take Anke inside, and I'll do it."

"Shall I put her upstairs in her crib?"

"Ne." Honor shook her head. "Just put her in her play yard in the kitchen."

Just then the barn door flew open, and Tanner ran out. "*Mam, Mam*, you're back!" Behind him came Elijah. Both wore coats, hats and mittens. "We fed up the animals."

"You did?" She nodded in approval.

"Me, too!" Elijah chimed in. "Fed the animalth."

"Where's Justice?" she asked.

"In the barn. With Luke. Luke helped feed up, too," Tanner informed her proudly.

Honor chuckled. "He helped you, did he?"

"Not much," Tanner bragged. "Mostly it was us."

"Tanner puthed Juthtithe out of the loft," Elijah said.

Tanner whipped around. "Did not."

"Did."

Luke appeared in the open barn doorway. Justice followed close on his heels. "You're home." Luke smiled at her. "I was wondering if you'd make it before dark. Let me take that horse for you."

She nodded appreciatively. The wind was picking up and a few snowflakes were drifting down. She didn't want the horse to stand in the traces long after the exercise of pulling the buggy home. The animal needed to be cared for immediately and the buggy put away in the carriage shed.

"Did you have a good visit?" Luke asked as he began to unhitch the horse. "Tanner, watch what I'm doing. You're old enough to do this with a little practice."

"We did," she said and explained about her change of plans for the day. "Everything go all right here?"

Luke glanced back at her. "Nothing I couldn't handle." He hesitated. "But there was something. Maybe we could talk about it later without the little ears—" he raised a hand to cup his ear "—listening."

Honor looked down at Tanner. "What happened?"

Tanner's face reddened and he stared at his boots. "Justice fell out of the loft."

"Not exactly," Luke corrected. "Tanner and Justice were roughhousing and Tanner pushed him."

"Were you roughhousing in the loft again?" Honor turned her attention to her two oldest sons. "Did he push you, Justice?"

Justice backed up and looked down at his boots.

Honor narrowed her gaze on her eldest. "Tanner, did you push your brother out of the loft?"

"He kicked me," Tanner defended himself. "And he threw hay in my face."

With a sigh, she looked at Luke. "I'm sorry. They

do this all the time. I don't approve of them fighting, but brothers—"

"Ne." Luke shook his head. "Tanner should know better than to push a younger child when they are up in the loft. He also used a pitchfork to fork hay to the cow and left it lying on the barn floor, tines up."

Honor's eyes widened and she brought a hand to her mouth. "No one stepped on it?"

"*Ne.* By the grace of God. But Tanner is old enough to learn that being careless with tools can cause great harm. One of his brothers could have been seriously injured." Taking hold of the horse by the bridle, Luke led it into the barn, leaving Honor with her boys.

"I didn't," Tanner protested. "He slipped and fell. I didn't push him." He sniffed and wiped his eyes with the back of his hands.

"*Ya*, you did," Justice whined.

Uncertain what to say, Honor glanced from one to the other. "Go in the house, all of you. We'll talk about this after supper." She clapped her hands. "Go on, now. Scoot! You, too, Elijah." She waited until they were all three inside and then followed Luke into the dimly lit barn. She'd had such a good day and now she felt terrible. "I'm sorry they were bad for you," she said.

"It's fine. They're children. And they weren't bad." Again, he hesitated. "But we did have a couple of incidents and…they need guidance, Honor."

"*Ya*, I agree. They do, and I try to give it to them. But Tanner isn't seven yet, and he—"

"He's old enough to know that a pitchfork can kill," Luke interrupted. "And that a fall can break an arm or a neck." He took a piece of burlap and wiped down the horse's neck and chest with strong, easy strokes.

"I think you're being too hard on him."

"I may be. But I think you're being too easy. A woman… A mother sometimes makes excuses for her child when he should be disciplined."

"Disciplined?" Honor struggled to hold back the surge of emotion that rose in her chest. She was angry that he would interfere. But she also felt a pang of guilt. She knew that sometimes she was too easy on them, but their father had been so harsh. "What would you have me do?" she asked. "Take a switch to him? Send him to bed without supper? Tanner is a rambunctious boy. It's only natural that he'd get himself into trouble once in a while."

"Honor, listen to what you're saying." Luke's voice was patient, but it had a thread of steel that she'd never heard before. "Do you think I'm the kind of man who would use physical force on a child? I didn't say anything about punishing Tanner. What I'm saying is that you should talk to him. He's a bright boy. He has to learn self-discipline. He's older and bigger than Justice. He has to set an example for the other three."

"So you don't believe a child should be spanked?" she demanded. "Doesn't the Bible tell us that—"

"I'm not a preacher or a deacon." He stopped what he was doing and turned toward her. "I think you need to show a child what is right. And violence against anyone is never right."

"Silas didn't believe that. He thought that it was his duty to not to spare the rod."

"I'm not Silas." He pushed open the stall door. "I'm sorry, Honor. It's not my place to tell you how to raise your children. I can't imagine how hard it must be, especially since you're doing it alone. I'm not criticizing you. I think you're a wonderful mother. But what happened here today can't keep happening. You need to make your son understand that his actions have consequences. I see how you love your children. Sometimes being a parent means delivering a tough message."

She stared at him, and the anger she'd felt crumbled, bit by bit. She didn't know why she'd tried to pick a fight with Luke over corporal punishment. She didn't believe in it, either. Mostly because she didn't think it worked. "Silas always said I was lenient with them."

Luke shrugged. "There's a difference between causing mischief and putting someone in danger. That's what you have to make them understand. I'm just saying this because…because I care about them and about you." He met her gaze. "And because you know why I'm here. You know what I want. I want you. And I want us to be a family."

Tears sprang to her eyes. Not knowing what to say, she turned around and walked toward the house.

Was Luke right? She couldn't help wondering if it would be easier to be a good parent if they had a man in their lives, a father who would make things easier for all of them…not harder. What was the right thing to do? With the children? And, maybe even more important, with Luke?

For several days, Honor prayed for guidance and wrestled with her conflicting emotions concerning Luke. Finally, she could take it no longer. Leaving Greta to watch Tanner and Elijah, and Luke to work on patching the roof over the kitchen, she loaded Anke and Justice into the buggy and drove to Sara's house. She hoped to find the matchmaker at home. If Sara was off somewhere, it would be a long ride for nothing, but Honor simply couldn't ignore her concerns for another day.

To her relief, she found Sara and Ellie in Sara's kitchen making a kettle of apple butter. Sara welcomed them in, poured hot chocolate with marshmallows for the little ones and whisked Honor off to her office.

"I don't want to bother you," Honor began, but she already felt better. Sara's office was warm and cheerful with sunshine streaming in the windows, a thick braided rug under her feet and blessed quiet. The scent of apple butter cooking and almond scones just out of the oven didn't hurt, either. Sara always seemed so capable and wise that Honor's worries didn't press quite so hard on her.

"No bother at all," Sara said with a smile. She looked as tidy as a Carolina wren this morning in her dark green calf-length dress, matching apron and starched white *kapp*. Tendrils of curly dark hair framed a round face that was dominated by her strong mouth and dark eyes, which missed nothing.

Honor's hands trembled, so she steadied the cup she was holding on her knee. "I need your advice," she blurted out. "It's about Luke. Weaver," she clarified. Then she felt silly. What other Luke could she be talking about?

Sara nodded. "I thought it might be. What troubles you about him?"

"Nothing… Everything." Honor glanced out the window. There was a bird feeder. Cardinals and blue jays vied with a red-bellied woodpecker for the choice spot at the suet, while a nuthatch crept down the tree trunk searching for insects. Honor sucked in a deep breath and tried again. Why was this so difficult? “He wants to court me,” she managed. “But, of course, you already know that.”

“What do *you* want, Honor?”

“That’s the problem.” She looked back at the matchmaker. Sara’s attention was fixed on her, but her demeanor was relaxed and peaceful. “I don’t know what I want,” Honor confessed. “He’s a good man, and the children like him. I think he would be a kind father to them.” She took a breath. “Kinder than their own father had been,” she added softly.

“And he’s an upstanding man in our community of faith.”

“He is.”

“Would he be a good provider?” Sara asked.

Honor nodded. She placed the mug on a small table. “He would. He…he fits all the requirements that would make him a good husband and a father—the things I told you when we discussed my finding a husband a few months ago. Luke fits well into our family. Having him there so much at the farm makes my life easier, but…but, Sara, I can’t forget what he did. He abandoned me! On our wedding day! It was shameful.” She couldn’t meet the matchmaker’s gaze as she fought tears in a rush of emotion. “He broke my heart.”

Sara was quiet for a moment. “It sounds to me as if you’re torn between what happened in the past and what would be the best for your future. Is that what you’re saying?”

Honor rose and went to the window. She pressed her forehead against the pane and closed her eyes. “Accepting him, agreeing to let him court me would be the easy thing to do. And…part of me wants that. I understand why he couldn't go through with our wedding. But…my head tells me that it would be foolish to risk the same thing happening again. How do I know what's sincere and what's charm?" Hugging herself tightly, she opened her eyes and turned to face Sara. "What do I do?"

Sara took a sip of her tea. "It's true that Luke is a charmer."

"Ya." Honor nodded. "And handsome. And I know that shouldn't matter, but it does. I'd told myself that I wouldn't look for that in my next husband, but…" She let her thought go unfinished because it sounded so silly. So girlish.

Sara chuckled. "But you're human. And young."

Honor gave a little laugh. "I don't feel young. I feel middle-aged some days."

"But you're not. And your time of mourning Silas is passed. It's time to marry."

"I have to think of my children. I have to make the best choice for them. If Luke left me again, he'd also be leaving my little ones. Who are already so attached to him."

Sara got to her feet and crossed the distance between them. She enfolded Honor in her arms, and for a brief moment, Honor rested her head on the older woman's shoulder.

"Aunt Martha thinks it would cause a scandal if I allowed Luke to court me now," Honor whispered.

Sara stepped back, looking indignant. "It isn't Martha who has to make this decision. It's *you*, my girl." A smile curved her full lips, and she wiped a tear away from Honor's cheek with the tip of one finger. "Now, no more tears. Let's put our heads together and think this through."

Honor nodded and Sara waved her back to her chair.

"Drink your tea while it's hot. Black tea soothes the mind and makes any situation more bearable."

Honor sat down and forced herself to take a sip from her cup. The tea was sweet and milky and so good. "Thank you," she murmured. She fumbled for a handkerchief. "You must think me a ninny."

"Not at all." Sara returned to her chair behind the desk. She steepled her small hands and leaned forward on her elbows. "You already know I approve of the match. Otherwise, I wouldn't have brought him to your home. So asking my opinion doesn't make a lot of sense, does it?"

Honor shook her head and then chuckled. "I suppose it doesn't. But I don't know who else to turn to. Everyone likes Luke. They'd take his side."

"Not Martha. I've already gotten an earful from that one."

Honor couldn't suppress a giggle.

Sara smiled but then grew serious. "Have you taken your problem to God?"

"I have." Honor nodded. "I've prayed for guidance, but… God hasn't answered my pleas."

Sara rubbed her hands together. "Perhaps, or perhaps He's answered, and you haven't been listening. I believe that He has a plan for each of us. We can't see that plan and I think often we wouldn't understand it if we could." She paused. "Honor, Luke came back into your life. Some might say that makes him part of God's plan." She paused. "So I suppose my question to you is, how important is your faith to you?"

"It's everything, of course," Honor replied in a rush. "My church, my God, are everything to me. I've never doubted that ours is the true path." She gripped the cup tightly. "Or that I am a weak woman."

"Not weak, but strong," Sara corrected. "You are a strong woman, a strong mother."

"I try, but so often, I fail."

"As we all do." Sara nodded. "But if you're sincere in your conviction that God's word is the truth, then it's time for you to forgive Luke for the wrong he did you all those years ago. God forgives us our sins, and we must try to forgive those who we feel have wronged us."

"You're right. I know you're right, but it isn't easy."

"*Ne*, child, it isn't easy because we're human. It's our nature to cling to hurts and ill-spoken words. But if we expect God to forgive us, we must do the same."

Honor looked up from her tea. "I think I can forgive, but can I forget?"

"Do you have feelings for Luke? Do you think you could give him the love a husband deserves?"

"I…think so. But then I have doubts. Maybe because…because agreeing to marry Luke nine years ago was the biggest mistake I ever made in my life."

Sara shook her head. "Then you have much to be grateful for. A mistake of the heart is a small sin, not one to carry as a burden. Let it go. Set aside your anger and hurt pride, and consider Luke Weaver for the man he is today. Not the man he was nine years ago. Do you think you could do that?"

Honor gazed out the window at the birds flitting on and off the bird feeder. God's creatures. "I think I can try," she said, as much to herself as to the matchmaker. She smiled, her eyes getting misty again. "I think I want to."

Chapter Ten

The following week, Honor and the family were invited to Hannah Yoder Hartman's farmhouse for a spaghetti supper. The invitation was extended to Luke, as well. It was Hannah's husband Albert's birthday.

Luke had met Albert the previous week when he'd come out to have a look at Honor's cow. A recent convert to the Amish faith, Albert had been and remained a veterinarian to the community. Born to a family of Old Order Mennonites, he had made the change from Mennonite to Amish as easily as a gardener might slip on a pair of worn leather gloves. He'd married widow Hannah Yoder and stepped into the respected role of husband, father and grandfather in Seven Poplars.

Luke pulled the buggy up in the driveway, not far from the porch. The temperature was just above freezing and a misty rain fell.

Almost before the wheels stopped rolling, Tanner pushed open the back door to the buggy and leaped out. Elijah and Justice followed his lead.

"I don't want you tracking mud into Hannah's house," Honor cautioned. "Leave your boots on the porch when you go inside. And be on your best behavior tonight. Remember we're guests in Hannah and Albert's house."

Luke glanced at Honor with a grin. They'd had a nice ride to Seven Poplars. Honor was in a good mood and they'd chatted all the way here. Not about anything important, just life's little things. The things he imagined a husband and wife would talk about. "I think they're excited about that birthday cake."

"Maybe Zipporah's been invited," Greta said as she climbed down. "Lots of buggies." Anke threw open her arms to Greta, and Honor passed her to the girl. Greta carried the baby to the back steps and shooed the boys up and inside.

As the back door slammed shut, Luke glanced at the murky sky. "I think I'll get the horse under cover, just in case. I wouldn't want to leave him standing in the rain all evening."

Honor turned toward him on the seat and hesitantly reached out to touch him on the arm. Just a touch, and then she drew her hand back. "I wanted to thank you."

Luke smiled at her in the semidarkness. It seemed as if they hadn't had more than a moment alone all week, between bad weather keeping the boys inside and him working hard to check one item after the next off the list they created together of all the things that needed repairing on her farm. "For anything in particular?" he teased.

Her cheeks grew rosy. She was so beautiful, particularly when she blushed or got flustered. "For everything you've done. You did such a fine job patching the roof, I don't even know that I need a new one, yet."

"We'll see. In the meantime, there's a lot more to

do—the siding on the house, those missing boards on the barn. And the barn definitely needs a new roof—" He broke off as a man stepped off the porch and came to greet them. "There's Albert."

The older man approached the driver's side of the buggy. "Luke! Honor! So glad you could make it. When the weather turned wet, Hannah was afraid you'd think it too far to come on a Friday night."

"Once the boys heard that there would be cake, there was no choice," Luke answered.

Albert laughed, adjusting a battered wide-brimmed wool hat on his head. "Boys do like cake. And who can blame them? Hannah's Ruth baked it, and by the size of it, you'd better all have a hearty appetite."

Luke had liked Albert from their first meeting. There was something that reminded him of his uncle in Kansas, who'd been like a second father to him. Honor was becoming friends with Rebecca and Leah, two of Hannah's daughters. Luke thought that it would be good for Honor to have more friends her own age, even if the young women belonged to the Seven Poplars church community and not her own. And he enjoyed any opportunity to escort Honor somewhere besides Byler's Store.

"I hope my children are on their best behavior tonight." Honor leaned forward on the buggy seat to speak to Albert. "They can be a little high-spirited."

"No such thing in youngsters," Albert insisted. "I say a child will be a child. Hannah and I have a bushelful of grands. The more the merrier. Nothing like a child's laughter to liven up a house full of old people." He rested a hand on the buggy door frame. "I knew your Silas, Honor. He was always one to take good care of his livestock. He never stinted on food or medicine for his cows and horses. That says a lot about a man, that he cares about dumb beasts. Too many don't, you know. I was saddened to hear of his passing. And you left alone with four little ones to care for. But we're not given to understand God's plan."

"Thank you," Honor said.

"It's true," Albert went on. "But you've done all anyone could ask, and your time of mourning is rightfully past. Silas has gone on to a better place."

Luke murmured something appropriate. Talk of Silas always made him uncomfortable.

"It was kind of you to invite us to your birthday supper," Honor replied.

"Pleasure's all ours. If it was up to me, I wouldn't have made a fuss over my birthday, but Hannah insisted. We're always pleased to welcome company, and this is as good an occasion as any. I can't tell you how pleased I was to hear that the two of you were courting," Albert continued. "Luke will make you a fine—"

"Oh, we aren't courting," Honor protested.

Albert chuckled. "Ah, like that, is it?" He nodded, smoothing his beard. "I understand." Drops of rain spattered against the buggy windshield and on Albert's hat. "Young people like to keep their privacy. Not a problem. Well, best get your horse out of the weather." He pointed toward a large barn with a sliding door standing open. "You can drive right inside. Tie up your horse, or better yet, unhitch it and turn it into a stall. Plenty of room in that barn. And don't mind the llama. Bought it to turn in with the alpacas, sort of a big guard dog, and they won't let it into the field with them yet."

"What I was saying was that you're mistaken!"

Honor called as Albert made a dash for the house and Luke flicked the reins over the horse's back. "We're not—"

"I'd heard Albert bought a llama," Luke said, ignoring what she was trying to tell Albert. "The kids would probably love to see it."

Honor turned to him. "Who told Albert we were courting?" She didn't sound angry, but she was clearly not pleased.

"Wasn't me. But someone at the mill mentioned it yesterday morning. One of Hannah's sons-in-law, I think." He chuckled. "Everyone seems to think we are."

"It has to be Aunt Martha," she muttered. "She does like to stir a pot."

He glanced at her. "So...if everyone already thinks we're courting, maybe we should be."

"Dream on," she huffed.

But something in the tone of her voice gave him hope. She didn't sound as if she was completely convinced it *was* a bad idea. Almost without realizing it, he began to whistle as he turned the horse toward the barn.

Suddenly, the rain began to come down in sheets, making it almost impossible to see, but the horse had sensed shelter and headed toward it at a trot. In no more than a minute or two, the horse and buggy passed out of the yard and into the big barn.

"Atch," Honor said. "Where did that downpour come from?"

"As my uncle used to say, it's coming down *katze un hunde*. Cats and dogs! There's a big umbrella in the back," he suggested. "We could grab that."

"I don't think the umbrella would do much good," she said, glancing over her shoulder. "The rain's blowing sideways. Just as well, my pie flopped. It wouldn't do to serve it wet."

Luke made no comment. Honor had made her special shoofly pie for Albert and Hannah, but somehow, she'd switched sugar for salt in the recipe. She wouldn't have discovered it if she hadn't tasted the filling before putting the pie in the oven. Unfortunately, there'd been no time to start a second pie.

Luke suspected that it hadn't been an accident and that Tanner or maybe Justice was to blame. Somehow the canisters had gotten mixed up. That was exactly the sort of trick they liked to play. They weren't mean children, but some of their antics, like removing the ladder when he was patching the shed roof, which they'd done the other day, were more dangerous than funny.

He didn't like to make assumptions when he didn't have the facts. Still, he strongly suspected that one of them had filled the sugar container with salt. Not only had Tanner been helping his mother in the kitchen at the time, but he and his brothers had found the mix-up extremely funny. But Luke didn't want to touch that subject tonight. Honor was quick to defend her children, even when their mischief got out of hand, and he didn't want to spoil the birthday outing.

Besides, it was nice being here in the dark barn, with Honor sitting beside him and rain hitting the roof and coming down outside. Cozy and intimate. He could smell the green-apple shampoo that she used. It was the same scent he'd always associated with her, because she'd used it since she was a girl. And being here, so close to Honor, he could feel that something had changed between them. He didn't know if it was the tone of her voice, the way she seemed at ease with him tonight or something too precious and fleeting to put a name to. But there was a difference, and for the first time, he was sure he had a real chance of winning her as his wife.

"A pity about the pie," Honor remarked. "I don't know how I could have done something so thoughtless as to add so much salt for sugar. The canisters in the pantry aren't even the same size."

Again, Luke bit back the urge to give his opinion on who might have been responsible. He could be wrong, and even if he wasn't, it wouldn't be his place to parent Honor's boys until after they were married. If things worked out the way he hoped, there would have to be more discipline in the household, but it wasn't something he was looking forward to tackling.

"Anyone can make a mistake," he said. "It was kind of you to think of making a pie for Albert and Hannah."

Honor sighed. "A waste of good sugar." And then she chuckled. "*Ne*, salt. Well, next time I'll be more careful."

She slid over toward the far door and he quickly got out and came around the buggy to help her down.

Other horses poked their heads over the stalls to nicker at Honor's. And then a creamy-white llama with large eyes and enormous eyelashes did the same thing only a few feet from where Honor stood. The driving horse snorted and took a few steps backward. Luke caught Honor's arm and pulled her away from the rolling buggy. "Careful," he warned. "I was afraid the wheel would crush your foot." He was afraid the llama might have startled her as well, but he didn't say that.

But Honor didn't seem in the least intimidated. "Look at it. Isn't it amazing?" She moved free from his grasp and picked up a handful of hay from the barn floor. She held it out to the llama.

"It might bite," he warned.

Honor shook her head. "No, it's gentle. Look at the eyes." She placed a small piece of timothy hay in the flat of her palm and held it out. Daintily, the creature nibbled at the treat, then carefully removed it from Honor's hand with its lips, closed its eyes and munched contently. "Good, llama. That's good, isn't it?" she murmured.

The llama bobbed its head up and down as if in answer.

"One of God's creations," Honor said. "I've never seen one this close up." And then she turned toward him, her eyes shining in the light from the buggy.

"Beautiful," he said, not thinking of the animal but of the woman standing in front of him.

She smiled at him. "We'd better make a dash for it. We don't want to make anyone wait on us. And Heaven knows what mischief the children will get in." She dusted the hay off her hands. "Maybe I will take the offer of that umbrella."

He grabbed the umbrella out of the buggy and opened it.

"It's a big umbrella," she said. "Room for both of us."

Together, they dashed through the rain to Hannah's back door. Raindrops hit him in the face and pattered against his coat, but he barely noticed. His heart was too full of possibilities and a sense that all would come right between the two of them—and that the woman he loved would never fail to surprise him.

* * *

Hannah and Albert proved as welcoming and cheerful as Rebecca had promised they would. Honor already met Leah, Susanna and Anna previously, and tonight she became reacquainted with Hannah's other daughters, Miriam and Ruth, as well as Grace, who was a Mennonite. Luke seemed to hit it off with Albert and his sons-in-law, and Tanner, Elijah and Justice quickly made new friends among Hannah's grandchildren.

Even Anke seemed to feel at home among their new friends, laughing and clapping as she was passed from one woman to another. By the time supper was over, and it was time to let the children play and the adults have their coffee, Honor felt at ease enough in Hannah's house to help Rebecca and Grace clear away the dishes and make fresh coffee.

"It's rare we eat in the big parlor," Rebecca explained, setting down a stack of dishes, "but *Mam* wanted to be certain there was room for everyone at the tables at one sitting."

Several children, including Tanner, a boy his age and a little girl in a green dress and a student's black *kapp*, dashed through the kitchen, apparently engaged in a game of tag.

"Amelia, J.J., slow down," Rebecca called. "This is your grandmother's house, not a racetrack."

"No running in the house," Honor admonished her son.

"Why don't you all go upstairs to the playroom?" Grace suggested. "I'll call you when *Grossdaddi* is ready to cut his cake. And if you see Koda, tell him that he'd better be a good boy, or else." She smiled and grimaced. "My Dakota is the dark-haired one, and he's a handful."

"No worse than Amelia," Rebecca said. "Winter's always the hardest. Caleb says you can hardly blame the kids. They have all that energy and can't get outside to run it off."

A burst of children's laughter came from the utility room, and the group trooped through again. This time, Honor counted five children, two of them hers. She wanted to tell them to go sit somewhere and find a quiet activity, but she didn't want to embarrass them in front of their new friends.

"We're a big family," Grace chimed in. She was another auburn-haired Yoder girl, with blue eyes and lovely features. Her Mennonite prayer *kapp* was smaller and her blue dress bore a pattern of tiny flowers, but she wore the same white apron as her sisters. "Keeping us straight must be confusing to those who don't know us well, but you'll soon sort us out. I'm so pleased that *Mam* and *Dat* Albert invited you to join us this evening. And I wanted to congratulate you," she said as she wiped down a kitchen counter. "I just heard the news."

Honor stooped to clean spaghetti sauce off Elijah's chin. Her boys had been surprisingly good at supper, so happy at being with a new group of children that she'd hardly heard a peep out of them from the long kids' table during the meal. "What news?" She brushed a lock of hair out of her youngest son's face and watched him dart off to find his brothers.

"Your courtship," Grace said. "You and Luke. He seems a fine choice, and he's so good with your kids."

Honor straightened and forced herself not to show

her impatience. "Luke and I aren't courting," she said quietly. "I don't know where the rumor got started. He's working for me, but Luke isn't my beau and we have no arrangement."

Grace's bright eyes widened in surprise. "You aren't?" She brought her fingers to her lips. "I'm sorry, I heard—" She glanced at Rebecca, who was dumping ground coffee into the commercial-sized coffeepot.

Rebecca grimaced. "My fault, Honor. Don't blame Grace. I'm the one who told her. We saw you together at Byler's twice, and someone told me…"

"It's okay," Honor intoned.

Rebecca rolled her eyes. "Now I'm embarrassed. I heard that the two of you are attending church services together, and we assumed that you and Luke were… Sara told *Mam* that you and Luke were a perfect match, and I thought…" She shrugged. "I am sorry."

"*Ne*, it's fine," Honor assured her. "I just wanted you both to know that it wasn't true. People keep assuming that just because—" She glanced at them. "People just assume," she repeated, feeling awkward that she was making such a fuss over the issue.

Grace chuckled. "That's what happens in a small community. We get involved in each other's lives, sometimes too involved. But, I promise, we mean well." She and Rebecca gathered up dessert dishes. "Can you grab those forks, Honor? We'd better get back to the party before we miss something."

"*Dat* Albert has a new Bible game that he wants to play before the cake," Rebecca explained. "It's something like bingo using Old Testament people and objects."

"That sounds like fun." Honor picked up the tray

with the forks and spoons and followed them out of the kitchen.

Albert's game was fun, especially when everyone began shouting out when they could fill a square on their card. No one else asked about her involvement with Luke, and she relaxed and enjoyed herself. Anke crawled up into her lap and nodded off to sleep, and Rebecca showed Honor a daybed in the adjoining room, where her own baby was sleeping.

"We'll leave the door open," Rebecca whispered. "That way, we'll hear them if they make a single peep."

Hannah's daughter Susanna, and Anna's oldest girl, Naomi, gathered the other children in the kitchen with crayons, colored paper, old magazines and paste so that they could fashion homemade birthday cards for Albert. That left Honor free to join the others in the next round of bingo.

The mantel clock had just struck eight thirty when Hannah suggested that it was time to cut the cake and get the little ones home to their beds. Honor was collecting bingo cards on her side of the table when there was a loud crash and a chorus of children's shouts from the kitchen. Luke jumped to see what had happened, with Rebecca, Charley, Ruth and Hannah right behind him. Honor hurried around the table and through the kitchen hall.

"Atch," Hannah exclaimed from the kitchen. Charley erupted with a belly laugh and moved aside to allow Honor to enter the room.

Honor froze and gasped, her hands flying to her head. The door to Hannah's pantry stood open, the doorway filled with a tide of dry dog food. Buried to his knees in kibble was a wailing Elijah, and Justice was tugging frantically on his brother's arm to pull him to his feet. J.J. and Amelia stood off to the side, giggling, and a smaller child hid, wide-eyed, behind Naomi. An olive-skinned little boy with dark eyes and black hair that stood up like wheat spikes had run to help Justice and was skating on the spilled kibble.

Honor stood frozen to the spot. Elijah was yelling too loudly to be hurt, and there was indignity rather than pain in his voice. Justice was obviously unharmed. The only one not present was Tanner. Heat flared under her skin. What had her children done now? Mortification mixed with her fear that Tanner might be hurt. She tore herself from inaction and started forward, but Luke was quicker.

He scooped up Elijah, judged him sound and passed him, still protesting, to Honor. A glance at Justice sent him running out of the kitchen. "It's not a big deal," Luke said. "Just some spilled dog food. Hannah? Could I have a broom and dustpan? We'll just scoop it up and put it back in the bin. What's it got to be fifty, sixty pounds, maybe? We'll have it cleaned up in a jiff."

"Tanner?" Honor called, wondering where he had gotten to. She clutched Elijah against her and gently bounced him. "Hush now, Elijah. Hannah, I'm so sorry."

Hannah laughed. "I told Albert it was silly to store that kibble in one big can. He got a good deal on broken bags at the store, and he insisted none of it go to waste. Someone's always dropping strays at our farm. He makes certain they're healthy and well mannered and then finds them homes. I think we're feeding five dogs now."

"Seven, *Mam*," Rebecca corrected. "The one had

two puppies this morning." She nodded to Luke. "The cake is on the top shelf." She pointed. "Do you think you could pass it to me?"

"No problem," Luke said, wading through the kibble. He took the large cake off the top shelf and gingerly made his way back to the pantry doorway, where he passed it to Rebecca.

Just then, Tanner popped up from behind a table in the pantry and darted for the doorway, sending dog food flying.

Honor reached for him but he slipped past her and ran through the kitchen, toward the parlor.

"I'm so sorry," Honor repeated to no one in particular. She put Elijah down, and he followed his brothers.

Ruth and Charley each returned with a broom and a dustpan. "I'll help Luke with cleanup," Charley said. "No need to worry."

"Let's leave them to it," Hannah declared. "Capable hands." She waved her family and guests back into the parlor. Ruth brought the coffeepot, and Rebecca, the cream and sugar.

"What was all the fuss about?" Albert asked when they all returned to the table.

Hannah laughed. "Kibble. Somehow, the bin of kibble tipped over. But your cake is fine."

"A good thing I put it up high," Ruth said.

They hadn't finished the first cup of coffee when Luke and Charley joined them, Charley carrying the cake decorated with a hand-carved wooden llama and a circle of candles.

"If that thing looks more like a goat than a llama, don't blame me," Charley said.

Everyone laughed and admired the cake.

"Your pantry is restored," Luke declared. "The dog food is all back in the bin with the lid on tight, and every piece accounted for."

"Not every piece," Charley teased. "I think Luke ate a couple."

Luke laughed. "That was you, Charley."

"Exactly *what* happened to my dog food?" Albert asked.

"Some of the children, who shall go unnamed—" Luke glanced at Honor and she mouthed a silent thank-you "—were admiring the cake from the top of the kibble can. The can tipped over and…" He spread his hands and chuckled. "The rest is history."

Laughter rippled around the table. "If Charley wasn't in here when the bin went over," Ruth said, "I would have suspected him. His mother told me he once fell into a barrel of pickles."

"He must have smelled like a dill pickle for weeks," Anna's husband, Samuel, said before topping all the stories with his tale of spilling a bucket of maple syrup in the middle of a church service at the bishop's house.

Someone lit the birthday candles, and family and guests joined in to sing "Happy Birthday" to Albert. Cake was enjoyed by all, coats and hats were found, babies were bundled up and men went out into the night to hitch up the horses.

When Honor carried a sleeping Anke to the buggy and made certain Greta and the boys were safely inside, the worst of her embarrassment had passed. Hannah and her daughters hugged Honor and told her again how happy they were that she'd come, and Albert told her to come back anytime.

The rain had let up, and a sliver of a moon peeked

out between the clouds as Luke guided the horse down the country road. With the children and Greta in back, Honor was all too conscious of the strong male presence beside her.

They were almost home before she finally spoke up. “It was wonderful, what you did for me tonight,” she said quietly. “For my children. Cleaning that mess up. Thank you.”

He chuckled. “It was a lot of dog food, wasn’t it?”

“I suppose Tanner was the culprit.”

“Possibly.” He looked down at her. “I think you’ll have to ask him that tomorrow.”

“The two oldest know better.”

Luke smiled in the darkness. “There was no harm done.”

“But they’re mischievous,” she said, feeling guilty again. “And I told them to be on their best behavior.” Would Hannah think she was a bad mother for not demanding answers on the spot? For not punishing them? For not even making them clean up the mess? Was she? She hadn’t known what to do. She still didn’t. But Luke had. Luke had come to her rescue. She sighed. “You are an amazing man, Luke Weaver,” she said.

“Isn’t that what I’ve been telling you?” he replied.

And they laughed together.

Chapter Eleven

Honor glanced up from her sewing machine to the mantel clock. The morning had slipped away as quickly as most days did. She'd fed the children, cleaned up the breakfast dishes, washed and hung clothing on the line, baked biscuits, put a chicken in the oven to roast for the midday meal and had churned some fresh butter to spread on the bread.

She did make good butter, she had to admit that. Good butter making was a gift. Not every woman possessed it, but she wasn't showing pride in acknowledging that hers was worthy of praise. Nothing that came from the store tasted as rich or as sweet. Luke had even said as much to Hannah at the birthday supper.

She'd had such a good time that evening. In spite of the mischief with the spilled dog food, she'd enjoyed herself. It was wonderful to be able to get out of the house and make new friends, but most of all, being with Luke—having him come to her rescue—had warmed her heart.

He seemed to know instinctively what to do with her boys. And, in doing so, he lifted a heavy weight off her shoulders. For the first time in her life, she felt that she wasn't alone in the responsibility for her children. It was silly, of course. She and Luke had no commitment to each other. Hadn't she told him that he was only here on her farm to work? She'd implied, if not said directly, that there was nothing between them and never would be again. The question was, did she believe that anymore? Had she been able to do what Sara had suggested? Was she letting go of the past and looking at the future?

She looked back at the half-stitched seam on Tanner's new trousers. A few more minutes and she could finish. He was growing as fast as a pokeweed. Sometime this winter, her precious little son had sprouted into a long-legged colt. His wrists were shooting out of his sleeves, and his trousers were suddenly bursting at the seams, too short to wear in public.

All three boys were outside, watching Luke repair the windmill, and Anke was napping. Greta was setting the table for dinner and keeping a close eye on the chicken. The previous afternoon, the two of them had made applesauce with apples that were growing soft and prepared potato salad. Earlier, she'd sliced carrots and onions to roast with the chicken, so putting the noon meal together would be a snap. She knew that she should put up the sewing and summon Luke and the children to the table, but quiet was rare in this household. She'd always enjoyed sewing, and she savored her time alone to think while her hands were busy.

She felt as if she had to make a decision about Luke. The thought had been nudging her for days. Should she agree to allow him to court her, as Sara so obviously wanted? Or should she send him on his way, as Aunt

Martha had urged her? She knew that she needed to make up her own mind. That was the problem. She didn't know her own mind. Luke seemed to be the answer to her prayers and to the empty place in her heart. But...

What if she couldn't let go of the hurt he'd caused? Maybe the small voice in her head that urged her never to trust him again was the voice of reason. But sending him away now? Could she do that? Could she be certain that another man would fit into her family so easily? Would she ever feel the kind of connection she felt with him?

God forgive her for thinking ill of the dead, but she and Silas had not been compatible. He had been a good man, but from the beginning, they had rubbed on together like a mismatched team of oxen. No matter how she bowed to his position as head of the house and father of her children, her heart had secretly rebelled. And she had done him a disservice by never loving him fully, as she should have done. Would it have made a difference? In time, would her desire to have a good marriage have won out over her own willfulness? She didn't know, and now she never would.

She pumped the pedal and carefully guided the material to finish the seam. She snipped off the thread and held up the blue trousers for inspection. She'd allowed for a wide hem, and that she could stitch up tonight after the youngest ones were in bed. She'd have the pants ready for Tanner to wear tomorrow. His best ones could go to Justice in the fall, and she had enough of the blue cloth left to make a second pair. Smiling, she turned the trousers right side out and had begun to fold them when her peace was shattered by a child's scream. The kind that terrifies a mother.

By the time Honor reached the yard, Greta was already there and had added her wails to those of Elijah. Tanner's face was white, and Justice stood with tears running down his cheeks. His mouth opened and shut but not a sound came out.

"What is it?" Honor demanded. She looked up at the windmill, but didn't see Luke. "Is someone hurt?" she asked. The temperature had risen sharply since the wet night they'd gone to Hannah's, and the ground was muddy. Water squished around Honor's shoes and soaked her stockings. Bewildered, she looked from one to another, and then she reached Tanner and gripped his shoulder. "What happened?"

He pointed toward the board fence that separated the barnyard from the field. "Luke fell," Tanner said in a thin voice. "He fell and..." Sobs wracked his small body. "He's dead. Luke's dead."

Honor stared at her son, frozen for a moment. "Don't say that," she admonished. "That's not funny. You don't make a joke about—" Suddenly, she had no breath left in her. Darkness threatened to envelop her. Dead? Luke dead? Impossible. What was the child saying? Gooseflesh rose on the back of her neck and prickled the skin on her arms. "Luke fell?" It came out a whisper, but Tanner nodded, still pointing toward the fence.

And then she saw a man's foot encased in a black high-top shoe on the far side of the bottom rail. Somehow she closed the distance in a heartbeat and climbed the fence. Hatless, Luke lay sprawled on his back in the mud. His arms were flung out on either side of his head, his legs as motionless as if they were carved of wood. Luke's face was as pale as bleached flour, his eyes closed.

"Luke?" She fell to her knees beside him in the mud, and her blood turned to ice. Luke appeared to be asleep. His waxen lips were parted slightly, and his features were smooth. He'd shaved this morning, and she noticed a tiny scratch where he'd cut himself along his jawline. She could smell the clean scent of Ivory soap on his skin. "Dear God," she whispered. "Let this be a bad dream." She pressed her palm against the side of his throat, trying to find any sign of breath. "Luke," she murmured. She turned to look at Tanner. "He fell? How far? Off that?" She pointed at the windmill.

Tanner nodded. "From the top."

Honor tried to shut out the sound of the children's cries as she tried to figure out what to do. Was Luke broken beyond healing? Had the fall snapped his neck? His back? She touched his cheek. The noonday air was cool and moist, but his skin seemed chilled. "Luke," she repeated.

She didn't know what to do. She pressed her fingers to his throat again. She thought she could feel a pulse, but what if she was wrong? If only she had a phone. But the nearest telephone was at an English neighbor's house, too far to send Tanner on his own to call for help. Sending Greta would mean leaving the baby alone in the house for too long.

"Luke!" She patted his face again, first gently and then harder. "Luke!" If only she hadn't lingered over her sewing. If only she'd called them to dinner five minutes ago. If only... The enormity of her loss washed over her in waves. Luke was dead and she'd never told him that she loved him. “Don’t be dead,” she whispered.

“He’s dead, isn’t he?” Greta peered between the boards, her eyes wide and frightened.

“He’s not dead,” Honor insisted. He couldn’t be. It was impossible that someone could have been laughing and teasing her only an hour ago and now lying lifeless in her corral. Desperately, she placed her fingers over his lips, praying for some sign of breath.

Nothing.

“Luke,” she ordered. “Wake up. Wake up, Luke.” She bent and brought her own lips close to his. Did she feel… *Ya?* Her heart hammered against her ribs. Surely it wasn’t her imagination. She’d felt something, hadn’t she? “Luke?” She seized his shoulders and shook him. “Wake up!” What was it her grandmother had told her about reviving a grandchild who had fallen off the barn? “Greta! Bring me a bucket of water! Now!”

She studied Luke’s face. No movement. Not so much as a muscle twitched. Not an eyelid fluttered. Time passed. Seconds? Minutes?

Greta dropped a sloshing bucket into the mud beside her. Honor looked from the clear water to the mask that was Luke’s face and back again. “Please, God,” she whispered as she dashed the cold liquid over him.

Luke gasped. His eyes flew open, and he coughed. He tried to sit up and then fell back into the mud. His eyelids fluttered, and he drew in a long breath.

“You’re alive,” Honor whispered.

He groaned. “I think so.” He exhaled slowly. “Did I…”

She nodded, wanting to shout, to throw herself onto him and to kiss him. “We thought you were dead,” she managed. She used her apron to pat the water off his face. Tears ran down her cheeks.

"So you tried to drown me?" His voice came low and rasping, but his eyes focused on her face and the corners of his mouth turned up in a crooked smile.

"You fell from the windmill," she managed, finding suddenly that she could barely catch her breath. She wanted to cover his face with kisses, to hold him in her arms. She clasped her hands together to keep from touching him. "I think you should lie still. You might have broken bones."

He groaned again and flexed first one limb and then another. "I don't think so." He sat up and put his hands on either side of his head. "The board broke," he said. "The one I was standing on. I didn't want to fall on the concrete pad or the fence. I think I jumped."

Shakily, Honor got to her feet. "Greta, take the little ones into the house. Make certain everything on the stove is turned off. Tanner, see if Anke is awake. If she is, you can get her out of her crib."

"He's not dead?" Tanner asked.

Luke scoffed. "Do I look dead?"

"I think you should stay where you are." Honor fretted. "You may have a concussion. Or you could have internal injuries." She turned to Greta. "Please see to the children."

As Greta rounded up the boys and led them away, Luke slowly got to his feet. "Nothing's broken. I'm fine. Just a little woozy." He took a step and staggered. Instantly, she was at his side, supporting him.

"In here." She helped him into the barn through the open doorway. "Sit," she ordered when they reached a bale of straw. "Even if you didn't break your neck, you've taken a bad fall. You probably knocked your brains loose."

"I'm fine," he repeated, but he did as she told him and sat. "The mud absorbed most of the blow…when I hit."

With her hopelessly muddied apron, she dabbed at his face again at the smears of dirt that streaked his cheeks. He'd lost his hat in the fall but that didn't matter now. "You're alive," she murmured. "I thought… I thought…" And then she lost whatever control she had and began to weep great sobs of relief. Tears blurred her vision, so that she was only vaguely aware when he stood again and put his arms around her. "I thought I'd lost you," she wailed. "And I hadn't told you—" She took a deep, gulping breath.

"Shh, shh," he soothed, rocking her against him. "You hadn't told me what, Honor?"

The words *that I love you* rose to her lips, but she couldn't utter them. Instead, she laid her head on his shoulder and drank in the strength of his arms and the blessed sounds of his breathing. It wasn't too late, she realized. God had given her a second chance. "I think," she began and then found herself racked by another sob. "I think I would…like to…"

"Like to what?" He patted her shoulder. "Don't cry, Honor. Please don't cry. It's all right. I'm all right. Tell me."

"Luke, I think we should… I want to…" She wiped at her tears with a muddy hand, trying to find the words.

He searched for a handkerchief, but when he pulled it from his pocket, it was as wet as his coat and trousers. She stared at it, and her sobs became gasps of laughter.

Soon, Luke was laughing with her. “Is this your way of saying you’ll marry me?” he asked. “Is that what you’re trying to say?”

“Ya.” She nodded, pulled free from his embrace and wiped her eyes with the backs of her hands. “If you still want...”

“Say it,” he urged. “Say the words.”

She covered her face with her hands and then sniffed. She glanced down at her apron and skirts. Her muddy stockings sagged around her ankles, her shoes were soaked and her apron was dirty beyond belief. “*Ne.* You have ask me properly, first,” she said, sniffing again.

“I’ll ask you a hundred times if I have to.”

He smiled at her, and her chest felt tight. She’d come so close to losing him. In those terrible minutes when she’d thought he was dead, all her doubts had evaporated, and all she could think was how much she needed him. Not only her, her children needed him. “My Anke... My boys need a father,” she whispered.

“And I want to be that father. I want to be your husband. So will you let me court you?”

“Ne.” She shook her head, fighting another wave of tears. She was so thankful for God’s grace. “I don’t need that. We’ve had our courtship, Luke. I think that’s what we’ve been doing here these last weeks.” She looked up at him. Took a breath. “I want us to marry... as soon as possible. I don’t want to be alone anymore. And you’re the only man I want, I’ll ever want for my husband.”

Now it was Luke whose eyes glistened with emotion. "I prayed I could win your love again. I was certain that God meant for us to be together. But I nearly lost faith that it could happen. But now God has answered my prayers. I'll be a good husband to you, Honor. I will be the best father to your children…to *our children* that I can."

"It was my foolish pride that kept us apart," she said. "But I never… Luke, I never stopped loving you."

He caught her hand and gripped it. "I love you," he said. "I've loved you since I was eight years old and you threw that ladle of well water on my head."

She laughed. "And now I've done it again, but this time with a whole bucket."

He turned her muddy hand in his and pressed his lips softly against the underside of her wrist. "If I'd known it would win you over, I'd have jumped off the windmill the first day I got here," he said.

He tugged at her hand, and she knew that in another second she'd be in his arms and he'd be kissing her mouth. And she wanted him to. But she made herself pull away from him. "First, we see you to a doctor and then to the bishop," she said. "I think it's wise we marry soon."

"The sooner the better," he agreed. "As soon as the *banns* can be cried."

She nodded, backing away from him. "I do love you, Luke Weaver," she said, and then she whirled around and ran for the safety of the house and her children.

"I haven't done this since I was sixteen," Honor said to Luke, holding on to his arm for balance. "I'll probably fall and break my neck."

"Skating isn't something you forget," he assured her.

She sighed. "I hope you're right." After a final glance over her shoulder at the campfire where members of the Seven Poplars youth group were helping her boys roast hot dogs, Honor made her way cautiously out onto the ice. Luke sat down to lace up his skates, and she took the opportunity to practice a few easy moves.

So much had happened in the past week that she could hardly believe it. Luke had gone to her bishop for permission for them to marry, and they were only waiting for certification from his Kansas church community to set a date. Most Amish weddings were held in November and December, but as a widow, she could marry at any time.

The only bad thing was that the bishop had asked Luke to stop working on her house until after the wedding, unless accompanied by others who could serve as chaperones. Since they'd made it plain that they cared for each other, the elders felt that the less time they spent together until they became man and wife, the more respectable it would appear to outsiders.

Honor could understand the bishop's decision, but she did miss having Luke at her table, and the children asked for him every day. Being with him tonight was even more special because he'd been absent all week. Typical of Delaware weather, the thaw hadn't lasted. The temperature had dropped to the single digits and the ice on the millpond had frozen faster and harder than it had in years.

"I thought you said you'd forgotten how to skate." Luke called, coming up behind her on his skates. "Race you to the far side."

Her response was to lengthen her stride, and she glided away from him. It felt wonderful to fly along on the ice with the wind on her face and the full moon illuminating the pond as brightly as twilight. Birds must feel like this, she thought. It was a glorious night, and her *grossmama* Berta's old skates fitted her as though they'd been made for her.

Honor and Luke had skated before, one cold winter when they were first dating, years ago. Tonight, it was almost as if those years had faded and she was young again. The moon was huge and bright, and the ice a sheet of silver. She could smell the crackle of apple wood on the fire and hear the sounds of children's laughter rising above the hiss of the skate blades. She felt as light as a feather…as free as a puff of wind as they skimmed over the frozen millpond. How could she have forgotten how much she loved Luke…how happy he made her?

Other Amish families and couples had gathered along the wooded shoreline of Freeman's pond, glad for an opportunity to get together for an evening of fellowship and pleasure. Anke was safely in the house with Katie and some of the women, and Greta and Zipporah were helping serve hot chocolate and marshmallows. A few Amish were on the ice, some with skates and some with sleds or just sliding along on their shoe soles, but she and Luke had most of the expanse of the large pond to themselves.

They reached the opposite bank side by side. She turned to avoid a tree root jutting out of the earth and spun out, landing on her bottom and sliding across the ice. Luke was immediately at her side, getting down on his knees beside her. "Are you hurt?" he asked.

She shook her head and laughed. "*Ne*, just feeling silly. Pride goes before a fall."

His gloved hand closed around her arm and he leaned close. “Do you have any idea how beautiful you are tonight?”

“Don’t,” she protested, but hearing him say so was sweet.

“Kiss me,” he said.

“Ne.” She shook her head, savoring the giddiness that made her tremble. “No kissing until we’re man and wife.”

“Just one kiss?”

His voice was teasing, but she found herself staring at his mouth. Wanting to press her lips to his. “*Ne*, absolutely not. We’re not teenagers, Luke.”

He groaned. “Honor, Honor, Honor. You’re right, but...” He sighed and got to his feet. He offered his hand, and she took it and he pulled her up. “Skate with me,” he said.

“All right.” She felt her left skate suddenly loosen. “Wait,” she said. “I think my lace came undone.”

Still holding her hand, Luke helped her to the edge of the pond. “Here. Sit here,” he said, motioning to a section of a tree that lay half below and half above the ice. She did as he told her, careful to keep her skirt in place over her thick stockings.

“Let me see your skate.”

Her heartbeat quickened as he took her skate in his hands and bent over it.

“Ah” He nodded. “The lace snapped. I think I can knot it so it will work.”

She breathed in the cold, clean air with its bite of cedar and pine. She could see the others on the other side of the pond and she assumed they could see her and

Luke, but here in the quiet semidarkness, it seemed as if they were alone in the world beneath this silvery moon.

He pulled off his gloves and unlaced her skate. "The rest of the lace seems strong enough," he said. He knotted it just above the break and then laced the top again, leaving an inch-long gap between. "If it doesn't hold, I can give you one of mine," he offered.

"Let me try. It feels all right," she answered. "We should go back to the group, anyway."

But she didn't want to go back. She wanted to go on skating alone with him, with her heart full and his strong hand clasping hers. Was it wrong to feel like this? She was a widow, a mother of four, but this couldn't be wrong, could it? She shifted her weight and skated a few feet beside him. "I think it's fine," she said.

And then they were off again, hand in hand, skimming over the shimmering surface, finding joy in being together and silently making promises to each other about the days and months and years ahead.

Chapter Twelve

"Boys, you're too noisy. Go outside and play. Better yet..." Honor stopped pedaling her sewing machine and looked up.

Freeman's mother, Ivy, had come to visit while her son helped Luke out with a project. While Honor worked at her sewing machine, Ivy was knitting. The two women had been trying to talk when the boys got too loud. "Get your coats on and go watch Luke and Freeman repairing the chicken house. Learn how it's done, so that you can mend your own buildings someday. They might even find work for you to do."

"We want to skate," Tanner said. "Can you take us to the millpond? I'm going to take my sled."

"Ne," Honor replied firmly, glancing down as she lifted the pressure foot of the sewing machine. "I've no time to take you anywhere today. We can't play on the pond, anyway. Freeman says the warmer temperatures are melting the ice."

Tanner pulled a face. "But we wanna go. We could stay close to the bank." Justice stood solidly behind him, the two of them united in a purpose for once, instead of quarreling or teasing each other.

Honor removed the shirt she was sewing and shook it out. "You heard me," she said. "Skating is only safe when it's very cold and the ice is thick. It may freeze again this month, or we could have to wait until next winter. We'll just have to wait and see."

"But we want to go," Justice insisted.

Honor took a deep breath and prayed for patience. Since the night of the winter frolic the previous week, Tanner and Luke had been wild to return to the mill with their sled. But the changeable Delaware weather made skating a rare treat. Some winters the temperatures never dropped and held long enough to make ice-skating safe at all.

"Please," Tanner begged.

"You heard me," Honor replied, becoming slightly embarrassed that the boys were being difficult in front of company. "The two of you go outside and play in the yard." She studied the shirt collar carefully, trying to decide if the seam was perfectly straight.

Justice looked pitiful. "But there's nothing fun to do in the yard," he said.

"What you both need is something useful to do," Honor replied. "See if you can figure out where the white hen is hiding her eggs."

Tanner shook his head. "She pecks."

"And scratches," Justice argued. "We should put her in the pot and eat her."

Honor didn't want to scold them in front of company, so she forced a cheerful expression. "The white hen is a good egg producer," she explained brightly.

"And she'll raise baby chicks for us in the spring. She's an excellent mother."

"I'll gather the eggs," Greta offered, coming into the kitchen. She crossed the kitchen and reached for her heavy shawl. "Come on, Tanner. Justice." Reluctantly, the boys trudged after her to put on their coats.

Honor returned to the table, where Ivy was knitting a blue baby cap. "It rained all day yesterday, and they've got so much energy that they get restless when they stay inside."

Ivy smiled and nodded. "I know about little boys and big ones. It's a pity about the ice. Freeman's father was very strict about the pond. When Freeman was little, he would beg and beg to be allowed to skate, but we never let him unless the pond was frozen from bank to bank. The ice must be two inches thick, and it's nothing like that now."

With Ivy there, not even the bishop could complain about Luke being on Honor's farm if they were chaperoned by such respected elders. And Honor liked Ivy and was glad for her company. She reminded Honor of her Grandmother Troyer, now passed on and greatly missed.

The men had carried Honor's sewing machine out into the kitchen so that the women could be at the center of everything while they did their needlework. It was so nice here, with the sun coming in the windows, that Honor thought she might move some of the furniture and keep the sewing machine there until spring.

"I hope Elijah's cold doesn't get any worse," she said to Ivy. Elijah had had the sniffles for several days and was cutting a molar, so after listening to his whining, Honor had tucked him back into bed at the same time she'd put Anke down for her nap. He protested for about ten minutes and then dropped off to sleep. She'd made chicken soup the previous day and had hoped some hot soup and plenty of rest would set him as right as rain. Her children were rarely ill and she hoped the rest of them wouldn't catch the toddler's cold.

"So long as your Elijah doesn't develop a fever or a bad cough, I think he'll be fine," Ivy commented. "He's a sturdy little one. And you're so sensible with him. You should have seen me when Freeman was small. If he sneezed, I was driving him to the doctor. Once, I took him to the emergency room for an infected mosquito bite." She sighed and smiled from under her black elder's *kapp.* Ivy's face was surprisingly unlined, and her eyes were bright. "He was our only one, you see," she said. "The only one who lived. And I was constantly in a panic that something would happen to him." She beamed. "But God blessed us, and he flourished in spite of my fears. Look at the size of him now, grown to a big, hearty man."

Honor paused from sewing a button on Tanner's spring jacket. Her heart went out to Ivy, having only one child and being unable to have any more. Honor couldn't imagine what she would do if anything happened to one of her four. Or the ones she and Luke might be blessed with… Her children were her life, and the truth was, she was looking forward to a bigger family. God willing, of course.

She swallowed and glanced around the kitchen. Soon Luke would be sharing her life permanently. He would help her with the farm and with the children. A small shiver of excitement spiraled up her spine. And with it came an icy thread of doubt.

"Ivy?"

"Ya?" The knitting needles paused, and Ivy rested them and the cap on her black apron.

"Do you think I'm marrying again too soon?" That wasn't what she wanted to ask. She wanted to ask Ivy if she thought that Honor was being foolish. Because she felt foolish. At times, she was downright giddy. There was no other word for it. She was giddy over Luke and the thought of making a life with him. Once, all those years ago, they'd shared a kiss behind the schoolhouse on the way home from a singing. She still remembered that kiss, dreamed about it…

"Why would you ask that?" Ivy said. "Of course not. A decent time has passed since Silas was laid in the earth. I've known women with children to marry again before the first year was up, and few thought to criticize them. A woman is meant to be married, and children are meant to have a father. It's God's way. It's our way."

"We nearly married before," Honor admitted. She wondered how much to reveal about Luke, but she felt the need to talk and Ivy seemed open to listening. "Before I agreed to become Silas's wife. But we… Luke and I…broke it off."

"I know about that," Ivy said with a wave. "Your almost marriage to Luke was common knowledge around the county. Yours was a different church community, but talk gets around. And don't think you two are the first or the last couple to call off a marriage at the last moment. Sometimes it's the wisest thing to do."

Honor looked down at her hands, now still. "It was Luke's doing, not mine."

"But you were both very young. Too young, some

would say. I think a woman needs to be in her midtwenties to know her own mind when it comes to marriage. Most women. I know that I would have been far too unsteady to have married sooner. Too much a girl to make a good wife if I'd married before I did. Marriage is hard. You have to put the other person first. We waited to exchange our vows, and it was worth it. He's gone now, my first husband, but a better man never walked God's earth. And I counted my blessings to have him. And now to have my Jehu. God is good."

"So, you don't think I'm rushing into this? With Luke? My aunt Martha does. She's against it. She thinks we'd be a terrible match."

Ivy glanced up from her knitting and chuckled. "Martha disapproves of a lot of things, but no one's asking Martha to marry Luke." Her eyes twinkled. "This has to be your decision, Honor. And Luke's. Not mine and certainly not Martha's. Besides, Sara Yoder thinks you've made a good match, and she's a sensible woman. And so is Hannah. She's so taken with you and Luke, she tells me that she's offered to have your wedding at her home."

"She did, but Sara offered first. It was so sweet of Hannah to offer, but we've decided to hold the ceremony at Sara's. The bishop is just waiting for a letter from Luke's church confirming his baptism. We want Katie and Freeman to be part of the wedding party, and Sara's already planning the menu. You'd think I was her daughter instead of just a client."

"You're more than a client," Ivy assured her. "You know Sara never had any children of her own. She thinks of all of her brides and grooms as her sons and daughters. She says so all the time." Ivy chuckled. "Sara may seem tough, but inside, she's as soft as new butter."

Honor nodded, reassured. She finished the last stitches on the shirt collar and then got up to check the roast. She was planning on making buttered noodles, a green bean casserole and scalloped potatoes for the midday meal. Ivy had brought a coconut cake and canned spiced pears to go with dinner.

Greta came in with the eggs. "Only eight today," she said.

"Are the boys staying out of Luke and Freeman's way?" Honor asked, reaching for hot mitts.

Greta nodded. "They hitched up the donkey to the sled and were driving it around the field." She removed her bonnet and retied the ends of her headscarf. "Want me to check on Anke?"

Honor nodded. "And would you make certain that Elijah is covered? He's as wiggly as a goat. Half the time his blankets end up on the floor. I wouldn't want him to take a chill." She slid the pan of scalloped potatoes into the oven. She felt a little better after talking with Ivy. She supposed that every woman must be nervous about a coming wedding. Marriage was a serious matter. God willing, she and Luke would be married for the next fifty years.

She loved Luke, she was certain of that. And she believed that he would make a good father for her children. It would be all right. They would be all right. In just a few weeks, she would stand before the bishop with Luke and they would be man and wife. She was scared, but in a good way, and the sooner they could make their promises to each other, the better for her and for her children.

It was a little after one o'clock when she finally had the food on the table and stepped out on the back porch to ring the dinner bell. "Come and eat!" she called.

The air was brisk, but the sun was shining. She judged it to be in the forties, not a bad day for February. She ran the bell a second time, and Luke and Freeman appeared at the far end of the yard.

She smiled to herself. How fine Luke looked, with his tool belt around his waist and shoulders wide and strong. He wasn't quite as tall as Freeman, but Honor's throat warmed at the sight of Luke and his friend striding toward her. She wasn't alone anymore. She had a good man who wanted to marry her and she had friends. Truly, she felt blessed.

She didn't see the boys, so she rang the dinner bell yet again. "Have you seen Justice and Tanner?" she called to Luke. "Are they coming?"

The two men drew closer. "Haven't seen them in a good while," Luke replied. "They had the sled hitched to the donkey and were taking turns riding around the field."

"I saw them," Freeman said. "An hour ago, maybe more. They were going down the lane. I thought maybe you'd sent them to pick up the mail from your box."

Honor went to the far corner of the back porch and looked down the driveway. There was no sign of her boys. "Maybe they're in the barn," she said, hoping that they'd tired of their game and put the donkey in his stall. She pulled the rope again, and the old bell pealed.

"I'll go look," Luke said. "They can't have gone far."

"You know how kids are," Freeman said. "When they get playing, they forget everything else, even dinner."

When Luke came striding back alone, Honor's throat tightened. A shiver became a chill, despite the fact that she now had her cloak on. "Is the donkey there?" she asked. He shook his head, and suddenly she was afraid. "They've gone to millpond," she said. "Tanner wanted me to take them. He was going to take his sled to play on the ice."

"*Ne*, I don't think they'd do that. They've never gone that far before, have they?" Freeman's expression darkened. "The ice on the pond has been melting."

Honor's hand flew to her mouth. "That's where they've gone. I know it. Luke, hitch up the horse for me." She came down the steps toward him. "We have to get to Freeman's. Katie's not home today. There would be no one there to send them home."

"You really think they'd go to the millpond? By themselves?"

She nodded, starting across the barnyard. "Once Tanner gets something in his head, he doesn't let go of it. I've got to go after them before something terrible happens." If Tanner and Justice got to the pond… But she couldn't allow herself to think of that. She'd go after them, find them along the road. How fast could a donkey carry two little boys?

"I'll take the horse," Luke said, walking quickly beside her. "I can go cross-country through the farm lanes and the woods. It will cut off nearly a mile."

"You can't expect me to stay here," Honor insisted.

"I'll take you in my buggy," Freeman volunteered. "Your little ones will be safe with my mother." He looked at Luke, who was already on the move. "There's a life ring with a rope on the pole by the spillway. You won't need it, but just in case."

Honor stifled a breathless moan. The image of her boys walking out on thin ice sickened her.

Luke stopped and turned to Honor. "Go back to the house and get your gloves. No sense in you catching your death if Justice and Tanner are playing somewhere along the road. I'm going to go right now but Freeman will bring around his buggy."

"God grant they are safe," she murmured.

She rushed to gather her mittens and tell Ivy where she was going, then came back out. By the time she walked down the porch steps, Freeman was bringing his horse and buggy to the back door. "Luke?" she asked. "Has he—"

"Already gone." Freeman offered his gloved hand to help her into the buggy. "He slapped a bridle on your horse and took off at a canter across the back field. Don't worry. If they did have any notion of going to play on the ice, he'll get there well ahead of them."

Honor's horse was a good one and had obviously been ridden before. Some driving horses balked or shied at a rider, but not this one. Luke hadn't seen a saddle in the barn, but he'd ridden bareback a lot in Kansas. His uncle's fields were vast compared to these farms, and what the elders didn't see, they couldn't object to. There was no gate at the edge of Honor's land but he'd brought wire cutters and he made short work of the three strands of barbed wire. No time to repair it today; that could wait. If the boys were headed for Freeman's pond, he needed to beat them there.

When the fence was down, he remounted, crossed another meadow and followed a lumber road through the woods. He knew the way; he'd walked this track once from the mill. He kicked the horse into a trot and then to a gallop. Beneath the trees, the ground was barely thawed and frost tinted the dry leaves. Ahead of him, a deer sprang up and vanished as soundlessly as a shadow. Luke urged his mount on.

Honor's sons knew that the pond, any pond, was strictly forbidden without an adult. Winter or summer. And they knew that leaving the property without telling their mother wasn't allowed. He couldn't help thinking that this is what came of being so lenient with them. Honor had allowed her children to grow willful and disregard her wishes. His own mother had been quick with a switch if he got out of line. That wasn't his way. He didn't believe in striking a child, in using any sort of physical punishment on any person, young or old. But there were other ways to discipline.

He left the field to ride along the edge of a farmyard and then reined the horse to a trot down their driveway to a paved road, the same route that led to the mill. The final quarter mile passed quickly with no sign of the boys. There was a grassy shoulder and Luke kept the animal on it at a steady lope.

"Let there be no one there," he muttered. "Please, let them have turned back."

A car pulled from the parking lot of the mill onto the blacktop and came slowly toward him. When the driver reached him, he came to a stop and rolled down his window. "Hey! There are two Amish kids out on the ice! I hollered to them but they wouldn't listen. I didn't know what else to do. Didn't seem to be any adults, so I called 911."

"Thank you!" Luke kicked the horse in the sides and galloped toward the edge of the pond. As he approached, he frantically scanned the ice for the children. A loud *eee-haw* came from the picnic area, and the horse whinnied as it caught the scent of its barn mate. Luke spotted the donkey tied to a picnic table just inside the trees. A small black Amish boy's hat lay on the bank. Frantically, Luke scanned the surface of the pond, catching sight of the two small figures about thirty yards from the shore. Tanner was tugging on a rope that held the partially submerged sled.

Luke vaulted from the horse's back. "Tanner!" he yelled, cupping his hands around his mouth. "Justice!"

One of them let out a wail.

"I'm coming! Lay down on your bellies!" he shouted in *Deitsch*. "Stretch out your arms."

Where were the rope and the flotation device Freeman had mentioned? He saw it and spent precious seconds to run to it and pull it free from the stake. Looping the rope over his shoulder, he eased out onto the ice. It crunched ominously, and a long crack zigzagged out to his left. Luke took another step and the ice gave under his weight. The heel of his boot sank through the surface. "God help me," he whispered. "Not by my doing, but by Yours."

Tanner flipped the sled over and then shrieked as one knee sank through the ice. Water welled up around him. Justice didn't make a sound. He lay flat, motionless, his face white under his black knit cap. About fifteen feet separated the two children.

Cautiously, Luke lowered himself to his hands and knees. "Tanner," he called. "Lay it on its back." The sled was a concave plastic disk rather than a traditional wooden sled; it might hold Tanner's weight if he fell through the ice.

Luke heard Justice whimper, but the boys were otherwise silent. Too afraid to speak, he imagined.

Luke inched forward, ignoring the groaning and snapping beneath him. One hand punched through and black water bubbled up. Far in the distance, he heard the wail of rescue vehicles. Luke kept moving, no longer on hands and knees but flat on his stomach, trying to push and pull himself across the ice.

Justice seemed secure for the moment, but Tanner was clearly in trouble. More cracks opened in the ice, and the child's knees crashed through the shimmering surface. Tanner managed to flip the sled over.

"That's it!" Luke shouted. "Hold on to it! It should float!"

Justice was quietly sobbing. His eyes were huge and frightened.

"Stay calm!" Luke urged. "Justice, I'm going to slide this life ring to you. Grab it and don't let go! Do you understand, Justice? Whatever happens, don't let go!"

On his first try, the ring missed the boy by six feet. Luke pulled it back and tried again. This time, it came within a yard of Justice. "Creep to the ring!" Luke ordered. "Slowly! There! You've got it! Now, don't move. Do you hear me? Do not move. I'll get you in a second."

He turned back to Tanner. Tanner was glued to the sled, cold water surging around his waist. Luke knew that time was against them. The water temperature could kill the children almost as quickly as drowning. He glanced at Justice. "Start crawling toward the shore," he called. Justice was the lightest of them. He might just make it to shore without falling through. "Whatever you do, Justice, don't let go of the ring!"

The shrieks of the emergency vehicles became

louder, but Luke was afraid that if Tanner went through the ice, they wouldn't get there in time. "Keep moving!" he ordered Justice. Then he turned back to the older boy, "Hold on, Tanner, I'm coming to—"

The ice cracked and parted, and Luke felt himself fall. Heard the splash. Water closed over his head, colder than anything he could imagine. His coat and boots filled with water and pulled him down, but he fought his way to the surface. His head broke the surface and he gasped for air. Both boys were screaming.

Tanner had gone down into the water, but the sled was holding him up. Luke attempted to crawl back up onto the ice, but every time he moved forward, it shattered and he sank again. He went under again and came up. This time his fingers touched the edge of Tanner's sled.

The boy had suddenly stopped screaming and was staring at him. Tanner held out a hand and Luke grasped it. He looked around, saw what he thought was a thicker section of ice, and shoved the sled as hard as he could. The sled glided up and over the ice, taking Tanner with it.

Luke's teeth were chattering so hard that he couldn't think. He was cold, so cold, and his boots were so heavy. Slowly, he used one foot to push off the right boot and then repeated the process with the left. His coat was next, but the zipper was almost more than he could manage.

He heard voices. On a bullhorn. The *Englisher* firemen were there, but he couldn't make out what they were trying to tell him. "Hold on," he tried to say to Tanner, but the words were as frozen as the chunks of ice around him. *Into Your hands*, he prayed silently. *In Your infinite mercy, spare these innocents…*

Luke kicked in the water, but he could feel himself sinking. He was suddenly tired, so tired. And then, the blackness closed over him and he didn't feel the cold anymore.

Chapter Thirteen

Luke sat up and looked around the cubicle in the hospital emergency room. "No," he repeated firmly to the nurse in scrubs adorned with multicolored cartoon characters. "I'm fine. I want to go home." He hated hospitals. He hated the smells and the sounds of sick people, and he could imagine how much money every minute he remained was costing him. The Amish didn't believe in medical insurance; the bill would be paid out of his own pocket. He'd certainly not have permitted anyone to take him to the hospital in an ambulance if he'd had his wits about him.

Although it was all pretty hazy in his mind, Luke knew that the fire company volunteers had reached him in time to keep him from drowning or dying from hypothermia. How they'd gotten to him, he wasn't so clear about. He'd coughed up a lot of water, and at one point he remembered an oxygen mask over his face, but he was all right now. He just wanted to get out of here.

The middle-aged nurse shook her head and spoke louder and more distinctly, almost as one would to a slow child. "The doctor would prefer that you remained with us for a few hours, Mr. Weaver, for observation."

Luke looked down, embarrassed to see that he was clad only in a scanty cotton hospital gown. Quickly, he pulled the thin, white blanket up to his neck. "Where are my clothes?"

She shook her head again. "I'm sorry, but the paramedics had to cut your things off when they treated you in the ambulance." She smiled.

"But the children are safe? Right? You said the children were fine."

She nodded. "Absolutely. I was told that the younger of the two didn't even need medical attention. The older boy is here with his mother, but they are just waiting for his paperwork. Apparently, he was more frightened than injured."

Luke closed his eyes for a moment. He remembered repeatedly asking the fireman about Tanner and Justice, but he'd been confused during the ambulance ride. He was relieved that the boys were okay and he said a quick, silent prayer of gratitude.

The nurse patted his hand. "Thanks to you, they were saved. That was very brave of you to go to their rescue. You nearly lost your own life in the effort. You're quite the hero, Mr. Weaver."

"Luke," he corrected. "My name is Luke, and I'm not a hero. Their lives were in God's hands. It is the Lord who deserves credit, not me."

"But a blessing that you came by when you did." She fluffed up his pillow. "Now, if you're feeling up to it, you have people waiting to see you."

"*Ya.* I mean, yes. And I want to see the doctor. I'm leaving as soon as I can get something decent to wear."

"I'll speak to him as soon as I can. One of our docs is out today, and we're all hard-pressed to care for everyone." She pushed a tall pole with tubes and a clear plastic bag hanging from it back away from his bed. "There's a gentleman in the waiting room, a Mr. Freeman. Perhaps he can help with your clothing. I am sorry that your things were ruined, but the hospital isn't responsible."

"No, I didn't think they were. Could you please send Freeman in?" He didn't bother to explain that Freeman was the miller's first name, not his last.

"I'll be glad to," she replied. She produced another blanket and laid it on the end of his bed. "You just lie back and rest. If you aren't warm enough, here's a second blanket."

"Warm enough, thank you."

The nurse gave him a final reassuring smile. "Don't be surprised if you make the front page of the *State News*," she said. "And the *News Journal*. There's a news crew parked outside. Everyone will want to know how you saved those children." As she left, she pulled the curtain closed, shutting off his cubicle from the rest of the emergency room.

Great, more newspapers, Luke thought. Just what he wasn't hoping to hear.

He didn't have long to wait before a grinning Freeman pushed his way through the curtains. "You know how to have a good time," he said. "Isn't it a little early to be swimming?" He was carrying a white trash bag and a man's straw hat in one hand. "Seems you have a problem hanging on to hats," he said, handing over the hat. "It isn't spring, but this was the best I could do. My uncle offered one of his wool ones, but I think his head's smaller than yours."

"This will do fine," Luke answered. He smoothed back his hair and settled the hat on his head. "And you've got clothes for me in there, I hope."

"I do." Freeman grinned. "I got there in time to see one of the fireman cutting your trousers and shirt off. I brought shoes and socks, too. I don't know what happened to your boots."

Luke shrugged. "Bottom of the pond."

Freeman grimaced. "A worthwhile price, I'd say. Are they going to release you soon? I think Tanner is about ready to go home. I promised Honor I'd see them safely to the house. If you can go home with us, great. If not, I'll come back for you."

"I'll be ready to go as soon as I get dressed." Luke closed his eyes, then opened them. "But the boys are okay?" The memory of seeing Tanner break through the ice wouldn't leave him.

"Boys are fine."

"And the animals? I think I let the horse loose when—"

"Horse and mule are in my paddock. I'll have someone take them back to Honor's first thing in the morning. She came in the ambulance with you and Tanner. I called a driver. Plenty of room for you to go home with us." He held out his hand and Luke gripped it hard. "You did good," Freeman said. "If she'd lost one or both of those boys…"

"God preserved them," Luke said sincerely. "And you did the most by having that life ring and rope handy. Without it, I don't know what I would have done."

"Still, I'm pleased to call you my friend." Freeman settled his hat further down on his head. "My mother was the one who came up with the idea for that ring. Insisted I buy it. It's been hanging there for three or four years and we never needed it."

"Not until today," Luke said. "I'd like to put these clothes on, and then we go."

"You go ahead. I'll go tell Honor you're going home with us. She wants to see you. She was just waiting until… She wanted to make certain that you were decent. No sense causing more trouble with the elders than we need to. They're already a little nervous over the Mystery Cowboy stuff from that newspaper in Pennsylvania. The bus accident. Not many of our people getting their pictures on the English television."

"Right. It wasn't by choice, I can tell you that." Luke glanced up at the clock on the wall. "Give me five minutes to get dressed, and then she can come in. I told the nurse that I wanted to leave. If they don't get back soon with my release papers, I'm going, anyway."

He had his garments on in two minutes. His chest burned, and his throat was sore. He had a little headache and water in one ear, but other than that, he didn't feel terrible, certainly not like a man who'd gone swimming in February. The pants and shirt had to be Freeman's, he judged. The shirt was a good fit, but the pants were long. Quickly, he adjusted the suspenders and slipped into the socks and shoes. He was just tying the last one when someone cleared her throat in the hall outside the curtain.

"Luke? Can I come in?"

It was Honor, and honestly, at that moment, he wasn't certain if he wanted to see her yet. Now that he was on his feet, he felt a little disoriented. And tired. So tired he could have lain down on the hospital bed and taken a nap. He took a deep breath, coughed and called, "*Ya*. Come in."

She stepped through the curtain and threw her arms around him, nearly knocking him back onto the bed. "Luke!" Her face was pale, her eyes red and swollen as if she'd been weeping, worry lines crinkling her flawless complexion. "I was so frightened," she said, switching from English to *Deitsch*.

Awkwardly, he hugged her back. He knew that this wasn't the time or place, but he was angry, and he couldn't hide it. Gently, he pushed her away. "Not here," he said. "We don't want the *Englishers* talking about our behavior."

"I don't care what they think. I love you. I have every right to hug you. Especially after what you did. You saved my babies. You—"

"They shouldn't have been there," he said. His voice came out gruff and rasping. "They had no business at the pond alone. Or on the ice at all."

"*Ne*, I know that." She swallowed, looking small and vulnerable beneath her bonnet, tugging at his heart.

But he would have his say. He couldn't let this be, couldn't hide his feelings. He'd done it long enough. He loved her and loving someone meant being honest with her. He truly believed that. "They could have died, Honor," he said. "Both of them. We could have lost them today."

Swirls of hurt glistened in her big brown eyes. Tears gathered and threatened to fall. "You think I don't know that? It was a terrible accident—could have been a terrible accident. But, by the grace of God and your courage and quick thinking, you saved them. You rescued my babies."

"*Ne*, Honor. It wasn't an accident."

"What do you mean?" She blinked, and the tears fell.

He felt as if a fist had stuck him full in the stomach, but he would do her no favors by holding back. "It wasn't an accident," he repeated. "It was carelessness."

"You're saying it's my fault? That I was careless with my sons?"

"You've let them run wild, Honor. You have allowed them to think they could do as they pleased, without consequences for disobedience. And your soft heart has nearly brought them and your family to ruin."

Her lower lip quivered, but she stiffened. "I thought it was *our* family. How can you say such a thing? I told them that they were never to go near a pond without an adult. They're children. They disobey sometimes. It's what children do." She wiped at her eyes with the back of her hands, trying to stop the tears. "That's a cruel thing to say, Luke. To blame me."

She began to sob, and his resolve crumbled.

He took her in his arms. "I'm sorry. I shouldn't have said that, at least not here. Not today. I know how you love them." She was weeping against his chest. "Shh, shh," he soothed. "I'm an idiot. I was so scared. I didn't think I could get to them in time. I'm sorry. But I've remained silent too often these last months, when I should have spoken. This is a serious matter, Honor, one we must settle before we marry."

She sniffed and looked up at him. "What do you mean?"

"You've made it clear that you don't want me to

discipline the children. How do you expect me to be a father to them if I have no authority?"

"They are my children. It is my place to make them mind me."

"*Ne*, Honor, it can't be that way. When we marry, they'll be my children, as if born of my flesh. Either I'll be a father and a husband to you and your family, or this will never work between us."

"So, are you telling me that you've having second thoughts? You're talking about backing out of our wedding again?"

"Where would you get that idea?" He crushed her against him. "I'm never letting you go. You and the children are a package. I want to be your husband and their father, but this is something we have to face. Something must be done about their willfulness. We've got to set rules and there must be consequences for disobedience, even for the small ones. That's how you keep children from breaking the more serious rules."

"You're right." She glanced up at him. "They do get into trouble. And I am too softhearted to punish them as I should. But…if you'd… If you'll help me…" She started to cry again.

He looked around the small enclosure, saw a tiny box of tissues and retrieved them. He gave a handful to Honor and she blew her nose. "I'm sorry. I didn't mean to make you cry," he said.

"I know that you're right. I've worried about the same thing. It's just that Silas was so… He could be so stern with them. Once, he threatened Tanner with a belt."

"Did he beat him?"

She shook her head. "He tried to. I wouldn't let him.

I told him that if he laid a hand on Tanner in anger, I would take the children and leave him. He was so angry with me. He didn't speak to me for two days. He never did strike them, but he sent them to bed without supper and spoke to them so harshly when they misbehaved. I suppose, I think, I just tried to make up for his behavior by being too easy with them."

Luke hugged her again, just for a brief second. "We have to sit down and decide how we will handle misbehavior," he said quietly. "There should be small punishments for the small disobediences and larger ones for the more serious. What's important, I think, is that we both always react the same way. We act as a team, and then the children will know where we stand. And that they can't run from one to the other and expect to get away with mischief." He kissed the top of her forehead. "One thing I can promise you is that I will never raise a hand to our children. My father never did, either. He would talk to me quietly and make me understand what I had done wrong and why. His words pushed me to never make the same mistake again."

"I think that's a good plan," she said and reached for some more tissues. "I've let them get away with bad behavior, and I promise to try to do better." She took a step back. "I'd best get back to Tanner. Freeman is with him, but—"

Abruptly, the curtain pulled back and Luke heard the whirl of a digital camera. "There he is!" a young blonde woman in high heels and a tweed jacket exclaimed. "It's him! The cowboy hero. What do you do? Just ride around the country, looking for drowning people to rescue?" She stepped aside and a red-haired man with a camera on his shoulder moved forward to begin filming.

"No pictures," Luke said. He snatched off the hat Freeman had brought him and used it to cover his and Honor's faces. "We don't believe in having our image captured. Go away, please."

"Who is this woman?" the blonde demanded. "Is she the mother of the children? Can you tell us their names and ages?"

"We're saying nothing." Luke stepped in front of Honor, turning his back to the camera, still shielding their faces with the hat. "We are private people."

"Just a few questions," the persistent woman reporter insisted. "How does it feel to be a hero?"

The nurse with the silly cartoon scrubs swept in. "How did you get in here?" she said to the reporter and her companion. "Leave. Now, or I'll call security and..."

But Luke didn't hear the rest of her comment. He'd taken Honor by the arm and used the distraction to make his escape. The two of them slipped past the nurse and the newspaper people, and hurried down the hallway. He heard the sound of Tanner's voice and quickly located the curtain cubicle it was coming from. They stepped inside and he pulled the curtain shut behind them. Freeman sat on the side of the bed, showing Tanner a small, wooden marble game. If you placed a marble at the top of the tower, it would roll down, flipping switches. Tanner, red cheeked and hale, was laughing so hard that tears were running down his cheeks.

Tanner looked up when the two of them entered the room. Luke put his finger to his lips, and they all waited in silence while the nurse escorted the newspeople out of the emergency room, still fussing with them.

"Ready to go home?" Luke asked Tanner.

The boy nodded.

"Me, too," Luke said.

"And me." Honor reached over and squeezed Luke's hand. "Together."

He nodded. "Together."

Chapter Fourteen

"Take your time. Look around, and if you have any questions, I'll find the answers. My husband and his uncle aren't here today." Ruth Lapp waved toward the display area. "I don't usually help out at the chair shop because the children keep me busy at home, but our office girl had a dental appointment this afternoon. Fortunately, my sister Miriam offered to take my older children, so we didn't have to close."

She smiled down at the sleeping infant she wore in a baby sling made from dark green denim fabric. "This one seems to like being at the shop. He's been sleeping like a lamb most of the afternoon. Maybe he'll choose to be a woodworker like his father."

"Danke," Honor said.

Ruth was Hannah's oldest daughter. Her husband, Eli, and his uncle Roman, along with several other Amish craftsmen, designed and built most of the furniture for sale here. Honor didn't know Ruth as well as she did Rebecca or Leah, because Ruth was a little older, but she possessed the same vivid blue eyes and seemed as pleasant and helpful as her sisters.

Luke smiled. “A good choice for a man, if he does. Our Lord was a carpenter.”

The phone rang in the small office, and Ruth excused herself. “Just come and find me if you see something you like.”

Honor glanced at the clock on the wall behind the counter. “I hope the boys are behaving themselves.” They’d been good since they’d gotten in so much trouble over going out on the ice, but she wasn’t confident that they’d really reformed. “I’d hate to think that they were unruly for Katie. Maybe I should have brought one or two of them with us.”

“Nope. Today is just for us,” Luke said. “We need to pick out new bedroom furniture, and I promised you supper that you didn’t have to cook.”

“But the children… They can be a handful.”

He smiled and shook his head. “You worry too much. Ivy and Katie are there to help Greta. I doubt much gets past Ivy. She’s had experience with children for a lot of years. And Katie promised to bake gingerboy cookies with them. They’ll love that.”

Honor grimaced, imagining her kitchen strewed with flour and dripping with molasses. “That’s what I’m afraid of.” But she smiled with him. Maybe she *was* being a worrywart. “It’s sweet of you to want to take me to supper,” she said. “But we don’t have to go out to eat. You’re going to enough expense, buying new furniture.” She hesitated and then said what she was thinking. “You know, I’m not even sure we need to be here. There’s nothing wrong with the bed and dressers I have now.”

“Nothing wrong other than that Silas bought them for you.” Luke glanced around to make certain that they were alone and then took her hand in his. "When we marry, I'll be moving into Silas's house, eating off his table—"

"*Ne*, that's my grandmother's table. She left it to me. The tall maple dresser in my bedroom was hers, too. You haven't seen that, but it's lovely. I'd hate to part with it."

"Let me finish," he said gently. "I don't really care where the table came from. It's a nice table. But, Honor..." He hesitated a moment and then went on. "The truth is that a man doesn't like the idea of another man's bed. I'm buying us a new one. After we're married, you can move the old one into one of the children's rooms, sell it or give it away. And you can certainly keep your grandmother's maple dresser for your clothes, but we need our own bed. Can you understand that?"

"Ya." She nodded, liking the feel of his hand holding hers. But they weren't *Englishers*. Hand-holding in public wasn't something they did. She slipped her fingers out of his. "It's just the cost I was thinking of."

"Don't worry about the cost. I told you, I have substantial savings, and I also have the inheritance my uncle left me. This is what I've been saving my money for all these years. For you, Honor. For us."

She met his gaze and was so touched that she feared she might tear up. She loved that Luke felt so strongly that they belonged together. That he was so sure about this marriage. It helped her work through her own doubts.

Luke walked over to examine a queen-size oak bedstead. "What do you think of this style?"

"Umm, nice," she said noncommittally. She had to

admit that the thought of new furniture was a little bit exciting, but it was troublesome, as well.

Silas had always taken care that she knew how carefully he watched his money. He'd said she was too young to realize the value of it, especially since he was the one earning the income.

Only once could she remember arguing with him over money. She'd bought a cookie jar at Byler's, a silly thing shaped like a fat hen. The children had seen it and loved it, and since the holidays were approaching, she'd used part of her grocery allowance to buy it. Silas had made her return it, saying that it was an irresponsible purchase. But had it been an irresponsible purchase? She didn't think so. The cookie jar had made her laugh. And it had made her children happy. Couldn't money be used sometimes to bring happiness to the ones you loved?

Once she married, she would spend the rest of her married life obeying another man's wishes. At least now, if she wanted to make a foolish purchase with her own money, she could. Luke didn't seem to be miserly with his money, but what if she was misreading him?

Suddenly, marriage to Luke was a reality. It had all happened so fast. She loved him, certainly, but…she hoped she wouldn't live to regret her decision.

A woman should be married. Everyone said so; the church said so. It was the natural order of things. And doubly so for a woman with children. The incident on the ice had proved that, hadn't it? She couldn't care for her children properly alone. Her judgment wasn't always the best.

"Honor?"

"Ya?" She glanced up at him and realized that he'd

walked a few yards away to inspect a heavier bed with pineapples carved on the top of the posts. It was pretty, but probably more expensive than the first, plainer one. "Sorry, I was thinking about something."

"I can see that." He smiled at her. "Have you thought about what I asked you earlier? About going away for a honeymoon?"

"I don't know, Luke."

"We could go wherever you like," he said. "Maybe out West or to Florida. I've never seen palm trees, and it's a lot warmer there. We could go in the ocean."

It all sounded like a wonderful idea, but she knew he wouldn't want to take four children on his honeymoon, and she certainly couldn't leave them. She'd worry herself sick about them. And what would they think? That she'd abandoned them? It would be difficult enough for them to get used to having a new father, someone they would have to obey, without upsetting their daily routine by her taking a trip. "I don't think that would be a good idea. Not right away." She hedged. "I think it's best if we all stay at home and get settled in."

Luke ran his hand over the carving on the bedpost. "Most couples do go away for a few days after their marriage."

She pretended to look at the matching dresser. "Most couples don't already have four children. You didn't expect to take them with us, did you?"

"On our honeymoon?" He chuckled. "Definitely not. What I was hoping for was time alone with you."

"If you take me, you have to accept them, as well."

"Isn't that what I've been saying all along?" He moved closer and took her hand again. "Honor, it doesn't make me a bad father because I want to be alone for a few days with my bride. But if you think it isn't a good idea, I'll accept that. For now. But later, maybe in the summer, once I have the crops in the ground, we'll go somewhere, just the two of us. I'll hire a driver. We could go to Niagara Falls or even out to Kansas. Lots of people have been volunteering to watch our kids, and you know Katie and Freeman would take good care of them."

"I know they would, but..." She sighed. She didn't know what was wrong with her. The last three months with Luke had been the happiest, best weeks of her life. Why couldn't she just accept God's gift of Luke, and the happiness he brought her and her children, and enjoy it? Why was she second-guessing herself? "It's not something we have to decide today, is it?"

She was feeling a little overwhelmed. It seemed there were so many decisions to make all at once. Luke had insisted on taking her out today and choosing furniture when she had so much to do at home. Her wedding clothes were cut out and waiting to be stitched up. And Sara wanted her to come by and help her decide what they would serve for the wedding supper.

Aunt Martha had wanted to visit this afternoon, and Honor had had to tell her that she wouldn't be home because she and Luke were going to town. In a way, Honor was glad to have an excuse. Aunt Martha had let everyone in the county know that she thought Honor was rushing into a marriage with a less-than-suitable man, and Honor was sure that she was only coming to try to get her to change her mind. Martha had been one of her mother's best friends, and Honor respected her for that. She didn't want to be rude, but the older woman was wrong about Luke. He was a good man, and Honor loved him. She was going to marry him, and that was that. But having Aunt Martha to deal with when she was already at her wit's end only added icing to the cake.

"So, which set do you like best?" Luke asked, walking away to stand back and have another look at the furniture. "There's the oak one over there, but I'm not crazy about the low dresser with the mirror."

She sighed. "I don't know. Whichever one you want," Honor said.

He shook his head. "*Ne*, love. It's for you to choose. I want to make you happy."

That made her smile. "I know that, I just..." She didn't finish her sentence because she didn't know how to articulate what she was feeling. It was almost as if she was afraid this was all too good to be true.

He stood there, looking at her for a moment. "It is a little scary, isn't it? The wedding?" he said, almost seeming to know what she was thinking. "Making such big changes in our lives. But Freeman says everybody feels the same way." He folded his arms across his chest. "Now, please pick out a bedroom set for us, unless you don't like any of them." He shrugged. "And then we can go somewhere else. I just thought we'd get the best quality coming here."

"No, no, these pieces are beautiful and sturdy and... I like the one with the pineapples," she admitted.

"Me, too. That's my favorite. Will there be room for the tall dresser if we keep the one you already have?"

"Ya." She nodded. "It's a big room."

"*Goot.* So, we'll take the bed, the side tables and the dresser, and I'll make arrangements to have them delivered out to the farm." He pointed in the direction of the office where Ruth had gone. "Let me pay for them, and then we'll have our driver take us to the mall."

"I thought we were going to supper."

"We are, but first, we need to go somewhere to buy sheets, blankets, towels, that kind of stuff."

She smiled at him as she traced the lines of the pineapple on a foot post with her index finger. "Are you sure? This is going to be a very expensive day."

"You're worth it," he assured her.

"I hope so," she replied, looking up at him. "Because once we're married, it will be for keeps."

The waitress, a teenager with a brown ponytail, brought their orders and put them on the table. "Be careful," she warned cheerfully. "Everything's hot." She balanced her tray expertly on one hip and removed two glasses of iced tea. "Anything else I can get you?"

"No, thank you," Luke said.

Honor looked down at her supper. It smelled delicious. The special tonight at Hall's restaurant was meat loaf and boiled potatoes. She'd chosen collards and green beans to go with it. This had turned out to be a wonderful afternoon. After she'd gotten over her nervousness at picking out the furniture, she and Luke had walked around the mall and bought crisp white sheets and a beautiful blue comforter for their bed, as well as some new towels.

This was really happening.

She was marrying Luke, and nothing would be like it had been in her first marriage. The shopping trip was proof of that. The first time that she was married, the only new things they got for their house were gifts given to her. Everything else was a hand-me-down.

Not that there was anything wrong with perfectly good used household items, but a young girl just settling into her first house with her new husband takes great pride in her housewifery skills, and a set of new dish towels or a fresh broom can go a long way to making a house a home.

"Grace?" Luke said quietly and surprised her by reaching across the small table and taking her hands in his.

She inhaled sharply and glanced around to see if people were looking at them. But the other diners were all busy with their own conversations. No one was staring at them. Their driver, Jerry, was seated at a booth near the side door with his wife, Jan, and there was even another Amish couple at another table. Hall's was a neighborhood restaurant in a small town where locals came for traditional food and friendly service. She could feel at ease here, even if most of the people were *Englishers*.

Honor bowed her head for silent prayer. She knew that her thoughts should be on giving thanks to God for all His blessings, and especially for this meal, but it was difficult to focus when she was so conscious of Luke's touch and the tingling that ran up her arms.

When he opened his eyes, he looked directly into hers and smiled. "It's been a good day, hasn't it?"

"It has," she answered truthfully. Excitement bubbled through her and she found that she was starving. She brought a forkful of the meat loaf to her lips and tasted it. "Mmm. Just as good as I remembered. I'd like to have the recipe, but the cook won't give it out."

"Maybe I should bring you here every week," Luke teased.

She chuckled. "Not every week, but now and then. They don't have meat loaf all the time, but they do make a good liver and onions."

He made a face. "Not on my list of favorites."

"*Ne?* And I was planning on cooking it every Monday evening." She chuckled at his expression. "Just teasing. The children don't like it, either."

"Then I'm saved." He smiled at her as he buttered his roll. "Are you happy with the furniture we picked out?"

"I am. I'm glad we liked the same set." She couldn't stop looking at him. He was so solid, so handsome, so full of life that it was almost too good to be true that he wanted to be her husband and the father of her children.

In many ways, this was the Luke she'd loved as a girl, but there was something more about him. He was stronger, steadier, and seemed to glow with an inner enthusiasm whether he was opening a hymnal or tackling a tough task in the field. How foolish she'd been to resist his courting. This was truly the man God had planned for her.

"At least we agree on something," Luke said. She must have looked confused, because he quickly added, "The bedroom suite. We both like pineapples." He chuckled, and they laughed together.

She tasted the collards. They were tender and seasoned perfectly. "It was nice of you to buy the new things at the mall," she told him. "My sheets were getting shabby."

"After we're married, we'll open a joint bank account with my savings," Luke said. "You can write a check for anything you need for yourself or for our household. And whatever Silas left you is yours, for your children or for your security. I don't want any of it."

"That's kind of you," she replied.

"Not kind," he said. "Fair. You should have security, in case I should die or become..."

She put down her fork. "Don't say such a thing."

"It's possible. Farming accidents happen. Illnesses happen, Honor. I want to be certain that you will be cared for, no matter what comes."

She shook her head. "For that, we must trust in God." She smiled at him. "But this was supposed to be our night out. Can't you think of anything more pleasant to talk about than you dying?"

He reached out and patted her hand. "We can talk about anything you'd like, or we can just sit here and eat and I can look at you."

"Don't say such things," she whispered, feeling her cheeks grow warm. But secretly it pleased her. It had been a long time since she'd felt pretty or that a man cared about what she wanted or what she thought. How easy it was to forget the years that she'd resented him and remember the good times they'd had together, the laughter and the fun.

Luke began to talk about the wedding, and she found that, despite her nervousness, she was looking forward to the day. She wished that her children could be part of the celebration, but by custom, the wedding would be just for adults. Friends would care for them until the following day. She hoped the kids would understand. The marriage ceremony was a serious ritual, and she needed to give all her attention to the words of the bishop and the preachers, and, of course, to Luke.

"You haven't met my cousin Raymond, but you'll

like him and his wife. They're coming to the wedding because I want you to meet them. They have two children. The oldest is six, I believe. Anyway, work has been slow for Raymond in Kansas. He's thinking of moving his family here. He'd like to raise goats for meat and for milk. His wife makes the best cheese." Luke took a mouthful of potatoes and chewed slowly. "I was wondering if you might be interested in selling them that acreage on the far side of the road. I can't think that we'll ever need it, and you said you'd wondered if you should sell it. The fields are in good pasture, perfect for a dairy operation. What do you think?"

She looked up in surprise. "I don't know. Do you think they'd want to be so far from Dover and the other Amish communities?"

Luke leaned forward, his expression enthusiastic. "I don't because here's why. I was thinking that one way to fix the problem of being so far from your Amish community is to attract more young Amish families out to where we are. Raymond has an unmarried sister who's been teaching school for three years. If he moves, she'll come with him. Our children need a school nearby. Tanner really should have started first grade last fall."

The implied criticism stung a little. But she knew he was right. "Yes, Tanner should have gone," she said. "But the nearest Amish school is farther than he could walk alone, and getting all the children organized to drive him back and forth would have taken a lot of effort, especially in bad weather." She felt her cheeks and throat flush. "Besides, he'd just lost his father, and—"

"Not just, Honor," Luke corrected. "It's been more than a year since Silas died. It's time Tanner was in school like every other boy his age. It is the state law. You can't continue to coddle him."

"I'm not coddling him," she defended herself. "I intended to send him this coming September."

"Good. We agree on that, too. And that's why having Raymond's boy in the neighborhood would be an asset. We can start a school with two children. We just have to figure out where we want to build it. And when Tanner's a little older, he could walk, or we could buy him a pony to ride to school."

"I'm not letting a young child ride a horse on the road. The traffic..."

Luke chuckled. "He won't be seven for long. He'll be eight and then nine. He'll be responsible enough to be trusted with a horse. And you have to consider that the other boys will need schooling. Not to mention Anke."

"Anke's just a baby."

Luke shook his head. "Freeman and I have talked about this. He and Katie are planning to sell off several plots, to encourage Amish families to settle near the mill. I think they're even considering donating a little land to build a school. With them expecting."

Honor looked down at her plate. It was unusual of an Amish man to comment on a woman being in the family way, but she thought she liked it. Too many men pretended babies just fell from God's arms out of the sky.

"Your relatives have moved, either west or to Virginia, because land is so expensive here," Luke went on. "But your soil is rich. For a small specialty farm or for those who are craftsmen, they don't need a lot of acreage. And you don't have the bitter winters we had in Kansas."

Suddenly Honor was feeling a little overwhelmed.

More decisions. She looked down at the napkin on her lap. "I'm still not sure that I should sell land. I have four children. Maybe I should save all of the farm for them."

"I don't want to put any pressure on you, Honor. But think of it. We could build a community like Seven Poplars. We're only two families now, but in five years..."

"I *will* think about it," she promised. "And I did know that Tanner had to go to school. I just didn't think that it would hurt him to start a little later. I needed his help with the younger boys."

But, as she said it, she realized how lame it sounded. Tanner really wasn't that much help around the farm. At least, he hadn't been until she and Luke had decided together that she needed to ask more of the children. It wasn't easy to suddenly let someone else advise her on what to do with her sons, but there was a relief in not having to do it all alone.

She gave Luke a small smile. "I've been doing things on my own since Silas died," she said. "I know everything will be different after we're married, and I also know that will be a good thing. But..." Her smile deepened. "You'll have to be patient with me, because this is all happening pretty fast."

"Not fast enough for me." He broke into a grin. "But then, I've been waiting for this wedding for a long time."

Chapter Fifteen

The day of their wedding dawned bright and sunny, with only the slightest breeze and more blooming daffodils and early tulips than Luke had ever seen surrounding one house. He'd arrived at Sara's at five thirty in the morning to find her already up and buzzing around the kitchen.

Two cups of her strong coffee later, he'd joined six couples in Sara's hospitality barn where chickens were being prepared for roasting and trays of creamed celery, stuffing, apple crisp and pies were being assembled, ready for the commercial ovens. And more helpers would be arriving for a wedding where they were expecting nearly a hundred guests.

Luke had wanted a simple wedding, but there was no arguing with Sara once she set her mind on something. Several of his cousins and his brother and family had come from the Midwest to share in the happiness of the day, but Honor had few relatives. Most of the guests would be friends and neighbors and the extended Yoder family, as well as several of Sara's clients. The awaited assurance of his baptism and standing in his home church had finally come through, and Honor's bishop had agreed to perform the ceremony. Three couples would be sharing the *Eck*, or wedding table, with them: Freeman and Katie; Rebecca and her husband, Caleb; and a longtime friend of Honor's, Mary Beth, and her husband, Moses, who had come from Kentucky.

Freeman helped Luke to set up chairs in the main room of the barn. The preaching service and the actual wedding ceremony would take place in the house, but the dinner and, later, the evening supper would be held here in the barn. This was a building that Sara had rescued and had remodeled for entertaining. As a professional matchmaker, Sara needed a place to bring couples together. The outside might look like a red barn, but inside the only similarity was the loft area. The downstairs space was spacious and as tidy as Sara's living room, and the commercial kitchen was more than adequate for serving large groups of guests.

At eight o'clock, Sara bustled into the barn and inspected the preparations. The *Eck* had been set up in one prominent corner. Other long tables filled much of the remaining space. By custom, and for practicality, the *Eck* hadn't been decorated with wedding flowers. Instead, there was a snowy white table covering, beautiful antique dishes and blue and white pottery pitchers, which would later be filled with cold water, lemonade and apple cider. There would be cakes, pies and candies, as well as bowls of apples and oranges. Sara made a few adjustments to napkins and place settings and pronounced the *Eck* perfect for the bride and groom.

"You'd better change into your good clothing," she said to Luke. "It's laid out for you in the men's bunkhouse." Sara chuckled. "Hannah sent over two new wool hats for you, since you seem to have such trouble holding on to yours."

Luke grimaced, but took the teasing with good humor. Though he and Honor had chosen to have the wedding here instead of at Hannah and Albert's home, Hannah had appointed herself his honorary mother. As part of their wedding gift, she'd sewn a complete set of clothing for him, including a black wool *mutze*, the formal coat wore by Amish men for church services and important events, matching trousers and a vest. The garments had taken hours and hours to complete, and Luke knew that, with care, they would last him for years.

As he walked to the small building where the matchmaker housed her visiting male clients, Luke could hardly contain his excitement. In just a short while, Honor would join him in an upstairs room of Sara's house, where they would meet with the elders of the church. There, one of the preachers would speak to them about the duties and responsibilities of marriage and be certain that each entered this union of their own free will. Below, the guests would begin the first hymn of the service. He and Honor would follow the elders and the bishop downstairs and would take their seats near the front of the room.

The sermon would be two to three hours in length, after which the bishop would invite him and Honor to come up and exchange their vows. Luke's heart beat faster and he thought of his promise to cherish and care for Honor, to respect her and remain with her for the rest of their lives. He would utter these words in front of God and all the witnesses, and she would repeat the same. A few more words from the bishop, and they would be married.

His chest felt tight; his throat clenched. So long he'd waited and prayed for this day. He was so happy that he might have been made of mist instead of flesh and blood, so light that he could have vaulted over the house in one leap.

Honor… His Honor. His family.

Almost feeling as if he was in a dream, he dressed, his fingers wooden as he fumbled to pull up his stockings and adjust his suspenders. The trousers, coat and vest fitted him perfectly. How Hannah had managed it, he couldn't guess. He'd never stood for a measuring. Honor had told him that she would be wearing blue. He loved her in blue. There would be no veil, no flowing train as the English women wore. Her new dress and apron, cape and *kapp* were exactly like those she wore to worship services, but after tonight, she would fold the garments carefully away to only be worn again on the day of her funeral.

He blinked, nudged out of his dreamy and pleasant thoughts by the prospect of Honor's death. God willing, that would be far-off, in His time, when they had grown old together. Hopefully, there would be more children, grandchildren and even great-grandchildren before their time on Earth was ended.

Today was no time to think of partings or of the eternal life in Heaven that awaited those who lived according to God's teachings. Today was about new beginnings, about taking up a life of promise and love, about being with Honor every day and every night. Together, they had promised each other. It was all he wanted. Together, they would make a home for their children and teach them the values that had been handed down through the generations by their faith.

"Luke!" After a quick knock on the door, Freeman opened it a crack. "Are you dressed? The preachers have arrived. You'd better move along. You don't want to keep the bishop waiting."

"Coming," Luke said, putting on the first hat he could lay hands on. That, too, fitted him as well as… He chuckled. As well as if it had been made for him. How had Hannah guessed the exact size of his head? "I guess mothers know these things," he murmured under his breath.

Luke joined Freeman outside on the sidewalk. "Is Honor here? Have you seen her?" He glanced around. Dozens of buggies were arriving. Teenage boys were taking charge of the horses. Clusters of guests were making their way into the house. Luke chuckled again. He'd thought he'd only been a few minutes in getting dressed. But he had been woolgathering. The time had flown. Excitement surged through him.

"Getting nervous?" Freeman asked. He strode shoulder to shoulder with him, a steady friend.

"Ne," Luke answered. "*Ya.* I suppose I am." He couldn't help thinking back to the last time they'd intended to marry. Had he felt this excited? He didn't think so. That seemed a lifetime ago, as though it had happened to another person. He'd been a boy then, too young and foolish to know what he wanted in life… too immature to realize what he was throwing away by walking out on her.

"There's the bishop." Freeman indicated the approaching buggy drawn by a gray mare. "You'd best get upstairs. Honor's probably up there waiting for you."

And scared out of her mind that I won't show, Luke thought.

He went in through the back door, crossed the kitchen full of women and walked up the stairs. He couldn't wait to see her...couldn't wait to see her face. To marry her as he hadn't been able to do that day years ago.

I'll make it up to her, he promised silently. *I'll never let her down again.*

The door to the designated chamber stood open. Rebecca waited just inside. But he didn't see Honor anywhere. There were the two preachers and the deacon. There was Freeman's uncle, a respected elder of the church. But there were no other women. He scanned the room twice before turning to Rebecca. "She's not here yet?" he asked her quietly.

Rebecca's concern showed on her lovely face. "Not yet," she confirmed. "But she'll be here any moment. Don't worry. Katie and Ivy are bringing her. It's quarter to nine. The service doesn't start for another fifteen minutes."

"It's just...it's not like Honor to be late," he said. Honor always wanted to be at church a half hour before the first hymn. She thought it disrespectful to come in last. He exhaled softly and edged to the window to look out. Was it possible something had happened to delay them? An accident or mishap with the buggy? The horse throwing a shoe?

The bishop entered the room and shook hands all around. "Bride not here yet?" he asked. Someone made a joke about women primping on their special day, and everyone laughed but Luke.

Luke removed his hat and placed it on a dresser

beside other hats. Warm dampness rose at the back of his shirt collar and he rubbed absently at his neck. The minutes ticked away. He went to the window again and then looked at Freeman.

"I'll go down and check to see if she's arrived," his friend said. "I wouldn't think Katie would let the time get away from her. Not today."

One of the preachers began to tell about a longer-than-usual sermon he'd heard on a visit to an Amish community in western Virginia. It was an amusing tale, but the bishop laughed a little too loudly. Somewhere downstairs, a clock chimed.

"Nine o'clock," the deacon remarked. He said something quietly to the bishop and then nodded at Luke as he exited the room.

"My apologies," Luke said to the bishop. "I'm sure she'll be here any minute." He followed the deacon down the steps. As he left the house by the back way, the guests were rising for the first hymn. Luke walked into the yard, empty now of boys and horses. He glanced down the driveway. He could see the road. There were no buggies in sight.

Freeman came up beside him. "Don't get yourself into a fever," he said. "She'll be here. She's just late."

Luke turned to him, shoulders stiff and hands tingling. "Honor's not late," he said, voicing the unthinkable. "She's not coming."

One hour earlier...

"What do you mean you aren't going?" Katie called through Honor's closed bedroom door. "I know you're nervous, but there's no time to waste. We have to hurry, or we'll be late for service."

"Is she ready?" Ivy's voice came from down the hallway. "Do you know what time it is?" Honor heard her ask Katie. "The bishop and the elders will be waiting. Not to mention the wedding guests. And Luke, poor Luke will be pacing the floor."

"She says she's changed her mind," Katie answered. "She said she's not marrying Luke Weaver today or any day."

Honor blew her nose.

"Atch," Ivy remarked, outside the door now. "Wedding jitters."

Honor wiped her eyes. "Common sense," she whispered, too softly for either Ivy or Katie to hear.

There was a rapping on the door. "Honor. Will you let me come in and talk to you?" Ivy called.

"*Ne!* There's no need. I made a mistake and I have to right it now, while I still can. I thought I wanted to marry Luke, but I don't," Honor said. "Please go and tell the bishop that I've reconsidered my decision."

"Luke will be devastated," Katie said, sounding close to tears. "Please, won't you let us in so we can talk about it?"

"I'm sorry. I just can't do it," Honor replied.

She heard the two whispering, and then Katie called out, "You're sure you want us to go without you? You're certain about this? You don't just want to take a minute to catch your breath? Maybe spend a few minutes in prayer?"

"I'm certain I want you to go," Honor answered, fighting tears. "Tell everyone I'm sorry."

There was more whispering, and then Ivy said, "If you're sure that's what you want."

What she wanted? Honor didn't know what she wanted, but she replied, "*Ya*, go, please." She heard Katie say something that she couldn't make out and then footsteps echoing down the steps. Minutes later she heard the rattle of buggy wheels. She went to the window to watch Katie and Ivy roll out of the yard.

Then Honor sank down on the bed and buried her face in her hands. What would she say to the children? How could she explain to Sara, who'd been so good to her? And how could she face Luke ever again?

But, for better or worse, her decision was made and she'd have to live with it. She should have felt relief, but instead, all she felt was sadness.

Luke tugged on the brim of his new hat. "Honor did this on purpose. She did it to get even for what I did to her," he said stoically. "She planned this all along."

"Ne." Sara shook her head. "I don't believe that, and neither do you. Not really. You're just smarting right now. Honor doesn't have a spiteful bone in her body."

Sara, Albert and Freeman had followed Luke out of the house and into the yard. They stood in the grass near the back porch. None of the wedding guests, except for Ivy and Katie, who had brought word, knew there was no bride.

"Here's my question to you. Do you love her?" Sara asked, looking Luke in the eyes. "If you could fix this, would you?"

He glanced away. Emotion brought moisture that clouded his eyes, and he was afraid that he'd make himself appear even more of a fool than he was. "It's too late," he answered gruffly.

"It may not be," Albert put in. "They're only on the second hymn. It will be a long sermon."

"I agree," Freeman said. "If you want to try to change her mind, there's time." He glanced at Katie, who'd come to stand beside him. "Did you know that we almost broke up right before we married? I was to blame."

"*Ne*, Freeman," Katie said, taking his hand. "We were *both* to blame."

Freeman smiled down at her. "My Katie left me and I had to chase her down." He chuckled. "It was a lot farther than you'd have to go."

Luke scuffed the ground with one foot, sending up a small cloud of dust. He rubbed his hands together as he fought to compose himself. He'd been so happy, and now everything was lost. "It's because of the children," he admitted gruffly. "I thought she let them get away with too much, and I said so. I told her it wouldn't be that way after we were married."

"I don't think it's about that," Sara insisted. "I really think it's cold feet. Her last marriage was difficult. I expect she's afraid that she's climbing out of the frying pan and into the fire."

"You think she's afraid of me?" he asked, looking up at the matchmaker. "I'd never harm her. I'd never make decisions that weren't the best for her and for our children. I'll always put them first."

"So, convince her of that," Sara said.

"Go talk to her, Luke." Freeman laid a hand on his shoulder. "If Honor's worth having, she's worth trying to hold on to. Don't let pride stand in the way of fixing this."

Luke stood there in indecision. He wanted to go, but—

"Do you have a driver's license?" Albert asked.

"What?" Luke turned to him.

"Are you allowed to drive, legally?" Albert asked. "I thought you mentioned to me you knew how to drive."

"*Ya*, I have a driver's license. I needed one in Kansas to deliver my uncle's grain to the buyer." Luke frowned. "Why do you ask?"

The older man pointed to a small black SUV parked next to the barn. "Take Hannah's daughter Grace's car. The keys are in it."

"Take her car?" Luke asked, unsure of what he'd just heard.

"She's my daughter, too," Albert said. "And Grace would be the first to agree that this is an emergency. Go get your bride, Luke. Or you'll have to explain to Hannah why she made you that fine suit and baked all those pies for nothing."

Luke banged on the back door of the house. "Unlock the door, Honor!"

She stared at the door, glad the window was still covered with a board. Rather than fix the window, she and Luke had decided to replace the whole door and they were waiting for it to come in at the lumberyard.

"Honor!"

She took a shuddering breath. She hadn't believed that he would come for her. And when she'd heard the motor vehicle come up the driveway, she wondered who he'd gotten to drive him over from Sara's.

Honor's heart was pounding so hard that she thought it might fly out of her chest. How had she allowed this to go so far? What had made her agree to marry Luke in the first place? What had ever made her think it was a good idea?

"Be reasonable! We need to talk!"

"*Ne!* I don't want to talk to you!" Honor slid the bolt. "Go away!"

"No one is going to force you to marry me," Luke said. "I wouldn't do that. I just want to talk to you. I need to know why."

"It's for the best!"

He knocked louder. "You're angry about the children, about my trying to interfere with your parenting. I understand. I'm just trying to help. Because I love them, too. But we can talk about this, Honor. We can figure it out."

"I'm not talking to you. Go away!"

"I will not go away until we've talked face-to-face," he hollered. "I'm coming in!"

Then she heard nothing.

"Luke… Luke?" Had he given up? She ran to a window and tried to see if he was still on the back step, but it was out of her line of vision. What she did see was a stepladder moving in the direction of the kitchen window. "You wouldn't," she whispered. Then she heard the squeak of the ladder being opened.

Luke's hat and then his determined face appeared on the other side of the glass. "I'm coming in," he warned and began to push up the window.

Honor dashed from the laundry room, through the kitchen and up the stairs into her bedroom. She heard footsteps just before she slammed the door and threw the latch. "There," she declared, spinning around to stare at the paneled door. That would put an end to this nonsense. She didn't have to talk to him if she didn't want to. She'd decided what was best, and that was that.

Footsteps pounded up the staircase. "Honor?" Her doorknob turned. "Honor, please."

"I'm not letting you in. I can't marry you." Honor began to push one of the new bedside tables in front of the door.

"Honor, listen to me."

"*Ne*, go away, Luke." She shook her head again and again, feeling a sense of panic. "I'm sorry. I'm sorry."

"You are going to talk to me," he repeated. He banged on the door. "Just open it."

"I have nothing to say to you."

"Well, I have something to say to you. I love you," Luke called from the other side of the door. "I want to make you my wife. Why are you doing this?"

"Because I love you," she whispered, too low for him to hear her. "Because I don't want to ruin your life or my children's."

"What?" he shouted. "I can't understand what you're saying. Are you going to open the door and talk to me like an adult?"

She didn't answer. Couldn't answer. If she did, she'd start crying again, and she'd wept too many tears.

"Please open the door."

"Ne."

She heard him walk away and her heart sank. Her knees went weak and she steadied herself against one of the beautiful pineapple bedposts of the bed he'd put together the previous day. For their new life together. He'd set up the whole room, but first he'd cleaned the whole place top to bottom, and it smelled of lemon wood polish.

She didn't deserve him. Luke needed a sensible wife, someone with good judgment, someone he could rely on. She knew that she'd hurt him, but in time he'd come to realize that she'd made the best decision.

She went to the window but didn't see him. The black automobile stood in the yard, and she wondered where the driver was. She looked at the mantel clock. Quarter to ten. The bishop would be preaching Honor's wedding sermon and she wasn't there to hear it. What would her friends think of her? Sara Yoder would be crushed by her rejection of the match. She knew that Katie and Ivy were disappointed in her. She'd failed them all.

The footsteps came back up the steps. "Last chance, Honor," Luke said. "Open the door, or I'm taking it off the hinges."

He can't do that, she thought. Hinges are on the inside, not the outside. But the bedrooms had had no doors when they moved into the farmhouse, and Silas had hung them all backward so that they opened out into the hall, not into the rooms. He'd made a mistake, one she'd wanted to tease him about, but hadn't dared. It was a mistake he'd promised to fix, but like so many of Silas's promises, he'd never kept it.

Metal scraped against metal and the top hinge squealed as Luke pulled out the pin. "One question," he called. "Answer one question for me."

She was shaking. "Will you leave if I do?"

"Maybe," he replied, as he pried at the bottom hinge. "What is it?"

"Can you tell me that you don't love me?"

"You'll go if I do… If I tell you that I don't love you?"

"I will. If you tell me to my face, not through a door."

She breathed a sigh of relief. God forgive her, all she had to do was to tell a tiny untruth. Just say the words, and he'd go away and leave her in peace. Simple. But it was the most difficult thing anyone had ever asked her to do. She opened her mouth and tried to speak. Nothing came out.

"Thought so," Luke answered. He removed the pin from the bottom hinge. "One to go."

She ran back to the second nightstand and began to push it toward the door, but she was too late. The door sagged and swayed, and then Luke lifted it and moved it aside. He shoved aside the first nightstand aside and walked into her bedroom.

"You can't come in here with me," she protested weakly. "It isn't decent."

"Ne," he agreed. "It isn't, but after tonight, it will be our bedroom."

"Why can't you understand?" she cried, bringing her hands to her cheeks. "Why can't I make you see that I can't marry you?"

Luke sat on the corner of the nightstand and folded his arms. He took off his hat and tossed it onto the top of the tall dresser that stood at an angle to the door. "Explain it to me."

She began to tremble harder. Her throat felt as if it was closing up and her stomach turned over. How fine he looked in his new clothing. She could see how angry he was. But she didn't feel afraid of him, as she had been with Silas. She knew Luke would never harm her.

"You love me, and I love you," he said quietly. "You promised to marry me, and now you say you don't want to. What have I done wrong, Honor?"

She shook her head. "Nothing," she said, hugging herself inside the knit wrap. "It's not you, it's me. I'm afraid. Terrified that if I marry you, I'll ruin everything for you and for my children."

He opened his arms.

She ran to him, finding solace when she laid her head against his chest. "Don't you see?" she sobbed. "I've made so many bad decisions. Over and over. I insisted you and I get married when we were too young. You wanted to wait, but I wouldn't. I told you that I wouldn't wait for you if we didn't marry then. And with the children… My boys almost drowned because I'm a terrible mother."

He cradled her against him. "You're not a bad mother, Honor. You're a wonderful mother. You're dedicated to your children. And you can't blame yourself for what happened between us nine years ago. We were both immature."

"But you left me the morning of our wedding."

"It wasn't you. It was always me," he said, burying his face in her hair. Her *kapp* fell back onto her neck, but neither of them noticed. "I left because I knew that you would never abandon your faith. And I didn't know if mine was strong enough…if I could live Amish. I couldn't ask you to leave with me."

She raised her head and looked into his eyes. "But you'd accepted baptism."

"That made it worse, that I doubted my faith after I'd given my pledge to remain true to our beliefs."

"But you didn't leave the church. And you believe now. Your faith is strong."

He nodded. "I do believe now. I grew up, Honor. God spoke to me, not to my ears, but in my heart. I knew that He was the right way, the only way. I wanted to come back for you, but by then, you'd already married someone else."

"That was another mistake I made," she told him. "Marrying Silas, staying with him once I knew what he was, letting him control our money, control me. If I was a good mother, I would never have let him be so hard with the children. I was supposed to protect them."

"And you did. You told me that you wouldn't let Silas strike them."

"But…but…"

"You're human. You make mistakes, just like I do. Once you were in the marriage, you stayed to try to make the best of it. But that shouldn't keep you from marrying me, from reaching for happiness, Honor." He tilted her face up with a big hand and tenderly kissed her lips. "Why didn't you come this morning…? Why wouldn't you talk to me?"

"Because I was afraid. Afraid that if I was making another mistake by marrying you, my children would suffer, you would suffer. If I messed up my first wedding and then did the same with the second, how could I be certain that the third would be any different?"

The barest smile appeared on his face as he looked down on her. "Do you love me, Honor?" he asked.

"You know that I do."

"Then join with me in marriage in the sight of God and our church. Today. Now."

She closed her eyes. Not knowing what to say, what to do. She knew what she wanted to do. "But what if..."

"Have faith, Honor. Faith in us, faith in the Lord God. That's all you need, a little faith. Because you won't have to make all these decisions alone anymore. We'll do it together. And if we make mistakes, which we will, we'll work to make them right again. Together. It's all any of us can do. Try, every day. Try to do the right thing and try to live as our beliefs teach us."

"But it's too late," she murmured, still holding on tightly to him. "I was supposed to be there at nine."

"It's never too late," Luke assured her. "I've got Grace's car. I can have us at Sara's house in fifteen minutes." He leaned back to look at her, still holding her in his arms. "Now, dry your eyes, straighten your *kapp*, and let's go. Because, unless I'm sadly mistaken, our bishop won't be halfway through his sermon."

"Do you think so?" she asked.

"I do. And if he's as hungry as I think he'll be when he reaches the end of his sermon, he'll still marry us so that he can sit down to that fine wedding dinner that Sara and Hannah have prepared."

She offered him a faint smile, wiping at her eyes as she took a step back from him. "We'll be a scandal. Showing up late to our own wedding. Together."

He met her gaze. Held it. "Enough to keep your aunt Martha in a spin for weeks."

"Let's do it, then."

She laughed, and he laughed with her, and her heart swelled with joy as her fears melted away. It would be all right. It would really be all right. She would marry Luke, and with the children they would be a family. Together they would face all the trials and happiness that life had to offer. And when she made mistakes or Luke did, they would ask God for forgiveness and try to do better. As Luke said, it was all anyone could do.

Epilogue

One year later...

"I can help finishing setting up the chairs," Tanner offered. "I'm not tired."

Luke shook his head. "You heard your mother, son. Bedtime. I'll expect you up by five to feed the livestock."

"Ya, Dat." He turned to his mother. "Should I wake Justice then?"

Honor gave Tanner a good-night hug, still unable to believe how he'd shot up in the last year. "Leave your little brothers to sleep. Justice can tend the chickens after breakfast." She tousled his hair affectionately. "Our first worship service for our new church is a special day of thanksgiving and celebration. We'll need you to help look after the younger ones." Tanner nodded, and she hugged him again.

"Good night, son. Don't forget your prayers," Luke reminded.

"*Ne, Dat*, I won't." With a final grin, Tanner left the parlor.

Honor watched him go, a lump rising in her throat. "He's growing up on us. Not just in height, but he seems so much more mature."

"Ya," Luke agreed. "He is. It's what children do." He unfolded two more chairs and added them to the women's row. "Do you need any help in the kitchen for tomorrow's midday meal?"

"I don't think so. I just hope I've made enough chicken salad. I have plenty of yeast rolls, but I wouldn't want to run out of salad."

He chuckled. "It's just six families, counting Freeman's and ours. We aren't feeding half of Kent County, not yet. And everyone else is bringing food. We'll have plenty."

She used her broom to reach a cobweb on the ceiling in one corner of the parlor. This newly expanded room would be plenty large enough for their first worship service. "Do you think I was selfish not to sell any of my land? Would Green Meadows have come together sooner, if I did?"

Luke shook his head. "Everything is in God's plan. If you *had* agreed, I'd not have gone to that English neighbor and asked him to let us know if he wanted to move. And you see what came of that?"

She smiled at him. "I still have a hard time believing it."

The neighbor had wanted to move to South Carolina to be near his grandchildren, so Luke and Freeman were able to purchase the ninety-four acres. They'd divided that three ways and found three Amish families to settle, including Luke's cousin Raymond's. And Freeman and Katie had just sold one of their lots to a young Amish couple who wanted to build a house, so they would soon join the new church community. Zipporah's family would also be joining them.

"We have our church," Luke said, sliding a big stuffed easy chair into position for one of the elders. "And our bishop and preachers."

They'd asked Bishop Atlee from Seven Poplars to help choose their first church leaders. According to tradition, God's ministers were chosen by lottery. The names were placed in identical Bibles and one picked at random by a designated elder. Freeman's uncle Jehu would be their first bishop, with Freeman and one of the newcomers, Abel Byler, as preachers. Some might be surprised that their bishop would be a blind man, but they didn't know Jehu. He had committed passages, stories and proverbs to memory, and he was full of wisdom and compassion. His capable, work-worn hands would help to mold the new community. And, surprising everyone, Luke was to be the new deacon, responsible for seeing that the Ordnung was followed.

It was all Honor could do not to feel pride that her Luke was chosen and that he had been so instrumental in forming the new Amish community, which they'd decided to call Green Meadows.

"...the school," Luke said. "Honor, are you listening to me?"

She felt her cheeks grow warm. "*Ya*... *Ne*, I was thinking how God has blessed us with good friends and so many opportunities. And *ya*, I am thrilled that we will have our own school just across the meadow."

"Thanks to you," he said. "You donated the land."

"What's an acre to see our children educated close to home? It was you and our new neighbors who built it. Without you, Luke, none of this would have happened." Her smile was tender. "My life changed when you showed up at my door."

"It's a good thing you opened the door that day. I was afraid you were going to leave me in the rain."

She laughed as Luke put his arms around her and hugged her. Then he kissed her full on the mouth. "You know that I love you," he said.

She nodded, too full of emotion to speak.

"And I love our four children. You know that, too?"

"*Ya*, I do. And they know it, too."

He smiled down at her, his arms warm around her shoulders, the familiar male scent of him enveloping her in a loving embrace. "I love being a father. And I have the woman of my heart for my wife." His lips brushed hers again, and she reveled in the sweetness.

"And I love you, Luke Weaver."

"Good. I want you to tell me that every day for the rest of our lives together." He drew his thumb across her cheek. "We should get to bed. Morning comes early."

She smiled at him, tears of joy clouding her eyes, her heart so full of happiness that she could hardly breathe. "I know, but tomorrow's the Sabbath," she worried. "I won't be able to make more chicken salad in the morning. I'm thinking I should make another batch."

"We have enough chicken salad," he said, bending to pick her up in his arms and swing her in a circle.

She squealed and clung to him. "Put me down!" she cried.

"Look around you, woman," he said, turning in a circle with her in his arms. "Your house is shining like a new penny, your cupboards, refrigerator and freezers are full, and we're ready to host our first worship service." He kissed her again.

"Put me down," she repeated, laughing. "What if one of the children should hear us?"

"I won't put you down until you agree to go away with me," he said. "Our honeymoon. We never did get it. I think next week would be an excellent time to finally take it."

"How long?"

"Two weeks?" he bargained. "No children. I've already talked to Katie and she's agreed to watch all four for as long as we want. And Greta will be here to help her."

"One week," Honor countered. "But where are you taking me?"

"That will be a surprise. And my final offer is ten days. Take it or—"

"Or what?"

"Or we'll stand here all night and greet our guests with me all red eyed from lack of sleep and you wearing your third-best apron and your oldest head scarf."

Honor laughed. "Eight days. And you have to promise me that you'll not get your picture in the newspapers or rescue anybody from drowning on our honeymoon."

"Sold!" He kissed her one last time and then set her lightly on the floor. "I'll try my best, unless it's you who's in danger, and then..." He shrugged. "Now, turn out the lamps and come to bed. It will be daylight soon, and we have guests arriving."

"Whatever you say, husband."

He locked the door, she turned off the lights and they walked up the wide stairs, her hand in his, with light hearts and high hopes for the days and years to come.

* * * * *

PLAIN JEOPARDY

Alison Stone

To my eldest daughter, Kelsey,
as you get ready for your next adventure.
I'm very proud of you. May all your dreams
come true. Love and kisses.
To Scott and the rest of the gang,
love you guys, always and forever.

Peace I leave with you, my peace I give unto you:
not as the world giveth, give I unto you.
Let not your heart be troubled,
neither let it be afraid.
—*John* 14:27

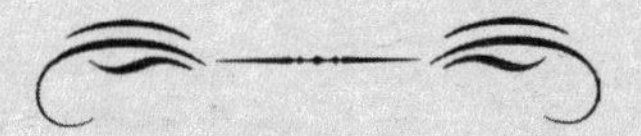

Chapter One

The traction-control light lit up on the dashboard, and Grace Miller clutched the steering wheel tighter. The tires quickly gained purchase on the snowy country road. *Phew.* Not as icy as she'd feared. All she needed to do was leave a little extra distance between her car and the car in front of hers, which wasn't too hard to do on the deserted streets of Quail Hollow, New York. Not a lot of cars—or wagons—out after dark. Most people were hunkered down at home doing sane things like watching TV or reading a book, not chasing leads on a story on a snowy night in the Amish community.

Grace reached across and touched the crumpled handwritten note she had tossed onto the passenger seat.

> I have info about drinking party. Meet at gas station. Main and Lapp. 8 p.m. Get gas while your there.

She could forgive the writer's misuse of the word *your* if it meant she had a new lead on a story that had, so far, produced nothing more than what had already been published in regional papers or played on the local TV stations out of Buffalo.

Grace had been surprised to find the handwritten note taped to the front door of her sister's bed & breakfast. She wondered why they hadn't knocked. She had been home alone most of the day, except for the window of time when Eli Stoltz, her sister's Amish neighbor, stopped by to care for the horses.

That would have been too easy. Instead, the author of the note had insisted on a clandestine meeting at a random location on a freezing night. Making her get out in the cold and pump gas, no less.

Already she didn't like the person. They better not waste her time.

Since she had zero leads, she didn't have much of a choice. The bishop had turned her away, and the sheriff's department had only given her the most basic of information regarding the party and the fatal accident that night. Even the few teenagers she'd tracked down had shut her out. However, Grace was not easily deterred. She had spent her days since graduating with her journalism degree traveling the world, writing in-depth articles featuring people or events that needed highlighting. The tagline under her online bio read Giving a Voice to the Voiceless.

Grace turned her car onto Main Street and was mildly cheered by the trees covered in twinkling white lights, even though Christmas had passed a few weeks ago. She supposed no one could fault the residents of Quail Hollow for looking for something to brighten up the long months of January and February in the great white north, where the days were short and the snow was deep.

It had been a long time since she had spent a winter up north. Her job afforded her the luxury of traveling the world, and when she had a choice, she chose warm, mild weather, certainly not polar-bear cold.

Before Grace's emergency appendectomy, she had finished a story in Florida about a young mother who had lost her job after she missed work due to cancer treatments. Grace's story led to a huge community outpouring of support and the promise of another job when the woman felt well enough.

That was why Grace did what she did.

But life's twists and turns—including a surprise appendectomy, infection and prolonged recovery—put her right in the middle of an exciting story while holed up at her sister's bed & breakfast in Quail Hollow.

Grace slowed and turned into the snowy parking lot of the gas station. The back of her car fishtailed, then she regained control. Prickles of anxiety swept across her skin. Boy, she hated driving in the snow. It didn't help that her sister's car probably needed new tires.

Grace pulled under the overhang meant to protect customers from the elements while they filled their tanks. The snow swirled violently, touching down in mini tornadoes. No overhang would protect the customers from those gusts. She shuddered, despite the warm air pumping from the heating vents. In the rearview mirror, she saw an Amish man with his collar flipped up, hunkered down in his wagon. He flicked the horse's reins and continued to trot down the street in a steady rhythm.

Suck it up, buttercup, she thought. At least *she*

wasn't exposed to the elements like the Amish man in his open wagon. How did they deal with the harsh winter? It reminded her of a story she had written about the homeless in Arizona. One man claimed he moved down there from Minnesota because if life had dealt him the unfair hand of being homeless, he would choose to live in the desert.

Clearing her thoughts, Grace scanned the gas station parking lot. She had to keep her head in the game. Stay focused. The gas station and surrounding stores were mostly quiet except for a couple of vehicles parked along the fence on one edge of the parking lot. One car, covered in a layer of snow, was probably an employee's. The other, a truck, looked like someone had recently parked and run into the attached minimart or a neighboring store on Main Street.

No sign of someone lingering around to talk to her.

Clicking her fingernails on the steering wheel, she watched the red digital number on the dashboard change to 8:01 p.m. Past experience told her that sources didn't always keep to a schedule. Dreading the inevitable, she wrapped her scarf around her neck and pushed open the door. The arctic air rushed in, making her wish she was covering a story near the equator. "Where are you?" she muttered under her breath as she climbed out and scanned the parking lot again. It didn't help that she had no idea who she was looking for.

Grace waited half a second before lifting the pump from its slot and jamming it into the car's tank, hoping that the letter writer approached before her ears froze off. She yanked down her hat. Sighing heavily, she swiped her credit card through the reader, selected 87 octane and began pumping. Because she refused to ruin her nice leather gloves, she didn't wear them while she filled the tank. Seconds seemed like hours, and she wondered if she'd ever be able to uncurl her frozen fingers from the metal handle.

She continued to sweep her gaze across the area while she pumped gas. The pump clicked off. If her secret informant was going to show, he'd better show now or she was getting back into her car and cranking up the heat before she turned into a popsicle.

She turned to hang up the pump when she heard the deep rumble of an engine roaring to life. She spun around. The reverse lights lit up on the pickup truck parked nearby. Strange, since she hadn't noticed anyone getting into it. She reached for the door handle on her car, convinced her pen pal had stiffed her.

The sound of tires spinning drew her attention back to the truck. Her heart jolted into her throat. The driver sped in Reverse, barreling directly toward her.

She dove to the side, fearing she'd be pinned between her car and the gas pumps. Visions of news coverage of fuel pumps ablaze and charred cars ran through her mind. She landed with an *oomph* and pain shot through her midsection from her recent appendectomy. Slushy wetness seeped through her clothes, adding insult to injury.

The sound of metal crunching metal filled her ears. She desperately tried to scramble away in an awkward crab crawl. Craning her head, she caught sight of the pickup truck tearing out onto Main Street. Relief that he was leaving wrestled with anger that he was getting away, making her forget the pain shooting through her numb hands. The world shifted into slow motion. A bitterly cold wind turned her vision blurry, making it difficult to make out the profile of the departing driver.

The back end of a vehicle had been smashed against the fuel pumps, leaving Captain Conner Gates wondering what had happened here. When Dispatch sent him on the hit-and-run call, he had expected to see a fender bender and two drivers arguing over who was at fault.

This was far more than a simple collision.

An uneasy feeling swept over him as he pushed open the door on the patrol car and climbed out. Despite having grown up in Quail Hollow, he'd never get used to the cold. Squinting against a blast of wind, he inspected the crumpled back end of the vehicle driven against the cement base of the fuel pumps. No sign of a second vehicle. Unease tightened like a fist in his gut. The images from the night of his cousin's fatal accident six weeks ago were seared into his brain. Well, technically, Jason was the son of a cousin, but he'd been like a brother to him. Jason's pickup truck had clipped an Amish woman's wagon then continued on, careening out of control and coming to rest wrapped around the solid trunk of a tree. Past experience told him no one could survive the brutal impact.

Past experience had been right.

Jason had died instantly.

Blinking away the graphic image of the young man's bloodied face, Conner muttered to himself that he hoped no one was injured tonight. He had long ago given up on prayer.

The dispatcher hadn't indicated any injuries.

Conner flipped up his collar and shrugged his shoulders against the punishing winds. The harsh glare of the emergency lights on his patrol car cut across his line of vision. He caught sight of a woman standing inside the minimart with a blanket wrapped around her shoulders. The woman next to her, Erin, the gas station clerk in her green uniform vest, waved at him frantically. Conner stopped at the minimart at least once a shift for some friendly chatter and hot black coffee.

He glanced around. There was only one other car in the lot, and it hadn't sustained any damage. He spoke into his shoulder radio. "I'm at the gas station. Send a tow truck." He yanked open the glass door and stepped inside. "You okay?" he asked the shivering woman. "Need an ambulance?"

Her red fingers flitted in a quick wave of dismissal. "No. No ambulance. I'm okay."

He nodded briefly and relayed the information to Dispatch.

Conner tugged off his leather glove and held out his hand. "I'm Captain Gates from the sheriff's department." Her hand was ice cold. "Can you tell me what happened here?"

"Someone rammed into my car and took off." Conner expected to hear fear in the woman's tone. Instead, he was met by the hard edge of annoyance. "It's my sister's car," she added, as if that might explain her tone.

"It was horrible." Erin rolled up on the balls of her orthopedic shoes and her eyes brightened with excitement. This was, after all, probably the most thrilling thing she'd witnessed in her fifty-odd years. "I've never seen anything like it. Always thought maybe someday someone would come crashing through the front of the store. You know?" She touched the arm of the woman standing next to her. If she had been looking for an ally, she didn't find one in the woman's steely gaze. The clerk continued, undeterred. "I see that all the time on the TV. But, wow, never seen anything like that in real life. He was aiming right for this lady's car."

"You saw the accident?"

"Yes," Erin said. "I looked up when I heard the tires squeal. At first I thought it was on account of the snow and ice. But no, this was *completely* intentional. He tried to crush her between the car and fuel pumps." The clerk's eyes grew wide. "I didn't catch the license plate. He pulled in and parked there shortly before this lady arrived. Never came into the store. I didn't think much of it because people use this parking lot all the time to shop at other stores. Easier than street parking."

"Did you notice anyone getting out of the truck?" Conner asked.

"Can't say that I did."

Conner directed his attention to the attractive woman who clasped a blanket tightly around her shoulders. Her attention was focused on the parking lot, or maybe her car. What was she searching for? "Any surveillance camera footage from that part of the parking lot?" Conner asked.

"Doubtful. You're free to look, though," Erin offered. "The only camera is pointed at the register."

"Do you..." He backed up his train of thought and turned toward the shivering woman. "I'm sorry. What's your name?" It wasn't often that he met strangers in Quail Hollow. It was one of those places where everyone knew everyone else or, at the very least, knew *of* everyone else. He most definitely had never met this brunette with watchful brown eyes. Yet something about her seemed vaguely familiar.

"Grace Miller." She blinked slowly, as if she had to think about it.

He made a mental note of it. Miller was a common Amish name around here; however, this woman was definitely not Amish. Not with her long brown hair flowing out from under her knit cap. Not to mention her expensive-looking boots, albeit not snow boots.

"Do you have ID?"

She held up her hand toward the smashed car. "My purse is on the passenger seat."

"No problem. We can deal with that later. Want to tell me what happened?"

A shadow crossed her eyes as if she were deciding how much to tell him. "I was pumping gas and some guy crashed into me. And took off." She seemed bored with the retelling. It was odd. Most people would have been completely panicked if someone rammed into their car while they pumped gas.

"Do you know the guy? Did you see him or get a license plate?"

"Of course I don't know him. And no, I didn't get a license plate. I was too busy diving out of the way." She twisted to get a better look at the slushy, black snow on her pants. She winced and her hand moved to her midsection. "I only saw a profile. Male. It was too hard to make out his face."

"Are you sure you don't need a doctor?"

"I'll be fine. I had my appendix out a few weeks ago. Landing on my side didn't do much for my recovery." Apparently sensing he was going to push the doctor thing again, she held up her hand. "I'm fine, really. I want to go home and change my clothes. I'm soaking wet."

"All right." Conner glanced around. The beeping sound of a tow truck backing up to her damaged car filled the night air. "Do you have someone you can call for a ride?"

"Um, no?" Her answer came out as a question. "I don't suppose Quail Hollow has Uber."

He suppressed a chuckle. "Let me take a few photos of the scene, talk to the tow truck driver, then I'll see that you get home."

A fraught expression tightened her pretty features. "That would be great."

"Wait here where it's warm."

Grace hugged the blanket closer around her and shuddered. "That's a matter of opinion." Her lips tilted into a weary smile, but he didn't miss the daggers shooting from her eyes.

For all the investigative journalism Grace had done over the years, she had never sat in the front seat of a patrol car. She had never sat in the backseat, either, for that matter. She'd come close a few times, but she had a knack for knowing when pushing law enforcement for answers had drifted from merely annoying to "let's lock her up."

The officer had started the engine, then climbed back out of the vehicle. She felt a little guilty about being coy regarding what happened tonight. She hadn't *just* been filling her gas tank. She had come here because she had received a tip on the story she was working on. However, the sheriff's department had been less than forthcoming with information when it came to the underage drinking party and subsequent fatal car accident.

Two could play at that game.

Besides, she didn't want to become part of the story. If she kept her mouth shut, the hit-and-run would be a little blurb on the back page of a local paper and not part of a larger story, one that she was trying to cover. That was, *if* Quail Hollow had a newspaper.

Grace hadn't dealt with this officer from the sheriff's department before. Maybe she could pry some information out of him before he realized she was a journalist.

Just maybe…

Just maybe that would be unethical, a little voice whispered in her head.

Stifling a shiver, Grace adjusted the vent on the dash, glad the officer had turned on the heat before getting back out of his patrol car to talk to the tow truck driver and retrieve her purse from the passenger seat of her car. She plucked at the fabric of her wet pants, eager to get home and change.

When the officer finally climbed behind the steering wheel, he handed her the purse. "Warming up?"

"Thanks. Yeah."

"Before we go, I want to see if you recall anything else from the accident. Anything else important you haven't told me?" His intense brown eyes searched her face. She wasn't ready to talk. Not yet.

Twisting her lips, she shrugged. "Not really." She pulled on the blanket she was sitting on to smooth out the crease cutting into her thigh. "I'd love to get home and change out of these wet clothes."

He hesitated a moment then asked, "Where are you staying? Do you have friends or family in Quail Hollow?"

Grace couldn't resist smiling. This was small-town life. Since he hadn't met her before, she couldn't possibly belong in Quail Hollow. And he wasn't wrong. Grace doubted she'd ever fit in here, regardless of her background. "I'm staying at the bed & breakfast."

The fluorescent lighting from the gas station overhang lit on the handsome angles of his face. A look of confusion flickered in his eyes. "The Quail Hollow Bed & Breakfast? It's closed for the season. The owners..." He stopped himself, perhaps realizing it wasn't prudent for law enforcement to reveal when the residents of their fine town were away on an extended vacation.

"Yes, I know. My sister and Zach are on their honeymoon."

The officer's eyes widened, and he pointed at her with a crooked smile. "I knew you looked familiar. It was bugging me. Of course, your last name's Miller. A lot of Millers live around here." He put the patrol car in Drive. "Let me get you home."

"I'd appreciate that." She turned and watched the driver tow her sister's smashed-up car away on the back of the flatbed truck. So much for successfully taking care of things while her sister was away. Her stomach bottomed out, and a new worry took hold: it would require writing a lot of articles to pay for the damage. Her sister most likely had insurance, yet repairs still meant an inconvenience to everyone involved.

She pushed the thought aside. The occasional voice crackled over the police radio, interrupting the silence that stretched between her and the officer. Something about a deputy taking their dinner break and something else about Paul King's cows blocking the road and that someone was sure to have a wreck if the animals weren't cleared from the road right away. At that, she cut a sideways glance at the officer, who seemed unfazed. "Bet you're glad you got taxi duty and don't have to deal with the cows."

He laughed, a weary sound, as if he had heard it all before. "Oh, I'm sure I'll be dealing with the cows once I get you home."

"Are cows blocking the road a regular occurrence around here?" Maybe she could somehow work that into her article about the dark side of Amish life.

"We've been after Paul to get his fence repaired. These things take time, I suppose. It's all part of a slower-paced life."

Grace snagged her opening. "I heard there was some excitement in town about a month and a half ago."

The officer seemed to stiffen. He kept his eyes straight ahead on the country road. "That's the kind of excitement we don't need or want."

"I heard there was a big drinking party." She ran her hand down the strap of her seat belt, choosing her words carefully. "Is it unusual for the Amish and the townies to party together?" She had a hard time imagining her quiet father, who'd grown up Amish, drinking a Budweiser with his buddies out in some field.

The officer made an indecipherable sound. "The Amish and *Englisch* grow up together in some ways. They overlap in jobs and in the community. It *is* a small town. It's not unusual, especially during *Rumspringa*, for the Amish to test their limits." The Amish didn't encourage their youth to misbehave during this period of freedom prior to being baptized, but she understood the theory behind it. The Amish elders wanted their youth to willingly choose to be baptized into the faith after exploring the outside world. Surprisingly, a majority of Amish youth did decide to be baptized. It was a fact that had jumped out at her during her initial research.

Despite being the daughter of Amish parents, Grace had only recently started to research the Amish. There had been a reason she had avoided exploring her past. However, now she wished her father had opened up more about his Amish upbringing. It would make writing this story that much easier. But after her father had left Quail Hollow and the Amish way, bringing his three young daughters with him, he refused to talk about "life before." Even the good parts. It was all too painful. And how could she blame him, considering the way her mother had died?

Grace plucked a small pebble from her coat. "How is the Amish girl who was in the accident that night?"

"She's in a coma. Her prognosis is uncertain." His unemotional tone made it sound like he was reading from a list.

"That's horrible. And the driver of the truck..." Grace purposely left the sentence open-ended, despite knowing the outcome.

"Died at the scene." The officer's grip tightened around the steering wheel, and a muscle worked in his jaw.

His reaction made her realize something for the first time, and her pulse thrummed loudly in her ears. "Were you on duty that night?" She studied his reaction, sensing she was on the verge of learning something fresh she could use in her story. Deep inside, a sense of guilt niggled at her.

Using someone else's misfortune...

No, she was writing a story that needed to be told.

A young man had partied and then recklessly crashed into an Amish wagon, most likely ruining a young woman's life. Grace's job was to bring light to stories that needed to be told. And she was good at her job. It allowed her to travel and be financially independent.

He cut her a sideways glance this time, before slowing down and turning into the rutted driveway of the bed & breakfast, which was covered in a fresh layer of snow. He shifted the patrol car into Park and turned to look at her. "Why didn't you tell me you were a journalist?"

Her stomach felt like she was riding a roller-coaster car that had plunged over a ten-story crest. However, there was nothing fun about this feeling.

Her go-to move was to feign confusion. "I'm..." She slumped back into the passenger seat, rethinking her plan of action. He knew. But how?

"Are you investigating the underage party?" he asked.

Without saying a word, Grace turned and stared up at the bed & breakfast in the darkness. The house gave off a lonely, unwelcoming vibe. She should have left on a light in the kitchen.

"Can you explain this?" The officer pulled a crumpled piece of paper from his pocket. It was the note from the anonymous source that she had left on the passenger seat of her sister's car. The officer must have found it when he retrieved her purse. For a fleeting moment, she wished she could disappear into the vinyl seat.

"Why didn't you tell me you were meeting someone at the gas station?" Captain Gates pressed. "Don't you think maybe this note and the accident are related?"

Chapter Two

"Yes, I *am* a writer. I don't think the accident had anything to do with my job." Had it? The words sounded wrong in her ears the minute Grace said them, but she was committed to her denial, because acceptance that someone had tried to hurt her—*kill* her—would put a serious crimp in her research. The sheriff's department wasn't likely to let this go unchecked, and she wasn't foolish enough to make herself a target.

Grace traced a finger along the armrest on the patrol car door and stared at the house. The house that had once been her grandmother's hunkered in the winter night like a monstrosity from her past.

"Really?" Grace shifted to face Captain Gates, astonishment etched on his handsome features. "You get a note to meet at the gas station. No one shows up to talk to you, then a truck nearly pins you between the car and the pump. You don't see the connection?"

"Now that you put it that way." Grace tended to use humor to deflect. Had she really been that obtuse? No, she had simply shoved the obvious to the back of her mind. She tended to be single-minded in her focus, and she certainly wasn't going to allow some jerk to deter her from the story. She'd have to be more cautious, that was all.

"This is serious," the officer said.

Grace unfastened her seat belt. "I've dealt with far more dangerous situations covering stories all over the world. I can handle a punk in a truck. Besides, if he wanted to hurt me, he would have. His goal was to scare me." She didn't know who she was trying to convince.

"Did he?"

"No, don't be ridiculous. I mean, I'm not too happy about what happened tonight, but I'm not going anywhere." She scratched her head under the edge of her winter hat. "I can't imagine why he wanted to scare me in the first place. I'm trying to get more details about the party the night of the fatal accident. Readers will be fascinated to learn that Amish teens have the same issues as everyone else."

"Who have you spoken to already?" The officer shifted, and the seat creaked under his weight. She lifted her legs a fraction from the seat, the dampness adding to her ill temper. She didn't need to be a deputy to follow his train of thought. Someone in Quail Hollow wanted to put an end to her investigation.

"Bishop Yoder wasn't helpful when I tried to talk to him about the party. He assured me that anyone caught acting in an inappropriate manner would be dealt with accordingly. Then he shooed me along like I was some unwanted flu bug."

"The Amish prefer to live separate. They're not going to be receptive to anyone shining a light on something negative like this. Law enforcement and the Amish have a tenuous relationship, too. They deal with us only if they have to. That's why, when a journalist comes snooping around, it makes our job harder because the Amish shut down."

"I'm not snooping around." Grace resented the accusation. "I don't force anyone to talk to me if they don't want to. I ask questions. They either answer or they don't." She preferred when they did, of course. "I also stopped by the victim's house," she continued, laying out the names of all the people she had already tried to talk to.

"Katy Weaver?"

"Yes, her brother answered the door and asked me to leave. Out of respect, I did."

"Have you tracked down any of the teenagers from town who were at the party?" His tone changed subtly to one of genuine interest.

"Not yet. Any teenagers I've met claimed they weren't there. I had hoped maybe tonight, after getting that note, I'd find out more information." She wrapped her chapped fingers around the door handle on the passenger side of the patrol car. "Listen, my pants are soaked. I'm freezing. I need to go inside."

Captain Gates pushed open his door, and the dome light popped on. She shot a glance over her shoulder at him. "You don't have to walk me to the door. I'm fine."

"You're not getting off that easy." His deep voice rumbled through her. Despite her frustration with the sheriff's department thus far, she wasn't sorry Captain Gates was going to escort her to the door. The surroundings were pitch dark in a way that can only happen in the country, far from civilization and light pollution. The memory of the truck barreling toward her flashed in her mind, and renewed dread sprinted up her spine.

The officer's hand hovered by the small of her back, and the snow crunched under their boots as they crossed the yard. Grace dug out the keys to the bed & breakfast and unlocked the back door leading into a mudroom adjacent to the kitchen. She turned around in the small, dark space to thank him, and was caught off guard when he stepped into the mudroom behind her.

She cleared her throat, debating if she should ask him to leave. "Thank you for the ride home. I'm really tired. I need—"

"Turn on a few lights. Change into dry clothes. We need to talk."

Conner made sure the windows and doors were secure on the first floor of the bed & breakfast. After he checked the last window, he turned around, surprised to find Grace watching him from the bottom stair with a determined look on her face. "I'll be fine. My sister has an alarm system."

It made sense. Heather Miller, Grace's sister, had been the target of a vicious stalker almost two years ago. Her ex-husband had escaped prison and found his way to Quail Hollow, where his former wife had hoped to start a new life. Thankfully, U.S. Marshal Zachary Walker had protected her, and duty had turned to love. Now the two of them were on their honeymoon. He wished them all the best. They seemed like a nice couple. He only hoped the challenges of a career in law enforcement didn't wreak havoc on their marriage like it had on his parents'.

He cleared his throat. "Can't hurt to check to make sure everything is locked up."

"Was it, Captain?" He detected a hint of sarcasm in her tone.

He lifted an eyebrow and couldn't hide his smile. Her cheeks were rosy from the weather. She stared back at him blankly. He could tell she was humoring him.

"Yes, everything was secure. Yet I don't like the idea of you out here all alone."

Grace's lips parted. "You're kidding me, right? Would you say that to a guy?" She glared at him, skepticism shining in her eyes. "I'm more than capable of taking care of myself. I don't need some big, strong law enforcement officer to protect me," she said in a singsong voice.

Conner had to consciously will the smile from his face, not wanting to stoke the flames of her anger. "I didn't mean to offend you. My job is to keep the residents of Quail Hollow safe. All of its residents, regardless of gender."

Grace dipped her head and ran a hand across her neck. She had twisted her long brown hair into a messy bun at the back of her head. She had also changed into gray sweatpants and a sweatshirt with the name of a university emblazoned across the front. He remembered the story his father had told him about how Grace's father had taken his three young daughters away from Quail Hollow after their mother was murdered. How different their lives had turned out. Grace would have never gone to college if she had been baptized into the Amish community. She'd probably be married with a few kids by now.

He shook his head, dismissing the image. “Are you warming up?”

“Yeah, let me throw another log into the woodstove. You said we needed to talk.”

“Yeah.” She opened the door and tossed in another log. The orange embers scattered and a new flame sparked to life. He feared if he offered to help her, she might bite his head off. She seemed the independent sort.

“How old were you when you moved away from Quail Hollow?”

She grabbed a second log and tossed it in. “Three,” she said, without questioning how he knew her background. That seemed par for the course in Quail Hollow, especially since he knew her sister. Grace straightened with her back to him.

“My dad was the sheriff when your mother…” He scrubbed a hand across his face. As hardened as he had become over the years, this felt too personal to casually toss out the word *murdered.*

Grace slowly turned around. “I didn’t know that. I haven’t done much research on my mom’s death.” She frowned. “I only have vague recollections of her. My memories are a blend of my own and stories told by my oldest sister, Heather. She was six when my mom died.” Then she seemed to mentally shake herself and held out her hand to one of the wooden rocking chairs in front of the wood-burning stove. “Have a seat. What did you want to talk about?”

“What is the focus of the story you’re working on? Why were you meeting someone at the gas station?”

She slowly sat in the rocker next to his and unwound

and rewound the fastener in her hair, as if stalling. The skeptic in him wondered if she'd tell him the truth.

She stopped fidgeting with her hair, placed her hands in her lap and angled her body toward him. "My editor asked me to cover the underage party and the fatal accident. The image of buggies lined up and police arresting the underage Amish drinkers has been splashed all over the news. My editor thought it made a fantastic visual. Like two eras intersecting." She held up her fingers in a square, framing the perfect shot. "Since I was already here recuperating from my surgery—" she shrugged "—it made sense for me to do a more in-depth story."

"Your surgery?" Then he remembered their conversation at the gas station. "Your appendectomy."

"Yes." She waved her hand in dismissal. "I'm fine. I'm still hanging around as a favor to my sister, keeping an eye on the bed & breakfast."

"I'm glad to hear it." He tapped his fingers on the arm of the rocking chair, deciding how to phrase his next question. "Did you ever think you'd have a much bigger story if you covered your mother's murder?"

She closed her eyes and tipped her head back on the chair. "I don't want to dig into that case. I like to keep my personal and professional lives separate." She opened her eyes and leaned forward. "Besides, that's old news." The haunted look in her eyes suggested otherwise.

Conner tapped his fist lightly on the arm of the rocker. The heat from the stove warmed his skin. "The case still haunts my dad."

Grace let out an awkward laugh, as if to say, "Yeah, it haunts me, too."

"I could set up an interview with him if you'd like. It doesn't mean you have to do the story. Maybe it'd provide some answers." He wrapped one hand around the other fisted hand and squeezed. "Truth be told, it might do my father some good to see that you turned out all right." His father often talked about the tormented look in the eyes of the three young Amish girls.

"Has your father ever talked to Heather?"

Conner shook his head. "From what I gather, she's forgiven the person who murdered your mom and has moved on. I'm guessing that's not the case with you." He wanted to ask about the youngest sister, but couldn't recall her name.

She shook her head quickly, but he wasn't sure what question she was answering. "My assignment is to write a story on the youth of Quail Hollow. The Amish. The drinking. The accident. Not something that happened almost thirty years ago." There was a tightness to her voice. "I hope you can understand, Captain Gates."

"Please, call me Conner. Otherwise I feel like we're in an interrogation room." He leaned forward and added, "I don't mean to add to your pain."

Grace smiled tightly. "No, not at all. That was a lifetime ago." She was obviously downplaying her emotions, and he regretted bringing up her mother's murder. No one ever got over losing their mother at such a young age. He still struggled with losing his mom, and she was still alive. After his parents got divorced, she married someone else and seemed perfectly content with her replacement family, never bothering to return to Quail Hollow.

He felt a quiet connection to this woman. Perhaps it

was from remembering the impact her mother's murder had had on the entire community. Perhaps from the pain radiating from her eyes. He understood pain.

"I'm going to lay it on the line. I don't want you covering the story because Jason Klein, the young man killed in the accident, is—was—my cousin's son."

She sat back and squared her shoulders. "Oh… I'm sorry. I didn't know."

"My cousin and I were like brothers. When Ben, Jason's father, was deployed with the army last year, he asked me to keep an eye on his son. A teenager needs a male role model, you know? Anyway, Ben was killed in a helicopter crash."

Grace seemed to stifle a gasp. "I'm sorry."

"Thanks." Conner paused a moment, not trusting his voice. "Turns out, I did a lousy job of looking after his son."

"Kids make their own choices. It's not your fault."

"I don't want this one night—this one stupid, stupid decision—to be what Jason's forever remembered for. I need you to kill this story."

Grace slumped in the rocking chair and pulled her sweatshirt sleeves down over her hands, feeling like someone had punched her in the gut. "Wow, I'm sorry, but—" she bit her lip, considering her options "—I have to do this story. It's my job. I can't afford to lose my job."

Conner stared straight ahead at the woodstove, the flames visible through slots in the door. A muscle worked in his jaw.

"It's my livelihood. I've already begun posting little teasers on my blog about the story. If I don't follow through, it'll look bad." The words poured from her mouth, as if she were trying to convince them both that writing this story was the right thing to do.

When Conner didn't respond, she added, "I'm sorry for your loss, but what about the Amish girl in the hospital? Who gives her a voice? She's innocent in all this." Grace tempered her response out of respect for his loss.

"My cousin's wife, Anna, is having a terrible time with all this. She lost her husband and now her son. Jason was a good kid who made a horrible decision. More publicity only adds to the pain."

"He hadn't been involved with alcohol or drugs before that night?" Grace found her journalistic instincts piqued.

"Off the record?" Conner met her gaze.

"Yeah."

"A couple weeks before his death, Jason had a few friends over for a bonfire at his house after a big football game. Anna called me, worried that there might be some drinking going on. So I showed up, drove some guys home and Jason dealt with some blowback from that night. Apparently drinking is grounds for suspension from the football team. The star quarterback was one of the guys suspended. They're a pretty tight group. They weathered the storm and moved on. Kids make mistakes. Most importantly, no one was hurt that night. Anyway..."

The story angles swirled in Grace's head, making her dizzy. Was she really this insensitive? A good story above all else?

"Jason swore to me he wasn't drinking at his bonfire. That the other guys brought the alcohol. I had no reason not to believe him. I gave him the riot act, anyway. I thought that'd be enough." The inflection in his voice spoke of his pain far more than his words. Yelling at his cousin's son for hosting a drinking party wasn't enough to stop him from being killed a few weeks later in an accident where he was impaired.

"How do you explain the drugs in his system the night of the crash?" she asked hesitantly.

"I can't." Conner pushed up from his rocker and began to pace the small space in front of the stove. "He made a mistake. Must have taken something he didn't know how to handle. Doesn't mean he wasn't a good kid."

"This isn't about good kids and bad kids. It's about making decisions and suffering the consequences. Maybe some other kid will read the story and think twice before experimenting with drugs or alcohol. Perhaps the fact that he was a good kid will make a stronger impression. Show that it only takes one time." Grace stood and folded her arms across her chest. Heat pumped from the stove, but it barely touched the chill in her bones.

"I'm sorry about your loss," she continued, "but I'm sure the young Amish girl is a good kid, too." The fact that she had just met this man stopped her from reaching out, touching his arm, offering him comfort. "I hope you understand that I have a job to do."

He stopped pacing and stared down at her. "You realize, besides causing Jason's mother tremendous pain, you're also making it exceedingly difficult for the sheriff's department to find out who provided the drugs the night of the party?"

Offended, Grace jerked her head back. "How?"

"The more you go digging around, the harder you're

making it for law enforcement to do the same. The Amish don't like to be in the spotlight."

"Maybe I provided you a lead tonight. Go find the truck that rammed my sister's car. Then you'll find someone who has something to hide."

"Trust me, we'll be working that angle. Meanwhile, I need you to stay put."

"Don't tell me to stay put." Anger surged hot and fiery in her veins. She didn't take commands from anyone, certainly not a man she had just met.

"I can't keep saving you if you're being reckless."

"I hardly think pumping gas is being reckless."

Conner held up his hand, then backed up. "Good night. Set the alarm when I leave." He pulled a business card from his pocket. "Here's my cell phone number. I'll respond quicker than a 9-1-1 call from a cell. Sometimes those calls are routed through a few substations before they can find the origin."

"If you're trying to scare me, you're not."

He set the card down on the table and looked at her intently. "I'm not trying to scare you. You need to understand how things are. Good night," he added tersely, turning to leave.

She stomped to the back door and turned the lock behind him. An ache in her hip from her heroic dive earlier this evening joined the dull pain from her appendectomy surgery.

The memory of the truck barreling toward her came to mind. She entered the alarm code and hit On, convincing herself she was safe. She had pursued far more dangerous stories in far scarier parts of the world. She wasn't afraid of some teenager in a souped-up truck, if indeed the accident at the gas station had been intentional.

She returned to the sitting room and slipped her laptop out of the case resting against her sister's fancy rolltop desk. She logged on to her blog, the one the editor encouraged her to keep updated. Since he was the one who assigned the stories, it was in her best interest to keep him happy.

"It gets the readers excited," he'd told her more than once.

She focused her thoughts, her fingers hovering motionless over the keyboard. The hurt and betrayal in Conner's eyes would haunt her. The dead boy had been his family. His responsibility.

The young man had made a horrible error in judgment that put a young Amish girl in a coma. People had to take responsibility for their actions.

No one had ever taken responsibility for her mother's murder.

She considered all the hurt and deceit in her life. Her mother's murder. Her sister's violent husband. People weren't always who they seemed to be. She had to shed light on the evil of the world. Give victims a voice.

This was her job. Her editor expected her to write the story.

She clicked New Post and started to type:

> The idyllic countryside is dotted with picturesque farmhouses and barns. The Amish people wear conservative clothing and use horses for transportation, as if living in another era. Yet the world changes around them at a dizzying speed.
>
> Alcohol. Drugs. And other evils.

The Amish choose to live an insular life with porous borders that provide no barrier at all. They are warned to live separate from the world.

But, apparently, no one told the outsiders, for they have found a way in.

Grace drummed her fingers on the edge of the keypad and reread her words. Too dramatic?

She closed her eyes and tried to remember her mother's face. It was hazy, the memory of a three-year-old little girl.

Her mother had been murdered and no one had paid for the crime. Justice had never been served. Were the answers still out there? Was it really too late? What could it hurt to talk to the sheriff at the time of her mother's death? Could she still ask Captain Gates to set up a meeting with his father? She hadn't been very sympathetic to his family's plight when he asked her not to write about Jason.

Conner must think she was as cold as the winter winds slamming the outside walls of the Quail Hollow Bed & Breakfast. Nerves tangled in her stomach, and she made one more check of the alarm.

All set.

She wandered back to the seating area and stared over the yard. In the window, her weary reflection peered back at her. A chill raced down her spine.

She backed away from the window, unable to shake the sensation that she wasn't alone.

Chapter Three

Late the next afternoon, after completing his shift, Conner strode around to the passenger side of his personal vehicle and opened the door for Grace. She had called him early that morning to see if the offer to talk to his father was still on the table. Conner considered this a good sign. Maybe they'd work out something mutually beneficial for both of them. She could get information on her mother's murder, and maybe she'd back off Jason's story.

When Grace didn't immediately unbuckle her seat belt, he asked, "Is something wrong?"

"Are you sure your dad's up for talking to me?"

"Yeah, come on. I called him earlier." He held out his hand, and she finally unbuckled her seat belt and slid out of the truck without taking it. "He generally doesn't like to discuss this case with outsiders, but that's not the situation here." Conner paused, not wanting to say that his father had always had a soft spot for the three little girls that Sarah Miller had left behind when she was brutally murdered. "He's willing to talk to one of Sarah's daughters.

"Besides—" he yanked open the back door and grabbed the takeout bags "—he's always up for food."

Grace held her scarf close to her neck as they walked up the pathway cleared of snow. Conner suspected his father had shoveled the flakes before they had a chance to hit the ground, whereas Conner preferred to put his four-wheel-drive truck to work each winter, creating two deep tracks in his long driveway. No shovel required. It was an ongoing joke between the two men.

"Watch out for the ice on the steps." The salt hadn't kept up with the sun-kissed icicles dripping from the overhang. He reached out for her elbow. She moved to the side and grabbed the railing instead.

"Any leads on the truck involved in the hit-and-run last night?" she asked.

"No, nothing on the surveillance video. But that was to be expected since it was positioned at the register and the driver never came into the store. All the officers know to look for a pickup with rear-end damage. If anyone tries to bring a truck in for repairs within a hundred-mile radius, we'll be notified."

Grace glanced up at him. "Why was it you answered the call last night when you obviously work the day shift?"

Conner smiled. "It's a small town. I was filling in for another officer who requested off."

She nodded.

"I've also—" The door swung open, stopping Conner midsentence. His father must have been waiting on the other side for their arrival. "Hey, Dad."

"Son." The former sheriff stepped back into the foyer, allowing him and Grace to enter. His father took the takeout bag from his son before grabbing their coats with his other hand. He shuffled off to the first-floor bedroom where he undoubtedly placed the coats on the king-size bed, like Conner's mother used to do when they entertained when he was a little boy. It baffled Conner that, even after twenty-some years, the memory of his mother's habits made him miss her like the day she had left.

Time had passed. The Miller case had grown cold. His father retired. Yet his mother never returned, having found happiness with a nice engineer with regular hours and little chance of getting shot on the job. Apparently, the replacement kids meant she didn't miss the one she had left behind in Quail Hollow.

"Oh, something smells good." His father's voice snapped Conner out of his dark thoughts.

"Yeah, I picked up a few burgers from the diner," Conner said.

His father nodded. "This must be—"

"Grace Miller," Conner jumped in. "This is my father, Harry Gates."

His father narrowed his eyes, and a frown slanted his mouth. "If my memory serves me correctly, the Miller girls were Heather, Lily and Rose. Not Grace."

Conner watched Grace, wondering what that was all about. His memory had been a little hazy on the girls' names, but he hadn't given it much thought because she was staying at Heather's bed & breakfast. And the striking resemblance to her mother…

Had this woman deceived him?

Conner was starting to feel protective of his father when she finally spoke up. "I'm Lily. Lily Grace. I started going by my middle name when I went away to college." She smiled ruefully. "I wanted to put distance between my name and the tragedy that shaped my life."

"Seems reasonable," his father said without much ceremony. His father's career and failed marriage had hardened him. What little sentimentality that remained belonged to the family of Sarah Miller. The family he had let down.

"Regardless of the name, there's no doubt you're your mother's daughter. You have the same face." His father tipped his head. "However, she was Amish and you're—" he scanned her modern clothes and gave her a crooked smile "—obviously not. Do you see the resemblance yourself?"

"I only have a vague memory of my mom. The Amish don't allow photos, so I can only rely on my memories. I was only three when she died."

His dad held up his hand. "Of course. You were very young. Such a tragic thing. It's going on thirty years, isn't it?"

"Getting there. A lifetime ago." Conner detected a vulnerability in Grace that had been lacking last night when she was focused on his cousin's story. Perhaps she had been wise to keep her professional and personal lives separate.

Conner caught Grace's gaze briefly before his father invited them farther into the house. When they reached the dining room, Conner was surprised to see retired Undersheriff Kevin Schrock sitting at the table, his chair angled to keep an eye on some TV program with a guy haggling to buy some other guy's stuff. The big-screen TV dominated the adjacent family room. Kevin stood when they entered, and his dad was the first to speak. "I invited Kevin over. Kevin, this is Lil… Grace

Miller. Grace, this is Kevin Schrock. He was one of the key investigators in your mother's case."

Grace shook his hand. "Thank you for taking the time to meet with me."

Kevin studied Grace's face, probably seeing the same thing that Conner's father saw: the likeness to the woman whose murder they had never been able to solve.

His father peered into the paper bag with blossoming grease stains on the bottom and sides. "Any chance you have an extra burger in here?"

"Of course." Conner pulled out a chair for Grace to sit down. "Plenty of food for everyone." He smiled at Kevin. "Nice to see you."

"Same here." Kevin picked up the remote sitting on the table in front of him and muted the TV program. He shifted in his chair to face Grace. "Boy, you certainly don't look like the little girl who left Quail Hollow in an Amish bonnet and bare feet."

Conner shot Kevin a stern look. These old-timers got directly to the point.

"I suppose not," Grace said softly.

"You've come back to find answers?" Kevin pressed, seemingly intrigued.

"That wasn't my intention. Not initially. I was staying at my sister's bed & breakfast for other reasons, and then my editor asked me to write a story regarding the underage drinking party involving both the Amish and the townies."

His father muttered something he couldn't make out, anger blazing in his eyes. He cleared his throat and finally spoke. "I'm sure my son told you that Jason Klein, the boy killed in the crash that night, was family."

Grace swallowed hard. "I'm sorry for your loss."

His father's expression grew pinched, and he faced Conner. "She's a journalist? I hadn't realized that."

"She wants to know about her mom."

Resting his elbows on the table, his father leaned forward. "If your motive is to drag poor Jason's name through the mud..." He shook his head. "Jason's mother has been through enough, hasn't she? First losing her husband in a horrible helicopter crash, now her son."

"That's not my intention, sir." Grace moved to sit on the edge of her seat. "I like to shed light on untold stories. I'm sure people would be fascinated to learn of the—" she seemed to be choosing her words carefully "—things that go on in an Amish community beyond farming and cross-stitch."

"You really did move away from here young." Kevin folded his arms, a self-satisfied look on his face. "The Amish do far more than farm and needlework."

Grace tucked a long strand of hair behind her ear. "I don't identify with the Amish at all. My father raised us in Buffalo. Please forgive me if I find this story fascinating. Others will, too. I'm sure of it."

"Oh, people will find it interesting," his father said. "They were all over your mother's murder, too."

Grace's face burned red, and uncertainty glistened in her eyes.

"Dad!" Conner scolded him. "Grace came here to talk, not to be put on the spot." Conner suspected his father's blunt comment was a result of wanting to protect Jason, his great-nephew.

"After your mother's murder, a young reporter thought she'd make a name for herself and wrote story after story about the Miller murder for the *Quail Hol-*

low Gazette. She inserted herself to the point that the Amish wouldn't talk to anyone anymore, not even law enforcement." His father fisted his hands in his lap, his anger evidently directed at a long-ago slight, not at the need to protect Jason. "The journalist was a huge detriment to our investigation."

"You never told me that." Conner studied his father's face. A vein throbbed at the elderly man's temple, his ire still palpable. His father had pored over paperwork and reports at the kitchen table long after the town had written Sarah Miller's death off to a tragic and random encounter with a stranger passing through town. Yet they had never been able to prove it.

Conner himself had never felt the need to read the newspaper accounts because the case had taken over his young life, leaving his father obsessed and his mother absent. Now, as a law enforcement officer, he understood the delicate relationship with reporters *and* with the Amish. He had recently tried to mind this relationship when he'd asked Grace to stop asking questions about the night Jason was killed.

"People would say my accusations regarding the reporter were only conjecture on my part," his father continued. "That *I* needed to take responsibility for not handling the investigation. That *I* was the only one responsible for not finding the murderer."

"My intention wasn't to upset you." Grace pushed back from her chair, stood and smiled sympathetically. "I'm sorry, sir. I was under the impression that your son had told you I was coming."

"He did. But I thought I'd be talking to Sarah Miller's daughter. Not a journalist."

* * *

"Please, sit down." Conner gently touched Grace's wrist and they locked gazes. He gave her a quick nod as if to say, "It's okay. Please stay." Trusting him, she sat down. If she hoped to learn anything about her mom, she didn't see that she had much of a choice.

She glanced over at the undersheriff. Tingles of awareness prickled her skin from the retired officer's intense focus. She hadn't realized she'd be ambushed when she arrived here.

"I'm sorry you had a bad experience with a reporter. I have no intention of making anyone look bad." Her only motivation was to reveal the truth. Let the rest of the chips fall where they may.

The retired sheriff grumbled under his breath, perhaps understanding more than most how these things worked.

Grace picked up a French fry and distractedly dipped it into the glob of ketchup she had squirted onto her paper plate. "I understand you put a lot of time into my mother's case. Why was this one more difficult than most?" She knew from her journalism career that all cases weren't neatly wrapped up.

Conner's father folded the corner of the takeout wrapper from his hamburger. "Murder is rare in Quail Hollow. Some might say I *was* out of my depth. I worked that case harder than I'd ever worked anything before. Or since." There was a faraway quality to his voice. "The best lead we had was a man who had been traveling through town. Eventually, we tracked him down, but he had a solid alibi. Rumors cropped up that there was another stranger in town. The locals needed to believe it was an outsider. It grew harder and harder to separate fact from fiction. But that's where we still are all these years later. A vagrant passing through town killed Sarah Miller."

"Were there any other suspects?"

The two retired law enforcement officers exchanged a subtle glance that she might have missed if she hadn't been so observant. A heaviness weighed on her chest, making the room feel close. When neither of them answered, she pressed, "What aren't you telling me?" A cold pool of dread formed in the pit of her stomach. *"What?"*

Kevin drummed his fingers on the table. She guessed it was a nervous habit. "In a murder investigation, the person closest to the victim is usually investigated."

She tossed aside the French fry and wiped her hands on a napkin. "That's not unusual." She shrugged, trying to act casual when her insides were rioting. *Her sweet father.* Her mother's murder had destroyed him. "You cleared my father and then moved on to this stranger passing through Quail Hollow." Her gaze shifted between the two men. Holding her breath, she waited for reassurance. *Of course* they'd cleared her father. Hadn't they?

Kevin finished chewing a bite of his burger and swallowed. "Your father moved out of town before we could one hundred percent clear him."

"Well, that's only partially true." Harry leaned forward and gave her a reassuring smile. "I knew your father a bit from town before your mother's murder. Your father and mother used to sell corn at the farmers market on the weekends. He was a friendly man. Talkative. You girls were his little helpers. After your mother's murder, he shut down. Her death broke him." He pressed his lips together. "Even though we never officially cleared him, my gut told me that he could never have hurt Sarah. *Never.*"

A lump of emotion clogged her throat. "Thank you." She averted her gaze, fearing she'd lose it if she didn't. This was the price of looking into her family's story, the reason she had avoided it all these years. The reason she'd probably leave here today and forget she ever came.

"What else can you tell Grace about the time surrounding her mother's death?" Conner asked the question Grace was now afraid to, because she was uncertain she could afford the emotional toll.

"The night Sarah disappeared, she had taken the horse and wagon into town to drop off a few pies. She had sold them to the diner. She left you girls home with your grandmother. A few people noticed her in town, but didn't see anything or anyone suspicious. She never came home."

She never came home.

Pinpricks of dread washed over Grace's scalp as if she were reliving her mother's last moments. She had vague memories of hanging out at the farmers market. Maybe the memories had been dreams, yet the images were vivid: the long dresses of the Amish women, the farmers' work boots and the fancy shoes of the *Englisch.* The occasional dog would lick her sticky fingers after she devoured a piece of apple strudel. The farmers' market was the highlight of the week. She figured the only reason she had those memories was because of how quickly her life had changed.

Amish to outsider.

Before versus after.

Conner's father glanced over at his former coworker. "Anything else to add?"

"No. Not really. It was a shame we never found the guilty party. It was like he vanished into the night."

"You mentioned a reporter at the time..." Grace watched the former sheriff flinch.

"Yeah," Harry said. "She worked for the now-defunct *Quail Hollow Gazette*. She was like a dog with a bone. Relentless."

"Do you know if she still lives in Quail Hollow?" Grace asked, hope blossoming. Another piece of the puzzle.

Can I really do this?

Kevin leaned back and crossed his arms over his chest. "Can't be sure. I believe she had some health issues and moved away to live with her daughter down south. Away from this cold."

"I imagine they have her articles on file at the library," Grace said, thinking out loud. "Maybe I'll do some digging."

After they finished eating, Grace and Conner carried the paper plates and glasses into the kitchen. Grace leaned on the counter while Conner put the glasses in the dishwasher. "I'm not sure I'm ready to look into my mother's murder."

Conner slowly closed the dishwasher door and turned to face her. "Your mother's sudden death had to be really tough on you. Leaving this community must have made it that much harder."

"I often wondered how my life would have been if I had grown up Amish. I look at the Amish men and women in town and try to imagine the path not taken.

Sometimes I wonder if this was all part of God's bigger plan." Heat crept up her face. "Don't get me wrong—I'd do anything to have my mom back. Yet no one could have predicted how her death changed everything about my life. Not all of it bad." She slowly ran a hand through her hair. "That sounds horrible, doesn't it?"

"No, life's twists and turns are hard to understand sometimes." He took a step closer to her, and she didn't move. "But some tragedies don't have any redeeming qualities."

"You're talking about Jason's death."

He nodded, a flash of hurt in his eyes. "I'm asking you not to continue to write about the death of my cousin's son. It's hard for our family, especially his mom. She lost her son and her husband in the course of a year. She's spiraling out of control. She's distraught."

A knot twisted in Grace's stomach. "I'm sympathetic. I really am, but you can't compare the two cases. Jason drove under the influence. *He* made a choice." She shifted away from the counter and glanced out the back window overlooking the snow-covered yard. The evening light was about to fade. "This is my job." Grace wondered how many times they'd go round and round on this topic.

"Everyone has a job to do." Grace spun around to find Kevin Schrock resting his shoulder on the doorway of the kitchen. "And sometimes it's best not to mix business with personal." How long had he been eavesdropping?

Kevin seemed unfazed that he had interrupted their private conversation. "His dad allowed your mother's case to get to him. Ruined his marriage." He pushed off the doorway and strolled into the room. "You have to trust your gut on these things. If you don't think you can live with what you find, maybe it's a story better left untold."

Grace stared at him, wondering which story he thought was better left untold.

A few days later, since her sister's car was still in the collision shop, Grace called the number for a car service in town. The Amish often hired drivers to get them from place to place when taking a horse and buggy wasn't feasible. The local district's *Ordnung* allowed the Amish to ride in the vans, but they couldn't own cars or drive themselves.

The driver, an older gentleman, dropped Grace off at the local library and promised to return in one hour to bring her home. Grace climbed out of the van and smiled at an Amish woman hustling past with three young daughters in tow. The thick fabric of their bonnets kept their heads warm. Their long dresses poked out from under black coats. The fabric brushed the edge of the shoveled walkway, collecting clumps of snow. Nostalgia pricked the back of Grace's eyes. Another generation ago, that could have been her and her sisters.

Grace held her collar closed and strode toward the main entry of the quaint library. Ever since retired Sheriff Gates had mentioned the articles in the *Quail Hollow Gazette* about her mother's murder, Grace couldn't get them off her mind. She tried Googling and using some of her research tools to find the articles online, but came up empty. At first, Grace took it as a sign that she needed to let the past stay in the past.

Her initial curiosity had been followed by a restless night and a growing determination that hollowed out the pit of her stomach. Grace hadn't become a top-notch reporter by allowing a dead end to stop her.

After alternating between "let it go" and "just read the articles already," she decided only the latter would allow her to move on. Besides, there couldn't be much to go on in the articles since no one had ever been arrested. Grace needed to squelch her obsessive curiosity, a quality that usually served her well.

She carefully made her way up the salt-covered walkway. She entered the library and drew in a deep breath. The smell of books filled her nose. Something felt familiar. Grace had always loved to read, and she wondered if perhaps her mom had brought her here. Instilled in her a love of reading.

Or maybe that had come later, growing up in Buffalo.

Grace approached the librarian. "Where can I find articles from the *Quail Hollow Gazette*?"

"Oh, the *Gazette* went under—" she hesitated, giving it some thought "—fifteen years ago."

"Do you have copies of the paper from the 1990s?" Grace didn't want to tell the librarian exactly what she was looking for because she didn't want to invite questions.

"We have clippings of the more important articles from the paper filed chronologically in the basement." The librarian emphasized the word *basement*, apparently trying to dissuade her.

"Is the basement open for patrons to do research?"

The librarian planted her hands on the desk and pushed to her feet. "Um, Linnie, I'm going to show this woman where the archives are in the basement," she said to her colleague, also behind the desk.

"Thank you," Grace said, hoping her gratitude would make the woman feel like her trouble was worth it. She had met all kinds during her travels, from those eager to tell her their life story, to those who seemed bothered by the idea of doing their job. Yet in Grace's experience, whatever her reception, she chose to be pleasant. It proved to be disarming—most of the time.

The librarian muttered something as she led Grace down a back hall marked with an overhead exit sign. She moved surprisingly quickly despite her short, choppy steps and the narrow purple dress she wore. She stopped at a door before the emergency exit. With the key on a lanyard around her neck, the librarian unlocked the door, reached in and flipped on the lights. "I'll show you the files, and then I have to get back upstairs to help Linnie. The library gets busy in the afternoon with all our after-school programs." She squared her shoulders with a sense of pride.

"That's fine." Grace preferred to do her research without anyone standing over her shoulder, anyway.

The fluorescent lights buzzed to life in the basement. The librarian led her down the stairs, past a row of shelves stacked with books with identical bindings to a series of gray filing cabinets along a cement wall. The librarian planted her hand on the top of the cabinet, then pulled it away and swiped her hands together. "It's a little dusty down here. Most libraries have this information on microfiche or digital but, well, we don't have the budget for that."

"I understand." Grace hoped her cheery yet sympathetic tone was effective. She didn't know how long she'd be here or if she'd need to come back, and she wanted the librarian on her side.

The woman clasped her hands in front of her. "What dates are you looking for?"

The filing cabinets were neatly labeled with month, day and year ranges. As long as the newspaper clippings were filed correctly according to date, she'd be able to search the articles at the time of her mother's murder. She touched the handle of the closest cabinet. "I see the files are labeled. I'll be fine."

"Well—" the woman pursed her lips "—don't refile anything. Place any files you pull out on the desk over there. I'll refile them at a later date. Because if you don't put them in the right spot—"

"No one will ever be able to find the article they're looking for in the future."

The woman leaned back on her heels, apparently satisfied. "When you're done, let me know. I'll be at the information desk upstairs."

"Thank you." Grace watched the librarian walk down the narrow aisle, the bookshelves lining one side and the filing cabinets the other, her heels clacking on the cement floor. The librarian disappeared around the corner, and Grace waited until she heard the basement door click shut.

Finally alone, Grace ran her fingers along the labels on the drawers and stopped on October of that fateful year. Her knees grew weak, and a darkness crowded the periphery of her vision. Was she about to open Pandora's box?

Should she or shouldn't she?

Drawing in a deep breath, she slid open the first cabinet drawer. She'd come this far. She'd check out a few articles, that's all. Inside the drawer, manila folders were labeled with exact dates. She slid out the folders from a few days before to a few weeks after her mother's body was found. She carried the stack to a desk at the far end of the aisle, pulled out a chair and sat. She squinted up at the flickering overhead lights, wishing there was a desk lamp. Not many people must use the basement.

She opened the folder dated the day after her mother's body had been found.

Amish Woman Found Dead.

Her mother's life had been reduced to a four-word headline. No name. Simply "Amish Woman."

The black words on the yellowed paper swam in her field of vision. Blinking, she traced the letters, as if it provided a connection to her mother.

As she slowly read the article, she imagined the writer, fingers flying over the keyboard, jazzed to write about something more substantial than cows escaping through broken fences. A quiver rippled through her stomach. Was she any different?

She shook the thought away and focused on the article. It didn't provide any significant information that she hadn't already known. Her mother had gone into town to sell pies. The waitress oozed with pleasantries on how wonderful a person Mrs. Miller had been and then digressed into the usual platitudes: what an awful tragedy, her poor daughters, how had someone dumped her body in the family barn without being seen? It was almost too much to read.

Breathing slowly through her nose, Grace tried to calm her nerves. She pulled out another article and squinted at the black-and-white photo taken from a distance. Was that her with her father and sisters? The hairs on her arms prickled to life. Her grandma's house—the site of her sister's bed & breakfast before it had been updated—stood in the background. She recognized the tree out front and the porch. Emotions she wasn't ready to explore coursed through her.

The buzzing and winking of the yellow fluorescent lights threatened to trigger a migraine. She slid the files into her tote bag, convinced the lighting would be better upstairs. She went over to the cabinet to close the drawer when the lights went out.

Her heart nearly exploded out of her chest.

Just great.

Frozen in blackness, Grace called out, "Hello, I'm down here."

The only response was the uneven sound of her breath.

"Hel-lo?" Her voice hitched. She didn't dare move for fear she'd trip over something in the blackness.

A muffled shuffling sent terror pulsing through her veins. "Hello? Is someone else down here?" She slid along the cabinets, the handles jabbing her side.

Hope made her change direction. Her phone was in her bag on the desk. It had a flashlight app. Or she could call for help.

A rhythmic creaking filled her ears, made louder in the blackness.

What is that?

"I'm down here!" she hollered in desperation.

"I know you're down here," an unseen man whispered. Tiny pinpricks of fear blanketed her scalp. She slid closer to the desk, realizing whoever was here had intentionally turned off the lights. And was coming for her.

Her hand found her tote bag on the desk. She reached inside and found her phone. She feared pulling it out and revealing her location, but she needed help. She swallowed hard. *Remain calm. You've been in far scarier situations.* Her usual response to those who warned her that her investigation was going to get her into trouble didn't seem to be doing her much good at this exact moment.

A loud, rhythmic creaking filled her ears. A groan of exertion cut through the blackness. She scrambled under the desk with her phone.

A loud crash exploded in her ears. A violent whoosh of air sent her hair flying off her face.

The bookshelves had crashed down around her, leaving her trapped underneath the desk.

Chapter Four

Conner braced himself against the cold winter blast as he strode toward his patrol car, careful to avoid oncoming traffic. He had let the teenage driver in her mother's minivan off with a warning, mostly because he believed her when she told him through sobbing hiccups that she hadn't been able to stop at the icy intersection. He told her it was a good thing he'd been the one to pull her over, because the sheriff had given all his officers a directive to crack down on all driving offenses, especially among the youth. And, more importantly, it was a blessing that her slide into the intersection hadn't resulted in a crash.

Everyone needed to slow down and be more careful on the roads.

Safely back inside his warm patrol car, he balanced his clipboard on the center console and entered the information into the laptop. A little less paperwork for the end of his shift, which he was looking forward to more than usual. He thought he'd stop by and check on Grace. It had been a few days since he had seen her. He had convinced himself his visit was to make sure she wasn't getting herself into trouble, not because the spunky reporter had caught his attention. Not that he was looking for anyone to catch his attention.

But she had.

His cell phone buzzed and he glanced at the screen. He smiled to himself and swept his finger across the screen.

"Hello, Grace." Conner wasn't sure what he had expected when he picked up the phone. But it wasn't what he heard next.

"Conner." Her panicked voice was barely above a whisper. "Conner, can you hear me?"

"Yes." He pressed the phone to his ear, fearing he wouldn't be able to hear her over the sudden surge of adrenaline pulsing through his veins. "What's wrong?"

"I'm in the basement of the library. I'm trapped."

Conner glanced over his shoulder to check for oncoming vehicles and pulled out onto the road. "I'm a block away. Are you hurt?"

"No… I don't think so…" Her voice cracked. "But I'm trapped. Someone was down here."

"I'm on my way." He flipped on his lights and siren. He punched his foot down on the accelerator. Silence stretched across the phone line. "Grace? Are you there?"

Silence.

He eased off the gas as the library came into view. He scanned the crowded parking lot and realized his only option was to make his own spot. His patrol car bumped over the curb and came to an abrupt stop on the snow-covered lawn of the library. With the patrol car lights still flashing, Conner jumped out of the vehicle and sprinted across the lawn, the snow crunching under his boots. He flung open the library doors. He forced himself to slow down to avoid barreling into a couple of toddlers who had escaped from the not-so-watchful eye of their adult. The pair were now making a break for it, hand in hand, toward the group of senior citizens in the newspaper section.

A thin woman in a purple dress with black-frame glasses and hair twirled in a bun was the first to make eye contact with him. She scooted out from behind the information desk. If he hadn't been in such a panic to find Grace, it would have registered that the woman making a beeline for him with her pinched expression could have been plucked out of central casting for librarians.

"Officer, is there an emergency?" She angled her head to look around him, toward the wall of windows, no doubt to his patrol car parked on the front lawn, complete with lights flashing. Once he collected Grace, he'd make it up to the librarian by scheduling a date to give the kids a peek at a real patrol car.

"Where's your basement?" He strode toward the back of the library and looked both ways. He continued down the hall, proceeding on a hunch.

The librarian chased after him with choppy steps. "What's going on, sir? A woman is doing research in the basement. We have old records stored down there."

"Here?" Conner pointed at the door, then turned the handle. It was locked.

The librarian nodded and flattened her hand over a key on a lanyard around her neck. "Yes, it's usually locked, though it shouldn't be now." A line marred the woman's pale forehead, and Conner had to resist the urge to yank the key from around her neck—*now.* "Like I said, a woman is doing research down there."

"Open the door," he said through gritted teeth.

The librarian hunched over and stuck the key into the lock without removing the lanyard from around her neck. She opened the door and took a step through the opening. Conner held up his hand. "No. Wait here. Keep anyone else from entering this back hallway."

"Oh." The woman's eyes widened underneath her thick lenses.

Conner pulled out his gun, reached in and flipped on the basement light. The darkness scurried into the far corners where he couldn't see. Where someone could easily hide.

The wooden stairs creaked under his cautious step. Grace was in the basement. He had no idea if she was alone.

A cramp shot up Grace's leg. It had been twisted under her for what seemed like forever, in a position no amount of exercise could have prepared her for. Pressing her eyes closed, she held the phone tight to her chest. She didn't dare talk more than she had to for fear of revealing her location.

She whispered a prayer of thanks when she heard the sound of a siren growing closer. Conner really had been close by. Her solace was short-lived when she opened her eyes and realized it was just as dark as when she had them pressed closed. A memory slammed into her, unbidden, and ramped up her panic.

It was a long time ago. Grace was a teenager. Heather, her eldest sister, had come home after a big fight with her new husband. Grace loved having her sister around, and they had spent a fun evening watching a movie and eating popcorn. Their other sister, Rose, had been at a sleepover at a friend's house. The credits for one of their favorite movies had begun to roll when Heather's husband, Brian, pounded on the door looking for "his woman." At the sound of his banging—his yelling—all the color drained from her sister's face. The woman Grace looked up to, admired, the big sister who had always protected her two little sisters in their mother's absence, had a sheen of terror in her eyes that shook Grace to her very core.

Heather grabbed Grace roughly by the shoulders and shoved her toward the front hall closet. Before Grace knew what was happening, she was curled up among the shoes, umbrellas and whatever stuff she had thrown in there the last time she'd quickly cleaned up.

Grace remained in the closet until the shouting stopped and the police took Brian away. Heather never took refuge in her childhood home again, because she knew that she'd be putting her little sisters' lives in jeopardy.

A rustling, then a snap sent light filtering from the far end of the basement and brought Grace immediately back to her current predicament. The fallen bookshelves in the basement of the library came into fuzzy focus in the dim lighting. Grace swallowed back the urge to call out. What if it wasn't Conner?

Dear Lord, help me.

She'd give up the scoop on the next big story in a tropical climate just to be able to stretch out her legs again. She tried to shift to ease the pain and bumped her head on the underside of the desk.

Ugh. Time had dulled the fear and now she was

frustrated. Annoyed. She angled her head and strained to see toward the stairs to determine who was coming down.

Footsteps sounded on the stairs, then legs came into view. She squinted. Uniform pants?

Emboldened by her certainty that Conner was here, she stretched out a hand and pushed the side of the metal shelving. It wouldn't budge.

She flashed back to the memory of being stuck in the front hall closet. Brian screaming at her sister. Heather crying.

An overwhelming sense of claustrophobia swept over Grace. She needed to get out of this confined space *now.*

"I'm over here! Get me out of here!" she screamed.

Grace pivoted and scraped her back on the underside of the desk. Ignoring the pain, she shoved with all her strength against the metal shelving with two hands. The metal scraped against the cement floor.

"Grace! Hold up!"

She sat back on her feet, her entire upper body hunched over to fit under the space of the desk. Her elation at seeing Conner overwhelmed her.

"Are you okay?" he asked.

She held up a hand to block the beam from his flashlight. "Yes. Now please get that light out of my eyes." Her panic made her irritable, and she suspected he'd use this against her. She'd heard the words countless times before from other well-meaning acquaintances. *Investigating this is too dangerous. You need to stop.*

But whatever happened here this afternoon only proved she was on to something important. Something she had to continue to investigate.

"Keep your limbs under the desk. I'm going to shove the shelving out of the way."

After some grunting and tossing books aside, Conner made a space big enough to reach her. "Grab my hand."

Grace slid her hand inside his solid one, and immediately the panicky feelings subsided. He started to pull her through the gap between the fallen shelving and the desk, when she squeezed his hand. "Hold up." She ducked back under the desk and slid the strap of her tote over her shoulder.

Grace found his hand again and let him pull her to safety over a stack of fallen books and mangled shelving. Once free and on solid ground, he held her out at arm's length. "You okay?"

Suddenly self-conscious, she pulled her hand from his and swiped at the back of her pants. She shook both legs to stretch them out. "I am now. My legs were falling asleep under there."

Conner glanced around, a muscle working in his jaw. "What happened?"

She tucked her elbow closer to the tote hanging from her arm. "I came down here to do some research and next thing I know, the lights go out, I'm under the desk, and the shelves come crashing down."

"Did you see anyone?"

Grace shook her head, thinking back to the pitch darkness. "It was a male voice. He said something like, 'I know you're here' or 'down here.'"

"Did you notice anyone following you today?"

"No, of course not." Grace's fear had morphed into indignation as she struggled to process what had happened. "Do you think I'd come down here alone if I thought someone was following me?"

"What happened down here?" The librarian had found her way to the bottom of the stairs and was clutching the lanyard at her neck as she took in the mess. Her eyes slowly shifted to Grace. "Are you okay?"

"I'm fine. Thank you. And about this..." She held up her palm to the mess. "I can help you put everything back in place."

The librarian shook her head. "No, no. We'll have to make sure everything is filed correctly." She rubbed her nose. "Maybe Linnie... Oh, dear." She shook her head and tut-tutted. Grace could see this woman reacting the same way to teenagers talking too loud in the quiet section of the library. "I've been so busy training Linnie. And then this..."

"I'm very sorry," Grace said.

Conner touched her arm. "You don't need to apologize. You didn't do this."

The librarian opened her mouth, but Conner cut her off before she had a chance to protest. "Did you see anyone who looked out of place in the library?"

One of the librarian's eyebrows drew down above the frame of her glasses. "We welcome everyone to our library. We don't—"

"I understand." Conner took a deep breath. "But did anyone stand out today? Someone who looked like they had the strength to knock over this shelving unit? Someone who usually doesn't come to the library?"

Grace leaned toward Conner. "I have to get out of here." Even though she had escaped her tiny hidey-hole under the desk, the basement felt like a tomb.

She smiled meekly at the librarian and tried to ignore the sweat dripping down her back. "I have to get air."

Conner nodded at Grace and guided her out of the basement with a hand on her lower back. They left the librarian in the basement to assess the damage with a warning not to touch anything. Not yet. He'd have to send a crew over to see if they could get fingerprints or any other evidence.

When they reached the top of the stairs, Grace pointed to the door to the right of the basement door. "Anyone could have run out through the exit."

Conner moved toward the door, keeping her safely tucked by his side. "There's a single track of footsteps in the snow headed toward the parking lot."

A cold chill skittered down her spine that had nothing to do with the swirl of snow flitting over the top of the lawn.

Someone had tried to kill her.

"I'm fine, *really*. Thanks for bringing me home." Grace stopped in the back doorway of the bed & breakfast, seeming eager for Conner to leave.

Conner placed his hand on the frame of the door. "We need to talk. I promise I won't stay long."

Grace's eyes lit up, then she turned to hang her tote on a hook inside the door. "Oh, you mean in an official capacity. You need to fill out your reports." He detected a hint of something in her tone. Yeah, he wasn't too thrilled about the reports, either.

"Yeah, reports." He smiled and shrugged. "The reason I got into law enforcement was because I love paperwork."

Grace's strained expression softened and a tired giggle escaped her lips. "Come in."

Conner slid off his snow-covered boots. He took off his hat and hung it on an empty hook. He could imagine the Amish men who had lived here a generation ago coming in from their chores and hanging their wide-brimmed hats on similar hooks in the entryway.

Grace busied herself in the kitchen. "Want some tea? Or coffee? I only have instant coffee," she added with a hint of apology. "I'm not much of a coffee drinker."

Conner waved his hand. "I'm fine. Don't bother yourself on my account. I need to get a full report of what happened today."

Grace finished filling the teakettle and set it down on the stovetop, but stopped short of turning on the burner. She turned around and leaned her backside against the counter and crossed her arms, not exactly looking receptive. "I don't know any more than I already told you. I went into the library basement to do research, and someone turned off the lights and knocked over the shelves."

Conner leaned his shoulder against the fridge. "You sure you didn't notice anyone suspicious following you?" She shook her head. "Did anyone know you were going to the library?"

She glanced up with a thoughtful look in her warm eyes. "Only the ride service I hired to drive me into town." A weariness had settled in around her eyes.

Conner ran the back of his hand over his mouth and levered off the refrigerator with his shoulder. "Can I ask you something?"

Grace blinked slowly, exhaustion evident on her face. "I've told you everything already."

Realizing Grace was shutting down, he tried to shift the mood. "I thought this B&B was supposed to be an authentic Amish experience."

"Um, yeah?" Grace looked up, her fatigue replaced by curiosity.

Conner jabbed his thumb toward the refrigerator. "Why do you have a fridge in here?"

Grace shook her head, and a smile pushed at the corners of her mouth. "I don't know. I suppose because it's convenient. I'm just housesitting. What does that have to do with anything, anyway?"

He took a step toward her. "You look serious. I thought maybe I could get you to smile. And I think I did. A little, maybe?"

Grace removed her ponytail and threaded her fingers through her hair, kneading her scalp. "I've had a really, really rough day, and even the muted light from the wall sconces that are, in fact, Amish approved, are hurting my eyeballs."

"Okay, then, I'll make it quick." He slipped the tote from the hook and offered it to her. Apprehension stole across her otherwise bland expression, confirming his suspicions. "What's in the bag?"

Grace's chin dipped as if she were carefully studying the floor.

"Grace," he said quietly, and that caught her attention.

She took the tote from him and their fingers brushed in the exchange. "I'll show you."

She carried the tote to the table next to the windows overlooking the yard and a gorgeous newly constructed barn. The Amish neighbors had all pitched in and had a barn raising to replace the one that had burned down in a horrific fire that nearly killed Grace's sister. And in that moment, Conner thought about all the hardships Grace had experienced through the tragedies in her family.

"Your family has had a rough go of it."

She gave him a level gaze, then glanced down at the manila folder she had pulled out of her tote. She opened it on the table. A yellowed newspaper clipping fluttered with the motion. "I went into the basement of the library to read the articles that were written about my mother's murder." If he hadn't been watching her closely, he might have missed the small shudder that shook her thin frame.

Conner sat down on the bench across from her, resting his back against the table. Twisting, he put his elbow on the table. He dragged the top folder toward him. "So, it's official, you're going to write an article about your mother's murder?" The burden weighing on him since Jason had died had lifted a fraction. But another part of him felt guilty. Had he added to Grace's burden while trying to ease his?

She smoothed her hand across a yellowed article, avoiding his face. "I'm *still* looking into the circumstances surrounding Jason Klein's death."

He ran his hand over the back of his neck. "Listen, you've had a rough day. I'll follow up and see if the deputies found anything in the basement. See if there's any video surveillance. Determine who did this."

She absentmindedly ran the tip of her finger across her lower lip. "I was thinking…" She opened up each of the manila folders and spread the articles out, and he studied the headlines in big black letters:

Amish Woman Murdered.

He scanned down to another.

No Suspect in Murder.

"See how big this headline is? The day after my mom died." He tracked her pink nail across several headlines, the font getting smaller, the articles getting shorter. "This is how it always goes. Big stories, big headlines, until the leads dry up and the story becomes an afterthought. The victim becomes an afterthought in everyone's mind except those they left behind."

He waited, sensing she wasn't done.

"That's why I do what I do. Well, partially… I don't want people who can't speak for themselves to be forgotten."

"The Quail Hollow Sheriff's Department did everything they could to find your mother's murderer."

Grace closed the manila folder, articles poking out from the bottom and sides. The librarian in the purple dress would probably burst a blood vessel if she knew Grace had smuggled out the articles. "My intention isn't to malign the sheriff's department. Not at all. What if a fresh pair of eyes…"

Conner couldn't decide why he felt conflicted, when this was exactly what he had hoped she'd do when he set up the meeting between her and his father.

"I know I was the one who suggested this story, but do you really think it's a good idea?"

"Because of today? We don't know who knocked over the shelves. Maybe it had nothing to do with my mom. No one knows what I was researching. It could have been someone trying to scare me away from the other story. The story even you don't want me to investigate." She threaded her fingers and placed them in front of her on the table, on top of the manila folder.

Frustration weighed on him. "Whether it's digging into your mom's death or Jason's death, someone wants to stop you."

"Including you."

His intention had been to protect his family. Now, he had a growing need to protect her. "I don't want you to get hurt."

Grace looked up slowly. "I appreciate the concern, but I'm done talking about this for now. I'm really tired."

"Okay." He started to leave, then turned back. "Lock up when I go, and activate the alarm."

She stood and followed him to the door. Conner left and waited until he heard the dead bolt snap into place. Without turning around, he lifted his hand to wave. Despite her bravado, he suspected his words had hit their intended mark. If he was unsuccessful in deterring her from her research—whether it be about Jason or her mother—he feared someone else would succeed.

Chapter Five

Studying the oranges and reds of the flames visible through the slats on the wood-burning stove door did little to ease Grace's nerves. Resting her feet on the hearth, she tried to turn off all the thoughts crowding in on her. Since her sister had wanted guests to experience a somewhat authentic Amish home and the Amish didn't watch TV, Grace didn't have the luxury of zoning out in front of one. Conner's crack about the fridge came to mind. Her sister could run a bed & breakfast without a TV, but a fridge, not so much. Or at least without experiencing a lot of hassle.

In the short time since she had met Conner when he answered the call of the hit-and-run at the gas station, she had grown to like the man and his sense of humor, but she didn't like his message very much. He was beginning to make her paranoid. She couldn't do her job if she was afraid. When she was on her own, she was very good at dismissing red flags, and she hadn't been any worse for it.

After the night in the closet when her former brother-in-law terrorized her big sister, Grace vowed she'd never allow anyone to make her afraid. Not if she could help it.

Grace turned toward the window at the front of the house. While she was lost in thought, the sun had set, leaving the landscape beyond the front window black.

Anyone could be out there.

She tended to have that feeling a lot since she had been left alone to care for the bed & breakfast. She suspected it had more to do with her isolation out here in the country, in the dead of winter, than with anything nefarious.

At least, she prayed that was the case.

Pushing to her feet, she wandered to the window and stared out. She had to search past her reflection to see the white blanket of snow, only broken up by tire tracks, footprints and then the main road. Sighing heavily, she reached up for the white roller shade and had to struggle with it to pull it down. Her phone chimed next to the rocker, making her jump.

She laughed at herself—apparently she didn't need anyone to make her afraid. Her imagination was doing a perfectly good job of that.

Grace debated ignoring the phone, then decided against it. Maybe it was her editor. She should probably give him an update. He'd been salivating over the recent turn of events and how her Amish story would generate lots of clicks on their website.

"Amish is hot," he kept saying.

That was the part of the business she didn't like; however, if she wanted to write full-time, she realized her stories needed to generate revenue for the online news site. An Amish story of any magnitude would generate lots of clicks.

Pushing that thought aside, she picked up her phone. Surprise rippled through her. Her sister's radiant face stared up at her from the display, a photo taken at her wedding last spring. Smiling, Grace swiped her finger to answer. "Aren't you supposed to be on your honeymoon?" A honeymoon they had to delay until after the bed & breakfast's busy season.

"Ha! Can't a big sister check in on her little sister?" Heather said, sounding far more relaxed than when she and Zach had gone racing out the door with all their luggage in tow, afraid they were going to miss their flight out of Buffalo because of the weather. But they'd made it and were now on a three-week cruise somewhere in the southern hemisphere.

"Why do I feel like you're checking in on your B&B and not your little sister?" Grace settled back into the rocker and put her feet on the hearth.

"Can't I do both?" Heather laughed, and Grace thought she heard Zach saying something in the background. Grace was grateful her sister had finally found a good guy. A *really* good guy.

"All is well here." Grace didn't want to worry her sister. Hopefully she'd have the car repaired before she got back home. No harm, no foul. Besides, when Heather and Zach left town, Grace was mostly on the mend. They had no idea she was going to be using her recovery-slash-housesit-the-B&B downtime to write a story about an underage party *and* investigate their murdered mother's cold case.

No rest for the weary.

"You're not bored? I thought maybe you'd be bored by now. There's not much to do compared to living in the city, and the cell reception can be spotty sometimes."

Grace smiled to herself, feeling a bit deceitful. "No, I'm fine." *I'm investigating two stories, and someone smashed your car and tried to crush me under library shelving. Beyond that...* "How's your trip going?"

As Heather told Grace about their ports of call and her sunburn, Grace thought she heard something at the back door. A soft scratching that made her freeze mid-rock in the rocking chair, straining to hear over her sister's update. With the phone pressed to her ear, she slid out of the rocker, crept toward the window over the seating area and tried to see who might be at the back door. Her view was obstructed.

Scratch-scratch-scratch.

Grace moved away from the windows and crept to the mudroom, the steady beat of her heart growing louder in her ears.

"Heather, is there a reason I'm hearing a scratching at the back door?" Grace laughed. Her nerves made it sound like an awkward squeak.

"Oh, that must be Boots."

Grace's shoulders relaxed. She couldn't imagine any ax murderer named Boots. "Is Boots a cat?"

"Of course." Her sister laughed.

"How come I've never met Boots before? I've been here for weeks."

"She's a stray. I thought she was gone for good. Haven't seen her in months. Thought maybe she had found her way back home. Oh, let her in. She must be freezing out there."

Really? Grace kept her thoughts to herself. Her mobile lifestyle meant she was used to caring for herself. Not stray animals.

"Okay..." Tucking the cell phone awkwardly between her ear and shoulder, she turned off the alarm and worked the lock on the back door. She opened the door a fraction, not quite sure what to expect, and a black cat with white paws slipped in and scampered over to the wood-burning stove and curled up on a pillow on the floor near the hearth that Grace hadn't noticed before. She turned the lock and followed Boots into the sitting room.

"She seems pretty comfortable." The cat licked her paws, effectively ignoring Grace.

"There's some cat food in the bottom cabinet by the oven in the kitchen. Boots will usually stay for the night and then want out in the morning. Poor thing was probably frozen out there. Oh, you're allergic. Maybe—"

"No, no, it's okay. I'll make sure she stays out of my bedroom. I'll be fine." Grace studied the cat, seemingly none the worse for wear. "I don't know how this kitty survived outside. It's freezing." A gust of wind beat against the side of the house, emphasizing her point.

"Your blood has thinned." Heather laughed. "After this trip, my blood might have thinned, too. The weather has been gorgeous."

"I'm glad to hear it. You deserve happiness."

"Thanks." After a pause, Heather added, "Is everything okay there? You sound a little subdued."

"Yeah," Grace said before quickly changing the subject. "You're sure Boots can stay for the night?" She crouched down and ran her hand across the cat's soft wet fur. "Dad would have never let us have an animal in the house."

"That was from his Amish days. Animals live in the barn." Heather cleared her throat. "It's hard not to think about Mom and Dad while you're at Mammy's old house, isn't it?"

"Yeah." Grace sat back down. *Even harder not to think of Mom when I've been researching her death.*

"I've gotten used to it after time. Mammy's home feels like my home now."

Grace traced the wood grain on the arm of the rocker. "Do you remember Mom?"

"Yes. Most of my memories seem dreamlike. You were three years younger."

"And Rose was just a baby," Grace said, staring at the flames in the stove. "She probably has no recollection of mom."

Heather's voice grew quiet. "Are you sure you're okay?"

"Oh, listen to me." She sat up a little straighter, feeling guilty for bringing up their dead mother while her sister was on her honeymoon. "Did I mention Rose sent me a nice fruit basket to wish me well on my recovery? She was always the thoughtful sister." She forced a cheery laugh.

"Who took care of you while you were recovering?" Heather said in mock disbelief. "Rose probably had someone in her office send it."

Grace smiled. It was a relief to both of them to know the youngest of the Miller sisters was doing well despite the tragedy that had befallen them as young children.

Grace stifled a yawn. "Sorry. I'm tired."

"Go curl up in bed with a good book. There's a library in the corner of the sitting room."

Grace had noticed the books. Maybe she would.

"Sounds nice. I might do that. Go enjoy your trip. Don't worry about things here. I've got it under control."

Zach yelled, "Hi, Grace!" in the background.

"Tell him to take care of you."

"I will." Her heart warmed at the smile she detected in her big sister's voice. Heather's happiness had been a long time coming.

On his way home, Conner swung by the grocery store to pick up a late dinner. Despite common misconceptions of bachelors living on takeout and cold cereal, Conner preferred to make a healthy dinner at home. The cooking relaxed him, and the food tasted better.

The automatic doors of the grocery store whooshed open, and a rush of hot air blasted him in the face as he grabbed a shopping basket. He would have offered to bring dinner over to Grace if he hadn't sensed she wanted time alone.

He reminded himself that she had a solid lock on the door and an alarm system.

Deciding that had to be good enough, he wandered through the produce section. He picked up a head of lettuce and inspected it.

"Exciting dinner plans?"

Conner turned to see Kevin Schrock, his father's former undersheriff, leaning one arm on the handle of an empty shopping cart and staring intently at him. Kevin and his father had worked together for years, and both bore the burden of never solving the only murder in Quail Hollow during their tenure.

"The life of a bachelor." Conner tossed the head of lettuce into his basket. He figured Kevin didn't really care what he was doing for dinner; he was merely looking for an opening to talk to him about something else.

"Don't I know it." Kevin sighed. A crooked smile hooked the side of his mouth. "But a young, good-looking guy like you shouldn't be a bachelor forever. Or at least you could get some pretty girl to offer to cook for you."

Conner pressed his lips together and shrugged. This wasn't exactly the type of conversation he cared to have.

"How's Grace Miller?" And there it was, the subject Kevin was angling to talk about.

Conner jerked his head back, unsure if Kevin knew about the incident in the basement library, or if he was simply making idle conversation regarding the new woman in town, who happened to be the daughter of the murdered Amish woman.

Conner decided to broach the subject directly. "You heard about the library?"

"Yes, a couple deputies were at the diner. Is Grace okay?"

"She's fine. She escaped without injury." Conner forced an even tone to his voice, trying not to think about how seriously Grace could have been injured.

"Do you know what happened?" It wasn't unusual for retired law enforcement officers to insert themselves into the thick of an active investigation, especially in a small town. Conner supposed it was more exciting than watching *The Price is Right* or whatever Kevin did in his spare time.

"We're still trying to figure that out."

"Do you think it has to do with the incident at the gas station? Because she's investigating Jason's death?" Kevin peppered him with questions, not taking a breath to wait for the answers. "What's in the library basement?" The retired officer straightened and ran his hand along the handle of the shopping cart. "Must be her mom's case, right? She was looking for those old articles your dad was telling her about?"

"We're still trying to figure that out, too." Conner took a few steps to his right and selected a cucumber for his salad.

"You need to be careful." Kevin pushed his cart closer to him, unwilling to take the subtle clues that Conner wanted to get his dinner and go home.

Conner tossed the cucumber into his basket and angled his head to give Kevin a curious look.

"Grace is a pretty girl. It's easy to look into those brown eyes and forget she's a reporter."

Conner bit back his annoyance. "I'm not really sure what you're getting at."

"Your dad told you how that reporter interfered during Sarah Miller's murder investigation."

"That was a long time ago."

"You're young. You're optimistic. Personally, I wouldn't trust Grace. If she finds something on Jason's accident and it comes out that you should have uncovered it first and missed it due to blind loyalty to family..." Kevin grimaced, suggesting loyalty to a fault would be a very bad thing indeed.

Anger simmered below the surface. Conner glanced

around to make sure no one was listening. "I'm not covering up anything. Jason's mom has been through enough. She doesn't need more news coverage on her son's death." He blinked away the image of Jason's bloody face from where it had impacted the steering wheel.

Kevin held up his hands and backed away from his cart. "Easy, man. I know, I know. Remember, Sheriff Flatt's retiring next year. If you have any hopes of running for sheriff, you don't want any stink attached to your name."

"Listen, I don't go about doing my job wondering what's in it for me. I do my job the best I can." Conner glanced around. An older woman gave him a curious look and continued past. He had raised his voice louder than he'd intended.

"You're great at your job. It's just—" Kevin shrugged "—your dad's worried about you. He knows firsthand what it's like to be burned by a reporter. I'm trying to help. Your dad won't say anything himself."

His father hadn't mentioned anything to him, but that wouldn't be unlike his old man. He was forever trying to protect his son—the best he knew how—from everything from the blow of losing his mom to his day-to-day frustrations. Instead of easing Conner's mind, the secrecy only served to make him worry more. What else was his father hiding in an effort to protect his son?

Conner lifted his shopping basket as if to say, "Well, I gotta go," and forced a smile. "Don't worry about me or my career. I've got it handled."

"That's what your father used to say, until the unsolved murder and the relentless bad press made him realize he'd never be reelected."

Conner shook his head in confusion and immediately realized his mistake.

"You didn't know that, did you? You thought he rode off into retirement." Kevin shook his head with a smug expression on his face. "Your father had no intentions of retiring until that reporter ruined his career."

"That was a long time ago, Kevin."

The older man tipped his head. "Time doesn't heal all wounds."

An unfamiliar sound broke through Grace's restless sleep. She rolled over and tried to get comfortable before she heard it again. She froze and held her breath, straining to listen, to understand what had woken her up.

Since she had come here a few weeks back to recover from her appendectomy, she had grown accustomed to the sounds of the bed & breakfast, even in the dead of night. The tree branches scraping against the side of the house on the windiest of nights, the battery-operated clock ticking away the longest stretch of the night and the occasional drip from the faucet when she forgot to turn the handle just a little bit tighter to the right.

But this was something different.

Scratch-scratch-scratch.

There it was again. Her sleepy mind finally registered, and relief flooded her system. Boots! The cat she had let in. She must have come upstairs looking for her in the middle of the night.

Thankful that it wasn't some intruder creepily dragging a nail across her closed—and thankfully locked—bedroom door, she pushed back the covers and climbed out of bed. The hardwood floor was cold on her bare feet. She slid on her slippers and shuffled to the door. She didn't want to let Boots into the room where she slept because she was mildly allergic. She could deal with the cat taking refuge in the main living quarters of the bed & breakfast. That shouldn't aggravate her eyes too much.

The lock snapped when she twisted the knob, the sound echoing in the quiet house. She opened the door a crack. Boots darted into the room and disappeared under the bed. Narrowing her gaze at the shadows in the hallway, Grace wondered what had spooked the cat.

Instinctively, she leaned out and glanced down the stairs, unable to make out much in the black of night. Was someone down there? No, she wouldn't let her imagination get the best of her, despite the fluttery whisper of dread upsetting her stomach.

She wandered over to the bed and got down on her knees. Groaning, she lay flat on her belly on the hardwood floor. She was ready to be done with the post-surgery aches and pains. "Come on, scaredy-cat, you can stay warm and cozy downstairs. You can't sleep under my bed."

In the blackness, Grace couldn't make out any discernible shapes under the bed skirt. She pushed up on all fours and reached to pick up her cell phone from the bedside table. Turning on the flashlight app, she shined it under the bed. Cat eyes glowed back at her, taunting her. With one hand, she reached out and, remarkably, Boots moved toward her.

For her reward, Grace sat cross-legged, rested her back against the bed and petted the cat, itchy eyes or not. After a few minutes, Grace got to her feet with the cat in her arms. She set the phone down on the nightstand. "Let's take you downstairs to your cozy bed, okay? You'll be nice and warm next to the stove." Grace laughed at herself. She wondered if someday, after living alone for years, she'd become the crazy cat lady who had full-on conversations with cats. "Don't start talking back," she muttered, running her hand over the cat's head.

Grace's slippers made a soft flip-flop sound as she crossed her bedroom to the hallway and made her way down the darkened stairs. She skimmed the cold railing with her free hand. When she reached the bottom stair, she put the wriggling cat down on the floor.

Boots shot across the room and darted behind Heather's rolltop desk. *What in the world?* Goosebumps blanketed Grace's cool skin, which made her realize it was freezing down here. Had the wood-burning stove gone out?

Then something fluttered at the corner of her eye, followed by a loud clack. The roller shade beat against the window frame. Holding her breath, she took a step closer, and terror sent a wave of prickles across her scalp. Behind the askew shade, the window yawned wide.

Frozen with indecision for the briefest of moments, Grace weighed her options. With a confidence she didn't feel, she ran to the window, reached behind the shade, and slammed it down, twisting the lock at the top.

Why hadn't the alarm gone off? She raced to the panel and noticed the light was green. It wasn't activated. Had she been too distracted when talking to her sister to forget to reset it after she let Boots in?

She strained her brain to remember. She couldn't.

What if the intruder was still inside? She glanced toward the shadows where Boots had disappeared. The cat would be fine. She, on the other hand, was exposed.

She ran to the staircase, taking them two at a time, and reached her room. She slammed the door and locked it, then raced to her bedside table and turned on the light, casting away all the spooky shadows.

She swiped her cell phone from her bedside table. Clutching it to her chest, she kicked off her slippers—they'd slow her down if she had to run—and crept to her bathroom. She reached around the corner and flipped on the light. With her jagged breath in her ears, she moved forward and snatched back the shower curtain, then heaved a sigh.

Empty.

She pressed her cold hand to her neck. She was alone. At least up here.

For now.

For all her bravado, when push came to shove, she hated being afraid. Being unsure. Being vulnerable.

Someone had opened the window downstairs, and it wasn't the cat.

Grace slammed the bathroom door and locked it. With her back pressed against the door, she dialed Conner's number.

Dear Lord, help him get here in time.

Chapter Six

"I'm pulling up the driveway now," Conner spoke to Grace on the phone, his words clipped. He canvassed the desolate landscape around the bed & breakfast. "Nothing visible out here. Everything okay on your end?"

He couldn't figure out why the alarm system hadn't gone off.

"Still safely locked in my bathroom." He didn't miss the trace of humor in her tone. It was a pleasant shift from the frantic call that had awoken him out of a sound sleep.

"I'm going to walk the perimeter." He climbed out of his truck and cringed when the cold air hit his exposed neck. "I'll see what's going on. Come downstairs in five minutes and open the back door." He didn't want to be distracted with the phone if someone was still out here.

When she didn't answer immediately, he added, "Okay?"

"Yes, thanks." The strain in her voice had been replaced by relief. For someone who claimed she didn't need anyone, it surprised him.

Conner slid the phone into the pocket of his bulky coat and lifted his flashlight. Out in the country on a cloudy night, it was dark like the bottom of a well. The beam of the flashlight bounced off the white snow. Footsteps dotted the driveway and the pathways to the house. He directed the light toward the barn and the other outbuildings. Footsteps led out to both. Nothing out of the ordinary, considering the horses had to be cared for by a young Amish man. According to Grace, he also did a few odd jobs around the bed & breakfast.

Conner walked toward the house, the beam from his flashlight leading the way. Grace had said a window in the sitting room had been opened. He made a wide berth around the house in an attempt to preserve evidence. The snow underneath the corner window had definitely been trampled. He slid out his phone, took off his gloves, and took a few snapshots of the boot prints. From first glance, the prints looked like they could be from any number of boots worn by half the men he knew, including him. The images would have to be enlarged and studied more closely.

The forecast was calling for more snow. Snow that would obscure the prints in no time at all.

He slid his phone back into his pocket and blew on his fisted hands to warm them up. On nights like this, he wondered why his dad hadn't retired to Florida by now. That was in Conner's twenty-year plan. Become sheriff. Retire. Move to Florida.

Conner stomped the snow from his feet on the back porch. "Come on, Grace." He quietly rapped on the door to avoid startling her. Just then, he heard her undoing the lock.

She pulled open the door, her hair mussed from sleep. She had pulled a fleece jacket over her pajamas.

"Are you okay?" Conner stepped into the small entryway.

"I guess I'm a trouble magnet."

Conner held up his hand. "Stay here. Let me check the house."

Grace's eyes flared wide. "You think he's still here?"

"Can't be too sure. Hold up." Conner did a quick canvass of the house, including the upstairs rooms that were often rented out to tourists during the warmer months.

When he came downstairs, he found Grace walking around the kitchen table, picking up the newspaper articles off the floor. Her long hair fell in a curtain, hiding her face. When she straightened, she tucked her hair behind her ear. She placed an article inside the manila folder. "I'm not sure if all the articles are still here." She flattened the paper with her hand. "Maybe this is what someone was looking for. It seems the wind from the open window blew them off the table." She bent over and picked up another one. "I wouldn't be able to tell you what's here or what's not. I haven't had time to study all of them."

A small piece of paper was tucked under the leg of the table. He leaned over and picked it up. The paper felt brittle. It was dated six months after Sarah Miller's murder. The first line read: *Local Amish family has yet to return after mother's murder.*

"Here's one more."

Grace took the piece of paper, glanced at it briefly,

then tucked it into the folder with the rest she had gathered. Her hip bumped the table, and the screen on her open laptop flickered to life. A photo of a smiling Grace beamed up at him from the screen. He caught sight of the title on the page: *Researching a Mother's Murder.*

His eyes met Grace's and she frowned. "My editor thinks this will go viral."

He furrowed his brow. "What do you think?"

Grace slowly sat down on the picnic-style bench and leaned back on the table. She threaded her hand through her hair and pressed her elbows together. "I haven't had a chance to think. When I arrived in Quail Hollow, I was sick as a dog. For the first few weeks, I was laid up in bed recovering from complications from my surgery. Once I was on the mend, I started to investigate Jason's accident, then my mom's murder, and—" she started to giggle and couldn't seem to stop "—it's been one thing after another."

She looked up and wiped the tears with the back of her knuckle. "Someone obviously doesn't want me to investigate something." She shrugged and took a calming breath to quell her giggle fit, the kind that struck when nothing was funny and you weren't supposed to laugh. "But what don't they want me to investigate? Jason's accident? Or my mother's murder?"

Conner sat on the bench next to Grace and nudged her shoulder. "We'll figure this out."

With a look of surprise glowing in her eyes, she opened her mouth to protest when he picked up her laptop from the table. "Nice photo."

"They caught me on a good hair day." She reached for the laptop.

"Wait. Can I read this?"

Her cynical expression said, "I don't know why you'd want to."

Conner skimmed through both the posts Grace had written and the teasers her editor had posted. It had specific details on her location as well as hints regarding her investigation. He tapped the screen and it flickered. "This right here makes you a sitting duck. This provides all the information someone needs if they want to hurt you."

Heat crawled up Grace's cheeks. She resented being treated like a teenager who had shared too much personal information on the internet. This was her job. Her job meant being visible online.

But had she foolishly put herself in jeopardy?

Normally when she was covering a story, she was staying in secure hotels, or she had long moved on to another town—another story—before her editor posted her work. Her extended stay in Quail Hollow and covering a story with a personal slant had been a game changer. Anyone with evil intent could know who she was and where she'd most likely be staying.

Annoyed and feeling more than foolish that she hadn't realized the risk, Grace leaned over and snapped the laptop closed. She took it from Conner's lap and placed it on the table a bit more roughly than she had intended.

"Most stories I write, I'm an anonymous reporter. I'm often done with the story and on to the next location before any information is posted online. People don't know where I'm staying." She pointed at the closed laptop for emphasis like Conner had. "My editor has insisted I post blogs until the bigger story is complete. I never felt like my safety was at risk." She pressed her palm to her neck and relished her cool fingers on her hot skin. "It's not like I can pick up and leave. I promised my sister I'd keep an eye on the bed & breakfast. It's the least I can do for her after all she's done for me."

"When will Heather and Zach be back?"

"The end of next week."

"You can't stay out here by yourself."

Instinctively, she bristled at his command. "I'll make sure I set the alarm this time." She dropped her hand and dipped her chin. "I must have forgotten to reset the alarm when I let Boots in." The green light glowing on the alarm display on the wall mocked her. "I don't know how I forgot. I needed to make sure Boots didn't go upstairs. I'm allergic. I mean, I'm okay, as long as cats don't roll around in my sheets." She smiled sheepishly, aware that she was talking too much.

As if sensing she had been called, Boots scooted out from wherever she had been hiding in all the commotion and brushed up against Grace's leg. If she wasn't worried about her eyes itching all day, she would pick up the cat and cuddle her. It wasn't Boots's fault that Grace had recklessly failed to reset the alarm. "I should have been more careful. I will be from now on."

Conner stood, planted his palms on the table and stared out over the yard. Grace turned to see whatever had captured his attention. Streaks of purple and pink stretched across the sky behind the barn. Today was going to be a very long day.

He pushed off the table and crossed his arms, ready to press his point. "I can't let you stay here alone."

Let her?

"I said I'd set the alarm. I won't forget again." She gritted her teeth to avoid saying something she knew she'd regret.

"Okay, you set the alarm," he said, his tone suggesting he was about to point out all the holes in her simple plan. "What do you do once someone breaks in again? The alarm's going off, blaring in the basement. You're out here alone. How long do you think it will take my department to respond? Do you know how many false alarms we get each day?"

"I'll call 9-1-1. Let them know it is an emergency," she bit out, frustrated that they even needed to have this conversation.

"Who knows what could happen while you're waiting for help?"

Grace fisted her hands. "I don't know. I'll get a gun!" she quickly added, determined not to be forced out of the bed & breakfast, despite her fear of guns. She had covered far too many stories where a gun in the wrong hands had changed someone's life with the pull of a trigger.

Conner closed the distance between them and glared down at her, using his height to intimidate her. "Do you know how to use a gun?"

"I can learn," she said with a trace of indignation, standing her ground.

"What do you do in the meantime?" Conner had a question for everything.

"I said I'd set the alarm."

"It seems we're talking in circles."

A quiet knock sounded on the door. Grace was relieved for the distraction and took a step toward it.

"Let me get it." Conner brushed past her and opened the door. A part of her wanted to bump him out of the way and tell him that it was *her* door. Someone had come to see *her.* A cooler head prevailed and she didn't act on her childish instincts, despite feeling humiliated.

Instead, she forced a cheery smile at the young Amish man standing at the door.

"Morning, Eli." Then, noticing the concerned look on his face, she added, "Is everything okay?" Perhaps he had seen something—or someone—in the barn.

"Um..." Eli palmed the top of his black knit winter hat. Blunt bangs jutted out, skimming the tops of his eyebrows. "Everything's okay. It's just..." His nose twitched. "Maybe..."

Grace slipped in front of Conner, thinking perhaps Eli was reluctant to talk to someone in law enforcement. Eli took a step backward, and Grace hoped she wouldn't have to follow him out into the snow. Clutching her collar closed, she blinked against the blowing snow. How did he work in these conditions? "Wait, Eli. Please come in. Conner is leaving if you'd prefer to talk in private."

"Um..." Something like regret, or maybe doubt, flashed across the man's face.

Curiosity had made Grace's nerve endings buzz, like when a story was about to break wide open.

"I'm not going anywhere," Conner muttered, standing directly behind her. Grace had to will herself not to nudge him with her elbow, fearing Eli would forget the whole thing and run off.

Eli flipped up his collar against the wind and tucked in his chin. Grace wished he'd come in the house already. "The horse needs to be fed." He mumbled a few words, then said, "I heard something."

"In the barn?" Conner's watchful gaze scanned the snow-covered field and stopped at the new barn.

"*Neh*, not in the barn."

"Come in." Grace pushed the door open wider, and Eli finally accepted her invitation. The Amish man didn't take off his hat or indicate that he had any intention of taking off his coat or coming in farther than the back mudroom. Conner must have also sensed the young man's apprehension, and he and Grace both waited for Eli to speak.

The worried young man studied the room, barely making eye contact. "I heard some guys talking at the hardware store yesterday." Eli bit his thumbnail, clearly more comfortable with the horses he tended than the people who owned them.

"Go on," Grace encouraged.

"They were laughing about the lady who got run down at the gas station."

Grace shot a look at Conner, who seemed more interested in watching Eli. Anticipation vibrated through her entire body.

"Do you know these guys?" Conner asked.

Eli shook his head. "*Neh.* I've seen them around, but I don't know them. The way they were talking, it made me wonder if they knew what happened to Miss Heather's car at the gas station."

"What else did you hear?" asked Grace.

"They said they heard the truck that hit you was parked behind Katy Weaver's barn."

"Katy? The young Amish woman who was hurt in

the accident after the drinking party?" Grace's heart raced in her ears.

"*Yah*, that's why I had to come forward. Katy's a *gut* friend of my sister's. Their family has been through a lot." Eli turned to Conner. "Maybe you can move the truck to spare the family finding it."

"Yes, absolutely," Conner said. "Are there any other males living in the Weaver household?"

Grace wondered if Conner's thoughts were heading down the same path as hers. Had someone in Katy's house been driving the truck? It all seemed a bit too coincidental.

"*Yah*, Katy's *dat* and her brother." Eli fisted and unfisted his gloved hands, before he stuffed them under his armpits and rocked up on the balls of his heavy work boots. "Levi."

A blanket of goosebumps raced across her arms, and her mouth grew dry.

Eli reached for the door handle, having said what he came to say. "I better feed the horses and get back home to my chores."

"Wait," Conner said, while Grace tried to process what she had heard. A part of her was ashamed that her brain automatically turned to crafting the first few lines of the post that would have her readers gasping: *Truck that narrowly missed me found behind the barn of the Amish girl fighting for her life after a separate accident.*

She stopped mentally composing her prose and said a quiet prayer that Katy's brother had nothing to do with the incident at the fuel pumps. They'd seemed like a close-knit family when she briefly met them, before they told her they wanted their privacy.

Grace ran a hand over her forehead. What purpose would it serve for Levi to hurt her? What was Grace missing about the night of the accident?

She snapped out of her wandering thoughts. "Would you recognize these guys from the hardware store if you saw them again?" she asked Eli.

"*Yah*, well, the way they were talking, it sounded like they were repeating what they had heard. Probably at school." He shrugged, the edges of his collar brushing against his cheeks. "I don't want to get into trouble. With everything else that's going on, I don't want to bring any shame to my family or my Amish neighbors." The Amish might not watch TV, but they had been well aware of the news reports that painted their community in an unflattering light.

"Thanks, Eli. You won't get into trouble," Grace said reassuringly.

The amount of information Grace gleaned because people failed to keep their mouths shut never ceased to amaze her. Far more criminals would get away with things if they didn't feel the need to boast, like whoever had bragged about parking the truck on the Weavers' property.

"I need to do my chores here and then get back home."

Conner nodded. "I appreciate your coming forward. I can't imagine it was easy."

"I had to. I saw you in the kitchen through the window. I hardly slept last night." Eli scratched his forehead under his bangs. "The outside world is evil." Then his eyes flared wide, realizing he may have offended them. "I hope they find whoever tried to hurt you." He flicked a look in her direction, then ducked his head and opened the door. Cold air filled the small space.

"Thank you, Eli," Grace quickly added, to reassure him. "You did the right thing." He took large steps across the deep snow to the barn. She closed the door and leaned against the cool wood, meeting Conner's gaze. "We have to go to the Weavers' house now. See if the truck is really there."

Chapter Seven

"Eli said the Weavers live three houses from the intersection of County and Pautler. It should be..." Grace tugged on her seat belt and leaned forward, straining to see past the wipers whooshing on high to keep up with the falling snow. Were they about to find out who rammed her car?

What if it's Katy's brother? The family would be devastated all over again.

"What are you going to say to Levi?" Grace asked, trying to focus on something productive and not all the what-ifs.

"Let's approach him and see what he knows about the truck." Conner adjusted the wipers to a lower speed.

"How likely is it that Levi's parents would allow him to store a truck at their home, even if it is his running-around years?" The irony that Grace had been born to Amish parents and had to ask Conner these questions wasn't lost on her.

Keeping his narrowed gaze on the disappearing road markers ahead, Conner said, "Some teens do drive cars, but their parents would hardly condone it by allowing them to keep the vehicle on their property. More often than not, if an abandoned vehicle is reported, it belongs to a young Amish man who has nowhere to park it but is eager to see what all the fuss is about. However, once they're baptized into the Amish faith, they have to give up cars and driving. It's a big decision for young adults to be baptized. In the end, most do choose to be baptized. It's what they know."

"That might explain why my dad knew how to drive when we left to live in Buffalo." She blinked the thought away, better left to explore on another day.

She pointed at a simple farmhouse with a long porch and no railings. "The Weaver house should be right here."

"Before we knock on the door," Conner said, "I want you to know I only agreed to bring you along because I didn't want you wandering over here alone."

She knew he didn't have to accommodate her. "I appreciate it. I'd really like to know who rammed my car—my sister's car—at the gas station."

"I need you to promise me you won't publish online any information we uncover here today until *after* we have things wrapped up."

"What constitutes wrapped up?" An edge of annoyance seeped into her tone. Some cases were never wrapped up, and she wasn't going to wait forever.

"Sit on the information until I give you the okay."

She leaned back in her seat, feeling like she was being confined by more than a seat belt. She worked alone. She preferred it that way. "I won't compromise the investigation," she said, unable to keep the defensive tone from her voice.

Conner nodded in agreement. He had called the tip

about the truck into the station, and the sheriff agreed that he could go to the Amish residence out of uniform in hopes they'd be more receptive to talk to him.

They parked in the Weavers' snow-covered driveway. A fresh footpath in the newly fallen snow connected the house to the barn. Even in the dead of winter, the animals needed to be cared for.

"Do you think Katy's parents saw the truck? Where did Eli say it was parked?" Grace wrapped her hand around the door release. "Behind the barn, right?"

"Yes, that's what he heard. And I doubt the Weavers know it's there otherwise they would have had it removed." Conner flipped up the collar on his coat, bracing for the cold. "Let me do the talking. See what's going on."

She opened her mouth to protest, and he cut her a sideways look. "Work with me, please."

Grace nodded. She decided she'd get more information if Conner was on her side. Up until now, the sheriff's department had blocked all her attempts at getting any information that wasn't already public knowledge.

"You ready?" he asked.

Grace wrapped her scarf around her neck and made sure her hat covered her ears. She'd never get used to this weather. "Ready."

They both climbed out of his truck. The snow made a squeaky, crunching noise under their hurried footsteps. Neither seemed willing to prolong this errand. Part of Grace hoped they found the truck—it would be a big lead—and another part of her prayed the Weaver family didn't have to face any more bad news.

"Before we upset the family, let's wander around behind the barn and see if we can find the truck. If there's nothing there, we can get out of here." Conner gently took her by the elbow.

He had read her mind. She had no interest in causing the family any more distress.

They moved past the well-worn path between the house and barn, through snowdrifts up to her knees. "Remind me why people live here?" she joked between chattering teeth.

A white cloud of vapor exhaled from his nose. He muttered something about taking up skiing.

When they reached the corner of the barn, they were met by a field of pristine snow. Grace fell back on the heels of her boots, and a clump of snow slipped into her boot. She tugged on the ends of her scarf, pulling it tighter. "There's nothing here." Grace wasn't sure what to feel beyond a growing eagerness to slip off her boots and warm her feet by the stove.

She sniffed. "Maybe Eli misunderstood what he overheard. We should talk to him again." She shoved her gloved hands into the pockets of her jacket. A snowflake landed on her eyelash and she blinked it away.

"There's another outbuilding across the field." Conner pointed to a dilapidated shed further back on the property.

Grace groaned. "The snow has to be two feet with drifts." She lifted one boot, then the other, already imagining her toes turning into ice chunks inside her boots—technically, her sister's boots. She hoped to never have a need for winter gear again.

"I'll go. Wait here or—" he handed her the keys "—inside the truck. Stay warm." Without waiting for an answer, Conner strode toward the building that had seen better days. It was the only other spot on the property where someone could hide a truck.

Disheartened, Grace turned to head toward Conner's truck, already envisioning the warm heat pumping from the vents. She didn't relish wet socks, but it'd be better than frozen toes. When she passed the barn, a young Amish man about Eli's age came out, a curious look on his clean-shaven face.

Levi Weaver.

Grace wasn't sure who was more surprised. A look of worry flashed in his eyes. Before he had a chance to speak, she said, "I'm sorry, I didn't mean to surprise you. You're Katy's brother." She had met him previously and he had chased her away. She hoped time had made him more receptive to talk to her.

"*Yah.*" The young man looked around, sensing that she wasn't alone. "Did something happen? My parents are inside. They were going to visit Katy today until the snow came."

"No, no..." She drew in a quick breath and measured her words. Her limbs instantly went heavy. He must have thought she'd come here with news of his sister's condition. She had tremendous empathy for the young man. She knew what it was like to have your family ripped apart by tragedy.

But what if he wasn't innocent?

Grace pointed toward the footsteps in the snow. Conner had disappeared behind the shed at this point. "Captain Gates is looking to see if a truck is parked behind the shed. Do you know anything about that?"

The young man fidgeted with the cuffs on his coat. "*Neh.*" He lifted his gaze to his home. His family was inside. Everyone except his sister. What had made him so jittery all of a sudden?

"Several nights ago," she started, "I went to the gas station to talk to someone about the party that took place the night your sister was injured. I wanted to find out what happened. Someone rammed my car with a big truck." She took a step closer to him. His downcast eyes were hidden under his long bangs made straighter by his snug-fitting knit hat. Snowflakes landed and melted from the heat of his head.

"My sister has been in the hospital ever since her accident."

"How is she doing?" Grace asked, encouraged that he was opening up.

A sad smile curved his mouth as he continued to study the snow. Soon he'd get married and a long beard would cover his jaw. "The doctors are encouraged. She woke up last night."

"That's wonderful." Grace reached out to touch his arm in a show of support, then let it drop, deciding it might not be welcomed.

"They're not sure when she'll be able to come home."

"I'll keep her in my prayers."

Levi finally lifted his weary eyes to meet hers. Didn't he believe she'd pray for her?

"Had you gone out the night of your sister's accident?"

"*Yah*, I took my courting wagon to the singing." Grace imagined it was exactly as it sounded. He hadn't been with his sister because he had been bringing a girl home. His words dripped with regret. "My sister had dropped off her friends, two sisters who live not far from the accident. It was a very *gut* thing they weren't hurt, too." His voice grew soft.

"I'm so sorry." The pain etched in his features broke her heart.

A dark intensity suddenly lit his eyes. "You need to leave before my parents see you."

"Okay." Grace turned to see Conner plodding through the snow toward her. From this distance, she couldn't tell whether or not he had found anything. "Here's Captain Gates now. We'll leave. We don't mean to cause you any pain. If you want to talk in the future, I'm staying at the Quail Hollow Bed & Breakfast."

Breathing heavily, Conner reached the snow-packed clearing where Grace stood with Katy's brother. Clumps of snow had attached to his pants. He gave her a subtle nod, indicating that he had found the truck. Her adrenaline spiked and she wanted to ask Levi a million questions. Yet she was empathetic to the young man's vulnerability and held back. "Captain Gates, this is Katy's brother, Levi."

Conner stuck out his hand, and the Amish man glanced at it, clearly uncomfortable. Realizing he wasn't going to take it, Conner slipped his hand back into his pocket. "Son, do you know how the truck ended up behind the building back there?"

The young man's eyes widened. *"Neh."*

"Did you see it?"

He shook his head, crossed his arms and seemed to sink deep into the collar of his coat. "We don't have a reason to go back there. That's the old barn. It's falling apart. We have this new one right here."

"Levi, I know you've had a tough time of it. If you *do* know anything about the truck parked on your family's property, you need to tell me." A muscle twitched in Conner's jaw. "Maybe we can clear this up without getting your parents involved. They've been through enough."

Conner looked into the fearful eyes of the young Amish man. His sister was in a coma because of Jason, his cousin's son. The Amish only wanted to live peacefully, yet the outside world—Conner's world—was forever encroaching on their attempts at a peaceful existence.

"If you know something," Conner repeated, "you can talk to us."

"I've explained that to him," Grace said. "Right, Levi? You know you can confide in us."

Conner caught the grief-stricken expression on Levi's face before the Amish man bowed his head to hide the emotions playing across his features. Conner's mind flashed back to the photo his father had kept of Sarah Miller's three young daughters, taken surreptitiously a few days after their mother's murder. Conner had never seen such a quiet display of unbearable grief as he had in the portrait of the three motherless girls. Perhaps until today. Conner's father had claimed that photo motivated him to keep pursuing the case until time and lack of leads made it fruitless.

"How is your sister doing?" Conner asked.

"She's awake and doing better." He kicked the edge of the snow.

"That's good to hear." He hadn't realized how good until a sense of relief flooded him. "How do your parents get back and forth to Buffalo, to the hospital?"

"They hire a driver."

"The weather is supposed to clear up. Maybe I can drive your family to the hospital later."

Levi shook his head. "That's okay. I don't think my parents would want to take a ride from law enforcement. We like to stay separate."

"That's harder to do more and more." Conner tried to connect with the young man, who seemed to be standing on the edge of making a decision, one that would keep him among the Amish or one that would forever separate him from his family. Grace touched Conner's arm sympathetically and stepped away, allowing him to try to talk with the young man without her hovering.

"I found a truck behind the shed. Any idea how it got there? I'll keep it in confidence."

"I've been explaining…" The frustration was evident in Levi's tone. "After my sister's accident, the bishop spoke to us all at Sunday service. He said the youth of this community are making all the Amish look bad. If anyone is caught drinking or breaking the rules of the *Ordnung*, they will be punished." His lower lip quivered. "The Amish have never condoned this type of behavior, but now there is no tolerance."

"I thought the Amish were all about forgiveness." Conner watched the young man carefully.

"The leaders are frustrated. They feel like they've lost control." Levi ran a gloved hand under his nose. "I can't take that chance of bringing shame to my family."

Levi wasn't going to give him anything worth pressing for. Conner glanced down the driveway and saw the engine running on his truck. At least Grace was warm.

Conner shifted to brace himself against the wind and jammed his hands into his coat pocket. "I'm going to share something with you." He took a calming breath. "I'm Jason Klein's cousin, and my entire family feels horrible that your sister was hurt in the accident."

Levi cut a look toward Conner, then looked away.

"Jason's dad was killed last year while serving in the army. I was supposed to look out for the kid. I failed him."

Levi shifted from one foot to the other.

"And I failed your family." Conner fought to keep his voice from shaking. "I know you're cold." He glanced toward Levi's house. "I'm guessing you don't want to go inside to talk."

Levi shook his head. "My parents are in there." He ran a hand over his mouth.

"The sheriff's department is going to have to tow the truck off your parents' property, maybe after the snow melts." Conner hadn't thought that far ahead. "We can talk to your parents. I'll assure them someone else dumped it there and that you had nothing to do with it." Conner was pretty good at reading people, and he suspected Levi was innocent in all this.

Levi let out a long, frustrated breath. "I was at that party with the kid—your cousin—who crashed into my sister's wagon," he muttered, his words almost lost on a gust of wind.

"Did you hang out with him?" Conner's heart beat wildly in his ears. This was not at all what he had expected.

Levi stared at him for a long moment, his nose growing red from the relentless wind. He chipped away at the flattened snow with the tip of his black boot. "Some guys were arguing with him at the party. They were blaming Jason for getting them in trouble. Jason left the party pretty quick."

"Trouble? What kind of trouble?"

"I'm not really sure. They were making pig noises."

Like he's a squealer? A million thoughts pinged around Conner's brain.

"Do you know those kids?"

"Yeah, from around."

Conner didn't know if it mattered. Didn't know if it played into Jason's death. Just because a few guys had words at a party didn't mean anything, necessarily. Conner scrubbed a gloved hand across his face. He and Grace had built the frame and grouped like colors, yet the final puzzle pieces didn't quite fit.

The tips of his ears stung from the cold.

"Listen, I'm not sure a tow truck can access the back of your property. Not until spring." He pulled out a piece of paper from his pocket. "I have the registration number of the truck. The sheriff's department will be able to determine who owns it. If you'd like, I can talk to your parents. Tell them it was abandoned. This way you won't get in trouble with them or the leaders."

Levi glanced toward the house wearily. "I'll talk to them." He shuddered. It was far too cold to be standing out here talking. "You think that's the truck that tried to run over your friend?"

Conner tipped his head. "There's some back-end damage. Could be."

Levi nodded tightly.

"Everything will be okay." Conner turned to walk away when Levi started to say something.

Conner turned back.

"Jason and I were friends. We met last summer while working for Able."

His young cousin had dug post holes all summer long while working for a fence company. "You worked for Able Fencing, too?" Conner felt like he was getting more bits and pieces of information the longer he talked to Levi. It would be his job to put the information together.

Levi nodded, and all the color drained from his face. "*Yah*, Jason was a *gut* kid. He didn't drink or do drugs."

Conner froze, the new information jolting his system. "Are you sure?" It didn't make sense, anymore than the final report that speculated Jason had taken a handful of prescription drugs during what kids called pharming parties. Conner could hardly believe Jason would participate in such risky behavior. But blood results didn't lie.

"*Yah*, we were hanging out that night. He only came to the party because a girl he liked was there. We had some hot chocolate, that's all. He told me he wasn't feeling well all of a sudden. When he was heading to the truck, some guys started yelling at him and chasing him. He tore out of the party right quick." Levi kicked the snow, and chunks shot in different directions. "One of the guys yelling at him was the mayor's son."

"Bradley Poissant? Are you sure? Jason and Brad have been friends since preschool."

"It was him. I've seen the kid around." That seemed to be the standard answer. Quail Hollow wasn't that big.

"But you don't know what they were arguing about?"

Levi slowly shook his head. "Look, I have to go in."

"All right then. Thanks for taking the time to talk to me." Conner walked back to his truck while Levi jogged toward his house.

Grace was tracking Levi's movements when Conner climbed back into the warmth of his truck. He was still processing the latest bit of news. Bradley and Jason had been arguing the night of Jason's fatal accident. Why hadn't Bradley told him? Perhaps guilt that their lifetime friendship had ended after a fight?

Conner tugged off his gloves and dragged a hand through his hair, shaking off the snow. He grabbed his cell phone out of the drink holder in the console between them and punched in a few numbers. "I need to know who registered that vehicle." He gave the deputy the registration information and hung up.

"Is it the truck that crashed into me?" Grace asked.

"It has damage."

"If it walks like a duck, talks like a duck..." She smiled wearily. He stared back, still trying to figure out why Jason was arguing with his best friend the night he died.

Grace shifted in her seat. "What happened back there? You and Levi seemed to have a pretty intense conversation."

Conner stared straight ahead, watching the dizzying swirl of snow. "Levi told me that Jason didn't drink or do drugs." This matched what Jason had tried to tell him the night Conner broke up the bonfire. He loosened his collar. When pressed, didn't most kids claim they didn't drink?

"What? How is that possible?" Grace had read the reports. "Perhaps he had a low threshold."

"I don't know. Levi claimed he wasn't taking drugs

or drinking alcohol that night. Levi said he left after saying he didn't feel well."

"What are you thinking?"

He shifted in his seat, avoiding her eyes. Was he taking a leap? "What if someone drugged him?"

"You mean, spiked his drink? He wasn't drinking."

"Levi said they had hot chocolate."

"Who would do that to him?"

Conner shook his head. None of this made sense. He'd been arguing with his best friend. No, none of this made sense. "I don't know."

His phone rang and he jumped. The dispatcher. "That vehicle is registered to a Paul Handler on Oak Grove."

"Thanks." He ended the call.

"You have a name?"

"Yeah."

Grace tapped the dash. "Let's go."

"I need to take you home."

"Aren't you going to take me with you? Keep me out of trouble?" She was hard to say no to.

"Yeah, I suppose you're right." Despite not wanting to put Grace in the center of his investigation, he preferred to keep an eye on her.

"Maybe I can ID him. I saw his profile at the gas station." Even Conner knew that was a stretch.

Before he lost his nerve and came to his senses, Conner jammed the gear into Drive. "Let's see about the owner of that truck."

Chapter Eight

Conner and Grace had almost reached the address of the truck owner when his cell phone buzzed. He glanced down and stifled a groan. The sheriff. His boss. He let it ring a few more times, debating if this phone call would somehow deter their little visit.

"You going to get that?" Grace asked, curiosity lighting her eyes.

Conner twisted his lips as if to say, "Maybe, maybe not." Who was he kidding? Of course he was going to get it, but he had to decide how he was going to handle it first. Letting out a long breath between tight lips, Conner grabbed the phone from his cup holder and swiped his thumb across the screen. "Sheriff." He forced a cheery tone that sounded stiff and insincere.

"How'd things go at the Weavers?" The men tended to dispense with formalities, getting right to the point.

"Fine."

"That's it? Fine? Care to elaborate? I hear you got a lead on the hit-and-run from the gas station."

"Yes, we did. I traced the owner. I'm at their address now."

"You're still in plain clothes, right?"

Conner rubbed his jaw with his palm. "Yeah." He was unable to hide the skepticism from his voice. His boss had given him the okay to stop by the Weavers' in plain clothes, hoping it would be less intimidating for the folks who didn't care to talk to law enforcement, even in the best of circumstances.

"Report for your shift, then track down the owner of the truck." The clock on the dash told him he was fifteen minutes past the start of his shift.

"I'm already here. I need to talk to the owner before word gets out. I want to catch him off guard. See what his excuse is." He thought back to the Amish man seeking him out this morning at the bed & breakfast. It was only a few hours ago, yet it felt like a lot longer, perhaps because now he had new information about his cousin. Information about him not feeling well prior to leaving the party. About not drinking. Conner shook his head, trying to clear it. He hadn't had time to process all the jumbled information and what it meant, if anything.

No matter how all this unfolded, at the end of the day, Jason would still be dead. The familiar fist of grief sat like a rock in his chest.

"See you in ten," the sheriff said, still pressing the issue that he report to the station immediately.

"I'm sitting in front of the residence now," he repeated to the sheriff, giving Grace an exasperated look. "Let me shake a few trees. See what falls out."

The sheriff's impatient sigh sounded over the line, and Conner imagined him leaning way back in his leather chair with one hand behind his head, his feet perched on the corner of the desk. "You got the reporter with you?"

Conner turned away from Grace, as if that would make a difference. "What's this about?" A sure way to act innocent: answering a question with another question.

"I hear you're getting chummy with her. Don't do anything stupid to jeopardize your career."

Gritting his teeth, Conner adjusted the vent on the dash to clear the frost from the windows. No, he didn't think he was getting "chummy" with the reporter. But he was limited in what he could say with her sitting inches away.

"Your silence speaks volumes." Conner imagined his boss's chair crashing forward, his feet slamming onto the floor and his face growing red with rage.

"Look, I have to go. I'll report back in after I talk to the truck's owner." Conner swiped the red button on his phone while the sheriff was still talking. It sounded like, "Who's the owner?" Conner would deal with the repercussions of hanging up on the sheriff later.

Grace casually gestured to his phone. "What was that all about?"

"Nothing."

She frowned, not exactly convinced.

"One problem at a time," Conner muttered, turning his focus on the situation at hand.

The Handlers' small white ranch house was ahead. His boss wasn't going to be happy with him for going against his request. It was a request, right? Not an order? He ignored the band of hesitation constricting his chest. Mentally, he was already calculating how much vacation he might be able to take if he needed to do some digging on his own. He had a sense the sheriff was about to put him on desk duty. And even if his boss did find the humor in his subordinate hanging up on him, Conner needed to be able to follow up on some things without the sheriff breathing down his neck.

There was no way Conner could give up exploring the path he was already on, because in the short time he had gotten to know Grace, he knew *she* wouldn't be easily deterred.

"I'm going with you," Grace said, hopping out of the truck before Conner even dared make the suggestion.

"And I'm doing the talking."

She twisted her lips in a wry expression. He'd accept that as agreement, but had his doubts even before they climbed the front steps of the Handlers' porch.

Conner lifted his hand to knock when the door flung open. Jenny Handler, a woman in her midforties, came up short, her purse swinging on the sleeve of her puffy winter jacket. "Oh." Surprise lit her eyes. Obviously, she had been on her way out and hadn't expected visitors to be standing on the other side of the door.

"Captain Gates." She tilted her head in recognition, and deep ridges lined her forehead. "Is something wrong?" She glanced over her shoulder, and her expression softened, perhaps after she had a chance to realize two things: her son was home and Conner was dressed in plain clothes, indicating he was unlikely to deliver bad news.

Maybe. Maybe not.

"Hi, Jenny. Is your husband around?" His name was on the truck's registration, after all, not hers.

Jenny leaned back on her heels and a cheerless smile slanted her lips. "You haven't heard?"

Conner frowned. "Clue me in."

"Paul took a job in Buffalo last summer."

"Ah, that's tough. Maybe the economy will pick up here soon."

She ran her hand down her fuzzy scarf. "Not sure it really matters." He didn't want to read more into that than he had to. Her marriage was none of his business. Right now, he needed to find out why her husband's truck was parked on the Weavers' property with damage consistent with a hit-and-run.

"What's going on?" Her gaze drifted to Grace.

"Where's Paul's pickup?"

"That heap of junk? Out in his workshop, I guess." She paused a moment and stared at him. "What's going on?"

"We found a truck registered to your husband on the Weavers' property."

"The family of that poor Amish girl who was in that horrible accident? I don't understand." She loosened the scarf from around her neck and pulled off her knit cap. Wisps of blond hair stood straight up from the static. "Come in." She waved to them. "Charlie!" she hollered, clearly annoyed. "Get in here." She smoothed her hair and glanced expectantly toward a short hallway. "Charlie!" she hollered again. "Now!"

Then, turning toward her guests, "My son has a late start to school because his first two classes are free." Conner smiled. At this exact moment, he wasn't worried if Charlie was truant; he wanted to know if he had used his father's truck.

Muffled grumbling preceded a door opening. A young kid appeared, pulling a sweatshirt over his bare chest. "What, Mom? What's wrong?" The teenager squinted at the three adults standing in the living room with the look of a person who had stepped out into the bright sun after an afternoon matinee.

"Hi, Charlie," Conner said. "I'm Captain Gates. This is Grace Miller. She was the woman nearly run down at the gas station the other night." Conner was watching the young man's expression carefully, but he took that exact moment to bend over and adjust his sock. Conner waited for him to straighten before continuing. "We found your father's truck."

Charlie's eyebrows scrunched up, and he shrugged. "Dad's truck?" He turned slowly, still seemingly struggling to come out of a dream state. "Isn't Dad's truck in his workshop out back?"

Conner was pretty good at reading people, and nothing about this kid screamed "liar." The kid was on edge, however. Maybe he was hiding something.

"Did you take out your dad's truck?" his mother asked, frustration weighing heavily on her slumped shoulders. "Please don't tell me you took his truck out and crashed it. I'll never hear the end of it. You know how your father is."

"No way. I didn't, Mom."

The kid was afraid of his father and wouldn't borrow his truck, even if his dad had taken a job in Buffalo and hadn't bothered to come home to know the difference.

Charlie pushed back the hood of his sweatshirt and scrubbed his cropped hair. "I don't understand. Where did you find the truck?" He turned to his mom. "I thought Dad had the Chevy?"

"He does."

"Do you know Levi Weaver?" Conner asked.

"The Amish kid?" He shrugged. "Yeah, I've met

him around." All the teenagers seemed to know all the other teens in town from "around."

"The truck was parked behind a run-down shed on their farm." Conner let the back of his hand brush Grace's, thankful she was allowing him to take the lead. She didn't make any indication that she recognized the kid as the driver of the truck that smashed into her. That would have been a long shot, anyway.

"How'd it get there?" Charlie's entire face scrunched up, as if he were trying to remember the formula to a complicated math problem.

"How many people knew the truck was parked in the workshop?" If someone knew Jenny's husband had left town, they could have taken the truck easily. Someone could borrow it without worrying about it being missed, for a while, anyway.

Charlie's eyes widened. If he had remembered something, he quickly tried to hide it by lifting his fist to his mouth and coughing.

"Did you remember something, Charlie?" Grace asked.

The young man turned to his mother with a hangdog expression. This was obviously a kid used to working his mom over to get his way.

"What is it, Charlie? Come on, spit it out." His mother unzipped her coat while speaking in a slow, methodical manner, as if she had grown weary of being a single parent to a teenage boy.

"It's nothing," he said through gritted teeth. Was he hoping his mother would "get it" without him saying whatever it was?

His mother took a step forward and turned around to stand next to her son. She put a hand on his back, clearly indicating she was on his side no matter what happened. "Charlie's a good kid. He has a scholarship to college this fall." She had the look of a woman who had already lost too much. "Please, he's on the right path. I don't think he'd do anything to screw that up." Conner wondered if this was wishful thinking on her part.

"A scholarship. That's great." Conner smiled at the young man, wondering if perhaps Charlie had gotten in over his head on something and needed an ally to open up to. Conner had gone away to school thinking he wanted to escape his small-town roots, only to return and follow in his father's footsteps. "What college are you going to?"

"University at Buffalo." The young man stuffed his hands deep into the pockets of his jeans, probably the same pair he had dropped on the floor next to his bed the night before.

"Any chance you let one of your friends borrow your dad's truck?" Conner used his most reassuring tone.

When Charlie didn't answer, his mother glared at him. "You let one of your friends borrow the truck? What were you thinking?"

"No!" The exasperation in Charlie's voice might have been a bit over the top to be genuine.

"Who knew the truck was there?" Conner kept his tone even. The kid needed to feel like he was on his side.

Charlie leaned back on the arm of the overstuffed couch. Apparently, he couldn't tell the truth with his mom standing next to him. "I had a few friends over last weekend. We were hanging out in the barn. That's where my dad has his workshop."

"What? Why would you hang out there? All your father's stuff..." A flicker of realization widened her eyes. "Aw, why, Charlie? You could lose your scholarship if they find out you're drinking."

"I don't think that could happen," Charlie said. "Besides, I *wasn't* drinking."

His mother looked like she was going to grind her teeth to nubs in an effort to keep quiet.

Charlie jerked one finger in her direction. "One beer. That's hardly anything."

Jenny put a hand over her mouth. "Charlie! Is it worth it?" She held out her open palm toward their visitors, indicating it obviously wasn't. "You might not lose a scholarship for drinking, but when teens drink, they do stupid things."

"Mom, you're being dramatic. One beer is nothing. Half my friends are—" He cut himself off short. No teenager was going to rat out his friends in front of the sheriff's department. Conner didn't need him to. He knew what went on at those parties. As an officer, he had broken up countless parties, including that one at Jason's house not long before he died.

"Were any of these kids at your house also at the party the night—" Grace lowered her voice, probably out of consideration for Conner, but it still stung "—Jason died?"

Charlie shrugged again and mumbled something that sounded a lot like, "I don't know."

"Give us a few names." Conner crossed his arms, trying to act casual, yet authoritative enough to demand some answers. What if one of these kids who had borrowed the Handlers' truck had tried to hurt Grace because she was getting too close to what really happened at the party the night Jason died? With the brand-new information from Levi that Jason wasn't drinking that night, it made it more imperative that Conner find out what really happened. *Had* someone drugged Jason's drink? If so, why? Had it been intentional, or had Jason picked up a drink intended for someone else?

A million questions swirled around his head, hurting his brain. He had to get to the bottom of it, for Jason. For Jason's mother. And for his own peace of mind.

"No one did anything. Come on," Charlie protested. Something akin to fear flashed in his eyes. What was he afraid of?

"How about I say a few names, and you tell me if they were drinking in your father's workshop?" Conner stuffed his hands into his jacket pockets, trying to act casual.

Charlie rolled his eyes in typical teenage fashion.

Conner made up a name and Charlie frowned. "No. I don't even know that kid. Does he live around here?" His tone suggested he thought Conner wasn't right in the head.

Conner didn't answer. "How about Bradley Poissant?"

"The mayor's son?" Jenny asked. She glared at her son. "Are you guys still friends?"

Charlie lifted one shoulder in a universal "whatever" gesture.

"Was Bradley there?" Levi had mentioned that Bradley and Jason were arguing the night Jason died. It didn't make sense. Bradley was a good kid. And the two teens were friends.

Charlie pushed off the arm of the couch and pleaded to his mom. “We weren’t doing *anything*.”

“Answer Captain Gates’s question.” Jenny planted her fists on her hips. “I’m not fooling around.”

“Yeah, Bradley and a few other guys were here.”

Conner stepped forward and clapped Charlie’s shoulder. “Okay, thanks for being honest. I have no interest in getting you in trouble with your mom. If there’s anything you need to tell me, tell me now.”

“Charlie?” his mother silently urged her son to come clean with the officer. A genuine look of fear haunted her eyes.

“No, there’s nothing else. Bradley was here with a few of his buddies. They’re jerks, anyway. I haven’t hung out with them since.”

Jenny pulled her arms out of her winter coat and tossed it on the couch. She tugged at the collar of her sweater. “Charlie, I can’t be at your side 24/7. You’re going away to college. You have to be responsible. You’ve got to…” She fisted her hands and clenched her jaw. She turned to Conner. “What happens now?”

“Do you know who took the truck? Where did you keep the keys?”

“My dad always kept them in a key box in the workshop. And no, I don’t know. If one of the guys took it, they did it without me knowing.”

“Okay,” Conner said, deciding to let that rest for now. “The sheriff’s department will tow the truck off the Weavers’ property as soon as they can get back there. See if the back-end damage matches the accident.”

“That’s fine. I don’t care about the stupid truck. If Paul wants it, I’ll tell him he can pick it up at the collision shop." Jenny scratched her head, as if trying to scrub the thought of her husband out of it. She took a step toward the door. "I have to get to work."

"I appreciate your time," Conner said, then turned to Charlie and handed him his business card. "If you think of anything else, call me."

Charlie took the card. A doubtful expression was plain on his face.

Once outside, Grace turned to Conner. "This Bradley Poissant's name has come up more than once. Maybe we should talk to him."

Unease sloshed in his gut. "I know Mayor Poissant and his family. They're good people. I can't believe he'd ram your car. It doesn't seem like him."

"People aren't always what they seem." She looked at him, and as much as he hated to acknowledge it, he agreed with her.

Chapter Nine

Later that afternoon, Grace watched Ruthie lumber down the stairs and lower herself into a rocking chair. "This baby can't come soon enough."

"How are you feeling?" Grace leaned forward on the matching rocker in the Hershbergers' sitting room. A cozy fire made her forget about the cold outside.

A hint of guilt reminded her that she hadn't been exactly honest with Conner. She had fully anticipated rereading all the articles surrounding her mother's murder in the *Quail Hollow Gazette* and spending the day at home. However, she'd stumbled upon the name Maryann Hershberger in one of the articles. Turned out Heather's right-hand employee at the bed & breakfast was none other than her daughter. Ruthie had stopped over to the bed & breakfast before Heather went on her honeymoon. Her sister had explained how Ruthie was the daughter of one of their mom's good friends from years ago. Once she had this piece of information, she had to take a drive to their home. Thankfully, her brother-in-law's truck made it out of the snowy yard.

"I'm doing fine. I'm curious how you're getting

along at the bed & breakfast. It's a shame I couldn't fill in while your sister is away." She smiled. "This baby has other ideas." Ruthie had the glow of a woman excited about her first child.

"It's really no problem. It's given me a chance to get to know Quail Hollow a little bit better."

"You should stick around until spring. Then you'll really get a feel for the area. Everyone's cooped up inside now." Maryann, Ruthie's mother, didn't look up from her needlework, carefully drawing the needle and thread through the fabric.

Grace couldn't imagine herself in this small town much beyond her sister's return from her honeymoon. She couldn't even stay at the bed & breakfast for the afternoon without getting antsy.

"Ruthie's been spending more of her days here than at home," Maryann continued. "I think she's afraid of going into labor and not being able to track down her husband on one of his jobs."

"He's a handyman," Ruthie said proudly. "He did a lot of the work on the bed & breakfast."

"It's beautiful." Grace cleared her throat. "I hate to intrude on your peaceful afternoon," said Grace, finally deciding to broach the topic on her mind, "but I was looking into my mom's death." *Death* sounded less bleak than *murder*. Everyone died. Only in truly awful cases did death come in the form of murder.

Maryann's head snapped up from her needlework. Then she immediately dipped it back down and seemed to struggle to get the needle through the fabric. Despite the older woman's obvious distress, Grace pressed on. "I read your name in one of the articles in the newspaper."

"I was a little girl then," Ruthie said, with an air of confusion. Then her eyes opened wide. "Oh, you mean *Mem. Mem* and Sarah were friends. Right?"

"Yah," Maryann said, a distant quality to her voice, perhaps lost in a pleasant memory. "We were." She smiled ruefully. "You and your sister resemble your *mem*."

"I regret that we never had any photos of her to remember her by," Grace said, wishing the room wasn't quite so warm.

"We don't believe in having photos. Yet the tourists don't seem to think anything of it nowadays. Always taking them." The older woman said *nowadays* with a longing for days gone by. The outside world was speeding up in a way Grace suspected Maryann could never imagine.

Grace blinked, thinking back to the photo someone had taken from a distance of her little family after their mother had been murdered. Even before the explosion of online news, local newspapers prided themselves on visual images. A photo like that would have sold a lot of papers.

The juxtaposition of the quiet Amish countryside with murder. The three grief-stricken girls left behind.

A familiar nagging worked at Grace, as if she were poking at a hornets' nest better left undisturbed. What did she hope to achieve, anyway?

"We were discouraged from talking to anyone back then," Maryann said. "The outsiders flooded Quail Hollow." She grew still. "What does the article say?"

"That you and my mom were friends. That you couldn't believe she was gone."

"Is that all?"

"Yes."

"True enough. I still can't believe she's gone, even after all these years." Maryann shook her bonneted head.

Grace opened her mouth to ask a question that had been on her mind, when Emma, Maryann's seventeen-year-old daughter, her youngest, came in through the kitchen and stomped her snowy boots on the floor mat.

"The greenhouse is okay." She smiled at her mom as she took off her coat. "We worried the heavy snow would crack the glass."

"Denki," Maryann said. "Now come in and get warm. This is Grace Miller, Heather's sister."

"Nice to meet you," Emma said shyly.

Ruthie groaned. "Emma, will you help me back upstairs? I need to lie down." She glanced at Grace. "Sorry, I'm not very good company."

"Oh, please, don't worry." Grace smiled, encouraged that maybe Maryann would be more receptive to talking about Sarah without her daughters around.

"Yah." Emma hung her coat on a hook near the fireplace to dry. "Want me to read to you some?"

Grace smiled, pondering a different life. Life with a *mem*, *dat* and two sisters in the quiet Amish community. A completely different upbringing from the one she'd had. Instead of reading books to each other, Heather, Grace and Rose tended to park themselves in front of the TV with frozen dinners while their dad picked up a second shift at the factory.

Emma held Ruthie's arm, helping her up the stairs. "Take care, Ruthie. I can't wait to meet that baby of yours."

Ruthie groaned and laughed. "Me, too. Me, too."

Grace rocked back and forth slowly, settling into the quietness of the place. For some reason, she felt content here with Maryann, whereas she was unsettled alone at the B&B. Perhaps she needed company.

"You're looking into Sarah's death?" Maryann asked, surprising Grace.

"I was looking into the underage drinking party. Then I got a little sidetracked when retired Sheriff Gates mentioned a relentless reporter who had covered my mom's death."

Maryann nodded. "I remember her. I shouldn't have spoken to her. She approached me in town. I was grief-stricken."

"You spoke from the heart. You and my mother were friends. And because of that long-ago conversation, I'm now talking to one of my mom's friends."

"True enough. Your *mem* and I *were* friends. *Gut* friends."

"Did my mom ever mention anything strange or unusual happening prior to her death? Something that had her worried?"

Sometimes people didn't realize they had valuable information. But Grace knew it was a long shot that Maryann would provide any new information after all these years.

"The sheriff asked me a lot of questions after Sarah's death." Maryann's eyes grew red-rimmed. "I was young. The loss was devastating."

"I'm sure you've thought a lot about my mom over the years. Did you ever remember something later that maybe was of significance?" Goosebumps blanketed Grace's skin, the same reaction she always got when she was about to get a huge lead in an investigation. It was nothing concrete. Just a feeling.

Maryann tilted her head, seemingly trying to discern if her daughters were within earshot.

Grace glanced up the stairs. She could hear the distant even cadence of a voice, someone reading. "Your daughters are close."

Maryann smiled sadly. "Your *mem* was like a sister to me. She was an only child, which is a rare thing among Amish families. We spent a lot of time together."

"What can you tell me about my mom? I hardly remember her."

Maryann gave Grace a sympathetic smile. "She was beautiful. Like you."

Grace leaned back in the rocking chair and let Maryann talk. The Amish woman touched the sides of her bonnet, a nervous gesture. "Before she married your *dat*, she had another suitor."

Grace smiled, having a hard time imagining her mom, younger than she was now, dating. "Do the Amish date a lot?" The longer Grace was in Quail Hollow, the more she realized how much she didn't know about her ancestry.

"He wasn't Amish." Maryann set aside her needlework and folded her hands in her lap.

Grace stifled a gasp. "Really?" What little fabric of her mother's life she thought she knew began to fray. A thread poked out at the edge. Did she dare pull it? "She dated an outsider?"

Maryann fidgeted with her hands, and pink splotches blossomed on her pale cheeks, suggesting she felt like she had betrayed her friend. "I'm not sure she was serious. I think a lot of Amish youth go through a rebellious phase. Some more than others." She angled her head when something sounded from the top of the stairs. She waited for a minute before continuing. "Your mother was happiest when she was corralling the three of you."

"Do you know who this man was?" Grace couldn't let Maryann gloss over this, even if it had nothing to do with her murder. "I mean, did my mom consider leaving the Amish?" Maybe Grace had painted a romantic notion of her father and mother that had never existed.

The conversation she'd had with the retired law enforcement officers came to mind. Her father had been a suspect. Had he been jealous? Heat pooled under her arms. Investigating her mother's death had been a mistake. Regardless of the outcome, she'd never be able to bottle up the questions that had escaped and now floated around her mind.

Maryann waved her hand, suggesting this new piece of information didn't matter. It was in the past, after all. "Oh, no. It was a harmless thing, I'm sure. Leaving the Amish would have devastated your *mammy.*" Maryann tapped the pads of her fingers together. "Once your dad made his intentions known, she never talked of this *Englisch* boy again."

"She loved my father."

"Of course! Your father was a *gut* man."

Grace released a shaky breath she hadn't realized she'd been holding. By all accounts, her father had loved her mother dearly. After her father lost her mother, he had never recovered. He loved her. He had.

Relationships only lead to heartache.

The familiar refrain whispered across her brain.

Best to live her life on her own terms, traveling the world, giving a voice to the voiceless. Not getting attached.

Maryann stood and crossed over to where Grace sat in the rocker. The Amish woman's hand brushed across her shoulder. "Your mother was a dear friend. I'm here for her daughters."

"Thank you."

"Tell me, how is Rose? She was just a little thing when your mother died."

"She's doing well. She lives in Buffalo and has a great job as a midwife."

Maryann tilted her head to the side and smiled. "That's wonderful. I hope she is happy."

"She seems to be."

"Is she married? Kids?"

"Oh, no." It was Grace's turn to laugh. "Seems only Heather has taken that plunge."

Maryann's face grew somber. Grace sensed her mother's old friend wanted to ask her about her romantic relationships, so she spoke up first. "I suppose I should go."

"Wait, can I get you something?" Maryann asked.

"I'm fine. Thank you all the same." Grace drew in a deep breath. "Perhaps Emma would like to help out at the bed & breakfast for a bit now that Ruthie's going to have a family?" The idea had just come to Grace. The final decision would be up to Heather when she came back. But for now, Grace could use some temporary help. Dust didn't take a break during the off-season. Besides, the thought of company at the bed & breakfast cheered Grace. And maybe Emma knew some of the Amish teens who were at the party the night of Jason's death.

A concern wormed its way into Grace's subconscious. *Is everything about the story?*

Grace couldn't help herself. Stories were in her blood.

Just because the bishop ordered the youth to avoid the parties, didn't mean Emma would. Grace found that when something was forbidden, it became that much more desired. She hoped she could be a positive influence on the young woman. Tell her how to be smart and sidestep trouble if she found herself at parties.

"I'll go get her." Maryann stopped at the bottom of the stairs.

Grace got to her feet. "No, let me run up. If that's okay?"

"Yah." Maryann turned and continued into the kitchen.

Grace smiled and jogged up the stairs silently in her socks. Emma was still reading to her sister. Grace knocked quietly and then pushed open the door. Ruthie had drifted off to sleep while Emma seemed engrossed in the story.

"Hi," Grace whispered. Ruthie's breathing was even. "I don't want to wake your sister."

Understanding, Emma put a string in the book to mark her page and set it aside. They both stepped out into the hallway. "I wanted to know if you'd be interested in doing a little light cleaning at the bed & breakfast while I'm staying there?" Emma must wonder why a single woman couldn't clean up after herself.

"*Yah.* Yes," she corrected herself. "When?"

"Whenever works for you." She reached into her

pocket and pulled out her business card, then realized how ridiculous that was. Her smile faded. "I was going to say you could call me."

Emma swiped the card from her hand. "We have a phone in the barn. We use it for business purposes. For the greenhouse. I'll come tomorrow."

"Sounds good." Grace glanced down the stairs. Maryann didn't seem to be within earshot. "Can I ask you something?"

Emma twirled the strings of her bonnet, and her cheeks flared pink at the attention.

"Were you at the drinking party that made the news?"

Emma glanced around, appearing to be searching for an escape route. "You're the one writing a story."

"I am." She spoke encouragingly. "I promise not to get you into trouble."

Emma shook her head. "No, I wasn't at the party. I went right home after Sunday singing that night."

Grace decided not to press. She'd get to know the young woman soon enough when she came to work at the bed & breakfast.

"You have my card. See you tomorrow."

"Yah." Emma slipped back into Ruthie's room, and her steady voice picked up where she had left off in the story.

Grace had only been home long enough to formulate a blog post to keep her editor happy when she noticed a patrol car pulling up the driveway. Perhaps Conner had news about Bradley Poissant, the mayor's son.

She waited by the back door, hoping not to appear too eager. She counted to five after Conner's knock, and pulled the door open. Her greeting died on her lips. A female officer was standing next to Conner with a bag slung over her shoulder.

What's going on?

"Grace, this is Deputy Becky Spoth."

Grace backed up and hit her heel on the open door. "Hello, deputy."

"Mind if we come in?" Conner asked, amusement edging his tone. He must have noticed Grace's befuddlement.

"Um, sure. What's going on?" Grace stepped out of the way and the two officers came through the door, looking very official in their uniforms. "Does this mean you found the guy who rammed me at the gas station?" What other reason would Conner have for bringing Deputy Spoth with him? What was with the bag?

Conner hooked his thumbs in his belt. "Sorry to say we couldn't locate Bradley. The mayor said he was away on a college visit with his mom. Just for today. We don't even know he was involved, but until we arrest who was, I'd prefer if you weren't alone out here."

"Do you think it was Bradley?" Grace's gaze drifted to Conner then the deputy and back. She was sensing he was having doubts.

Conner took off his hat and scratched his head. "It's a stretch. I've known the mayor a long time. I've known Bradley his entire life. He's a good kid. Made a mistake drinking out back behind Jason's house. His parents were grateful to know what their son was up to. He's on the straight and narrow now."

"You trust him that much?" Grace leaned back and gripped the counter behind her. "But that's not the end of it, right? Did you find out why he was arguing with

Jason? Does the mayor know why you're looking for him?"

"We had to tell him something. I told him I had questions regarding the party. That I heard he was there with Jason," Conner said. "For all he knows, he thinks I want to know more about Jason's last hours, being family and all. And as far as the fighting, kids argue, right?"

"Sounds like you've talked yourself into this theory." Grace watched him closely. A shadow crossed his face, suggesting perhaps she was right.

"The mayor seemed pretty wrecked about Jason's death," Deputy Spoth added, looking toward Conner for confirmation. "It's a sad situation. After the boys were caught drinking at Jason's, Bradley lost his starting position as quarterback—part of school district policy if caught with drugs or alcohol. He said his son realized it was a wake-up call."

"To a teenage kid, missing out on a big game is a big deal. It was perhaps the end of his football career." Although Grace didn't have kids, she had heard more times than she could count that teenage brains weren't fully developed. That they did stupid things for stupid reasons. Acted irrationally. The officers had to know that better than anyone.

"I'd hardly call it a career," Conner scoffed. "His parents said he had no plans to play past high school. They looked forward to the day he hung up his cleats. The game's tough. Don't go grasping for reasons for him to get revenge on Jason that don't exist."

"Why are you shutting me down?"

"I know these people." Conner leveled an even gaze

at her. "They've known Jason a long time. They want to know the truth, too."

"Not if it means taking their son down."

Conner pressed his hands together and touched the tips of his fingers to his lips. "Okay, I'll do a little more digging."

"Thank you," Grace said, and pushed off the counter. "Now, about Deputy Spoth staying with me?" She pointed at Deputy Spoth's bag.

"You didn't run this by her ahead of time?" The deputy shook her head, giving Conner a skeptical look. Already Grace liked this woman.

"You need protection out here," Conner said as if that trumped everything.

Grace was beginning to miss her quiet hotel rooms in various cities where she could come and go without everyone worrying about her. "I thought we've been over this. I have the alarm." She sighed. "I won't forget to turn it on if Boots comes knocking." If only she hadn't forgotten that one step, she wouldn't be stuck entertaining this sheriff's deputy.

"I'd feel better if you had more than an alarm. I got authorization to have Deputy Becky Spoth stay with you."

Grace squared her shoulders. "No offense, deputy, but I don't need a babysitter."

"Please, call me Becky." Self-consciously, she touched one of the long braids pinned on top of her head.

Grace was beginning to feel a bit like a heel, but Conner had given her no choice.

"Humor me." A slow smile crept up Conner's face, and Grace's heart melted. *Traitorous heart!* If she stayed in Quail Hollow much longer, she'd be in jeopardy, and not only from some testosterone-fueled punk in a big truck.

Grace held up her hands, too tired to argue.

Conner took a step, retreating toward the door. "I have to follow up on a few things. You going to be okay?"

"Sure," the two women said in unison, then looked at each other. Grace smiled, figuring the young deputy probably didn't want to be here any more than she wanted a babysitter.

Once Conner stepped outside, the deputy moved to the door and locked it. "What's the code for the alarm?"

Grace told her, and the deputy set it. "I'm sure they'll track down whoever is harassing you, and then your life will go back to normal."

Grace was beginning to wonder what normal looked like. She had never had a normal life.

Grace opened the fridge and stared inside at the expired quart of half-and-half as well as a bruised apple and a withered pear left over from the fruit basket Rose had sent. She had hoped something good to eat would spontaneously appear. If she were here alone, she'd probably eat a granola bar or a bowl of cereal. *I wonder if my guest would enjoy that?*

Grace turned around and planted her fists on her hips. "You hungry? We could order takeout."

"No one will deliver out here." Becky strolled over and pointed at a door off the kitchen. "Pantry?"

Grace nodded. Her sister had mentioned the pantry, but Grace hadn't even opened it. She wasn't much of a cook.

Becky opened the door of the well-stocked pantry and studied its contents. "I can whip something up."

"Really?" Grace glanced over the deputy's shoulder at the cans, jars and containers that struck her more like a last resort during a snowstorm, when you were willing to risk botulism versus starving to death. "My sister had an Amish woman run her kitchen."

Earlier today she had watched Emma helping a very pregnant Ruthie up the stairs. Grace reached in and read a date on the can, but they hadn't come from any manufacturer. The Amish must have canned the food. "Hmm…she must have stocked up before she went on maternity leave. I never thought to look in there for something to eat." Living on the road always meant eating out. Since her sister left, she had been living on a few fresh foods stored in the fridge, cold cereal, granola bars and prepared food she had picked up in town. She wasn't fussy.

The deputy gave her a strange look and laughed quietly to herself. She undid the buttons on her cuffs and rolled back her sleeves. "If it's okay with you, I'll make us something for dinner. I promise you it'll be good."

"Sure." Grace hoped the single word of agreement didn't show her doubt. "What can I do?"

The deputy handed her a basket of potatoes. "You can peel these while I see what vegetables you have."

The two women worked in companionable silence. Grace never realized that peeling potatoes could be a nice distraction. Becky, as the deputy insisted on being called, finished preparing the meal, and the two of them sat down at the table to eat something that resembled Shepherd's Pie. Grace had to clear the paperwork and her computer from the table.

Grace took a bite, and the flavor exploded in her mouth. It took her back. Made her think of home.

A home she had lost the day her mother was murdered.

"Where did you learn to cook like this? It reminds me of my childhood." Grace wasn't even sure that was possible. Her mom had died when she was three, and her dad had moved his young family away shortly after.

A small smile hooked the corner of the deputy's mouth. The young woman had a flawless beauty, and Grace suspected she wasn't wearing any makeup. "I grew up Amish."

Grace laughed. "Really? I did, too. Well, not really. I left a long time ago."

"I know," Becky said. Of course she knew. "I'm sorry. I didn't mean to offend you. Everyone who grew up around here knows about your *mem*." It was strange to hear Pennsylvania Dutch coming from the deputy's mouth.

"How old were you when you left?" Grace took another bite. "This is really good," she added quickly, pointing at the food with her fork.

"Thanks." Becky seemed pleased, as if she hadn't cooked for anyone in a long time. "I left when I was seventeen."

"Did you leave all by yourself?"

Becky swallowed and smiled ruefully. "Yes."

"Yet you stayed in Quail Hollow?"

"Call me a glutton for punishment." Becky dragged a fork through her mashed potatoes, making Grace think about how she had done the same when she was a child. She liked to pretend she was paving roads through the mountainside in her mashed potatoes. “It’s not too bad. I still have family here.”

Grace suspected this was the true reason the young woman had stayed in town despite leaving the Amish faith.

“They’re okay with…” Grace held out her hand to the uniform, indicating the life of an *Englischer.*

“No, my parents are disappointed. They didn’t have to shun me because I left before I was baptized, but I’m certainly not welcome at home.” Her voice grew soft. “They consider me a bad influence on my sister.”

“Please forgive me if I’m overstepping for asking this question. Wouldn’t it be easier to move away?” Grace folded a corner of the napkin and ran her finger over the fold. “Make a clean break?” That’s why Grace suspected her father had left. Easier to move on from the past if it wasn’t always poking you smack between the eyes. If truth be told, her father had never moved on. He’d gone through the motions, providing for his family, until he suffered an early death.

Becky dipped her head, and her cheeks grew feverish. “I don’t know much beyond Quail Hollow. When I decided to leave the Amish, a woman who lives about thirty minutes away took me in. She helps other youth who decide to leave. I caught up with my education and took classes at the community college.”

Grace took another bite of her potatoes, allowing Becky to talk. Grace had never considered that there would be people who helped in the transition of runaway Amish. “How did you end up back here?”

“After community college, I looked for a job. Admittedly, I didn’t look far. The first job I was offered was in the sheriff's department. One thing led to another, and I eventually became a deputy."

"Interesting."

"The sheriff thought perhaps I'd be able to form a bridge between law enforcement and the Amish. However, the Amish are as skeptical of law enforcement today as they ever were. Maybe more so."

"That's got to be tough."

"Many people lead tough lives." Becky covered Grace's hand, her gaze reaching inside her soul. "There are far worse things than living in a town where the majority of the residents think calling you a fence jumper is going to hurt your feelings."

"Fence jumper?" Grace asked, curious.

"Yes, someone who left the Amish." Her eyes twinkled in amusement.

Grace scooped up more mashed potatoes. "From one fence jumper to another, this is awesome." Maybe having a bodyguard wouldn't be so bad.

If only Grace and Conner could figure out who wanted her to leave the Amish community again, once and for all.

Chapter Ten

After finishing his shift, Conner changed into shorts and a T-shirt and made his way to the small room in the sheriff's department designated for physical fitness. He started running, hoping hard footfalls on the relentless conveyor could beat the frustration out of him. He couldn't wait for the snow to melt. Then he could run his usual three-mile course along the country roads, up hills, alongside fields and barns and past buggies and wagons. There was something therapeutic about it. However, until the snow melted, he'd have to settle for the treadmill and the local news coming out of Buffalo on the small screen in front of him.

Thankfully, the wild-party clips from the news stations had died down, even though Conner was generating more questions in his own investigation on that exact same story. He hoped the answers he uncovered didn't generate another cycle of news stories. This evening, the news anchors were spending an inordinate amount of time discussing the weather. Nothing novel about that. A snowstorm warning was in effect for tomorrow, bringing a potential nine inches of the white fluffy stuff.

That meant more time on the treadmill.

Just great.

Annoyed, Conner snapped off the TV and jammed his earbuds, connected to his phone balanced precariously on the tray in front of him, into his ears. Arms pumping, he got into a rhythm. All the conversations he had had over the course of the past few days bounced around his head. Despite all his protests to the contrary, he couldn't shake Grace's concerns. *Was* he overlooking Bradley because the case was too personal?

He wiped sweat off his brow and allowed his mind to drift back to the night he had received a call from Anna, Jason's mother. She thought Jason and his friends were out back drinking. A visit from the sheriff's department would set them straight.

Sure enough, when Conner arrived, a few guys were pounding back beers. After seeing that each of the young men made it safely home, Conner took it upon himself to follow up with their parents. Perhaps his first mistake was not following through more with Jason. Conner had no idea that his actions would have a domino effect, getting the mayor's son suspended from the football team and effectively ending the small town's run in the playoffs.

Was the mayor dismissing how big of a deal that missed opportunity really was? Again, had Conner allowed his friendship with the mayor to cloud his judgment regarding his son?

Bam-bam-bam.

The soles of his shoes slapped the conveyor belt, sending a jolt through his entire body.

Could Jason's best friend really have lashed out at him? Drugged his drink to mess with him, not grasping the true danger? Not realizing that Jason would get behind the wheel of a truck and kill himself and seriously injure a young Amish woman?

Bam-bam-bam.

His footsteps landed heavily on the treadmill belt. He turned the music up in his ears, trying to drown out his thoughts. Could Conner have been that blind?

If this kid was desperate enough to drug someone for payback, what would he do to a reporter trying to uncover the truth?

Despite cranking his music up mind-numbingly loud, Conner still couldn't turn off his thoughts.

Bam-bam-bam.

Exertion usually helped Conner calm down. Not tonight. His frustration was ramping up with his heartbeat.

He hated punks. He hated being duped.

Conner swiped the back of his hand across his sweaty forehead. He'd have to come up with a plan. He knew he couldn't keep Grace under his watch—or the watch of a fellow officer—forever. Grace was much too independent. First chance she got, she'd be back out there, asking more questions.

Questions that someone obviously didn't want her to find answers to.

Arms and legs pumping, music cranking, thoughts swirling, Conner pretended he was outside, climbing the crest of the road winding through the cornfields. If only he was smelling the country air and not whatever greasy mess one of his coworkers had warmed up in the microwave in the nearby break room.

A shadow crossed his line of vision, and Conner pulled out an earbud, then the other. Heavy breaths from his exertion sounded loud in his ears. He didn't try to pivot to see who was there because then he'd have to break his stride or risk flying off the treadmill. There were too many cameras situated around this place to risk that. He was not about to become a viral video.

"Captain Gates." The sheriff's commanding tone was unmistakable.

Conner hit the stop button and grabbed the handlebars as the treadmill came to an abrupt stop. Forget the usual cooldown. He grabbed the edge of his T-shirt and wiped his forehead, a preemptive effort to prevent the sweat from stinging his eyes.

Conner gave his boss, dressed in a crisp uniform, a sly smile. "I find I get a better workout if I change out of uniform."

The sheriff stared back at him, clearly not amused. "We need to talk."

Conner stepped down from the platform. His legs vibrated from the sudden ceasing of motion. He wiped his forehead again. "How can I help you?"

"The mayor called."

Conner got a sinking feeling and waited for the sheriff to continue.

"What's your endgame?"

Conner leaned forward and planted his hands on his thighs, trying to catch his breath. He angled his head to look up at the sheriff. "I'm trying to understand what happened the night Jason died. I have new information that suggests he wasn't drinking or doing drugs. That maybe he was drugged."

The sheriff faltered for a moment before continuing. "You have to let it go. Jason's death was a tragic accident." The sheriff shook his head. "These other kids feel awful that they didn't stop him from drinking, doing drugs, and driving."

Conner could feel a muscle working in his jaw. Something didn't make sense.

The sheriff pinned him with his gaze. "Maybe you need to take some time off."

Conner froze and straightened. He plucked his damp T-shirt away from his chest. "What?"

"You've been working long hours. You lost your cousin, then his son in a short period of time. Take a week off. Pull yourself together."

"What am I supposed to do with a week off in the middle of winter?"

The sheriff curled his hand and tapped his fist on one of the treadmill's rails. "I've made my decision. I don't want to see you back here until next week."

Conner swiped his towel from where he had draped it over an unused piece of equipment. The first twinges of a headache hammered behind his eyes. "See you next week," Conner gritted out as he stormed from the workout area, afraid if he said anything more he'd be out of a job for far longer than a week.

Conner showered at the sheriff's department, changed into street clothes and drove over to see Anna Klein. This unexpected week off might give him the time he needed to finally get some answers. He doubted that was the sheriff's intent, but that was Conner's plan.

When he reached his cousin's wife's house, it was dark. It was too early for someone to be in bed but not too early for someone who had lost everything to be taking a nap or doing something to otherwise make herself forget.

But Anna had never been much of a drinker and certainly not a drug user. Neither had his cousin Ben; that's why it had come as such a blow that their son had driven under the influence.

From the front stoop, he could hear music. It only took him a couple notes to recognize the Buffalo band that had made it big. A band he and his cousin had taken more than one road trip to see.

Sorry I let you down, buddy. I didn't do right by your son.

If for no other reason, Conner owed his deceased cousin answers about his dead son, and Conner wouldn't stop until he had them.

What a nightmare.

Conner drew in a deep breath and knocked. After a few seconds, the music cut off and then the curtain on the door pulled back. Anna gave him a lopsided smile and dropped the curtain. She released the dead bolt and opened the door.

Anna ran a hand over her mussed hair. "I wasn't expecting anyone."

"Sorry." He hadn't given her a call in advance because he feared she'd beg off from a visit, and he needed to ask her some questions about Jason's relationship with Bradley.

Anna led the way to the family room. She turned on a light as she passed and lifted up the remote from the couch cushion to place it on the coffee table. The image of her lying in the dark listening to music was more than he could bear. What would his cousin think about his heartbroken bride?

"How are you doing?"

"How do you think I'm doing?" He could see it all in her haunted expression.

"I need to ask you a few questions." Conner got right to it. "Did Jason suffer any backlash after the party I broke up here?"

Anna sat down on the edge of the couch, sinking into the soft cushions. She held up the palms of her hands. "How would I know? I'm his mom… The mom is the last to know." Her words had a sad resignation to them.

"How did he seem after the bonfire here?"

"Moody. That's to be expected, right? His mom called the sheriff's department on his party."

Conner sat down on the coffee table near her and touched her hand. "It's not like you called 9-1-1. You called me. I'm family."

"Family in the sheriff's department." Anna sighed heavily. "I'm not sorry I called you." She frowned, and a silent tear trailed down her cheek. "I'm thinking I didn't call you enough. My kid was out of control and I couldn't stop him."

"You can't beat yourself up over this." If only Conner could take his own advice.

She picked up a decorative pillow and held it to her midsection. "I've got nothing else to do but think and analyze and wonder what else I could have done." She started to push to her feet, offering him something to eat or drink.

"No, no. Sit…"

She plopped back down and met his gaze. He had been a bit envious of his cousin Ben, who was ten years older, when he met Anna and had a son. They seemed to have the perfect family, unlike the broken home he had come from.

Now look at what remained of that perfect family.

Conner was cynical about relationships. Too much potential heartache.

"What is it?" The look in Anna's eyes suggested there wasn't much more she could hear that would faze her. She had already lost everything that was important to her.

"I heard some rumblings that Jason and Bradley had a run-in the night Jason died," Conner confided in her. "Had they been on the outs?"

"I don't know. I mean..." Her eyes moved quickly back and forth, searching her memory. "Kids go through phases. Bradley and Jason were joined at the hip growing up. They had other friends, too. I never thought much of it. Boys don't have the drama that girls usually do, or so I've heard." Anna dragged a hand across her tired face. Grief had aged her in the past year.

"I guess not." Conner glanced around at the small space. In the corner near the back sliding door to the deck, he noticed a pair of sneakers. Based on the size and style, they had to belong to her deceased son. One shoe was tipped on its side.

He turned back to Anna, realizing she wasn't going to provide him with any new information on her son's relationship with Bradley. "Is there anything I can do for you?"

She sat upright and stretched to drag the laptop that was sitting on the far end of the coffee table closer to her. "Maybe there is." She flipped open the laptop, and a professional photo of Grace smiled back at him. "Maybe you can get this lady to stop writing about Jason."

Conner spun the computer around to face him. He skimmed the blog entry dated today.

I never intended to be in Quail Hollow for this long. Maybe it's part of God's plan. My life started in Quail Hollow, then tragedy pulled me away. I've often fantasized about what my life might have been if I'd grown up Amish, yet I resisted coming back to face my past. To see what I had lost.

Now that I'm here, I've been blessed to meet people who knew my mother when she was younger than I am now. That's hard to believe. And I've learned that the Amish can have complicated lives, despite trying to live simply.

And, tragically, I've learned that despite their attempted isolation, drugs and alcohol can play a deadly role in their lives. You can't share the same stores, restaurants and roads without crossing paths with exactly what you're trying to avoid.

That was never more apparent than a fateful autumn night when a young man named Jason Klein, an *Englischer* as the Amish call them, clipped his truck on the wagon of Katy Weaver, a young Amish woman.

But the longer I'm here, the more I'm discovering answers aren't always black-and-white. Sometimes there are shades of gray. I'm determined to find those answers before life calls me to my next location.

Hopefully someplace without snow.

Conner snapped the lid of the computer closed, a failed attempt to keep his anger in check. How could Grace still be writing about Jason after everything they'd learned? After he warned her that she was putting herself in jeopardy?

"I'll talk to Grace."

Anna nodded. "I thought you might know her. People in town said you were hanging around with a reporter." Conner detected a hint of disappointment in her tone.

"It's not exactly what you think." He had a job to do. He had to protect Grace.

The smile on Anna's lips didn't reach her eyes. "I'm hoping I can find peace if people stop hounding me." She placed her hand on top of the laptop. "Someone from a Buffalo news station called, asking me to comment on those posts." She pulled her shoulders forward in a shrug. "I can't stop reading her posts. Punishing myself." She dragged a hand through her hair. "I need her to stop posting things about the accident."

Conner placed a hand on Anna's shoulder. "I'll take care of it." He had made a promise to Ben and failed him. Now, protecting Ben's wife from further pain was a promise Conner was determined to keep.

Early the next morning, a loud knock on the back door made Grace jump. The sight of Conner's personal truck calmed her nerves.

"That man has got to learn to call," she muttered as she placed a hand over her thundering chest.

She glanced up at the clock.

Why isn't he at work?

Becky had left a full hour ago for the start of her

shift. She wanted to make it into work before the forecasted snowstorm hit. It made Grace wonder who was paying her for her overnight shift. It didn't seem likely the sheriff's department would put Grace's safety ahead of keeping their overtime budget in check.

Not her problem, she supposed.

She lowered the lid to her laptop, slid off the bench and stretched her back. The smile slid from her face when she opened the door and saw Conner's stern expression. He seemed strung tight, and his muscles twitched in his jaw.

"What's wrong?"

He hesitated a fraction of a second, as if waiting for an invitation, then when he didn't get it, he pushed past her. "I thought we had an agreement."

She held up her palms in confusion. "What are you talking about?"

He strode over to her laptop and jabbed his finger at it. "What were you doing just now?"

Conner had shown himself to always be a gentleman, but she had never seen this side of him. In the blink of an eye, she was a teenager hiding in the closet while her brother-in-law screamed at her sister.

An icy pool of dread settled in her stomach, and she took a step back and squared her shoulders. Conner must have seen her reaction, and he relaxed his posture and lowered his voice. "Listen, you have the right to do whatever you please. However…" He pointed at her laptop again. "This is not helping."

"*This* is my job." She reached around him and tapped the lid of her laptop for emphasis.

Conner sat down slowly on the bench. "I saw Jason's mom last night."

Grace crossed her arms and leaned against the wall. "Oh?"

"She's been following your blog." He lifted his eyes to hers. "It's causing her more pain."

"My editor is pressuring me to push forward with the story. Did you read my recent post?"

"Yeah."

"I didn't say anything that would jeopardize the investigation. I thought it was rather masterful how I touched on current events without giving anything away." She tipped her head and lifted her eyes, seeking his approval.

"People are finding your posts and then calling Anna for comment."

"I'm sorry." She really was, but she wanted to keep her job. "Maybe Anna could get an unlisted number." She ran a hand across her eyes, which were gritty from staying up late last night, rereading all the articles that had been written about her mother's murder. No matter how many times she read them, nothing struck her as new.

Because there *was* nothing new.

Except for the information that Mrs. Hershberger had shared. An outsider had been courting her mother before she married her father.

She sat down on the kitchen bench and glanced at Conner. She should probably be focusing on one story or the other, but her head told her this could be something bigger, the combination of an accident on a lonely road between a wagon and a truck and the murder of an Amish woman almost three decades ago. There were probably countless incidences—many far less newsworthy—that would make a fascinating read of the true-life stories of the Amish.

Yet her compassionate side told her it might be too revealing. What would her parents think? Even though they had both been dead for a long time now, she often guided her life by imagining what they would do. It kept her honest.

Most of the time.

"I'll be more thoughtful in the future," she finally said.

Conner nodded and unzipped his jacket, but didn't press her for more concrete promises. He probably knew her too well.

"Why aren't you at work?"

"Funny story."

"What?"

He shifted, his thigh accidentally brushing against hers. "I'm on forced vacation."

Grace's hand flew to her mouth. "On account of me? Oh, I hope not."

He ran his hands up and down his thighs. "The mayor called the sheriff. Suggested I was too close to the case."

"I thought everything was okay when you talked to the mayor?" Her pulse whooshed louder in her ears. "Maybe their son isn't innocent." Excitement edged her tone. She couldn't help herself.

Conner cut her a sideways glance. "Can we let it rest? For five seconds, maybe?"

"Okay. Can I ask you something about my mother's murder investigation, then?"

"Sure."

Grace's cell phone rang at that exact moment. Before completely ignoring the call, she checked caller ID. It was a local area code. Curious, she held up her finger. "Excuse me a second."

Emma Hershberger was on the other end of the line, asking if it was okay if she came over another day to help out because of the snow.

"Of course," Grace said into the phone. "Call me the next time you have a free day and it's not snowing."

She ended the call and turned back to Conner. "Sorry about that. I wanted to ask you if Harry ever mentioned investigating any old boyfriends of my mother's?"

"I was a kid. I heard bits and pieces. My dad didn't discuss the details of the case with me. I'm sure he'd be willing to discuss it with you again, if you'd like."

"It's such a random angle. Something that Emma's mom said got me thinking. Mrs. Hershberger and my mom were good friends." She ran a hand over her mouth. "It's probably a dead end, but one I'd like to ask the retired sheriff about."

"Okay..." He planted his hands on his thighs and stood. "And you'll hold off on the blog. Until—"

"Until? There will never be a time that this tragedy won't hurt Jason's mom. It doesn't matter if I write about it or not, she'll still be hurting. Except maybe if I—if *we*—ask enough questions, she'll have answers to what really happened. Answers I never had regarding my mother's death."

"You can justify this any way you want. Anna is hurting now. I need to help her."

"I feel bad for Anna. I've kept her in my prayers," Grace said softly.

"How can you have faith after everything you've been through?"

"How can I not?"

Conner seemed to study her for a long minute before taking her hand and threading his fingers through hers. Warmth raced up her arm. Staring at their entwined fingers, her chest grew tight. "I'm on your side. Really, I am." He kissed the back of her hand. "I'm worried about your safety."

Grace pulled her hand away from his lips, but not out of his clasp. "Why are you so worried?"

A deep line creased his forehead. "What do you mean? Someone's harassing you."

She slid her hand out of his and stood. "You've gone above and beyond for me. You've put your job on the line." She lowered her head. "Why? You can't possibly do this for everybody." Her heart raced in her ears as she held her breath, waiting for his answer.

Conner searched her face in a way that made Grace very self-aware. Too self-aware. She shook her head and added, "Never mind, I shouldn't have asked."

He reached out and touched her elbow, the whisper of a touch that sent waves of awareness coursing through her. "No, you have every right to ask. It's something I've had to ask myself." A hint of a smile touched his eyes. "You've gotten under my skin."

She raised her eyebrows and her face grew warm. She didn't know how to respond to that.

Conner rubbed his forehead, obviously second guessing his confession. "I shouldn't have crossed the line. My job is to protect you."

"You didn't cross the line." She finally found her voice. "I'm only in Quail Hollow temporarily. My job has me traveling the world." The words felt like an excuse. For the first time in her adult life, the thought of planting roots didn't seem like such a crazy idea.

But what about Dad's heartbreak when Mom died? Heather's pain when her husband turned abusive?

Grace sat back down slowly. "I'm not in a position to date anyone." She looked up to meet his gaze. "Don't take it personally."

A light came into his eyes and he laughed. "Hard not to take it personally. But I do understand." He took a step backward toward the door, as if to make a hasty retreat. "I'm pretty much a confirmed bachelor." He shrugged. "I didn't exactly have the best role models while growing up. My dad was a workaholic and my mother bailed when I was just a kid."

Grace caught a glimpse of the hurt little boy in his wry expression. "I'm sorry. I didn't know that." A part of her felt guilty. Everything about their relationship had been about her. Grace knew far less about him. "Do you stay in touch with your mother?"

He shook his head. "She moved on. New husband. New kids."

She pushed to her feet and approached him. She looked in one eye then the other. Mustering courage she didn't realize she had, she reached out and cupped his smooth cheek. "I'm sorry."

"It was a lifetime ago."

"We both know that time doesn't heal all wounds." She leaned in and brushed a kiss across his warm lips. Fearing she'd never be this brave again, she tried to memorize the moment.

Chapter Eleven

Conner ran his hand down Grace's long silky hair and she blinked slowly. Time didn't heal all wounds, but this woman just might. The realization surprised him. He cleared his throat. "Despite our determination to both stay single, I'm curious, have you ever thought you could be happy in Quail Hollow?"

"I'm happy now." A light shone in her eyes, then she suddenly looked down, but didn't step away from him. "My mother's death broke my father." She shook her head, as if trying to dismiss some horrible memory. "And I saw firsthand how wrong relationships can go with my sister and her first husband. I just..." She looked up and met his gaze. "I'm not cut out for this. I'm content traveling and writing. That's all I need."

He wondered if she were trying to convince herself.

"But if I was looking to stay in some really cold, snowy place, Quail Hollow would be the top of my list." She laughed, obviously trying to lighten the mood.

Conner tucked a strand of her hair behind her ear, deciding not to push the topic. He didn't want to scare her away. "Perhaps if we were two different people with very different pasts."

"Perhaps..." They stared into one another's eyes for a long moment, then she said, "We should probably focus on the task at hand."

"I suppose you're right." Maybe at another point in time they'd be willing to explore whatever was going on between them.

She shifted away from him. Immediately, he missed the fragrance of her hair. The warmth of her proximity.

But she was right. They had work to do.

Grace filled the teakettle at the sink. "You mentioned you talked to Anna last night," she said, getting right down to business, and the warm and cozy mood that had surrounded them dissipated.

"Did Anna indicate if Jason and Bradley had been in a fight the night of the party?" Grace continued.

"She didn't know."

Grace reached for two mugs and set them on the counter with a clank. "Pretend you don't have a personal relationship with Bradley. Do you think he is in any way capable of ramming a truck into my car? That's pretty violent behavior."

His stomach sunk and he shook his head. "I don't."

"What about breaking into the bed & breakfast to scare me?"

"I can't imagine any of it. And, most of all, I can't imagine Bradley drugging Jason. They grew up together."

Grace turned around and grabbed two tea bags from the cupboard, tore them open, then placed one in each mug. She leaned back against the counter, apparently to wait for the water to boil.

"Keeping emotions out of it, let's think logically," she said. Conner had been down the logical road and hadn't liked what he'd seen. "Bradley gets in trouble for drinking at Jason's house, ruins his dreams of winning a state title in football and, despite what his parents claim, he *is* mad. Really mad. This was supposed to be his moment of glory. Star quarterback. Big game." She screwed up her face, thinking. "A lot of people peak in high school. That game could have been a story Bradley told for the rest of his life. Instead, he gets in trouble for drinking and he's done. School policy. So—" her eyes grew bright "—he decides to have a little payback. He spikes the drink of the kid who got him in trouble. Show that Jason, cousin of Captain Gates of the sheriff's department, is not a Goody Two-shoes like he claims to be."

"Jason didn't call the sheriff's department. His mother did."

"Doesn't matter. In the eyes of a teenager, Jason's at fault. And what better way to show his mother that Jason's not such a good kid than by sending him home drugged up? A nice reminder to his mother to keep her nose out of their business."

"Isn't that a huge risk to take? Look what happened."

"Bradley didn't think through all the ramifications."

"If he drugged Jason, why not stop there, especially after the horrific consequences? Pray to God for forgiveness and that no one ever finds out and then move on with your life."

Grace's eyes widened. "That's exactly it." And Conner knew it, too. "He can't stop. Not now. He has to make sure no one ever finds out he's responsible for the accident. Whatever hopes he had for his future—football or not—would be destroyed."

"Maybe..." Conner still wasn't ready to believe Bradley Poissant was guilty of all that. "But why come after you? I've been investigating, too."

"Don't you see? He knows you'd never suspect him. You said it yourself. You've known him since he was a boy. He was Jason's friend. His best friend. Even now, you're doubting it's possible."

"We work on more than theories. We need proof."

"Yes, and I'm the writer in town, investigating the night of the accident. I'm the one he needs to stop."

"Now I can tell why you're a writer."

The kettle whistled and Grace spun around to fill the two mugs. She carried them over and sat down next to Conner. "Too out there?"

He pulled his tea bag out of the mug and set it on the napkin. "I wish it was. In this line of work, I've seen how dark people's hearts can be. I never imagined Bradley had it in him." He took a long sip of the piping-hot tea. "But even at that, we need proof. If he is involved, he's only digging himself in deeper."

Grace tapped her fingers on the table. "You're officially off duty because you're too close to Jason's case." Staring off in the yard, her eyes tracked something only she could see. She seemed to be plotting something.

"Yeah, and probably because I'm too close to you." He lowered his gaze to her mouth, and her breath hitched. He shifted in his seat and took a long sip of the tea. If he wanted to solve this case and respect her wishes, he'd have to check his emotions. She had made it clear she wasn't going to stay in Quail Hollow long term. And, quite frankly, why did he think their relationship wouldn't eventually implode? All his previous relationships had.

The corner of her pink mouth quirked into a grin. "Vacation, huh? What are you going to do with all your free time?"

"Make sure you don't get in trouble." He glanced around. "Where's Becky?"

"She left for work. My understanding is that she only had to guard me overnight. Make sure someone didn't murder me in my sleep." Grace laughed nervously.

"Nothing's going to happen to you. Not while I'm around." He still didn't like Grace out here all alone, day or night. This forced vacation meant he could protect her during the day.

She jerked her head back, and a strand of hair fell over her forehead. He resisted the urge to push it off her face. Her expression grew serious. "I appreciate your being here for me. I'm used to going it alone."

"You don't have to anymore." He wrapped the napkin around the teabag and stood. He tossed it into the garbage can. "Why don't we track Bradley down? See what he has to say?"

"Now?"

"Sure, the schools are closed because of the snow. We might get lucky and catch him at home."

Grace ran upstairs to grab a sweater out of her dresser, stuffing her arms into the sleeves as she walked briskly toward the bathroom. She snatched her lip gloss off the glass shelf and caught her reflection in the mirror.

She stopped and stared. A hint of a shadow lingered under her eyes. She had lost a lot of sleep lately between her illness and the two cases she had been investigating.

"Make sure you dress warmly," Conner hollered from the bottom of the stairs.

"Okay." She peered out the window. The falling snow was blanketing all the out buildings. The new red-stained barn with accents of snow could have been a postcard photo.

Mem's body was found in the old barn.

For a woman who left Quail Hollow at age three, there were far too many haunting memories. She couldn't stay here despite her growing feelings for Conner. And a short-term romance wouldn't be fair to either of them. When Grace made all her life plans—writing and traveling the world—she had never imagined meeting a man as kind as Conner.

Hadn't Heather once thought Brian was nice?

Grace grabbed a fastener off her dresser and twirled her hair into a messy bun. She grabbed a hat and gloves out of the closet, then turned to run back downstairs.

Focus on the investigation.

That was the safest thing to do for everyone.

"The house is up here on the right," Conner said distractedly while adjusting the windshield wipers in a futile attempt to keep up with the driving snow.

"Are you sure this is a good idea?" Grace's sudden apprehension did nothing to squash the little critter of doubt scurrying around Conner's brain, making him wonder if it was a good idea to pay Bradley Poissant a little visit. "Are you sure neither of his parents are home?" She leaned forward against the seat belt and squinted out the windshield.

"I called the mayor's office. The mayor is there, making sure all services are being provided during the storm. And since schools have been cancelled for the day, there's a good chance we can catch Bradley at home."

"What about his mom?"

"Also at work. I checked," Conner said. Mrs. Poissant was an insurance agent at some office just outside of Quail Hollow. Probably not very busy on a day like today. "If we catch Bradley at home, we'll chat unofficially, since I'm technically on vacation. And Bradley's eighteen." Conner wasn't sure who he was trying to convince. A cautionary voice grew louder, warning him that what he was doing could blow up in his face.

Would *surely* blow up in his face.

His father, the retired sheriff, certainly wouldn't approve. He dismissed the thought. Conner was his own man. He'd deal with whatever fallout came his way. He had to follow all the leads on this investigation. And Bradley Poissant, Jason's friend, was one of those leads.

Conner adjusted his wipers again. "It's snowing a lot harder than when we left the house. We better not waste time here or we might not make it back home." His four-wheel-drive truck was good in snow, but even it had limitations, especially in snow that was coming down at a clip of three inches per hour. "The house is right here."

A quaint yellow house came into view. It had a wide porch now coated with a fresh layer of snow. Conner debated pulling up the driveway, then second guessed himself. The street plows had left a large pile of snow chunks at the end of the driveway that he'd never get through. Apparently the mayor didn't ask the crews to give him any special treatment. The mayor was a pretty stand-up guy, which was why checking in with his son when he wasn't home felt a little underhanded.

The tires brushed against the snow piled on the side of the road. He pulled away from the curb to give Grace room to hop out.

Conner put the truck in Park and turned to her. "Okay, if you recognize him at all from the gas station, brush the back of my hand."

"I only saw his profile." She seemed to be searching her memory. "Let's do this. If I think it's him, I'll touch your hand."

"I'll do the talking. See where we get."

"Are you going to give me this same drill every time we talk to someone?" Grace smiled at him, and he couldn't resist smiling in return.

"Sorry, can't help myself."

Grace followed the path Conner created through the foot of snow. A two-foot drift was gathered alongside a car parked in the driveway. He reached back and took Grace's hand to steady her. "You good?"

She nodded and mumbled something that was muffled by the scarf wrapped across the bottom of her face.

The newly fallen snow made the house seem empty. Still. Maybe no one was home. That theory was quickly dismissed when a pounding sound came from inside, like someone racing down the stairs. Had Bradley seen them walking up the driveway?

Conner fisted his gloved hand and pounded on the door. A shadow slowed behind the smoky glass insert on the front door. "You expecting someone?" a female voice shouted from inside. Conner and Grace exchanged glances.

"Do we have the right house?" Grace whispered.

"Yes." Conner raised his eyebrows. Bradley was an only child. "Looks like while the parents are away, the kids will play."

"But it's a snow day."

"You grew up in Buffalo. A snow day means no school. It doesn't mean kids aren't going to find a way to hang out, especially if they live near each other."

Grace frowned. "Snow days were meant for curling up in bed with a good book."

"Different strokes, I suppose." He lifted his hand to knock again, and the door swung open. A young girl with long blond hair answered the door with a surprised look on her face.

"Is Bradley home?" Conner asked, holding the storm door open.

"Yeah, we're hanging out. Watching movies. Can I tell him who's here?" Score one for the teenager. She didn't allow a stranger into the house.

"Who's there?" Bradley appeared in the kitchen, visible at the end of the hallway. He wore sweatpants and a T-shirt with a few small holes in it. Recognition lit his face and he strode toward them. "Hey, Captain Gates, how are you?" An eyebrow twitched. "Is something wrong?" The young man tried to look out the door beyond Conner and Grace. His attention slipped right past Grace.

Probably a good indicator that he didn't have it out for her.

"Hi, Bradley. Do you have a few minutes to talk?"

"Yeah, sure." Bradley stepped away from the door, giving them room to enter. He placed a hand on the young woman's shoulder. "This is my girlfriend, Suze."

"Nice to meet you," Conner said. "I'm Captain Gates, a friend of the family. And this is a friend of mine, Miss Miller."

"Nice to meet you, too," Suze said, smiling warmly at Grace.

"Have you met Miss Miller?" Conner asked Bradley, scrutinizing the young man's reaction.

Bradley's mouth grew pinched. "I don't think so." He offered his hand and Grace took it. She didn't seem to be registering any concern that she recognized him from the hit-and-run at the gas station.

Suze pointed at Conner casually. "You're the officer that's related to Jason Klein. I remember you from the bonfire."

Conner tapped his fingers on his thigh. "Jason was my cousin's son."

"Real sorry about his death. He was a nice kid."

"Thank you. Suze, were you also at the party the night Jason died?"

"No." She shook her head for emphasis. "My parents wouldn't let me go."

Good parents.

"Bradley was there." She linked hands with her boyfriend and rested her head on his shoulder. "He feels so bad. Right, Bradley?"

"Yeah, if I had known he was wasted, I would have stopped him from driving."

"You didn't see Jason drinking a lot the night of the accident? Or taking pills?"

"Everyone was drinking. Some were taking drugs.

I avoid that stuff." Bradley dragged his toe along the seam between two oak floorboards.

"Did you guys want to come in?" Suze asked, her gaze drifting from the visitors to her boyfriend and back.

"We're not going to stay long. It's really coming down out there. I just wanted to get a few more details straight about the night of Jason's accident."

"I told you everything already." Bradley scrubbed his hand across his face.

"I need some clarification. I've heard recent stories that Jason wasn't much of a drinker, and that he definitely didn't do drugs. In hindsight, him being *wasted* doesn't make a lot of sense."

"We all make mistakes." Bradley held out his free hand toward Conner. "Like that night at the bonfire. Boy, was I stupid." Bradley put on what Conner suspected was his best oh-golly tone. Why hadn't Conner noticed it before? "I'm happy to put the partying phase behind me."

"I hear you were on a college visit yesterday. Have you decided where you're going?"

If Conner hadn't glanced down at that exact moment, he might have missed Bradley giving his girlfriend's hand a quick squeeze.

What's that all about?

"I haven't made a decision. Not yet, anyway."

"It's a big decision. I'm sure you'll make the right one." Conner unzipped his jacket. "I have a theory, and I wanted your take on it."

"Oh yeah?" Bradley jutted out his lower lip and blew his bangs from his forehead.

"Since I heard rumblings that Jason hadn't been

drinking, what if someone spiked his drink the night he died?"

"That's your theory?" Bradley frowned, giving it some thought. "That might explain why he was messed up."

"You know anything about it?"

Bradley's eyes grew round, as if he were shocked. Conner quickly held up his hands to reassure the young man. "I'm not suggesting you had anything to do with it. But perhaps you've heard talk."

"No way. I can't believe someone would do that."

"It's hard to believe," Conner agreed. "Well, if you hear anything, you know where to reach me."

"Sure do." Bradley dropped his girlfriend's hand, crossed his arms and smiled tightly.

"We'll see ourselves out." Conner opened the door and Grace slipped in front of him.

Bradley retreated into the kitchen while Suze was too polite not to see them out. Just before they stepped outside, Suze asked in a hushed voice, "Did they ever find out what Jason was on the night he died?"

Conner debated giving her a straight answer. "Yeah, he had a mixture of prescription drugs in his system." He listed a few of the brand names. "Do you know anything about that?"

"No," Suze said a bit too emphatically. The rims of her eyes grew red. "I was curious, that's all."

"Okay, then," Conner said. "Have a good day. Stay warm."

Grace paused and reached into her pocket. She smiled at Suze. "I'm writing a story on how the Amish and local teens hang out with each other despite their very different lifestyles. If you'd like to be part of it, let me know." She pressed her business card into her hand. Suze seemed confused, but took the card and slipped it into her back pocket before closing the door.

Conner and Grace bowed their heads, bracing against the wind. When they were back inside the truck, Grace turned to Conner. "Did you see that? Suze looked concerned. Like maybe she wanted to say something more, but couldn't."

"I thought the same thing. Smart move on giving her your business card. Maybe she'll feel more comfortable calling you rather than the sheriff's department. Less threatening, maybe."

Grace plucked off her gloves. "Do you think we should have pressed her more before we left?"

Conner shook his head. "If she talks, it'll be when Bradley's out of earshot." He started the engine and turned on the wipers. The blades swept off the light dusting of snow. "We'll have to wait and see if our little visit pays off."

Retired sheriff Harry Gates lifted the glass coffee pot out of the automatic coffee maker and set out two mugs. Grace drew in a deep breath, the smell of strong coffee filling her senses. Despite not being much of a coffee girl, Grace felt nostalgic when it came to the scent. Her dad had been a big coffee drinker.

"Have a seat." Harry carried the two mugs over to the small table next to a window overlooking the driveway. "Nice of you guys to stop by. It's really blowing out there." Outside the window, Conner had powered up the snowblower and was slicing a path down the driveway, the snow shooting up in an arc and the wind blowing it back into Conner's face. Grace shuddered.

"Not much of a hardship for me." Smiling, she lifted the mug to her lips and took a small sip. "I'm sitting in the cozy, warm kitchen with you."

"My pleasure." Harry smiled. "Have you made any progress in your investigation?"

"Which one?" Grace tried to read the older gentleman to determine if he was still upset she was a writer, considering the trouble he'd had with the reporter from the *Quail Hollow Gazette.*

"Ah, you couldn't resist following up on both stories. Any new leads?"

"A few things. But it's been tough. I'm persona non grata around here."

"I may be retired, but I still hear things." Harry set his spoon down, and a brown stain spread across the napkin. "Regardless of my feelings for reporters, there's no excuse for what's been happening to you. Are you okay?"

"I'm fine. I think someone is trying to scare me away." She bit her tongue before saying more. She imagined the retired sheriff was also friends with the mayor.

"Did you ever ask yourself why they're trying to scare you?"

Grace angled her head in confusion. "Because I'm looking into the night of Jason's death, and someone doesn't want me to find out what really happened."

Harry lifted his mug to his lips and took a long sip. Above the mug, his eyes drifted to the weather outside. He seemed lost in thought. "That's one reason." He put the mug down and redirected his gaze toward her. "You're an easier target than, say, someone in law enforcement. However, either way, they're only attracting more attention to themselves."

"Criminals aren't always rational thinkers." She and Conner had had a similar conversation.

"True." Harry scratched the top of his head. "It seems they want to stop you before you uncover the truth. How many years has it been since your mother's murder? That's a deeply buried secret. I wonder if maybe you've stumbled upon something in your mother's case?"

If she had found something of value in that case, it had eluded her. "I believe I'm drawing attention because of Jason's death."

"I don't know."

"Really? What if the harassment is related to my mother's murder?" She studied the retired sheriff's face. "That would mean someone who was involved way back then is still around." Nerves tangled in her belly. "What's the likelihood?" She shook her head, the absurdity of the thought settling in. "No, it has to be related to the night Jason died."

Harry tapped the handle of his mug. "You're probably right. Kevin and I have been rehashing the case of late. We're still coming up blank." His eyes slanted in a thoughtful gesture, and Grace realized for the first time how much Conner resembled his father.

Grace took another sip of coffee, then set her mug down. "Nothing much to report. I did hear something strange, though." She took a deep breath, measuring her words, then smiled, feeling a little embarrassed to keep bringing up a nearly three-decades-old case. "When you were investigating my mother's death, did you uncover anything about former boyfriends?"

The retired sheriff's forehead furrowed. "Can't say that we did." He took another sip of coffee. "From what I gathered, your mother married your father when she was eighteen. I'm sure she had her usual running-around period. Most Amish do. By all accounts, she didn't waste time getting baptized and married to your father. No other Amish suspects came under our radar. Why? What did you hear?"

Grace's mouth went dry. She struggled to find her voice. Could she ask if her mother had considered leaving the Amish with an outsider? It felt too much like a betrayal of her mother's memory.

Grace ran her fingers across the edge of the table, realizing she was making this personal. This was a story and a good one at that.

But how can I not make this personal?

"I was wondering if someone who wasn't Amish showed a special interest in my mother."

Harry got a faraway look in his eyes. "Your mother was beautiful." A blush of pink infused his cheeks. "If you don't mind me saying so. However, I had never heard anything about her dating an *Englischer*." He rubbed a hand across his jaw, rough with stubble. "No one mentioned anything like that." He met her gaze. "If I were you, I wouldn't be wasting time on that theory. Your mother was a good Amish woman. No one ever said otherwise."

Grace nodded her agreement, unwilling to call into question her mother's character. That certainly wouldn't help the investigation.

Inwardly, Grace tried to shed the growing confusion that tracking this story had caused. Thinking she could do a story in Quail Hollow had been her first mistake. Believing she could be impartial had been her second.

"I haven't been able to find any real new information on my mother's murder. Maybe it was a silly idea to try to write a story on it. Perhaps I'll focus on the original story." She smiled. "But, happily, I got to know the Hershberger family. Maryann knew my mom."

"Maryann was quiet. It was hard to get any information out of the Amish. Your mother's death really impacted the community."

"They can be quiet." Grace dragged a hand through her hair. "The Hershberger family seems to be warming up to me. Maryann's daughter Emma is going to start working at the bed & breakfast."

"That's great." He leaned toward her. "I really like you, Grace. You might just change my opinion about your profession after all."

His comment caught Grace off guard and she laughed. "Was that almost a compliment?"

"Maybe it was. But I hope you remember that there are people behind your stories. Namely, Jason Klein and his grieving mother."

"I'll do my best to respect that." Her mind drifted to Conner's request that she hold off on posting updates online because of their impact on Jason's mom.

Harry smiled tightly as if he doubted that was possible.

Just then, Grace felt her cell phone vibrate in her sweater pocket. Something told her to check it.

"Excuse me a second," she said, pushing away from the table. "I should take this."

"Go for it."

Grace stepped into the family room and lifted the phone to her ear. "Hello?"

"Grace Miller?"

"Yes." Grace pressed the phone to her ear, fearing she'd miss what the caller was saying.

"This is Suze, Bradley's girlfriend."

"How are you?"

"Okay, um…" She was soft-spoken. "My grandmother's medication is missing. I didn't want to say anything until I went home to check."

A slow, steady beat thrummed through Grace's ears. "What kind of medication?"

"The kind found in Jason's system the night he died."

Grace shot a glance toward the kitchen. Harry seemed focused on Conner clearing the driveway. She turned back around and spoke quietly into the phone. "Would Bradley have had access to the drugs?"

"Yes, he used to joke that he could make a lot of money by selling them at school. I blew him off. I thought it was a stupid joke. Well, my grandma died last fall—"

"I'm very sorry."

"Thanks…" Suze sniffed. "I forgot all about it until earlier today when the deputy said something."

"Does Bradley know you checked your grandma's medication?"

"No! Shortly after you left, I told him I wasn't feeling well. I went home and checked my grandma's bathroom. She lived with us before she died. I know my mom hasn't gotten around to clearing anything out." Her voice shook. "Do you think Bradley drugged Jason? I can't imagine…"

"I don't know. I need you to do me a favor. Don't say anything to Bradley. Okay? Promise?"

"I promise."

"I'll talk to Captain Gates. He'll follow up."

"Okay." Suze sniffed again. "Did I do the right thing by calling? I don't want to get Bradley into trouble, but...if he did that to Jason..." Indecision, disgust and uncertainty dripped from her tone.

"You did the right thing. Now, don't say another word about it to anyone until you hear from Captain Gates."

Grace ended the call and stood motionless in the living room. Had Bradley stolen the prescription? They'd need proof.

Grace returned to the kitchen and detected a shift in Harry's posture. Staring out the window, he set down his coffee mug, and the brown contents sloshed over the edges. She drew closer to the window to see what had caught his attention. A car was parked in the road, and a man in a long black coat was charging up the driveway.

Plowing the snow, Conner seemed oblivious to the man approaching. He adjusted the chute on the snowblower, narrowly missing the man with the arc of white snow.

"Who is that?" Grace asked, staring intently.

"The mayor. And he doesn't look happy."

Chapter Twelve

Hunkering down in the collar of his winter coat, Conner pushed the snowblower up his father's driveway. At the rate snow was falling, he'd have to swing by and clear the driveway again in a few hours. Conner hated to see his father out in the cold, even though he was more than capable of clearing it himself.

Who was he kidding? *He* hated to be out in the cold, too. Good thing he didn't mind putting his truck into four-wheel drive and zooming up his own driveway that rarely saw a shovel or a snowblower.

Conner reached the top of the driveway and cranked the chute to blow the snow to the far side of the driveway. He came up short when a black form charging toward him caught his attention. Adrenaline shot through his veins, making him forget about his frozen face, despite his winter hat tucked low on his head.

Conner shoved the snowblower into Neutral, then, when he realized it was the mayor, he turned it off. "How can I help you, Mayor?"

"I thought maybe you'd be here after stopping at my house."

"I'm helping my dad out."

"Listen, Conner, I'm real sorry about your cousin's son, but you have to stop bothering *my* son."

Conner tucked his gloved hands under his armpits. "I wanted to ask him a few questions about the night Jason died."

"Haven't we covered that ground more than once? The kid is wrecked." The mayor's nose had turned bright red, matching the tips of his ears. The guy needed a hat. "I want him to move on. Go to college. I don't need you to keep dragging him back to that night. The poor kid feels awful."

Something about his choice of words bothered Conner. "Why does he feel awful?"

The mayor fell back on his heels. "What do you mean? He lost his best friend. Of course he feels awful."

"How did you know I was at your house, anyway?"

"A neighbor recognized you. Said you were with some woman." As if sensing "the woman" was close, the mayor's eyes drifted to the house, then returned to him. "We need this whole situation to go away."

"Situation? Jason died. It's never going to go away." Conner's cheeks grew fiery hot, despite the polar wind whipping his face.

The mayor seemed to deflate a little, realizing what he had said. "I'm sorry. This whole situation—I mean, Jason's tragic death—has thrown everyone for a loop. Bradley is struggling. Really struggling. I'm worried about his mental health. I need for him to move on. I love my son. I don't want this to derail his life."

Conner bit back the argument that Jason didn't have the option to move on. Yet no one could fault the mayor for wanting only good for his son. Maybe that was the best thing. Besides, without any evidence, their theory was all conjecture at this point. Would they needlessly ruin another young life?

"I talked to the sheriff, and he said you're supposed to be on vacation."

Conner raised his eyebrows, but didn't say anything.

"Come in before you both freeze," Conner's father called from the front door, sounding very much like the authoritative sheriff he had once been. "Come in, both of you."

The mayor strode toward the door, traipsing over a few inches of fresh snow. Conner had just cleared that walkway. It was going to be a long day, for more than one reason.

Conner made sure the snowplow was off and followed the mayor into his father's home. His father grabbed two mugs from the holder and proceeded to fill them up.

He handed one to the mayor and waited for Conner to take off his gloves before offering him the other.

Conner set the mug down, afraid the coffee would upset his already roiling gut. He yanked off his hat. Chunks of snow fell to his father's hardwood floor. He pulled his arms out of his heavy coat and tossed it over the chair.

"What brings you here in this weather, Mayor?" his father asked.

The mayor hesitated for a moment before answering. "Checking on why Conner and his friend here were at my house talking to my son."

"Like I said in the driveway, we were following up on some things, that's all."

The mayor set down his coffee mug forcefully. "I don't know why I came in. I don't have time for this. Thanks, Harry. We'll catch up at the diner one of these days."

"Sure," Harry said, taking a step toward the mayor. "You pick the time. I've got lots of it."

"Mayor?" Grace spoke up for the first time. "Everything I've heard about you leads me to believe you're a stand-up guy."

"Is there something you want?" The mayor lifted his chin, practically puffing out his chest. "I don't believe we've met."

Grace smiled and held out her hand. "Grace Miller. My sister Heather opened the bed & breakfast."

"Yes, yes..." He strolled toward her and held out his hand in the easy way of politicians. He pumped her hand twice before pausing and adding, "You were the woman at my house talking to my son?"

"I was. I'm working on a story about the night Jason died."

The mayor visibly flinched. "I was telling Conner that my son has taken Jason's death hard, and I'd appreciate it if you stopped asking questions. It's too painful for him."

"I can imagine." There was a coldness to Grace's words that struck Conner. She seemed to be calculating something. She met Conner's gaze, then looked at the mayor. "Would you give the sheriff's department permission to search your home for some prescription drugs?"

The mayor jerked his head back. "What are you talking about?"

Conner stared at Grace. Obviously something had

transpired between the time he put his jacket on and went outside to clear his father's driveway and now. He wanted to take her to another room and talk privately, but something told him he had to let it play out. To trust her.

"I know you love your son. However, I think he may have done something very stupid. Something that may have led to Jason's accident."

The mayor shook his head. "No way. You're wrong."

"Perhaps you'll allow Conner to call the sheriff's department. Allow someone to search the house, perhaps your son's room, for prescription drugs that don't belong to him."

The mayor crossed his arms. "Is that what it will take to make you both stop?" The mayor's gaze bounced from Grace to Conner.

Conner studied Grace for the briefest of moments before facing the mayor and nodding.

"Make the call then." The mayor reached for the door handle. "One condition—neither of you can be involved."

"That was a pretty gutsy move," Conner said, pacing back and forth in his father's kitchen. Once the mayor had left, Conner called Sheriff Flatt to conduct the search of the Poissant residence. His boss wasn't too thrilled on how things had unfolded, but he couldn't ignore Conner's request, especially since the mayor had given them permission.

"Perhaps I should have waited and discussed it with you first. If I had, Suze might have folded and told Bradley what she had done. I couldn't take that risk."

Grace crossed her arms and leaned back in the kitchen chair. She shuddered as the wind pelted the glass.

"Time was critical here." Harry looked at Grace with something akin to approval. "The mayor and his family have been friends of mine for a long time. If their son drugged Jason—" he shook his head slowly "—that will be hard to forgive. But the kid needs to pay."

Conner smiled sympathetically at his dad and placed his hand on his arm. "Let's wait and see." Grace could tell Conner was still hoping Bradley was innocent in all this.

A sense of loss knotted Grace's stomach. She missed her dad. For years it had just been her and her sisters, and Grace had chosen to travel the world rather than connect with either of them. Of course, Heather's violent husband had had a hand in keeping her isolated.

Grace glanced at the clock on the wall. "How long do you think it'll be till we hear something regarding the search?"

"Not long."

A knock sounded on the door. "It's like Grand Central around here," Harry muttered as he shuffled to the door in his slippers. "Ah, Kevin." Harry's voice traveled from the front room to the kitchen where Grace was waiting with Conner.

"There's a lot of commotion at the mayor's house. Do you know what's going on?"

"Come on in." Harry led Kevin to the kitchen. "Want some coffee?"

"Um…" Kevin seemed to come up short when he noticed Grace.

"Hello," she said. "Quite a storm out there."

"Sure is." He unzipped his jacket and shrugged out of it. "Any chance you know what's going on at the mayor's house?" When no one answered right away, he added, "Aw, come on. You know I'll find out soon enough. I'm a retired undersheriff. Don't be such a stickler."

"Have a seat," Conner said, and he explained the situation. "Since it's only speculation at this time, please keep the information confidential."

"Of course," Kevin said, a million thoughts behind his bright eyes. "It's a shame when a decent guy like the mayor is saddled with a kid who thinks the world owes him everything."

"Why do you say it like that?" Grace asked.

"The kid has everything going for him, makes a few mistakes, stumbles, then decides to take down those around him. Shame." Kevin shook his head in a world-weary way.

"Let's wait and see if they uncover anything," Conner suggested.

Grace's phone chimed again, and she answered. Emma wanted to see if maybe she could start working next week, after the storm had passed. The young woman must have been eager to start her new job to call again. Grace ended the call and smiled at the three pairs of eyes staring at her. "Emma Hershberger is going to start work at the bed & breakfast."

"Hershberger..." Kevin seemed to roll the name around on his tongue. "Maryann Hershberger was a friend of your mom's. Any relation? A lot of these Amish have the same name."

"Emma is Maryann's daughter. I went to talk to Maryann about my mom."

Kevin nodded. "You don't leave any stone unturned."

"Not much else to do while I'm cooped up here." Her face immediately flushed, realizing she had probably offended everyone in the room.

Conner's phone rang. He swiped his finger across the display. "Captain Gates."

Grace studied Conner's face for any signs that prescription drugs had been found at the mayor's house. After a frustrating series of one-word answers that told her nothing, Conner said, "I need to be the one to tell Anna." A muscle worked in his jaw. "Thank you. I understand. Yes." Conner ended the call.

"They found two prescription bottles under Bradley's mattress. Two of the same drugs found in Jason's system." Conner relayed the information.

Grace grew light-headed.

"They had the name Elaine Jankowski on them."

"Suze's grandma?" she asked.

Conner slowly nodded. "Suze's grandma."

"Unbelievable," Harry said.

"How hard will it be to prove that Bradley drugged Jason?" Grace asked.

"Not hard at all. After one of the deputies found the bottles, Bradley cracked. He confessed to drugging his friend. He had no idea things would turn deadly." He met Grace's eyes. "Your theory was right. He wanted people to think Jason wasn't such a good kid after all."

Grace took no pride in being right. Not in this case. She slowly sat down, feeling oddly sorry for Bradley, but even more so for Jason and all the lives ruined because of the young man's reckless decision.

"Did he confess to ramming the car at the gas station?"

"He claims a friend of his did that. They wanted to stop you."

"Hmm..." Grace gave it some thought. "No wonder Bradley was falling apart. Every bad decision he made led to two more."

"He hasn't confessed to anything else," Conner said to Grace in a somber tone. She assumed he was talking about the incident in the library basement and the break-in at the bed & breakfast. "I'm sure once we track down his friend, all the pieces will fall into place."

"Did the sheriff give you the friend's name?" Kevin asked. "Your dad and I still know a lot of the troublemakers in town."

Conner rubbed his jaw. "Some kid, last name Younge."

Kevin gave a knowing nod. "Must be Jimmy Younge. Comes from a long line of delinquents."

Grace wrapped her arms tightly around her middle. "Sounds like everything is unraveling. We caught a break when we ran into Suze at Bradley's house this morning. If not for her..." She let her words trail off.

"Sometimes that's how cases are solved. A matter of being in the right place at the right time," Kevin said.

"That's for sure," Harry added. With that, he turned his attention to the storm outside. "The snow doesn't show any signs of letting up."

"Let me finish the driveway, then get you home." Conner smiled at Grace while he reached for his jacket. "I'll hurry up. We don't want to get stranded."

Chapter Thirteen

The following evening, Grace stepped away from the table after snapping her laptop closed. She had spent most of the day working on her article about the events that had unfolded here over the past few days and weeks. The story was good. *Really* good. Now she had to wait for the right time to post it.

She rolled back her shoulders, easing out the kinks from hunching over her laptop for hours. It wasn't often the son of a mayor set in motion the tragic events that ruined lives and intensified the focus on an otherwise sleepy little town. She blinked her eyes, surprised to see that it was already dark outside. She really could get lost in her work.

Good thing she had declined Conner's offer for dinner. As much as she wanted to spend more time with him, she feared they were getting too close. A romantic relationship wasn't in her plans. They had already settled that.

Standing and stretching, she strolled over to the fridge. She was grateful for the leftovers. Conner's father had made a mean meatloaf last night and insisted she take some home. She could get used to the family and friendships in Quail Hollow, yet she still had no plans to stay. Her writing took her out into the world. Gave her financial freedom.

She dug her cell phone out of her purse when it dinged. It was her editor.

When are you going to get me that piece? Amish won't be hot forever. Followed by a clock emoji, as in, "Tick tock, your time is running out."

She smiled ruefully. She felt that way about a lot of things of late: time was running out.

Not in the mood to deal with her editor, she set her phone facedown on the counter. She ran her hand across her chin and stared at the plate rotating in the microwave. There was a bigger story here. Maybe a book.

Did she have what it took to write a book? It would take a long time, and she wouldn't make any money for a while.

She bent her arm over her head and tugged on her elbow with the opposite hand, savoring the muscle stretch. Her phone chimed—this time, a phone call.

She flipped over her phone. It was a local number. Maybe Conner was calling her from a different phone. She slid her finger across the display and pressed the speaker button.

"Hello?"

"Hello," came a shaky female voice. "Grace?"

"Yes, this is Grace." She moved the phone closer to her mouth and spoke louder, as if that would help her hear the caller better. "Who is this?"

"Em…ma." The single word wobbled over the line.

Grace's heart dropped. "What's wrong?"

"I had to run some errands, and a deputy pulled my wagon over."

Grace blinked rapidly, trying to process what was going on. She had heard the sheriff's department was cracking down on underage drinking parties and driving under the influence. But Emma surely hadn't done anything.

Grace didn't want to ask the question over the line when a deputy was probably standing right there, allowing Emma to use his phone.

"The deputy said he'd let me go home if someone came to pick me up."

"Okay, I'll be right there. Where are you?"

Emma gave her directions. She wasn't too far. Grace grabbed her coat and ran out the back door. With Bradley's arrest, they hadn't felt the need to station Becky at Grace's home again tonight.

Grace slowed down when she remembered Zach's truck was buried after the heavy snowfall. It would take her forever to dig it out. She ran back in and dialed Conner's number. Maybe he could give her a ride. His phone went to voicemail and she paused, then hung up without leaving a message.

A little voice in her head cautioned her. She couldn't keep calling on Conner when she needed something *and* push him away at the same time. She wasn't being fair to him.

Grace's gaze drifted to the bulletin board in the kitchen with a list of local services. She dialed the number and seemed satisfied that she had done the right thing when a short time later a white van pulled up along the bottom of her driveway. He probably didn't want to risk getting stuck in the snow.

Grace ran outside and hopped in. The driver explained that he had just dropped someone off nearby.

She said a silent prayer of gratitude. After everything that had gone wrong lately, she was thankful for a timely ride. She hated to leave Emma out in the cold for long.

Grace gave the driver directions. A short time later, snow and slush kicked up under the van's tires as the driver slowed and pulled over on the opposite side of the road from Emma's horse and wagon.

"Who pulls someone over in this weather?" Grace muttered, not expecting the driver to answer. She released her seatbelt and leaned forward to study the pickup truck with a flashing dome light on its dash.

Strange, not a regular patrol car.

The deputy, his face obscured by the brim of his hat, stood next to the wagon. Emma was still sitting on the wagon's bench, wearing a heavy black bonnet and winter cape. Something didn't feel right. Grace grabbed the handle of the sliding door. "Wait here, please," she told the driver. "I shouldn't be long."

She hopped out, careful to avoid the patches of ice. The harsh wind slapped her in the face. Holding the collar of her coat tight at the neck, she crossed the road to where the officer stood with his back to her, talking to Emma.

"What's the concern here, deputy?" Grace said, both confused and angered by the situation. Her only restraint came from her gratitude that the deputy had allowed her young friend to call her. Emma wasn't a troublemaker or a drinker, not that Grace knew, anyway.

The officer turned around and Grace jerked her head back. "Kevin?"

"Hi, Grace. I understand you've come to rescue Emma."

"I'm confused. I thought you were retired."

Kevin rubbed his gloved hands together against the cold. "The sheriff hires some of us back on a contract basis to keep the streets safe. I'm sure you understand."

"Not exactly. In fact, I'm sure this must be a misunderstanding."

"*Yah*, I was careful," Emma said.

"You were weaving all over the road. I think you might have had too much to drink. I pulled you over for your own protection and that of anyone who might come into your path."

"Were you drinking?" Grace stared into the frightened Amish girl's watery eyes.

"*Neh.* I promise. I'm coming back from checking on my sister. She's expecting a baby."

"Is Ruthie okay?"

"*Yah.* I don't think the baby is ready to meet us." A small smile flickered on the young woman's sweet face.

Grace squeezed her hand and whispered, "Don't worry. I'll handle this and get you home."

"Thank you. I'm not sure my *mem* would be too happy if the sheriff's department brought me home."

"I understand." Grace let out a long frustrated huff and turned her attention to Kevin. "What do you do in situations like this? Obviously, you allowed her to call me. Can I promise you that I'll see her safely home?"

Kevin seemed to ponder this a minute. "She needs to be more careful. It's dangerous out here on the roads at night, especially for young ladies who've been drinking." The underlying meaning of his words sent fear skittering up Grace's spine: women, alone, night.

"I wasn't drinking," Emma insisted. Grace touched the young woman's arm, reassuring her. Kevin was going to let her off with a warning. No harm, no foul. It seemed pointless to argue.

"I can take you home, Emma. Let's go."

Emma started to scoot off the bench of the wagon when her eyes grew wide. "My horse. I can't leave her on the side of the road." Emma looked even more panic stricken now.

Grace glanced at Kevin. Surely they've run into this predicament before. "What do we do about the horse?"

"I can't allow you to drive." Kevin's tone lacked compassion.

"Please, I'm not…" Emma let her words trail off in exasperation.

Kevin turned to Grace. "Do you know how to handle a horse?"

Grace pressed a hand to her chest. "Are you kidding me?"

"Okay, I have an idea. You drive my truck—you can drive, right?—and I'll take the horse back to the barn at the bed & breakfast. It's closer than the Hershberger farm."

"Yes," Grace agreed, eager for a solution. "I can have Eli bring the horse and wagon to your home in the morning." She addressed the last part to Emma.

"Okay," Emma said, clearly not sure about any of this.

Grace walked Emma over to the van and pulled open the door. She could feel Kevin's eyes on them from across the road. A fluttering feeling settled in her belly. Grace leaned in close. She needed a plan. A backup in case something went wrong.

But you know Kevin. You're just cautious because of recent events. But…

Unable to shake her misgivings, Grace leaned in close to her Amish friend. "Emma, I should be home in thirty minutes. Once I get home, I'm going to call the business phone in your barn. If you don't hear from me by then, call 9-1-1 and ask to speak to Captain Conner Gates. Tell him exactly what happened. Tell him that Kevin Schrock was the man who pulled you over. Kevin," she emphasized. Grace considered jumping into the van with Emma and leaving the scene.

"I don't understand…" Emma started.

"What's going on?" Grace jumped when she realized Kevin was standing right behind her. He took her arm firmly, and she looked up at him with a question in her eyes.

He eased his grip a bit. "Come on. Let's get the horse safely home." Kevin grabbed the door handle and slammed it closed with Emma inside. He handed the driver some money through the open driver's side window, then tapped the roof of the van. "Safe travels." Then he turned to Grace. "Let's get this horse settled." Despite his innocuous words, a dark shadow lurked in the depths of his eyes.

"The driveway is plowed and the walks are shoveled." Conner took off his gloves and hat, then stomped his boots on the carpet just inside the entryway at his dad's house.

"I'm more than capable," his father hollered from his recliner in front of the TV toward the back of the house.

Conner walked through the dining room and took

off his coat. He threw it over the chair "I know. But I don't mind."

His father laughed. "You don't even plow your own driveway."

Conner tilted his head. "Just gives me more time to do yours." He sat down on the edge of the couch in the adjacent family room.

"Actually I'm surprised. I thought you'd be trying to charm your lady friend before Heather and Zach get home from their honeymoon." Conner's father took a sip of his soda and leaned back in his recliner. "I don't imagine she'll be sticking around town much longer."

"Yeah, well, you know me. More the bachelor type." And she had refused his dinner invitation.

His father aimed the remote at the TV and turned the volume down. Setting his soda on the side table, he shifted in his chair to get a good look at his son. "I've never been one to speak from the heart. And my motto's always been live and let live, unless, of course, that involves going against the law."

"Not sure I'm following." He and his father discussed sports, weather, the occasional case. Not feelings.

"I have to say my piece. Up until now, you've dated here and there. I always bought into your claims that you preferred bachelorhood. The freedom of it all. I can see why you might think that's true." He held out his palm and plastered on an exaggerated smile, indicating his own living situation. "Sometimes I think you chose to be alone because of how your mom and I hurt you."

Conner held up his hands, not willing to get into this with his dad. Conner's mom had hurt both of them when she walked out after Sarah Miller's murder case took over his father's life. She claimed she could never compete with a dead woman for his father's attention. His father claimed his mother never understood the stresses of the job. At a standstill, they never reconciled.

"I know you had a job to do and Mom didn't understand. It's an important job. I get it."

"I don't think you do. Don't let this job consume you. If you can find happiness, grab it. Grace needs a guy like you. A good guy. Show her what a good guy is like."

Conner dragged a hand through his hair. "She's witnessed a lot in her lifetime. Losing her mom to violence. Knowing her former brother-in-law terrorized her sister. That shapes a person."

"You can change that. For both of you," his father pleaded.

Conner lifted a shoulder, unable to see how their very different lives would fit together. Starting to feel uncomfortable at all this touchy-feely talk, he asked, "Did you order the pizza?"

"Yep, should be ready."

Conner went to the front hall and pulled his father's coat off a hanger. "My coat's wet. I'm going to grab yours."

"No problem. Pick up more pop while you're out," his father hollered from his cozy spot in front of the TV.

"Sure thing." He stepped outside and the wind felt raw on his exposed head and hands. The key was to dress for the weather, only then could people embrace it.

Grace wasn't a fan of the cold weather. He couldn't

help but wonder if she could be convinced to make Quail Hollow her home.

Driving Kevin's truck, Grace pulled out behind Emma's wagon with Kevin behind the reins. He told her to follow him with her flashers on in his truck. Something about this seemed very wrong.

But would a man who bothered to care for a horse mean her any harm? Perhaps I'm overreacting.

She reached into her pocket and pulled out her phone. She didn't like to use her phone while driving, but figured this couldn't wait. She dialed Conner's number and held her breath. Her shoulders sagged when it went to voicemail again.

"Where are you?" she muttered.

"Leave a message..."

"Conner, it's me again. Listen, Emma Hershberger got pulled over by Kevin Schrock. He said he was working with the sheriff's department on a contract basis." She tried to keep her voice even. "Just seemed odd. I put Emma in a van home and right now I'm driving his truck back to the bed & breakfast behind him. He's driving Emma's wagon. Strange, right? I don't know." As she rambled on, she began to question why she called. "Just call me when you get this."

Grace ended the call and glanced at her phone's display. Who else could she call? She didn't want to call the sheriff's department because she didn't want Emma to get into more trouble if Grace's "bad feeling" turned out to be paranoia. What if they sent a deputy to Emma's house? Maryann would be upset. She slid the phone into her pocket and turned her full attention to the road.

Dear Lord, please keep me safe and quiet my racing thoughts.

Surprisingly, Kevin seemed comfortable behind the reins of the horse. It took longer to get back to the bed & breakfast than it had taken Grace to drive out. She didn't envy the Amish form of transportation in the bitter cold of winter.

Kevin stopped the wagon near the end of the driveway to the bed & breakfast. Grace pulled the truck in front of the horse. She gave Kevin a few minutes to unhitch the horse and guide it toward the barn.

She hopped out of the warm truck. Her instincts told her to go directly into the bed & breakfast, but she had to give Kevin his truck keys. She jogged over to the barn.

Grace waited in the doorway of the barn, stuffing her hands under her arms to keep them warm. "Looks like you're all set. Eli comes in the morning. I'll see that Emma's horse is fed and cared for until we can get her home. Here's your truck keys."

Kevin pushed the door of the stall closed and patted the horse. "All set." He approached her and took the keys.

"Good night." She turned and picked up her pace toward the house, still unable to shake her nerves.

"Hold up." With heightened awareness, she tuned into Kevin's steady stride, fast approaching behind her. All her self-defense moves she never practiced floated to mind.

She knew she couldn't outrun him so she spun around and squared her shoulders. "Yes?" She hiked up her chin in a show of confidence she most certainly didn't feel.

"Would you like to go for coffee?" His expression was unreadable in the heavy shadows of the winter night.

Heat immediately pooled under the collar of her heavy coat. "No, thank you, I'm really tired." She turned again to walk toward the house. "Maybe another time," she quickly added, only to be polite.

Solid fingers latched on to her wrist, and Grace bit back a yelp. "No, you're coming now."

Conner returned to his father's house with the piping hot pizza. He set it on top of a hot pad on the dining room table. "Pizza's here."

Harry lowered the footrest on the recliner and stood. "Smells great." He gestured casually to Conner's wet coat slung over the back of the dining room chair. "Your phone's been ringing."

"Oh, yeah?" Conner frowned.

Just as he slipped his hand into his coat pocket, the phone rang. He pulled it out and glanced at the display.

It was Dispatch. He slid his finger across the accept button. "Captain Gates."

"I have Emma Hershberger. She's anxious to talk to you."

He recognized the name. "Does she know I'm on vacation?"

"She insisted on talking to you."

Apprehension had Conner holding his breath. "Put her through."

"This is Emma Hershberger. Grace wanted me to call you." He pressed the phone closer to his ear, making sure he caught every word. "She wanted me to tell you that Kevin pulled me over. I promise, I wasn't drinking. The deputy let me call Grace to come pick me up."

Conner turned his back to the TV and walked toward the front of the house, focusing intently on the words spilling out of the young woman's mouth. "When Grace got there, the deputy let me leave with the hired driver while Grace and Kevin saw that my horse and wagon got safely back to her barn. She said to call you if she didn't call me in thirty minutes. I tried calling her myself but she didn't answer."

Conner listened to the long, winding tale. Not much of it made sense. One thing, however, stuck out: Grace had insisted this young lady call him. Grace must have sensed something was off.

"Did she say why she asked you to call me?" He turned and saw his father approaching out of the corner of his eye.

"She looked worried. I think she wanted you to know it was Kevin. She said make sure you tell him Kevin pulled me over."

"Where did you last see Grace?"

"On the side of the road with Kevin, the sheriff's officer."

"Is there a number where I can reach you, Emma?"

She rattled off the number and told him she had an answering machine in the barn and to leave a message if she didn't pick up.

Conner ended the call and noticed the missed calls from Grace. He listened to her message. She seemed concerned, but not overly. He tried to call her back. It rang a few times, then stopped. He hung up and dialed the sheriff's cell phone number. When he picked up, he asked, "Did you hire Kevin Schrock perhaps on a contract basis?"

"*Retired* Undersheriff Schrock? Um, no," the sheriff said. "I don't know what you're getting at."

"We might have a situation. I'll call you if I find anything out." He ended the call and explained to his father what Emma had told him. "Has Kevin ever pulled anyone over after he retired?"

"He's not allowed to. And you can go to jail for impersonating an officer."

He jammed one arm then the other into his damp coat sleeves. "Want to come with me? See what's going on?"

"Absolutely."

"Let's go." Conner swiped his keys from the table, tamping back his mounting fear. "Something's not right."

Grace tried to yank her arm away from Kevin's tightening grip, but he was stronger. "Please let me go," she said forcefully. "I called Conner from the truck. I'm expecting him any minute. He'll wonder where I am." She prayed a little white lie might derail whatever plans Kevin had. She had no idea why he was pulling her toward his truck.

"Your boyfriend won't make it here in time."

Her chest tightened and she tried to dig in her heels, but he was stronger. She pulled and wriggled and dropped like dead weight. She landed on her backside in the snow and scrambled backward. She'd have to get to her feet if she hoped to outrun Kevin.

"What are you doing?" he asked, his tone a mix of curiosity and disgust.

"I'm not going anywhere with you."

He stomped toward her punching holes in the snow with his boots "I thought you wanted to know what happened to your mother."

Grace wasn't going to take the bait. "Leave me alone. I'm not going with you."

His heavily shadowed face grew darker. "Now you sound just like her."

Grace's insides turned ice cold. She scrambled to her feet and debated if she could beat him to the house. "What do you mean, 'I sound just like her'?"

Kevin smirked. "Oh, don't get riled up. You know how much you look like her. It's only natural that you'd sound like her, too."

His words seeped into her brain. Her arms and legs trembled. There was more to their meaning than he was letting on.

Dear Lord, help me remain calm.

She doubted she could run to the door, unlock it and get in before he grabbed her. Perhaps she could keep him talking until Conner showed up.

If Conner showed up. She said a quick prayer that Emma called Conner as she had told her to. Or perhaps he had gotten her voicemail and decided to investigate.

Grace hiked her chin and tried to speak calmly. *Show no fear.* "Did you know my mother before she died?"

A slow smile tilted the corners of his lips. A wicked glint lit his eyes in the moonlight. Sadness prickled the backs of her eyes. Her phone rang and a burst of hope rippled through her. She locked eyes with Kevin. Could she answer it before he stopped her?

Quickly, she reached into her pocket. Saw it was

Conner. Frantic, she tried to accept the call, but Kevin slapped the phone out of her hand. "Not so fast. No more games."

Her phone sliced through the snow and disappeared. Her one source of communication was lost. A link to survival.

Kevin Schrock, the retired undersheriff, grabbed her arms and pulled them behind her. He shoved her toward his truck. Knowing this was her last chance, however feeble, she screamed and it echoed off the snow and barren trees. She wanted to cry, knowing it wasn't likely anyone had heard.

Kevin cursed, lifted his fist and slammed it into her head. Grace's all-consuming fear turned to blackness.

Chapter Fourteen

"None of this makes sense," the retired sheriff said from the passenger seat of Conner's truck. "Kevin Schrock pulled a young Amish woman over? Why would he do that?"

"I don't know. Maybe it was some kind of misunderstanding. Grace asked Emma to call me if she didn't call her in thirty minutes. Now Grace isn't answering her phone. Emma was under the impression that they were going to take her horse and wagon to the barn at the bed & breakfast for safekeeping. Let's go there. Clear this up."

"What are you thinking?"

"Kevin was acting outside his authority to pull someone over." Conner swallowed hard. He considered the fact that Kevin wanted to get to Grace somehow. How did that play into all this? The puzzle pieces didn't quite fit. Kevin had been his dad's longtime friend and subordinate. This was out of character for the man who had worn a badge for most of his adult life.

"You're friends with Kevin. Anything unusual going on in his life?"

"As much as it might surprise you, us guys don't talk about our feelings much."

Conner scrubbed a hand across his face. Maybe he should try another angle. "What role did Kevin play in Sarah Miller's murder investigation?" Something niggled at the back of his brain. Despite not seeing how all this would play out, Conner was convinced he was on the right path.

"What does that have to do with anything?"

"Dad, answer the question." He pressed down on the accelerator and the truck's engine roared. He prayed he didn't hit any ice. He didn't want to fishtail and end up in a ditch. Not tonight.

"He was my right-hand man. Sarah's case nearly killed me. I could never get her daughters out of my mind. I won't lie—it got emotional for me, whereas Kevin could separate his job from his emotions. He kept me focused. Kept me from charging off in all sorts of directions where I would have been wasting time and resources. You need to have focus with investigations like these."

Conner slowed at an intersection, glanced both ways and then sped through. "Were there any leads on which you felt he redirected you?"

"What are you talking about? Are you suggesting Kevin purposely interfered with the case?" Conner hadn't heard this hard-edged anger in his father's voice in a long time. He hated to be challenged.

Conner gripped the steering wheel tighter. "I'm throwing out ideas. Trying to keep myself focused. Otherwise I might go mad imagining why Grace isn't answering her cell phone. Why would Kevin pull over an Amish girl when he's no longer working for the sheriff's department? Can we play around with a few what-if scenarios?"

"Yes." His father's answer was clipped. "Kevin was convinced a vagrant passing through town killed Mrs. Miller. And it was our best lead. Once, I thought we even had the guy, until he produced a rock-solid alibi. The guy was in Buffalo, locked up in the county holding center the week Sarah was murdered. But then we got information on another stranger seen in town that week." He fisted his hands. "Never could track him down."

"Who got that lead? The one on the second stranger?" Conner asked, keeping his eyes on the road.

"I don't know." His father grew silent for a minute. "I'm pretty sure it was Kevin." His father muttered under his breath. "I can't..."

"I wonder if Kevin generated this lead because he was trying to redirect your focus."

"I can't imagine."

"Were there any leads you *didn't* pursue, perhaps on Kevin's insistence?"

"A rumor surfaced that Sarah Miller may have dated an *Englischer*. We quickly put that to bed. It was hard enough for the family. We didn't want to drag Sarah's reputation through the mud."

He considered the exchange between Maryann Hershberger and Grace. Maryann claimed her friend had had an *Englisch* suitor. "What did Kevin think about that theory?"

"Not a lot. We were on the same page. No sense hurting the family more with baseless allegations."

Conner slowed and turned into the snow-packed

driveway of the bed & breakfast. A wagon sat at the end of the driveway. "Looks like they made it here."

Conner and his dad hopped out of the truck at the same time. Conner ran to the back door and pounded on it. He canvassed the trampled snow while they waited. Either a few kids had been playing out here, or someone had had a struggle.

His father checked the barn and the two men met back in the center of the snowy yard. "There are two horses in the barn."

"The bed & breakfast only has one horse." Conner glanced around and noticed the tracks in the snow. "Looks like they brought Emma's horse and wagon here like she said. But there's no sign of Grace or Kevin."

The retired sheriff studied him with watchful eyes. "What's going on?"

Conner shook his head. "I wish I knew." He jerked his head toward his dad. "Call Kevin. Don't let on that we're looking for him. See what he says."

His father gave him a quick nod and opened his old-school flip phone. Conner paced outside the barn. Puffs of white vapor floated out from his mouth and disappeared into the black of night.

His father snapped the phone shut. "No answer."

"I'll try Grace again." He dialed her number. From across the yard, he heard a chirping noise. He followed the sound, made easier by the glowing light under a layer of snow.

He ran over to it, his boots crunching on the snow. Holding his breath, he bent over, stuck his hand in the snow and grabbed the phone. The screen displayed his name and number.

"Wherever Grace went, she left in a hurry," his dad said.

"How far does Kevin live from here?"

"He doesn't live far from the sheriff's department." The two men's eyes locked. Conner knew exactly what his father was thinking. "I'll call it in. Have someone go by and check his house. They'll get there before we possibly can."

The throbbing in Grace's head was the first thing she tuned into as she regained consciousness. The second was the stale smell of something closed up for far too long. The third was the set of events leading up to the pounding headache.

Fighting to keep her breath even so Kevin might think she was still sleeping, she opened her eyes a fraction. She had no idea where she was or the time. The room was dark, and a thin line of light seeped in under the door. The sharp springs of a cot poked her back.

She couldn't see much of anything. She held her breath and avoided any conspicuous movements. She didn't sense Kevin in the room with her.

She dared to open her eyes wide and study her surroundings. The heavily shadowed room came into focus. The thick drapes over the windows masked the time of day. She was in a room—a cabin decorated hunter chic—and the exit was about twenty feet away.

Dear Lord, help me get out of here.

Flattening her hand on the cot, she pushed herself up to a seated position and the springs groaned. Her aching head joined the protest. The room spun and what little was in her stomach threatened to make a second appearance. She lifted a hand to her aching head and was surprised to feel something. A prayer *kapp*? A bonnet. Blinking away her confusion, she touched the fabric gathered around her legs. A dress.

Head swimming, she pushed to her feet and crossed to a dresser and turned on a dim light. A full-length mirror sat in the corner. Someone had pulled her hair into a bun, placed on a bonnet and dressed her in Amish clothing. Frantic, she lifted up the hem of the gown and saw her jeans. The cuffs of her shirt poked up from the sleeves of the Amish dress. Someone had dressed her over her regular street clothes. She took small comfort in that, even as an underlying dread pulsed ever stronger through her veins.

Whoever had done this was sick.

Fearing Kevin had become unhinged, she knew she had to get out of there. As she quickly scanned the room, her thoughts grew scattered, and her face felt heated. If she hoped to make a break for it, she'd have to find her shoes and coat. Without them, she'd escape only to be found frozen to death in the harsh elements. She didn't see them anywhere.

A rustling sounded at the door. She grew rigid with indecision, uncertain if she should get back into bed and pretend she was still unconscious, or charge the door.

Her mouth went dry as the door swung open.

"Stay on the line with the deputy," Conner said to his dad. "Tell him we're headed to Kevin Schrock's house now. We're twelve minutes out. If he's there, make sure to keep him in sight. We're looking for Grace Miller. We can't risk him getting desperate."

His father nodded in the passenger seat, his phone pressed to his ear. He relayed the information. Conner could see the old fire in his dad's eyes. Conner hoped they'd find Grace safe and sound.

The thought of losing Grace forever forced all his true feelings to the surface. He had tried to stuff them down to be effective at his job. And because he knew she wasn't going to stay in Quail Hollow, anyway. That made it easy to pretend he didn't feel what he felt for her.

But the thought of losing her forever…

Hadn't his dad's inability to separate his feelings been his downfall? Or had his right-hand man purposely derailed the investigation?

A fist knotted his stomach as the pieces of the case started to click together.

As Conner raced toward Kevin's house and his dad waited on the phone, Conner asked, "Do you think Kevin was capable of hurting Sarah?"

His father stared straight ahead. "He was my friend. We don't even know that Kevin has Grace." His square jaw was set in determination.

"If he does, do you think he'd hurt Grace?"

His father sighed heavily, as if finally resigned to the fact Kevin wasn't who he thought he was. "I don't know anymore. I'm going to have to question everything I knew about Kevin. *If* he's involved." His dad straightened in his seat and turned his attention back to the person on the other end of the phone. "Yeah… You sure?… Okay." He ran a hand across his jaw. "Keep us posted."

His father flipped the phone closed. "No sign of Kevin at his house."

Conner eased off the gas, annoyance coursing through him. "Did they put out an alert for his vehicle?"

"Yes."

Conner pounded the steering wheel. The vehicle emitted a wimpy honk when his fist unintentionally made contact with the horn. An idea zipped through his mind. "Does Kevin have other friends, places he might go if he's desperate? If he needed someplace to hole up?"

His father bolted upright in his seat. "He's got an old hunting cabin. Goes there to clear his head. He brought me up there once a long time ago."

Conner's adrenaline spiked, and he had to consciously will himself to calm down. "Do you think you could find it now?"

"Yes!" His father's voice vibrated with excitement. "Turn left at the next intersection. It's about thirty minutes away."

Chapter Fifteen

"You're awake." Kevin stood with an armload of firewood. His demeanor was that of someone who had simply returned from a quick errand, not of someone who had kidnapped a woman and dressed her in Amish clothing.

"I'm awake," she replied, studying him carefully. "What are we doing here?" She tried to keep her tone even, nonaccusatory.

"I'm lighting a fire. It gets cold in here." He stretched out a hand and flipped on the light switch. "This provides better light than that old lamp." He dragged one hand over a piece of dusty furniture. "This place could use a good cleaning. I haven't been up here as much as I'd like."

Grace nodded slowly and winced. The pain ricocheted around her aching head. Kevin unloaded the firewood in the stand next to the fireplace in what seemed to be the master bedroom, yet he had set her up on a cot and not the bed that took up half of one wall. He rushed over to her like a doting boyfriend. "Does it hurt?" He studied her face in a way that made her skin crawl. He cupped her cheek, and she could feel gritty pieces of wood and dirt on his fingers. "I didn't mean to hurt you, but you were making such a fuss."

Grace leaned back a fraction and lifted her chin in a show of strength. "I need you to take me home now, Kevin. People will be looking for me."

He studied her face with an intensity that made her eyelid twitch. "You're not going home, Sarah. It'll be different this time."

Cold dread pumped through her veins. She knew it, even before he called her by the wrong name. Her mother's name. His link with reality had shattered to the point where Kevin thought she was a woman he had likely killed almost thirty years ago.

The walls closed in on her.

Kevin Schrock had been her mother's *Englisch* suitor. And when she rejected him he had ended her life.

It was the only thing that made sense.

"I never, *ever* meant to hurt you." Kevin narrowed his gaze, lost in thought. Lost in another time. Lost in the face of another woman. "We could have been happy if you had chosen me. You were too stubborn, self-righteous." A vein bulged on his forehead, and Grace knew she had to put on a performance.

She smoothed the tips of her trembling fingers across his forehead. She swallowed her revulsion. "It's okay. I'm here now."

Kevin let out a shaky breath and seemed to relax his shoulders. He even closed his eyes for the briefest of moments. "You are, aren't you?" He stared into her eyes, and it was all Grace could do not to blink.

Not to cry. Not to lash out at this man who had killed her mother.

Dear Lord, help me.

"Why don't you light the fire?" She made an exaggerated show of shuddering to emphasize how cold she was.

Kevin searched her face for a long moment, then ran his hand down her arm. "Okay, honey. Stay here. I'll take care of it."

She nodded slowly, wishing her head would stop throbbing.

He took a piece of newspaper from the stack near the fireplace and crumpled it up for kindling. Grace's mind raced. How could she get out of here? She still had no jacket or shoes. How far could she get in the snow?

While her mother's murderer built the fire, he muttered something about taking care of the horse this time because people seemed more concerned about the horse than they had about a murdered woman. People didn't always have their priorities straight.

Grace had read about her mother's horse being found wandering Quail Hollow after she had been killed. She quickly shoved the thought aside, determined to remain strong and focused if she hoped to survive.

Grace took a chance and stepped toward the bedroom door. Kevin froze like an animal sensing a shift in the environment. He pivoted on the balls of his feet and slowly rose, a dark cloud floating behind his eyes. "What are you doing?"

With her pulse thrumming in her ears, Grace swallowed hard and forced a smile, fearing Kevin would notice the twitch in her cheeks. "I thought maybe I'd make us tea." Her eyes wandered toward the bedroom door. Maybe she'd find a weapon in the kitchen.

Kevin considered her suggestion for a moment before telling her to sit on the cot. He was the host. He'd make the tea.

"Okay." She slowly sat down and clutched her hands in her lap. He flicked the lighter and a flame caught the piece of newspaper under the firewood.

Kevin rubbed his hands together. "We should have a roaring fire before long. It's a good thing I came along when you were stuck on the side of the road."

What?

Grace pressed her lips together, determined not to contradict him. Her nerves hummed as she plotted her escape. The longer he was in the cabin, the calmer he became. Maybe he'd eventually let down his guard. Until then, what would she endure? She wanted to ask him so many questions about her mom, about the recent attacks and break-ins, and how Bradley and his confession fit in. But she feared his precarious grasp on reality would further shatter and put her in imminent danger. He thought he was her rescuer. He was blending events…from tonight? And from almost thirty years ago?

"Are you warm?" he asked, coming to sit next to her and taking her hand in his. She fought the urge to yank it away.

"Yes…" She purposely let the word hang out there, preying on his need to please her.

"What is it?"

Grace smiled, doing her best to act shy. "I'm embarrassed to tell you this. I'd like to use the bathroom."

Kevin blinked rapidly. Then all of a sudden he stood

and grabbed her wrist, pulling her up with him. "It's back here." He strode toward a door in the corner of the room.

Grace stopped and stared at him. "I need privacy."

He watched her, his eyes dark and unreadable. It was like part of him was seeing Grace and not trusting her, and another part of him was seeing Sarah, the woman he had fallen in love with. Become obsessed with. She prayed he'd be fooled long enough to give her time alone in the bathroom.

"I'll give you five minutes. I'll be standing right outside the door. Don't lock it."

Grace smiled tightly. She had no idea if it even mattered.

She went inside the bathroom, and a wave of nausea nearly doubled her over when she realized there was no lock on the door. Panicking, she knew she'd have to move fast. A tall, narrow glass shelving unit sat in the corner on the same wall as the door. Working quickly, she removed the tissue box, an ornamental duck and a few rolls of toilet paper. Silently, she slanted it across the door, forming a diagonal. It wouldn't keep someone out for long, but it would certainly slow them down.

At least, she prayed it would.

Tearing off her bonnet and stepping out of the Amish dress, she crept toward the window. She stretched up, felt for a lock on top of the window and twisted it.

Panic sent gooseflesh racing across her skin.

She planted two hands on either side of the window and froze. She glanced over her shoulder. If this window made any noise, Kevin would come charging in.

"Everything okay in there?"

"Yes. I'd feel better if you weren't standing right outside the door."

She thought she heard a little chuckle.

She turned both taps, opening the faucet full blast. It would mask the sound, but it might make him suspicious.

Quickly, she planted her hands on both sides of the window again and shoved. A horrendous rumbling noise sent the window up. A cold blast of winter assaulted her face.

Thank You, God.

At that exact moment, the sound of glass shelves exploded behind her.

Bam. Bam. Bam.

Kevin was busting through the door.

Not wasting any time, she hoisted herself through the small opening, her hips getting caught on the narrow window. Wiggling fiercely, she finally pushed her midsection through to the other side.

Just as she was about to pull her legs free, solid fingers grasped her ankle and wrenched it.

Grace released a bloodcurdling scream.

"How much farther?" Conner's nerves hummed in constant rhythm with the winter tires on the country road.

"Up here." His father leaned forward against his shoulder harness, searching for a landmark visible only to him. Then he pointed frantically toward a narrow break between the trees. "There! There! That road leads to his cabin."

Conner slammed on the brakes, threw it in Reverse

and narrowed his gaze. “Here? The path between the trees?”

“Yeah, yeah, turn here. That sign is familiar.” Sure enough, the headlights flashed on a sign with the words No Trespassing and the silhouette of a growling dog underneath.

Conner engaged the four-wheel drive and turned onto the small path. A single set of tire tracks told them someone had been down this way recently. “I would have never found this in a million years, Dad. Thank you.”

“Don’t thank me yet,” his dad said, his voice somber. “Let’s go rescue Sarah’s daughter.”

Conner pressed his foot on the accelerator, realizing for the first time that finding Grace safe meant more to his father than he had realized. It was his justice for Sarah.

“Dad, you can’t blame yourself.”

“I should have known. I never suspected Kevin. After me, he was closest to the case and probably used misdirection every chance he got.” His father muttered something under his breath that Conner didn’t quite catch.

“He had a lot of people fooled.” Conner navigated the truck through the snow under a canopy of trees.

“I was the sheriff. The buck stopped with me. I failed Sarah. I failed her family.”

Conner carefully navigated the snowy road, knowing nothing he could say would convince his father otherwise.

“Are you going to be able to drive all the way to the cabin?”

“Looks like Kevin’s truck made it.”

"It's not that much farther."

The rocking and slipping on the snow-covered road slowed their progress. As they rounded a curve in the road, a cabin with lights glowing could be seen set back among the trees.

"That's it," his father said, excited. "Right there. There's his cabin."

Conner stopped, cut off his engine and manually shut off the lights. "I don't see Kevin's truck, but someone's definitely there." He turned to his father. "You okay to walk from here? Gives us the element of surprise."

His father playfully patted his son's thigh. "This ain't my first rodeo." He zipped his jacket all the way up and put on his winter hat. "Let's go." Without waiting for a response, the retired sheriff pushed open the door. Conner slipped out of the vehicle. They both closed their doors at the same time with a quiet click.

They met at the front of the truck. "Snow's pretty deep," Conner said. "Let's follow the tire tracks until we get about fifty feet from the cabin. Then you go right, and I'll go left around to the back. Assess the situation."

Conner's gut tightened at the thought of what might be happening to Grace at this very moment. He found himself saying a quick prayer. He hadn't done that since his mom took him to church when he was a little kid.

His father nodded, and they both set off. The sound of their breathing was punctuated by the squeaking of their boots in the snow.

As Conner broke left, a scream pierced the night.

His blood ran cold.

Grace.

Conner took off running at the sound of her scream, his legs and arms pumping as he struggled through the deep snow. He turned the corner. Light—and Grace—spilled out of a window. Grace had her hands propped on the snow and was flailing. Kevin had his head and one shoulder out the window, and he had a firm grasp on Grace's ankle, after what was obviously a failed escape attempt.

"Let her go," Conner ordered.

"Get out of here!" Kevin growled, not taking his eyes off Grace.

"You're in a tight spot there. There's nowhere to go. Let her go," Conner repeated as he pulled out his gun.

Kevin shifted, revealing the gun he was barely able to squeeze out on the other side of his body. "I may not be able to get you, son, but I have a clear shot at Sarah here."

"Her name is Grace," Conner enunciated slowly, trying to break through whatever alternate universe Kevin was in. Conner directed the beam of his flashlight at Kevin's face.

Kevin blinked a few times, anger sparking in his eyes. "She was supposed to marry me and get out of this awful town. If she couldn't love me, she wasn't going to have anyone."

Kevin began to sob. Conner crept closer.

Suddenly Kevin released his grip on Grace's ankle and crumbled on the windowsill as if someone had cracked him from behind. The gun fell from his hand and disappeared in a tunnel of snow beneath the window.

From inside the bathroom, retired sheriff Harry

Gates hadn't missed a beat. "I've got him." He yanked Kevin back through the opening.

"Everything under control?" Conner shouted.

"Yep, got this jerk in handcuffs. How's everyone out there?" his father hollered out the window, his focus on his prisoner.

Conner bent down and scooped up Grace. Her head fell against his chest. "Are you okay?"

She shuddered against him. "I am now."

"Let's get you home."

Thank You, God, for keeping her safe.

Chapter Sixteen

Grace tried not to giggle as Conner touched the ticklish spot around her ankle, inspecting where Kevin had grabbed her and twisted in an attempt to keep her under his control. She leaned back in the rocking chair by the wood-burning stove in her sister's bed & breakfast and tried to think of serious things to stop her silly giggling, which wasn't too hard.

Her gaze drifted to the stairs where Becky had disappeared only moments ago. "Do you really think it's necessary to make Becky stay?"

"Hey!" Becky called from the upstairs landing. "You're going to give a girl a complex."

"Sorry," Grace called back, "no offense meant. Just hate to waste your time. All the people that have had it in for me are in custody. Or am I missing something?"

Becky came down the steps. "You should be safe. Conner wants me to stay another night or two. He thought you'd like the company after everything that's happened."

"You don't mind, do you?" Conner asked. A tingle raced up her foot from where he was still holding it.

"I certainly don't mind the company." She smiled at Becky, trying to ignore the effect Conner was having on her.

"Listen, I stopped over at the Hershberger residence on my way over," Becky said. "Emma's relieved you're okay."

"Did you explain to her mom that she didn't do anything wrong? I'd hate for her to get in trouble with her community."

Becky waved her hand. "Yes, she's fine. Their family wishes you a speedy recovery. Emma said she'll stop by in a few days. See about helping you around here."

"Sounds good."

Becky pointed toward the kitchen. "Mind if I grab some tea and head upstairs? I have a good book waiting for me."

"Sure thing," Grace said.

"And I'll make sure the alarm is set." Conner patted Grace's foot, gently placed it on the rocker next to him and stood.

Grace groaned. "What more could go wrong? You already have Bradley in custody for drugging Jason, and obviously Kevin's not going anywhere. That pretty much covers all the stories I was digging into here in Quail Hollow." She crossed her arms and settled back in her chair. "I promise."

Conner studied her with an intensity that made her toes curl. "You're not going to ruin Becky's evening. I think she enjoys getting away at the bed & breakfast."

"She's good company. I don't mind. I appreciate her taking the time."

Conner brushed his hand across her shoulder, seeming hesitant to leave. Grace understood. They had been through a lot together. "Things will be wrapped up soon."

Despite Kevin's break with reality, he did have the wherewithal to tell his side of the story. He had hired some guy to knock the shelves over in the basement of the library to scare Grace away from her mother's story. He was rightfully afraid of what she'd uncover. A deputy had been sent to pick up the guy he'd hired.

"What about the person who rammed my car in the parking lot?"

"One of Bradley's teammates wanted to protect his friend. Misguided loyalty. He felt the team had suffered enough by missing the playoffs. He didn't want Bradley getting in trouble for spiking his friend's drink, too." Conner bowed his head and rubbed the back of his neck. "I fear for the next generation if they think hurting someone else is a form of loyalty."

"They're not representative of our youth. There are a lot of wonderful people in this world. I've met them while covering different stories. I have faith we're on the right track." She rubbed her arms absentmindedly.

He leaned over and picked up her foot from the rocking chair, sat down and rested her foot on his knee. "I admire that about you. You have faith despite all the horrible things you've experienced."

"My faith is the one thing that keeps me going."

Conner studied her foot while massaging it. He seemed hesitant, as if he was trying to figure out how to tell her something. He lifted his eyes to hers. "I found myself praying that I'd be able to save you. I haven't done that in a long time."

Grace reached forward and covered his hands with hers. "Thank you for being there for me."

"I wouldn't have had it any other way."

He set her foot down, then leaned in to brush a soft kiss across her lips. "You sure know how to have a quiet vacation in Quail Hollow."

"This was never meant to be a vacation. I came here initially to recover from an appendectomy." Her hand went to her side. "That seems so long ago."

"I'd hate to see what kind of trouble you could have gotten into if you hadn't been sick."

Grace cupped his cheek and ran her thumb across the stubble on his jaw. "Well, thankfully, I'm fully recovered."

"Thank goodness." Conner took her hand from his face and kissed it. "You're okay? Kevin didn't hurt you?"

"Just a few bumps and bruises."

A hint of a smile danced in his eyes.

"I'll be okay. I promise," she whispered. The air in the room grew charged with an energy of expectancy that made butterflies flit in her stomach.

"I didn't realize how much I cared for you until I thought I lost you." He held her hand. Warmth spread up her arm, and she pushed the blanket down from around her shoulders.

"Did I thank you for saving me?" She hated the nervous squeak in her voice.

"More than once." He sat up straight and dropped her hand, as if he had switched gears.

Grace scooted toward the edge of her rocking chair, causing it to dip forward. She reached out and covered his hand resting on the arm of his chair. "I care for you, too."

"I sense a *but* coming on."

"We lead different lives. Your home is here. Mine is wherever the story takes me." She knew that stuff was superficial. The only thing truly keeping her from committing was her fear of relationships after losing her mom and witnessing her sister's violent relationship. If her dad were still alive, he'd no doubt tell her he'd marry her mother all over again, in spite of her heartbreaking murder. And Conner was not anything like her sister's ex. She had been using her fear as an excuse. Until now, she had never met someone worth taking the risk. Worth pushing aside her worries.

All her thoughts were jumbled and the only words she found were yet another excuse. "This would never work."

"I guess you can't blame a guy for trying." Conner laughed, a mirthless sound. "You'll have a great story to tell about your adventures in Quail Hollow."

She gently rubbed the back of his hand. "More than that, I finally have answers. My sisters will have answers. And my mom will have justice."

"I'm glad. I'm sorry it took this long."

Grace stifled a yawn. Conner covered her hand with his, keeping it warm. "I'll let you go to bed." He started to rise, and she stood with him. He took the opportunity to cup her cheek and kiss her, slow and gentle. After a moment, he pulled away. "I'm really going to miss you."

She nodded, unable to swallow around the lump of emotion in her throat. Unable to find the words to tell him she cared for him. Deeply. Too much had happened to make any sweeping promises she might regret in the light of day.

When she didn't respond, he cleared his throat. "Follow me to the back door and set the alarm after I go."

"I will."

"Oh, and I'll send someone over to plow the driveway. I don't want you to be snowed in."

"Thanks." They walked in silence and she saw him out, then set the alarm and waited for the sense of loss to pass.

The next morning, Grace headed downstairs after a dreamless sleep. Despite the things she had yet to face, she finally had peace. Her mother's murderer had been caught.

When she rounded the corner into the kitchen, she came up short. "Hey, Becky. I didn't expect you to still be here."

The young sheriff's deputy smiled. Sitting at the table, she lifted her book with one hand and her coffee with another. "You know how it is when you say you're going to read just one more page?"

Grace laughed. She was really growing to like this woman.

"Conner wanted me to let you know they arrested the young man Kevin hired to attack you in the basement of the library."

"What about whoever broke in here?"

"Kevin confessed to that. He said that you reminded him of Sarah. He wasn't really clear on how he got through the window here at the bed & breakfast or how he unlocked it. I'm sure he learned tricks over the years as a sheriff's deputy. He said he wanted to get close to you. See if you had uncovered anything about Sarah Miller's murder." Becky spoke as if Sarah wasn't related to Grace. "He hadn't expected you to come downstairs that night. He ran off instead of confronting you."

Grace's stomach knotted at the thought of surprising Kevin in the middle of the night. "I'm lucky Boots notified me of his presence. I hate to think..."

"Speaking of Boots, I haven't seen the kitty around in a while." Becky furrowed her brow and glanced around.

"She took off. My sister says she comes and goes and not to worry."

"Not to worry. Sounds like a plan." Becky gave her a sympathetic smile. "You have to move on. There's no way to understand the thought process of someone who's mentally ill. It seems Kevin eventually became obsessed with you, much as he became obsessed with your mom." She placed her book facedown to mark the page and stood. "I'm really sorry you had to go through all that." Becky flipped over the book, folded a corner of the page and then closed it. "You can finish that story you've been writing."

"Yeah..." The weight of indecision pressed heavily on Grace's chest. Maybe she was too close to the story to be objective.

Voices floated in from outside, and Grace leaned over to look out the back window. "Oh, wow, my sister and her husband are home. Already?" Had she been that preoccupied that she'd lost track of the days? She hadn't thought so.

Becky stood and set her mug in the sink. "Looks

like my cue to leave." She slowed and touched Grace's arm. "Take care, okay?"

Grace nodded. "Thanks for everything." The two women exchanged a brief hug.

"You're welcome." Becky picked up her overnight bag from the floor and slung the strap over her shoulder. She greeted Heather and Zach as she slipped out the back door.

Heather appeared suntanned and well rested. And happy. She flicked her thumb toward the yard with a confused look on her face. "Booking overnight guests while we're gone?"

"Long story." Grace hugged her sister fiercely. "You guys are back early."

"A few days early," Zach said with a broad smile.

"Miss this place too much?" Grace asked, confused.

"I was feeling a little queasy on the boat. We caught an earlier flight home from one of the ports."

Grace studied her sister. Heather glanced at her husband, then back at Grace. She placed a hand on her midsection. "I'm pregnant." She hunched up her shoulders and a smile crept up on her face. "Morning sickness." Her happiness was contagious.

Grace hugged her sister again, and a tear tracked down her cheek. "I'm thrilled for you." She reached out and playfully tapped Zach's cheek with the palm of her hand. "And you. You guys deserve all the best."

"So tell me," Heather said, as she sat down at the table. "How have things been around here?" She glanced around the bed & breakfast, her pride and joy. "Looks like you held down the fort. I hope your stay in Quail Hollow was uneventful."

"Why don't you and Zach get settled first? We'll talk

later." Grace didn't want to throw a wet blanket over their happy homecoming by telling her sister about her car. Hopefully, the collision shop would have it repaired soon so that her sister wouldn't be inconvenienced.

Heather pushed to her feet. "Sounds good." Zach breezed past with the luggage, and Heather followed him upstairs.

Grace turned and stared out the window. A wicked wind sent the top layer of snow into a mini tornado. She shuddered and wrapped her arms around herself.

The sound of another vehicle made her glance toward the driveway. Conner's patrol car. She had thought they said their goodbyes last night. A lightness sent butterflies fluttering in her chest. She hustled to the mudroom, threw on her coat and opened the door, not caring if she seemed too eager to see him.

Upon noticing her as he walked across the yard, he took off his hat and smiled. Her heart melted a little bit more. He reached the back porch in a few long strides. "Becky filled you in?"

"About the arrests? Is it really over?"

Conner nodded. "Everyone involved has been arrested."

"Good." She rolled up on the balls of her stocking feet in the doorway.

"I've been doing a lot of thinking. I hope *we're* not over."

Grace tilted her head. Emotion trapped the words in her throat. A harsh wind whipped up and blew the hair from her face.

Conner stepped closer. "I couldn't let last night be the end. I don't want to say goodbye."

Tears burned the backs of her eyes. She'd be lying

if she claimed they were from the wicked winds. "Neither do I, but I couldn't find the right words last night." She met his gaze. "I've always been afraid to get hurt, but I've never met anyone like you."

Conner took her hand and stepped into the mudroom and closed the door behind them. "I understand. I promised myself I'd never repeat the mistakes of my parents. That I'd somehow protect my heart if I never risked it." He reached up and cupped her cheek. "But after thinking I'd lost you last night to that lunatic, I realized I'd been foolish." He traced her jawline with his knuckle. "You're too special to let go because I made a promise to myself to remain a bachelor when I was young and naïve."

Her face grew warm, despite the cool touch of his hand. A smile tugged on the corners of her lips. "Looks like we both had time to reflect last night."

He ran his fingers through her hair. "These feelings had been growing for awhile. The events of last night jolted me into realizing I couldn't keep ignoring them. I was afraid you'd leave before I had a chance to talk to you in person."

Grace reached up and wrapped her fingers around his wrist. "But where do we go from here?"

"I have an idea." He stepped closer and pressed a kiss to her lips.

Grace tasted like good coffee and morning sunshine. Conner hadn't slept much last night after nearly losing Grace. Then, this morning, he had gotten a quick phone call from Zach when they landed. Conner couldn't risk Grace leaving without knowing how he truly felt.

He stepped back and Grace tenderly touched her

lips. Dipping her head, she slipped past him and into the kitchen. "I imagine you have to get back to work? Can I get you a coffee to go?"

"That would be great." He watched her open and close the cabinets, probably looking for a to-go cup. Sensing her unease, he stepped up behind her and gently touched her back. "How about I stay for the coffee?"

"Oh, sure." She grabbed a mug, filled it and handed it to him.

He took a sip and decided to update Grace. Give her a minute to settle down, to process everything they shared. "This is great. Hey, I have good news about Katy Weaver. She went home from the hospital yesterday. The doctors feel she's on her way to a full recovery." The young Amish woman injured in the crash would get to live her life.

"What a relief."

"For everyone."

"How's Jason's mom? It had to be excruciating for her to know Bradley was responsible for Jason's death."

Conner nodded. "Having answers will go a long way toward providing her peace."

"I get it. I never thought we'd find my mother's murderer." Grace's eyes brightened. "I can't thank your dad enough for leading you to the cabin."

"It brought my dad some measure of peace to know he didn't let down Sarah's daughter." He smiled.

"He didn't let down my mother either. That's on Kevin." Grace squeezed his hand.

Conner gestured with his coffee mug toward the interior of the house. "Your sister's home."

"They're upstairs unpacking." She smiled brightly and leaned toward him. "They came home a few days early because my sister was getting queasy on the ship." She lowered her voice. "They're expecting a baby!"

"That's great."

Grace met his gaze. "It looks like things are finally working out for the Miller girls."

Conner set his coffee mug down and took her chin gently between his fingers. "Things *are* working out. Remember that. Don't start second guessing things when I leave here."

She nodded.

"We have a lot of things to figure out, but we'll do that together." He covered her mouth with his. He pulled back a fraction and whispered, "I love you."

She tilted her head back and smiled. "I love you, too." She narrowed her gaze, then laughed. "Does that mean I have to move to the great white north?"

Conner raised his eyebrows. "Not if you don't want to. I could find a job somewhere else, as long as I'm with you. That's all that matters."

Epilogue

Six months later...

The early morning sun streamed into Grace's bedroom. She sat on the chaise lounge with her laptop, finishing up the reader letter to be inserted at the back of her book about life in the Amish community. She stopped typing, pressed her fist to her mouth and reread:

> My mother lived her entire life in the Amish community. I don't think ever in her wildest dreams could she have envisioned the lives her three daughters would go on to live after her untimely death. My memories of my mom are vague. But deep in my heart—despite the Amish caution against pride—I believe she would be proud of all of us.
>
> Proud that we persevered through difficult times.
>
> Proud that we've found happiness despite all the sadness in the world.
>
> Proud that we chose to live life with hope. And faith.

With a great sense of satisfaction, she closed the lid of the laptop. Grace was confident she had done everyone justice with this book with her thorough research. She had returned the articles to the library. She was pretty sure the librarian had forgiven her because she had been more than helpful with the follow-up research.

Setting the laptop aside, Grace stood and stretched out all the kinks from sitting too long. Perhaps she'd tweak the letter again later. Writing was rewriting, after all.

Opening the bedroom door, Grace stepped into the hallway of the bed & breakfast. Although Heather didn't expect her to, Grace had gotten into the habit of starting the coffee and putting out a few baked goods for the guests who were early risers. Emma would prepare a warm breakfast at nine o'clock sharp for the guests. She had taken over now full-time for her big sister now that Ruthie was the mother to a beautiful baby girl.

Heather and Zach had invited Grace to stay at the bed & breakfast while she wrote her book and planned her wedding to Conner. The least she could do was help out here and there.

After getting the coffee and baked goods set, Grace put on her sneakers and headed out for a run, another new habit. It was amazing how easily she'd adjusted to small-town life. It was far easier during the summer than the winter, but she was learning to take it all in stride. And Conner assured her theirs would be the type of relationship where she could travel the world to write her stories. He'd come with her when he could. Quail Hollow would be their home base. But more and more, she found contentment with writing longer features right here at home.

Home. After years of writing stories about other people, to give them a voice, it felt wonderful to have overcome her fears to find a voice of her own.

She paused at the end of the driveway and smiled when she saw Conner's truck pull up. They had gotten into a routine of jogging on weekend mornings when he didn't have to be at work.

He pulled over and hopped out of the truck. "Am I late?"

"No, you have perfect timing." She smiled up at him, and he leaned down and kissed her.

A light twinkled in his eyes. "Good morning."

"Let's get moving." Grace stretched her arms over her head.

"I still can't believe you've taken up jogging."

"I'm full of surprises." She jogged in place as Conner checked the laces on his running shoes.

"Do you think you'll take up skiing this winter?"

"One sport at a time, buddy." She shook her head and laughed.

"The key is to wear the right clothes."

"So I've heard," she said, sounding skeptical. "Hey, did you see? Zach put out the sign last night on the front lawn."

"I did." They both glanced over to the Conner Gates for Mayor sign.

"Are you having second thoughts?" she asked.

"I never have second thoughts. Are you?" he asked teasingly.

"About you running for mayor? That means I'll be the mayor's wife." She held up her chin proudly and gave him a regal smile. Bradley's father had resigned after all the negative publicity regarding his son. "Why would I have doubts about that? You'll make a great mayor. It wasn't exactly your plan. But plans change. You would have made a great sheriff, but that was before this opportunity presented itself."

"I'm excited about new possibilities." He paused. "But that's not what I meant." He planted his hands on her waist and pulled her toward him. "Our wedding is in less than two weeks. Are you getting cold feet?"

She leaned up and pressed a kiss to his lips. "Absolutely not." She patted his chest. "I've never been more sure of anything in my life. Except that you're going to be the next mayor of Quail Hollow."

"Ah, from your lips to God's ears."

She cupped his face in her hands and smiled. God had certainly answered her prayers.

She gave him another quick peck and then spun around and started jogging toward the road. "Come on, slug. Try to catch me."

Grace didn't give Conner much of a chase. She laughed as she heard him approach from behind.

"Come on. You can run faster, can't you?" he asked.

Grace nudged his shoulder with hers. "I could, but why would I want to if it meant leaving you behind?"

* * * * *

SPECIAL EXCERPT FROM

Love Inspired®

After returning to his Amish community after losing his job in the Englisch world, Aaron King isn't sure if he wants to stay. But the more time he spends training a horse with childhood friend Sally Stoltzfus, the more he begins to believe this is exactly where he belongs.

Read on for a sneak preview of
The Promised Amish Bride *by Marta Perry, available February 2019 from Love Inspired!*

"Komm now, Aaron. I thought you might be ready to keep your promise to me."

"Promise?" He looked at her blankly.

"You can't have forgotten. You promised you'd wait until I grew up and then you'd marry me."

He stared at her, appalled for what seemed like forever until he saw the laughter in her eyes. "Sally Stoltzfus, you've turned into a threat to my sanity. What are you trying to do, scare me to death?"

She gave a gurgle of laughter. "You looked a little bored with the picnic. I thought I'd wake you up."

"Not bored," he said quickly. "Just…trying to find my way. So you don't expect me to marry you. Anything else I can do that's not so permanent?"

"As a matter of fact, there is. I want you to help me train Star."

So that was it. He frowned, trying to think of a way to refuse that wouldn't hurt her feelings.

"You saw what Star is like," she went on without waiting for an answer. "I've got to get him trained, and soon. And everyone knows that you're the best there is with horses."

"I don't think everyone believes any such thing," he retorted. "They don't know me well enough anymore."

She waved that away. "You've been working with horses

while you were gone. And Zeb always says you were born with the gift."

"Onkel Zeb might be a little bit prejudiced," he said, trying to organize his thoughts. There was no real reason he couldn't help her out, except that it seemed like a commitment, and he didn't intend to tie himself anywhere, not now.

"You can't deny that Star needs help, can you?" Her laughing gaze invited him to share her memory of the previous day.

"He needs help all right, but I don't quite see the point. Can't you use the family buggy when you need it?" He suspected that if he didn't come up with a good reason, he'd find himself working with that flighty gelding.

Her face grew serious suddenly. "As long as I do that, I'm depending on someone else. I want to make my own decisions about when and where I'm going. I'd like to be a bit independent, at least in that. I thought you were the one person who might understand."

That hit him right where he lived. He did understand—that was the trouble. He understood too well, and it made him vulnerable where Sally was concerned. He fumbled for words. "I'd like to help. But I don't know how long I'll be here and—"

"That doesn't matter." Seeing her face change was like watching the sun come out. "I'll take whatever time you can spare. Denke, Aaron. I'm wonderful glad."

He started to say that his words hadn't been a yes, but before he could, Sally had grabbed his hand and every thought flew right out of his head.

It was just like her catching hold of Onkel Zeb's arm, he tried to tell himself. But it didn't work. When she touched him, something seemed to light between them like a spark arcing from one terminal to another. He felt it right down to his toes, and he knew in that instant that he was in trouble.